Time is so short and I'm sure
There must be something more
--Coldplay

My Own Personal Fanfare

A great movie trailer never tells; it evokes. So imagine your life right now cut and calculated into a hundred interesting pieces to fit inside two minutes. Not to fill time but rather to expand it, to make others want to know more. What would they see? Could an artist possibly create some kind of poetry with the scenes and statements and songs from your life?

If your answer is no, that's okay. I made a living creating exceptional trailers. I didn't realize I could have spent it creating an exceptional life. But sometimes, something has to end in order for you to realize a truth you should have known from the beginning.

So let me start at the beginning. Which, in a bit of dark irony, begins when my life ends.

The Almighty Drop

There's a moment when you die where you don't see bright lights but you see a trailer that sums up your life. It's better than one I could ever make because it's so damn moving, with its melancholy *what-ifs* and its passing *almosts*. The sensation of leaving is almost better when someone alive is watching it unfold, wondering what if it was them, full of regret and wonder.

It's Christmas Eve and I've just finished watching *It's a Wonderful Life* for the twentieth time. I still wipe my eyes as if I didn't know how it would end. *There's no way he comes back and the town shows George Bailey some love and that angel Clarence gets his wings.* It gets me every time. I'm a sucker for things like that. But then again, maybe I'm just a sucker. One taken far too young.

Forty-two years old. What's that mean? Is there symbolism? Did Coldplay call it with their song titled "42"? I don't know. The questions are endless but so is the sky I'm drifting in. Like some kind of ember floating above a burning fire that's getting dimmer and dimmer.

I email myself a quote that I might use sometime down the road. I always do this. Email myself notes and thoughts and songs and anything and everything I can use in my craft. There's irony here because I'm about to die but it doesn't matter.

"Strange, isn't it? Each man's life touches so many other lives. When he isn't around, he leaves an awful hole, doesn't he?"

There's foreshadowing, and then there's this. I won't even have a night left to sleep on these words.

Soon the boom drops like every electronic song out there and every bad, clichéd trailer. The darkness covers and I'm lost. For a while.

Flickering like Falling Stars

So I should introduce myself. Or the me I used to be.

Or maybe you need a more interesting prologue.

Do you have access to the internet? Google Radiohead's "Everything in Its Right Place." Always thought this was just a brilliant piece of music to put into a movie trailer until Cameron Crowe beat me and used it in both the trailer for and the movie *Vanilla Sky*. I tried desperately to get the rights for "Paranoid Android" but just couldn't. It would've helped the movie I wanted it for to double its ticket sales. I still believe it even though I'm dead.

So yeah. I made movie trailers. Always an interesting job to describe at all the cocktail parties I attended (make that pretty much none).

I was great at what I did. Seriously.

There were lots of things I don't think I was good at in my life. Marriage was one. Fatherhood was another. Friendship . . . yikes. Faith. Ugh. But making movie trailers. I really was an artist.

The awards and accolades don't matter. I could share but that's like reading a résumé. Plus who knows and cares. The South California Who Gives a Flying Rip Conference for Baboons Movie Trailer Award. And wow—it's shaped just like a banana. No. You and I really don't care, do we? Just trust me. Lots of people valued my services. Not to make me a wealthy or happy man but to help them out (which in industry language means "they certainly value my work").

I got called by Spielberg once when I was changing a diaper. I love telling that story.

David Fincher once claimed I was ripping off his style in one of my trailers. He said that when I met him at a Hollywood thing. It was a joke that's not a joke. And you know what, Fincher? *I was.* #ConfessionsOfADeadMan

Oh, Lord. I just did a hashtag.

A ghost just did a hashtag in the narrative of his life. I think that's pretty sad.

But it will be over my dead body before I use the acronym I most despise.

LOL

Well, yeah. I can use it since I'm—well, yeah.

So more about me. I'm the guy to make you laugh. To make strangers laugh. To make the irritated waitress laugh. I think I did a good job making people laugh in my life. It stems from the deep insecurities residing in my soul that hate seeing others sad and hate hearing any kind of silence. I'd break all awkward anythings in every single way I could.

The irony is that I stopped making my wife laugh a long time ago. I know they say laughter is a good thing for a marriage. I think for us, it was necessary, and it had been long gone.

Yeah. No need to be subtle there.

"No alarms and no surprises, please."

Yeah, that's Radiohead and I'm in a Thom Yorke frame of mind.

I remember the car crash I survived almost a decade ago and I remember walking on the road afterward thinking, *God saved my life and He's got some great plan for me.* But maybe I never got back into a vehicle to figure out the grandness of His plans.

I still always believed, however. That at some point sometime I was going to do something great.

He pulled me out of the car crash but I never became anybody's superhero except those little ladies who looked up to me.

I miss them already the way a shipwrecked man misses signs of life. My girls. My daughters. My heart, lungs, and soul.

I can't exactly figure out an exit plan because I just jettisoned out the big exit doorway of life. And right now I'm floating in some kind of way. I'm narrating and telling but I'm not doing or seeing.

Bear with me. This is present tense and I'm trying to figure it out as we go.

I know Tamara has got to be a teeter-totter of despair and relief. I wonder which side is more heavy. I'm sure there's this quiet, secret sense of *finally* that she lets out whenever nobody's around. God knows I didn't offer the security, not in these final few turbulent years. I'm not saying she wanted this or is celebrating it but I know there's this tiny piece that's just glad. The fractured uncertain shadow

10

is gone.

That sounds pretty bleak, I know. But we were never going to cut the cord like some couples. That was most certainly never gonna happen before the princesses came. And after . . . well, yeah.

Absolutely impossible.

I like to always offer a caveat to things like that. In my younger, more defiantly stupid years, I made declarations that resemble epitaphs. I was a confident jackass. And one day all those statements followed me down a mountain kicking and screaming.

I know now and have known for some time but some things are difficult to lose the older you get. A padded waistline. A heavy debt. A non-erase graffiti of regret covering your soul.

I know now but sometimes the now is far too late.

So I float and drift and wonder and find these thoughts flickering like falling stars in the deep of night. I see them but then they're gone.

Going Down Now

Go find "When the Levee Breaks" by Led Zeppelin and put on some headphones before you read this.

Go ahead.

No, seriously, go.

. . . .

You're reading this and you're not doing as you're told. Come on.

Go ahead. I'll give you a few more moments.

. . . .

Okay, for those *few* who actually did it. Start the song.

This is your life.

One damn day after another dreaming the dream.

Pipe dreams droning on like some whining piper pounding.

You're four and you move and you're five and you move and all along this song is playing in your head but you don't know it and you can't imagine it but it's restless and it pounds away and it will stay until you die.

Yeah, I know 'cause I'm dead.

But you keep on keeping on and you find yourself forty-two and it's raining and the levee finally breaks.

The rain pounds down and the levee breaks and you have no place to stay.

The mean world beats you down.

The meanness makes you mean.

But you got what it takes and you know. *You know.*

Maybe you're wondering what this has to do with anything but stay with me and the song.

There's a little bit of glory here.

The guitar chimes in and you keep going and you follow all paths to Chicago.

The money's in LA but your heart's in Chicago.

Drone on, baby.

Forty-two years old and successful and in search of something more successful, more fulfilling, more real, and you suddenly choke.

Boom.

Boom.

Just like that.

And it's not fair and not right and you're leaving so much behind but yeah the music plays on just like this song. Loud, obnoxious, pounding away.

Pound.

Crying won't help you and prayer won't do you no good.

And breathe 'cause the levee's gonna break.

It's gonna break.

And you're gonna wake up and wonder where the hell you are.

Yeah. That's me.

And then there's you.

And here I am breaking some kind of fourth wall. But it's okay.

Still listening? Am I going too fast or slow?

Left ear higher right ear lower.

Awwwwww. Awwwww. Awwww.

So we begin.

The levee has broken and I'm on the other side. So yeah. Let's go.

Let's *see* what happens from here on out. 'Cause I'm not knockin' on Heaven's door and I'm not hearing hells bells.

And to that I will say, Thank God.

But still. Sitting. Wondering. Waiting. And yeah.

Let's find out together, shall we?

Inside

The first visible thing I see (and obviously it has to be *visible* since I'm seeing it, stupid) is the Fox River. I'm hovering over it, floating—no, wait. I'm leaning over a brick wall staring down at it. And that's when I realize I'm still down here. Still on earth. Still left around for some reason.

I stand and look down at myself. I'm wearing the same clothes I was wearing on Christmas Eve. The jeans and the black-and-white Arcade Fire T-shirt that says *The Suburbs*. Ah, the irony for an audience of one to enjoy.

Now I know for sure I'm a ghost. It's so obvious. Why didn't audiences realize the same thing with Bruce Willis's character in *The Sixth Sense*? He wears the same clothes the entire movie. Sure, he takes off his overcoat. And sports coat. And a vest, right? Oh, well. I won't be standing in shock at the end of this, dropping a coin and realizing I'm dead. Nope. I sorta already know.

Yep.

I touch my chest wondering if my hand will go through it like the cloud in your backyard after a long night of rain. But nope. I feel my abdomen. As soft as someone's gut might be after so many years at a desk. In a chair. In front of monitors. My brain is the only thing I ever built up. Sometimes I used to think it resembled Arnold Schwarzenegger's arms from his Conan days.

It doesn't feel like it's Christmas Day or the day after. It feels actually a little warm. So I wonder how I got here and what I'm supposed to do.

I head down the sidewalk toward the coffee shop and I enter.

Nobody looks at me.

I try to say something but I think that nothing comes out. Nobody looking, nobody bothering. Can I go behind the counter and make myself a coffee?

But instead I have to sit on a couch and think. My body is shaking. I'm scared. Which is the exact opposite thing I should be, right? Shouldn't I be the one making others shake? Scaring them out of their minds?

I see a couple pass. They don't notice me. This happens a few more times and it's depressing. Of course it's going to happen. I'm not here. I'm here but not.

The coffee aroma still weaves its way into my nose. I'm reminded of all those times sitting in a semidarkened room, listening to music and looking at other people. Being here but not really here. Maybe that was my training. Maybe this is my destiny.

Still, the wind outside nudges me back. The cars passing make loud sounds. I feel warm, hot almost from a humid evening.

I still have my wallet. Okay. But no keys. So I can be identified if they find my body but I can't drive a car.

#GhostRules

I start to head back there. Back home. Back to them. Back there. But I also suddenly flashback and see myself sitting on a train.

This could be a nice sort of trailer but it's not. It's real and it's happening to me and I'm in two alternative universes as they're unfolding at the same time and I'm really, seriously confused.

But I see the house we bought and the one they still live and sleep inside and somehow I manage to slip inside.

But the train rumbles and I'm headed to the city.

I see the pillows up like they always used to be so our dog wouldn't run up the stairs. She's a shih tzu and she doesn't hear me and it's further proof I'm a ghost because she would always, *always* bark at any noise once we had gone to sleep.

The house sleeps as I'm sure they do and I don't feel sad. I feel like some stalker for some reason. Like I shouldn't be here. Like I'm going to get in trouble. Like someone's going to kick me out.

But the seat is empty and this car only contains four other souls and I wonder if they're real or ghosts like me.

I take the steps and hear the fan and wonder what I'm going to do. Will I go in the twins' room? Will I go in our eldest daughter's room? Will I brave the creaks by our bathroom in order to hear my wife sleeping?

What exactly am I doing here anyway? Hoping to make a sound, hoping to break through a barrier, hoping the live people will hear the dead?

The rumbling of this endless train represents my heart and soul trembling in the night without being cold.

I stand at the top of the stairs and know the twins are behind that closed door, know our eldest is behind another one.

Know they're all so close.

But I can't. I move back down and move back out and decide to get away.

It's too soon to start haunting people I haven't told goodbye to. But I don't feel sad. It's weird for me to not feel this way but I don't.

On the train I feel more frustration than anything. Impatience.

I want—no, I *need* to figure things out. But there's nobody here to help explain this to me. No angel or demon or ghost or child who sees dead people.

No. I need to do this on my own. I'm on my own.

I wait until the train arrives. The Windy City awaits.

A dark giant beating heart of a city along some dark restless unmoving lake.

I will figure things out amidst the people. But there aren't as many memories down here. Only lights and motions and restless souls.

I'll blur beside them like the wind that cuts through their lives.

That house is no longer my home. But that doesn't mean I can't figure out a way to say goodbye.

I think the only reason I'm still here is to do this.

How I do it will be the mystery I have to solve. But I guess I have time now.

I have lots and lots of time.

Swan Song

This homeless man is watching me and wondering what in the world I'm doing here.

I smile at him across the street and he smiles back.

He's sitting and he also happens to be the laziest man I've ever seen. He can stand. He can walk. He can even run because I've seen him do it all on his way to get his Dunkin' Donuts coffee. But then he sits back down and takes the empty coffee cup and cuts half of it and makes it look like he pulled it out of a dumpster in order to get a few bucks.

Bucks he gets. His thick beard and wild hair and his general help-me-God look works on everybody but it's not fooling me.

I know this kind of guy.

He doesn't have to be homeless. I know he doesn't and I know he's fooling people.

Yet he can see me and I can see him. I wave and he waves back. It's a game for a while until I decide I'm tired of the game.

Okay, fine, some people can see me. Maybe he's got a side job of ghost hunting or something. But I bet he calls in sick. A lot.

I've been walking the streets all night and all morning. I'm not tired. I have this weird sort of energy like I'm on wild meds or taking a drug or something. I walk and keep walking and occasionally, like the beggar on the street, I find someone who can see me.

I think of my death and demise. The moment you die should really be a glorious thing but I'll be honest—I'm not ready to leave just yet. It feels like I'm still hanging around like some kind of dejected senior dumped on prom night still wearing the same tux and playing the same tune. The problem isn't humming the tune "If You Leave." The problem is declaring "Don't You (Forget about Me)."

The more I've thought about last night, the more I've realized my mission. So here's the thing I'll solve right away 'cause I like getting to the point. My journey is gonna be about somehow trying to figure out how to communicate one last time with my girls. The wife and the three little ladies. Last night I played Casper the Ghost but didn't even manage to knock over a decoration in the house. My goal in this journey is for one last swan song, a kind that sings goodbye, a sort that spells out sorrow in a thousand different ways.

I wanna wrap my arms around this entire world one last time but I can't even hold a spinning globe. I can, however, make a conning beggar grin. That's something, right?

I'm waiting and I'm stuck and I know that something's gotta happen because that's how stories begin. Right? Some inciting inferno needs to rip out my insides and tear away the very fabric holding me back right now.

"Will you call my name?"

So I wait. Wiggle around. Wrestle with the night. Wonder with held breath. So watchful and so very me. Still me in the same old awful ways.

Still singing eighties tunes like they were filling the big screen, the screen I knew so well, the one I gave my heart and soul to.

Maybe I should have given them to someone else. But it's too late for that.

My First Love

I think . . .

Look, I don't know what to think.

I've spent so long thinking. Analyzing. Layering. Burning. So deep.

Now no comprehension, no analytic, no desire can help me out here.

I'm still around, but for what and why? Should I haunt her and them and if so how and what for? Should I try to spy or study or simply walk the streets alone?

I feel like I wear flesh but I'm unseen. Like wearing the most ordinary sort of clothes to neither offend or impress. Passing through like a Ford you can't name.

I try and think of the first film that meant something to me. There have been so many that it's hard to remember what got me here in the first place. Or there in the first place now that I'm in that second place.

Star Wars is, of course, the clichéd answer. I was born in 1971. That means I was six when it was released. I don't remember seeing it that young. I'd like to think that yes, I saw it, I was blown away, and the trajectory of my life was changed. But no. I don't think it was *Star Wars*.

Empire Strikes Back now . . . yeah. That was a nail in the coffin in a sense. Because I know I eventually saw that and that was it.

But I think it was another Harrison Ford classic. The wonder, the adventure, the sarcasm, the epic *Raiders*.

I don't need to really finish the title, do I?

I remember talking to a college class and asking them how many loved *Raiders of the Lost Ark* and several hadn't even seen it.

THEY HAD NOT SEEN *RAIDERS OF THE LOST ARK*, ONE OF THE GREATEST FILMS EVER MADE.

Call it popcorn fare. Give me a jumbo bag and an extra giant-size Diet Coke and send me back into the jungle thank you very much.

I remember being in the theater for *Raiders*. And I was there in the jungle. At the beginning of their trek toward *something*. The master, the meister, John Williams, supplying the perfect score. So

19

brilliant. Epic. Spielberg when he wasn't a legend just yet. And George Lucas still having fun with his career and his stories before something changed and he turned into the Walmart of directors more worried about toys than story.

Ah, yes, *Raiders*.

Remember when you first see Indiana Jones? You're like, *That guy is cool. He's awesome. He's Han Solo's cooler brother. He's tougher. Meaner.*

Yeah. Way more awesome.

And he's heading into the dark cavern of the great unknown and the John Williams score is building and building and you know something bad is going to happen. And it all feels so fresh, so real, so alive, so unknown.

That moment he makes it to the idol. So close but . . . oh no.

And that score again. I'm telling you, the music does it. It's ethereal. You think this must single-handedly be the most amazing thing in the entire world and it's Harrison/Han/Indy in a dark tomb of death and oh my Lord the film is only like ten minutes into it and how could this possibly be any better and wait a minute he gets it and . . .

Phew.

Wait.

No. No. No.

And then the races. And they're off. And he's sprinting and crashing through the trees.

Crazy. Faster. Arrows flying. His hat—don't lose your hat, Indy. It's already become iconic. It's funny and meanwhile he's almost dying.

"Start the engine!"

He sounds so weak and helpless. He sounds like one of us. It's kinda amusing and thrilling at the same time.

"Start the engine!"

He's screaming as a whole tribe of evil Amazonians are following him.

Who they are and where he is—doesn't matter.

And then.

20

Yes. He flies off and away. Into the sunset.

And for the first time we are introduced to Indy's theme and our lives have suddenly become a little better. We are a little more whole thanks to Steven Spielberg and Harrison Ford and John Williams.

And this could be it. The entire movie. Boom. We're sold. The beginning. The end.

"I hate snakes!"

Well, of course he does. Because Indy is funny and human and we love him and we will go wherever he takes us.

Ah, yes. This was my first love. I still remember her fondly. I still write love letters to her.

Guess I just wrote one now.

I just thought you should know since film was really and truly my first love.

Maybe, unfortunately, my last too.

Something

A man who resembles a young Paul Newman approaches me on the street and I just assume he's not going to see me until he says my name.

—Hello, Spencer.

It's not as if he just said hello to me. That would have been weird enough. But he said my name. And I stop and stare and wait to see if he's another ghost or crazy person.

—I do believe you *are* the only Spencer on this sidewalk.

He's even got that wry, charming grin that Newman used to have.

A gust of wind cuts through us as I remain still and speechless. I see the man extend his hand, so I shake it.

—That's just to prove that I'm real, he says.

—Am I?

The man laughs.

—I like that question. And yes, you are very real, and this is very much happening.

—Can you sum up the "this" that you're referring to?

—I can, he says. But I won't. That's part of this all. "The object of the game is to discover the object of . . . *The Game*."

For a moment, I have to think of that line. Normally I would know in a heartbeat, but this whole thing of meeting on the sidewalk close to the bridge talking about "things" makes me a bit wonky.

Then, yes, obviously. One of my favorites.

—That's from *The Game*.

The man nods.

—Of course.

I feel disoriented for a moment just like Michael Douglas' character in the film.

—What's happening?

—I'm Matthew. And I'm here to help.

—Well, great. But so far you've made things even more strange while quoting David Fincher movies.

—I know you speak the language of film.

—I also speak the language of common sense.

—So tell me, Spencer . . . what does "common sense" tell you about all of this?

I want to be witty or say something funny or try to find some kind of amusement out of all of this but I can't.

—I'm not here to make you feel stupid, Spencer. Or to offer riddles for you to solve.

—So what are you doing?

—I'm here to answer the questions you haven't figured out to ask yet.

Even though I'm dead I still have my sense of humor (if you want to call it that).

—You're starting to talk like Yoda, I tell him.

—That's a shame because there's no Luke Skywalker in this picture.

I laugh out loud.

—I died. Right? I'm dead. So why am I standing here? Why am I here? And how can I be talking to you? Are you like my guardian angel?

A gust of wind blows through us. Not a kind that seems to answer my question, but more in a flowing, this-is-really-happening way.

—The world has turned titles like that into children's books and Hallmark films. The same way they've turned Satan into a cartoon in a horror movie.

—So is that a yes? I ask.

—You are here because there is something you must do. Something that must be done before you're able to move forward.

I think of those last two words. *Move forward.* Move to where? To heaven, hopefully? To a waiting place? To that *other* place?

—What is it? What am I supposed to do?

I can hear Clarence from *It's a Wonderful Life* talking.

"You've been given a great gift, George: a chance to see what the world would be like without you."

The thing is, I don't want to see what the world would look like without me. I'm fine with the world letting me be a part of it. The real, human, touchable, and knowable guy. I really was happy.

—I hope this doesn't involve heights. I'm not such a fan of heights.

—It only involves what is necessary.

I wait for more. It seems like I can see the sun falling and rising again before he's going to share anything else.

—Okay . . . so are you going to give me any sort of hint what you're talking about? Is this when the journey begins?

That good-looking grin shows up on Matthew's face.

—Have you ever heard the expression "Something borrowed, something blue"?

I nod and wait for him to continue.

—So consider this my borrowed-blue bit.

—What are you talking about?

—Listen carefully so you know exactly what you might have been thinking of, he says.

I shake my head and start to say something but his expression suddenly seems to be a red light on a freeway of free thoughts.

—These are the things you must seek, Spencer.

He pauses and I want to fill in the blanks like my mind and soul always do.

—What things?

He smiles.

—Something sun-sheltered. Something hidden. Something underwater. Something make-believe. Something spinning round. Something without sorrow. Something not there. Something soaring in prayer.

I just stand there.

What the hell was that?

—I don't understand.

—Of course you don't, he says. And that is the great mystery you must solve.

—I have to solve for what?

—For you. Not some stranger, some viewer in the dark, but for you. To see the things that aren't there, Spencer.

Which he probably knows is ironic considering who he's saying this to.

—But what if . . . ? What happens if I just . . . ?

—You must, you *must*, you absolutely must find the things you were thinking of, Spencer.

—But what . . . ?

My words echo off his back as he escapes into the night. But right before, he leaves me with this nice little quote, handwritten on a notecard. All his wonderful little *somethings*.

Something sun-sheltered. Something hidden. Something underwater. Something make-believe. Something spinning round. Something without sorrow. Something not there. Something soaring in prayer.

The ironic part is they've all left me pretty much with nothing.

Dream Is Collapsing

I'm breathing—no, panting—no, sucking-in-air-hyperventilating—as water streams over my head down my cheeks dousing my body. I'm leaning against ceramic tile and I'm saying over and over and over again.

—This is not happening.

I can't be feeling this way.

When is this? Is this now? Is this a dream? Is this back then?

—I'm going to die right here.

But of course I didn't because I died at a different time. This is a flashback. But it doesn't feel like a memory.

—God, help me, God, help, God, please.

But it doesn't feel like God's been there for a long time. The water pours and drains and I watch it disappear underneath me and I try to breathe but all I do is start to choke.

Me

It's not like I don't know myself and that this search for those many *something*s is supposed to be all about my inner journey to find my mysterious, missing self. I'm not missing and I'm definitely not mysterious. I'm just Spencer.

But let me start with me. The narrator. Imagine my voice is Morgan Freeman and I know you will absolutely love this story. Morgan's voice has that effect.

People love to rain down praise on my work, but I think I'd be simply soaked if it wasn't for my hidden weapons. My truly endless supply of music.

I believe it's an art to match a sound bite of a musical track with moving images that don't belong to you. I've done this for the last twenty years. I'm not rounding the number, either. It's been twenty exact years that I've been working with movie trailers in one form or another. Somewhere in those two decades, the time was right and the opportunity existed and I simply got lucky.

My name is Spencer Holloway. Since I'm a ghost I might not have many sit-down shake-the-hand sort of meetings where I introduce myself, so assume I'm doing this now. I'm forty-something. Over forty. Did I already tell you my age? And speaking of which, do ghosts age? Do they celebrate birthdays? I don't know. I have no answers for you. I'm detailing all of this in order to try to figure some answers out.

My career trajectory isn't worth detailing. I guess some details will spill out here and there. But the journey went from *I really want to be Steven Spielberg but I guess I'll do this* to *So I guess that's not gonna happen but I'm a lot better than all of them* to *How in the world did that happen?*

Dreams can be strange things. They're never fully formed. They're single snapshots in your mind, while the living-out-the-dream becomes a miniseries.

I'm a Chicago guy. Grew up a little bit of everywhere before settling down in a Chicago suburb. My office or offices or whatever you'd like to call them ended up being in Chicago. During the heyday.

27

But since then I moved out to be closer to where I live. I'm in the suburb of Appleton. That's where my offices are. We live in the neighboring town of Geneva. Or *lived* there. That's where my family still lives.

Ugh.

This stuff bores me.

Look. In about five seconds I'm going to go into some dark space and be confronted with the demons of my past while slaying the dragon. Just wait.

Four.

Three.

Come on, Two.

One.

Yeah.

Okay, maybe not. Maybe I'm still standing here rambling on.

Maybe it means something. I don't know.

I'm not Frodo. Or Bilbo. Or any of those.

I'm not carrying a ring.

I'm no comic-book character (and please don't get me started on the state of comic movies in cinema because I will blow a gasket . . .).

So yeah.

Look, blah blah blah. Successful or not. Life or not. I died. End of story. But I'm still here. Ah, intriguing story.

Let's just move on, shall we . . .

I mean—I *have* to move on. Right?

Right?

I Remember

—Savage.

—Yes it is.

My wife always had a way with words. The wind shouted against the house siding since there were only toothpick-thin trees stuck around it.

—I feel stranded.

—I do too.

I didn't need to know what would happen on this deserted island. Just the two of us in such a big house. We could go downstairs or upstairs or stay here on this new love seat and it would be the same.

—I'm cold, she said, tucking herself into me.

—Let me get you warm.

—Think it's going to snow all night?

—I hope.

And I did.

I hoped we'd be snowed in for a week.

I remember her slipping away and telling me to wait for a while until she put on something less comfortable for her but a lot more inviting for me. She had a lot to choose from and we had a lot of time to kill.

Like the snowflakes that fell, all we had was time.

And I waited and heard the wind rocking the new house and I didn't realize that this would eventually end. I just waited with anticipation and expectations that I always carried with me.

I believed things would always be like this. The two of us. Quiet and hungry and making the cold air warm with our love.

—Spence, she eventually said.

The restless beating fury of the outside couldn't find us. It couldn't come inside. We were safe here and we always would be and it would always be like this moving up these steps and smelling that perfume and seeing the glow from our bedroom and knowing that soon I'd be spent and soon the staggering outside would be like stereos in my dreams.

Dreams, indeed.

I still remember.

They're like fantasies that I make up because those times seem so long ago. And they were.

The winds didn't die down. Somehow, they found their way inside, changing our sanctuary into something else.

First Sight

It's a winter many years after that one. I'm not sure of the actual date. I mean—it's not like I've been keeping an address book. I remember those planners that were really popular back in the late nineties. Mine was a Franklin planner. It was impressive because it was actual *leather*. My daily to-do list. I carried that thing around everywhere. It had motivational quotes at the bottom of each page because this was a *special* kind of planner. It gave quips from leaders because I tried to think I might be one. People thirty and under will have no idea what I'm even talking about because all they have right now are their smartphones. Enough to plan the day and talk to others in Moscow and to watch the latest trailer for the next Star Wars movie.

Technology is a beautiful thing. Memories, on the other hand, can be subject to change, depending on the time and the day and the mood you might be in.

A strange thing happens. I'm walking down the street and it's cold and windy. The kind of cold and windy that makes you not walk down the street. The kind that tells you to stay in the car, to not go to that store, to not bother getting out even if it's for five seconds. It's brutal. And even though I feel it I think it shouldn't really bother me, right? But I'm still shivering in my long black overcoat.

I see a figure approaching on the sidewalk. Surely going into the coffee shop. That's where I'm headed. Not that I'll actually order a coffee but I'll people watch like I usually do. And this woman in a long coat and a cap with long dark hair spilling out and flickering about approaches and I stop for a minute. I already know she won't see me. She won't pause or look or do anything. She'll just keep going.

But instead, she looks up at me.

At *me*.

And then she does something shocking.

She smiles.

I look behind me but no. There's no one. We're the only two on this sidewalk. She gives me that smile for a few seconds and then she heads into the coffee shop. I don't follow. I still stand outside, wondering how she could have seen me. Wanting to know if I could actually talk to her.

Then worrying she might be another ghost that I'm seeing. Yet I see her in the coffee shop and she's as alive as any human might be. And considering that smile . . . well, she's a little more than alive.

She's a lot more.

And she saw me.

Hearing & Seeing

"Strange, isn't it? Each man's life touches so many other lives. When he isn't around, he leaves an awful hole, doesn't he?"

I found myself typing this with the tears still in my eyes.

You'd think someone who has seen as many movies as myself wouldn't get like this, but I blame our girls.

Christmas Eve and I'm emailing myself this quote from *It's a Wonderful Life*. Ah, the sweet story of redemption. It's one of my favorites. And it never gets old. Never.

I think about that now and wonder if I'm going to leave a hole and if it's going to be awful. I don't know. I'm no George Bailey. And I didn't *want* to go. I didn't. But you know—when it's time, I guess, it's time.

Christmas Eve. That's when I remember ending a busy and fulfilling day feeling chest pains.

I watch a movie and then suddenly. Boom.

Just like that.

I mean, I knew that could happen. That's what they always say. But I'm only—I *was* only forty-five years old. I mean forty-two. Wait, why am I forgetting?

I'm still hung up on this past and present tense thing. Is there such a thing as future tense? Because I'd love to start speaking in it.

That's all I know. It was late and I started to feel chest pains and then I couldn't breathe. I thought, of course, it was something I ate. I don't have heart trouble in my family. I'm healthy. Pretty healthy, at least.

But then my left arm began to get numb. And that's when I began to think, *Uh-oh.*

And now I'm here. Still here. Still watching. Still walking around even though nobody can see me.

I remember the first time I spoke with someone. Not Matthew the angel or ghost, but a real human being. The first time someone could actually hear me. He was a homeless guy who looked like he might be about thirty minutes from joining me in that next place. I remember saying something to him and seeing him turn his head and respond.

—I got your back, he said.

—Do you hear me?

—Yeah I think so even though my hearin's not so good these days.

I wanted to ask if he saw me too but I didn't. I couldn't.

—You hear me? I asked.

—Yeah. You hear me? Most ignore me.

—I hear you, I told him.

—You have any money for me?"

Wow. Even in the afterlife, the beggars could berate you for some dollar bills.

But I reached in my pockets and found a couple of twenties. I gave them to the guy. Sure, they could be wasted on jack and gin. But the guy heard me. And my money was real.

Soon after that I went into a coffee shop and got promptly ignored. Nobody noticed me and nobody could take my twenties. So I just waited. And this is where I would go just to watch and wait.

Little did I know I'd meet her here.

But I've never been the best of knowing. I just do. And I figure things out later.

The Pile

I sleep on a couch in my old office. I wonder what's going to happen to it but it remains the same. Day after day. Nobody is coming in to check on things. To look through my stuff or to start to dissect it or simply take it away. I always wonder whenever I'm here and hearing footsteps in the hallway. But nobody ever opens the door. I assume nobody will ever know. If they do, then I'll get really spooked.

I got this office after we found out about the twins. It's only seven minutes away in the nearby town of Appleton. It's an office building that I always joke looks like a prison. I remember when I once worked for a company on a team. Then I had my own business at home in an oversize bedroom complete with three Macs in it. Now two of those Macs followed me here.

Tonight, I'm not sleeping. I'm just roaming around the two offices that have lots and lots of things I've ignored for years. I'm looking through them like some guy who's going through his house when there's a wildfire approaching.

To say I have lots of DVDs is an understatement. I have them for various reasons. Some are for research, some for inspiration, some have been given to me by studios and companies I've worked for. They're grouped in genres. Thrillers, comedies, *romantic* comedies, sci-fi, on and on.

Yeah, I know they're *DVDs*. Next you'll ask me where my 8-track tapes are. Except, no. Most are too young to even know what the hell those are.

I used to take pride in saying there were truly few movies I hadn't seen. But once the girls came . . . well, that changed for both Tamara and me. I still watched movies all the time, but it was different. Middle row opening Friday nights were a thing of the past. I could still justify them, of course, but I justified time with those little wild girls more.

Tonight—the time unsure, the numbers irrelevant—I assessed my collection.

Every Kubrick film, of course.

Spielberg. Fincher. Hitchcock. Woody Allen. (Do people just say

Allen? I don't know but I never have).

There were some random movies here. Some fun ones to remember once again. I see *Chopper*. Great little film. Violent.

There's a collection that I stop and scan and have to try to figure out why they're grouped in this way. *Beetlejuice* next to *The Sixth Sense* doesn't exactly make sense. But then I see *Ghost* and *Ghostbusters* and *Poltergeist*.

Ah, yes, my ghost pile.

Perhaps assembling them all together should have been a warning.

Somewhere between scanning and searching through the movies, I find a slim DVD case with a black Sharpie marked *Grace* on it. I stop everything and then slip out the disc to watch.

GRACE (Trailer #1)

A white title floating on the black surface. The one-word movie. **GRACE**. Then seeming to swirl around down a drain until . . .

The screen explodes into a morning sun–colored cyclone while the music begins. A contemporary track I found. This undiscovered indie singer equally talented with a swelling voice and the brilliant strumming of a harp. But like the image at first, it's simple until the music expands.

A girl runs with trails of golden childhood bouncing over her shoulders. Our five-year-old heroine Grace in the grass. Then she turns and sprints sideways until you see Jennifer Lawrence running in her place. In the same backyard. Only twenty years later.

Then scenes begin from all over the film. Telling the whole story and none of it. All while Elton John's "Tiny Dancer" plays. It's an iconic song from an iconic artist. It's perfect for the picture being highlighted.

When we get to "Hold me closer tiny dancer," there's a couple holding hands. You can't see their faces. Then you see Steve Martin with Jennifer Lawrence. Both laughing. Then the unknown male lead.

Then the tagline.

EVERYBODY HAS A CHILD IN THEM WAITING TO WAKE UP.

The Perfect Trailer

You're given two minutes. Or in my world, one hundred and twenty seconds. Because in my world, seconds count. It can be one simple image caught on the screen. One snapshot can mean absolutely everything.

So what's the secret of a brilliant trailer? Well, whenever I'm asked that, I jokingly tell people to google the answer. But I'm actually being a bit serious. There's no answer to that. It's like asking a musician, "How do you write a really amazing song?" There's no answer to explain the things that move us. Maybe we could if we were still standing in place, able to analyze their impact.

Conflict we need the conflict get in some damn conflict . . .

Yes. Of course, Director Know-It-All. I certainly will, especially since this is the first trailer I've ever done.

(I've actually done over 50 trailers.)

Conflict is good. But there's more. Seriously more. And it always starts with evaluating what's at the core of the film. Not the genre—God no. Not the story. What's the heart of the film look like and how fast is it beating?

You figure that out first.

Then you toss around some ideas.

Should we mislead the audience? Should we give them some of the money shots right away? Should we capitalize on the star or the headline or the sound bite? Should we shock or surprise or simply try to bring a little awe into their popcorn-eating souls?

Those inevitable questions.

I try to get some of them figured out. Early in my career, I'd answer them myself and then start down some path that could be brilliant or disastrous depending on the answer and the producer and director. I've learned. Or . . . I should say I *had* learned.

Past tense. Past tense all the way.

Tone is everything. Everything.

I remember the trailer I did for *Tremble*. Some little indie thriller that had a love story at the core. We got permission to use the absolutely insane track from *Inception* called "Time." The last track in that movie, the one that the guitarist from the eighties English band The Smiths played in.

I'm inadvertently working with Johnny Marr from The Smiths and yes it's fantastic.

Oh, and Christopher Nolan, too. Not that either had *anything* to do with *Tremble*.

So this video. So beautiful. The director told me to do my Spencer thing. I had laughed and then wondered what the hell that meant. But it ultimately was him giving me license to do something different and moving and amazing.

Once I had "Time" in my possession . . . oh, Lordy, was I set loose.

You can do *so* much with the perfect track.

You fill in images with the chords.

You paint a smile and a couple and a love alongside the major chorus.

You shove an action with a minor chord.

You fill the colors to match the mood.

As the orchestra begins to play and fill the senses, you add images to match. Emotion. Someone crying. Someone yelling. Someone moving. Someone losing.

And you try to tell the viewer that this isn't just another film. You state that this is them. This is their life and a shadow of it is being captured. You wrap a hand around their neck and bend them toward you and whisper in their ear that the only thing they can do is come watch their story unfold opening night. There's no other choice. Because this burst of two minutes is like puncturing the side of their mouth with a giant hook from heaven above that's going to rip them out of their seat and bring them up to the surface to finally survey the wonderful glory awaiting them.

Then you make sure to give them the date their average life will change. It will just so coincide with the release date for the movie you've summed up in this short two-minute trailer.

If you don't think your life can be summed up in two minutes, then you're wrong.

Anything and everything can be condensed and woven together in that amount of time.

Give me average, offer me some meandering, then toss over some nuggets. I will take them and work a little bit of wonder.

Sometimes focusing on a simple image and accentuating it.

Sometimes harping on a simple bit of action and overdoing it.

Sometimes taking a simple scene and surrounding it with emotion.

Sometimes just doing my job and doing it well and doing it the way nobody else might and expressing my voice and my style and my soul where I'm not singing and I'm not seen and I'm not surveying any sort of background.

I'm just assembling and structuring and storytelling.

For some crazy reason, I continue to work on the film I was working on. In my previous life.

The trailer isn't done. But it's close. So very close.

Fatherhood Footsteps 1

I see the colors of the rainbow sprinkling the ceiling. I'm slightly color-blind so God only knows if it's blue or purple I'm seeing. Or green or brown. I do see the pink. A horse and a panda along with those stars. Moving and dancing and prancing and silently laughing. I hold M's hand and listen to breathing begin on both sides of me while those shapes stream above me. When I was young I had a bright night-light plugged into the wall that always stayed the same. Now we have color meteor showers crawling over walls lulling the kids to sleep. And usually doing the same for parents.

But this night I just watch. Still holding her hand, still waiting, but watching above.

And I picture myself falling. Bouncing. Streaming. Sailing.

The world with its worries hovering off with silent waves of goodbye.

Bursting through air and oxygen and gusts and jets.

Darting down and feeling so free for the first time.

Imagination is a wonderful thing, the way it can grab and take and then skip and hop toward hope. Ripples surround you with their smiles of affirmation.

Fatherhood has these fleeting moments that are gone and impossible to quickly bottle up into some meaningful memento. The quiet hush of two little souls breathing in their sleep right next to you. Then the crack of the floorboard and the creak of the door and then you're kissing their elder sister good night underneath another colorful display.

Breathe a sigh of relief. Time for wine and unwinding and music and imagination.

Yet sometimes the high is the thing you've just left behind.

And it takes time to realize that so fully.

Go

—Hello?

Her voice again.

Like sampling some kind of wine, I try to detect the hints behind that sound. Sadness? Exhaustion? Relief, perhaps? Annoyance to find no voice on the other end?

—Hello? Anybody there?

So close, so real. Tamara never liked talking on the phone. Such a patient soul in life could be so short on her cell.

Irony is getting lost on a country road only to wind back around to where you first started out.

The call ends. She's gone. The cheap prepaid cell phone I found doesn't have a recognizable number. Okay, fine, I stole it. But can that really be considered stealing? It's not like I can buy it, right? I can call but I can't call out. I can't hear but I can't answer. I can't take but I can't replace.

I hold the cell.

It reminds me of all the times I avoided conversation and communication.

Gotta focus don't have time.

I hate these things. Reminders of failures. Not the loss after but the complete idiocy of the loss I chose *before*.

Ghosts can't go back, but I guess they can hold samples of the past in their hand.

I wasted so much. Is there a way I can construct something, even if it's only something little, before my time here is really, truly done?

Go find the woman the ghost the girl—maybe she can tell you.

This particular moment and story could be summed up by a nice panic-packed Radiohead song. "Give Up the Ghost."

There you go. The title for your movie in the making.

There are no more movies to make. Even if I can try to in this sort of state.

Go.

That word, wading around like a broken paddle next to the canoe. Never sinking, but never helping.

42

Oh, to go back. To switch into some kind of time-travel tale and step out and realize I have every ability to make things right.

God only knows I'd still probably mess things up really bad.

Go. Gotta do and try and run and give it all. I write down notes trying to devise ways to make at least a handful of things right as long as I'm still here.

And how long might that be, Spencer my boy?

That's the question. The urgency. The worry.

Time here, however, is the thing. Is a day a true day? Are they blurring together? Am I six feet under remembering the past and imagining the present?

I think of other mild things to try to do now that I have time. Now that time isn't something so important for me. It's not like I'm worrying about collecting some kind of invoice. My will is the only thing that's going to be collecting anything, and thankfully it's a decent amount to help my family.

To help.

Such nobility in death. I'm *helping* them.

I'm a loaded crock today.

I head out to the streets. The sun seems to be peeking out and maybe it'll help me spot her. The only soul out there who seems to be able to spot me.

Moments outside, the weather doesn't cooperate. It suddenly dawns on me the sun must be a female, stubborn in its refusal to listen to me. That's okay because the moon was always a constant companion anyway.

LITTLE THINGS (Trailer #2)

Figures fogging up the windows already cloaked on the outside with white flakes. The engine off with no need to run it. With no need for the heat on this wintry night.

"Do we have to go?" he asks, a voice patient and caring.

"Not yet," she says, a voice soft and wanting.

"I don't want to get you into trouble," he says without much conviction.

"I don't care," she says with quiet conviction.

The scene doesn't become erotic or even suggestive but rather pans out to show the snow-covered car lost in others in a parking lot late at night. A soft melody begins to play, and one wonders if this is some type of Hallmark movie.

Then the music and the scene and everything all become a bit . . . off.

Then the hands separate. The sound of a simple keyboard—a children's keyboard almost—begins to play. And we see a story played out.

Passion. The best thing life can offer and the worse sort of road map to follow.

Stares of hate. Figures as lonely as prisoners. The silence. All while the song continues.

It's an odd, voice-in-a-vacuum cover of "Enjoy the Silence." At least that's what most viewers will think. They won't know it's the demo version of the classic upbeat song from the electronic English band Depeche Mode. The core of the song—the thing people don't understand—is that the tune is a heartbreaker.

All they ever wanted and all they ever needed was right there in their arms. But words and life and history and love come in like violence and break this blissful silence.

LITTLE THINGS. Coming soon to a theater near you.

Watching the River

Wandering and searching in snow and rain with my forehead raw as a windshield with broken wipers, I'm alone and cold and feeling like Michael Jackson is singing to me like a Stranger in Moscow. Odd how the scenes and songs of another life wrap over and try to wreck my lack of one.

Streets can be sober while I'm looking for a little wine. A little heart. A little soul. Somebody to come bumble beside me. But I don't find anybody except my solitary shadow and the memories of a thousand moments.

I didn't think it'd be like this, to be honest. Melancholy moments more than I can count. I thought I'd be free. Or maybe waiting in the white. Something like that but not like *this*. Imprisoned in ice while the rest of the world begins to thaw.

Hearing the laughs.

Seeing the lights.

Tasting the sweet tongue.

I'm missing it all. But I keep walking, hoping I can outwalk this, this lonely drowning.

Wondering if I'm still here to do something. Wishing I could figure out some kind of formula to let it all go. Waiting on some moment to slide by and scrape up the pieces like a passing snowplow.

How does it feel, Spence?

Alone and cold inside and still feeling like I've felt for a while.

A heart can be frozen while fiddling around with the locks before bedtime. A soul can still be empty despite the Bible verses inscribed on the walls. A mind can still be confused even if it claims to have all the answers.

The night knows. The midnight moments are so aware. They hold their breath, watching and waiting without worrying about anything.

The wind and the stone walls and the river below and the sheet of black above all know. The crevices the dark seeps inside. The echoes and the wandering and the dying.

What am I supposed to do?

I don't know. I'm walking to figure it out.

I was never the sort to sit down in the middle of an afternoon watching the river below drift by. Just watching and reflecting and sitting and staring. People who did that used to make me nervous.

I guess I didn't know that you would get to do that after you died.

Not sure if I'd call it heaven or hell.

But sitting on this bench on the edge of the sidewalk and the railing of the bridge, I see a figure walking across the street.

It's her. The woman I saw.

The woman who saw me.

I glance around for some reason. Not that anybody's seen me. Not that I have *any* reason to look around. But I do anyway. Then I stand and start walking toward her.

Can ghosts be stalkers? Guess we can find out.

When I reach the end of the sidewalk I scan the street she walked down. I can't find her. So I look at the different options she might have disappeared into. A salon/spa. A yoga place. A pizza joint. A pub.

I blink and see her and wonder where she might have gone.

And what are you going to do if you spot her?

It's a good question. I'm not sure.

Her hair looked quite fine and she didn't quite seem like the yoga sort. Or the pizza sort. So I head to the pub.

Certain doors can decide our destinies. Pulling them open or holding them for a moment or standing and seeing them shut. Life drifts through doorways, some familiar and some still unfound.

They're no longer shut and locked for me. I can't wait to see which ones open or close. I'm no longer given those chances. I had mine but no more.

But maybe—I don't know.

The frigid freezing finding me standing here in this deep feeling.

Go on in.

Maybe my chances are up and my open doors are finished but I just know that I need to open this one and try to find this woman to figure out . . .

To figure out the things I need to know. Maybe in some way she can help me.

Table for One

I see her again. And once again, the woman smiles.

Tall. So tall. Lean like some kind of dancer or athlete or gym instructor. It's hard to tell fully with the long coat but I can tell enough. The carved cut of her jawline. The sleek curves of her neck, so long, like some kind of scripted-out V.

I'm walking down the street and she looks up and sees me.

Sees.

Me.

Then she smiles.

And then she passes and she's gone. Except for this. I stop. Turn around. Then I start to follow her.

Isn't this what ghosts are supposed to do?

I want—I *need*—to know. What's going on here and how can see she me?

So I follow. Cross the street. Then cross another. Then make it to the pub she walks into before the door fully shuts.

In the corner, under a red lamp, the outline of that model-like face suddenly punctuated like she planned it, the woman sits on a barstool at a tiny table for two. The other stool is empty.

She stares at me as if I'm supposed to sit down.

Then I see another figure slip in there. Someone. Some guy. Looking cool and fit and handsome and, yeah, very much alive.

I stand there and wonder if she can see me. She smiles at the man across from her. This bothers me even though I don't know this woman at all. I've seen her—what?—two or three times. But somehow, in some weird way, I'm jealous.

It's weird.

I go over to the bar and so want a beer. The bartender ignores me but I see a glass just poured—dark and thick and spilling over the top—just sitting there. Just waiting.

So I grab it and I chug like a college student. I do a good job. I still got it.

Dead man chugging.

I drain the IPA and instantly feel something. An actual buzz. It's good.

Then I put the glass down on the bar and start to walk away.

I assume long legs and lines isn't looking my way, but I turn to glance anyway. And she's sitting alone again, staring at me, glowing like some kind of angel.

Then she smiles as I push the door and go back outside back to wander and then withdraw for the night.

I know that she's someone. I don't know her but I want and need to know her. I'm curious to see her fully and to see who she is and what she's all about. There's something about her. I just know.

But how?

Is this how I'm supposed to communicate?

But the great thing is this: I can find out.

I don't have to punch a time clock tomorrow. Or today, I guess I should say.

I don't have a boss breathing down whatever side of me he feels like scorching. I don't have commitments and deadlines.

I'm able to find her again and then find out what she's all about.

I can see her from behind and from in front and can stay and study. To look and to listen and to figure out who she is.

Is she a soul I'm supposed to haunt? 'Cause I will, gladly.

But I don't think so.

I don't think she's going to be frightened by anything even if I tried. But I don't want to try.

I just want to see if she spots me again.

What a glorious thing, being seen.

When it's been so long since it's happened, you can't help but burst open when it happens again.

Anyone's Ghost

Lost and tripping over the lanes, I can see my past flipping over like cards.

Third-grade joy.

Fifth-grade terror.

Eighth-grade hormones.

Tenth-grade confusion.

The full deck has forty-six cards but I wish that somehow I could cut them in half and start shuffling over again.

The things I know now, the roads I've traveled down, the words I've spoken and heard—I'd love a redo. Like a film, I'd love to reboot myself. My trilogy of the heart and mind and soul.

Grateful is the word I often hear. And yes, grateful is something I feel. But sometimes, I just dip my hands into this murky pot and pull them out as if they're dripping with black tar. A kind I can never fully wash off. A kind that accumulates a little more every day and every late night.

I'm in this office once again, and I'm cold. Cold. How in the world can I be cold? I'm not angry at the owners because I don't assume they heat the offices at night. But a ghost shivering instead of making others do the same? This is crazy.

Yet I need to somehow figure out why I'm still here.

And the only glimmer of hope that's come lately is that brunette beauty that's passed me by several times and always—*always*—seen me.

Can angels have dark hair? Can the living see the dead? Is she a fellow ghost waiting to start some kind of book club where we read Stephen King and discuss life on the other side?

"Didn't want be anyone's ghost."

Ah, yes. The National humming inside my head.

All I know is this.

I need to find her and talk to her to figure out what's going on. Or at least figure out who she is and why she can see me.

And also . . .

I'm so freaking cold.

Suddenly and Maybe and Only

God, the past claws at the skin on your back you can't reach. I'm feeling full tonight. Full of the whole clinking, clanging cans of curiosity following a car driven by a pair of newlyweds. The noise and the ocean and the so-so-so of voices of despair asking, *Why are you still here, Spencer?*

I don't know.

But standing and watching, I see her again. So I follow her.

This time it's that small Italian restaurant I always told Tamara we should go to. Some romantic place that fit all those others in life that resembled some kind of romance. We were an IHOP commercial, to be honest. Actually, I'm not sure if those are still around. Bakers Square? Denny's? Whatever this picture might convey, this is the one that we suddenly resembled. We were the spokespeople for it. The ambassadors of the mediocre family food fare where kids could hang over the seats and seventy-year-olds could look over with grumpy stares as they devoured three-dollar-meals.

I open the door of possibility and regret because there's some kind of answer waiting for me.

Every single time I've seen this woman, she's been alone. She's been passing and looking and passing more and looking more.

It's beyond obvious.

Inside this restaurant, it's beyond dreamy. Will I wake up from all of this like Alice in Wonderland? It's all a dream and how crappy can that be but let's celebrate the book for all eternity anyway? Oh, and that Tim Burton movie . . .

The server doesn't see me. Of course. It must be because I look so damn disheveled. Or wait, hold on . . . maybe it's because I'm DEAD.

I'm okay at saying that. Like some kind of song on a *Dora* episode. "Hola, what's *your* name? Are you the living or the dead? Okay, you're dead! Come on, *vamanos*. Everybody who's dead!"

Dora still rings in my head. I'm in some sultry, red-filtered bistro and I'm thinking of Dora songs. I'm such a loser.

Dark eyes spot this loser, and I know that at least I'm known. So I head to her this time. I'm not going to leave. I'm going to try to find out something.

A long-sleeved black T-shirt. Fitting her like the hands of a child on a Christmas present recently unwrapped. With some designer image something on the front. Probably something very cool that I'd know if I were cool. Her posture—upright—not proper but more so poised. Like some kind of model properly positioning the body in order to get the right view and angle and all that.

I stop right at the chair.

So let's try.

So I do.

—Is this seat taken?

Will she hear?

Will she reply?

Will she do anything?

Her smile resembles two hands opening up as if to grasp whatever might be falling down from the sky.

—I'm hoping it will be in the next few seconds.

It's a response. And not only that, it's one that legitimately feels like a hook in a fish's mouth. Yet it's gentle and feels so good.

—You look like you're seeing a ghost, she says.

—Do you mind if I sit?

This a question James Bond would never ask. Jason Bourne would never ask that. Some alpha male full of Jim Beam would never ask it.

Why are you suddenly full of men with abbreviations of JB?

Maybe it's a sign or a foreshadowing.

NOTE TO READER: BEWARE OF A CHARACTER NAMED JOE BURNS.

—I'd mind if you didn't.

So she says. The so-very-right answer to my so-very-wrong question. So I do as she wishes.

I'm a catching-my-breath just waiting to happen. A mumble and a look away. The very obvious, pitiful, billboard of an I've-seen-this-before. Yet she still seems interested and gracious and so insanely beautiful.

—I'm Lissie Hale.

I look around. I'm not sure why or what I'm looking around for.

Someone to come and take our orders? A boyfriend to break up this moment? But there's nothing to break it. I see a glass sitting in front of her. But again . . . again I'm still completely confused by all of this.

—I'm Spencer.

I don't give a last name. Because . . . because maybe that will be just too much. I'm dead but God forbid she look up my name on Twitter or try to friend me on Facebook.

She smiles and nods and then for the first time since seeing her she looks familiar. For some reason. It's like—it's like I've spent time with her. Hours, in fact. In another place and time, the kind that nobody else knows about.

—Nice to meet you, Spencer.

She says my name in a serious tone.

—Did I sound like that?

—A little, she says.

—Sorry. I just . . .

—It's okay. No need to apologize. No need to feel bad. Okay?

I nod but think, *Easier for you to think that.*

But then again, I don't know her. I just know that she can see me.

Those lines. God. So glorious. I can imagine feeling with my fingertips this face looking at me. Just following it like some kind of map to the undiscovered city in the middle of the Amazonian jungle. Everything about this woman feels like it's striking something. Her looks and lines and the way her lips curl up with this slight grin that feels like someone sliding a hand against my thigh.

Where's your mind and where'd that come from, Spencey?

—For some reason, I don't know . . . you look familiar.

—I've heard that before, she says.

—No, seriously. That's not some kind of line.

—I think you and I are past those kind of lines, wouldn't you say?

I nod but I don't know. I don't know what the hell I should say. I don't. I'm like a rock skipping over a blue surface of uncertainty just hoping to sink.

—I'm not quite sure what to say.

—That's okay because you're talking.

I nod.

—At least you can hear, can know that I'm here, I say.

—I was wondering when you'd actually decide to come and talk.

—What is happening?

She brushes back the dark tresses from her shoulders as if to say, *You've had enough—wait your turn.* Then I realize I just referred to her hair as tresses and wonder what I'm thinking here.

—Well, you are sitting in front of me, she says. And maybe we'll talk and get to know each other like normal people do when they're strangers.

—Do you know me?

—No.

—And yet you can see me? I mean—how can you—?

—It's okay, Spencer.

—You say that like . . .

—Like what?

But I don't finish my thought.

Like you've been around me for two decades. Like you've woken up by my side all that time. Like you've said my name many, many times.

I simply smile and blink and then it's like several moments have passed because I suddenly have a glass of red wine sitting in front of me.

When I spot it, I look at the glass then at Lissie then back at the glass.

—None for me, she says. I'm the designated driver.

I don't hesitate. The sip I take is probably more defined as a gulp. Lissie doesn't look at me in any other way than she has been looking. Which is good because it's different from other kinds of looks I've gotten and maybe I've deserved those looks but it doesn't matter now, because not much really matters. Or does it?

—You're very anxious.

I nod and laugh.

—Yeah. You'd think that I don't need to be anymore, right?

—Not necessarily.

She says this but nothing more. I want to ask her to say more, to expand, but she keeps talking before I can.

—I remember late morning walks. How they'd be my breath, my bundle of grace every time 10 a.m. suddenly showed up. I still need those. Now maybe more than ever.

—What's happened? Why am I here?

—Spencer?

Her voice, my name, the question, the tone. I suddenly can't breathe.

—Yes?

—You sit down across from a woman you've never met. Do you need to ask questions about the meaning of the universe within the first ten minutes?

I look around. I can't help it. I swear I'm thinking this is some kind of crazy dream that I'm going to wake up from. They always feature the beautiful, unattainable girl. But also me acting like a schmuck and not being able to do anything about it.

—I'm sorry.

This is all I can say.

—Don't be sorry. Please, don't even *think* about being sorry. I'm just saying. The meaning of life and the whole figuring-this-thing-out . . . ? Maybe we can just talk for a little while and you can enjoy your wine. How's that sound?

I want to ask a lot of things and I want to say a lot of things but all I can say is one simple thing.

—Okay.

Because sitting across from her—this stranger, this beauty, this sudden shock of oxygen—makes me suddenly shed the I-don't-know to be clothed in some kind of okay.

Reel around the Fountain

The most meaningful conversations don't have to be repeated verbatim. There's simply a collective sharing of the soul that occurs, a distinctive vibe, a definitive connection. One that will find you forever recalling even when the words can't necessarily be quoted. How do you quote learning about another? How do you quote falling in love? Words only capture a part of the whole experience. All you can do is hang on and then one day look back and wish you were on the ride again.

Lissie . . . where had this woman come from? This woman who knew me or at least acted like it and who seemed like my biggest fan and friend in the world. She was the living embodiment of an emoji, and thinking back over the twenty or thirty minutes or more I had spent with her suddenly seemed to stagger me. Only then do I realize we've been talking two hours.

—We haven't even ordered, I tell her.

—We haven't seemed to want to, Lissie says.

She's right, too, even though I've been helping myself with glasses of wine.

—I feel like we've just started talking.

Lissie only smiles.

—That's because we have.

As if to answer my words, a song begins to play in the background.

—Do they have a jukebox here? I ask her.

—Why?

—What Italian restaurant plays The Smiths?

—A really awesome one, Lissie says.

"William, It Was Really Nothing" plays and I know I'm in a dream. What kind, I'm not sure.

I'm lost in the song and her gaze and the glow of this early late sort of hour.

Maybe I'm back in my office bombed and dreaming.

Maybe I'm just simply dreaming the sort of weird, vibrant dreams a ghost can dream.

Or maybe . . .

—What difference does it make? she asks, quoting the next song that starts to play.

I smile.

—You're not looking very old tonight, I tell her.

—I never imagined someone could use a Smiths lyric as a pickup line.

—Aren't we past the point of the whole picking up thing?

The glow around her grin. The effervescence around her eyes.

I'm so drunk, listen to my thoughts, I just said effervescence, good Lord.

—Picking up usually refers to going somewhere, Lissie says.

—We can just stay here. I'm pretty happy here. But I know—I swear, there's a jukebox back there. The whole *Hatful of Hollow* album? Come on.

—I used to play this and my friends hated it. *Hated* it.

—Where were you living?

—I'd just moved to Illinois.

—Really?

I was genuinely surprised.

--When?

—Junior year.

—Me too.

She shares a date and I share a similar one. A similar school, a similar year. The same stranded shores. Isolation and feeling alone. Embracing this English band and many others and ultimately embracing this alone sort of life. Commonality combined with The Smiths' "How Soon Is Now?" is an intoxicating cocktail.

—I had a boyfriend break up with me to this song, Lissie says.

I think I'm genuinely in love.

—I made a mixtape for a girl with this playing on it over and over like twenty-five times, I say.

—What happened?

—She broke up with me, of course. I was boil-the-rabbit material.

—It's nice to talk to someone who knows what that means.

—Are you saying we're old?

Lissie laughs.

—I'm saying youth is wasted on the young, she says.

The glorious, most famous Smiths song plays and I've never known it to be like some kind of crazy drug. Johnny Marr's guitar feels like it's pulling something out of me, like every lame fiber is peeled off, allowing the human and loved parts to stay.

—Did you like this song? I ask.

—Did you wish high school would end? she replies.

So put together. So composed and assured. Not just with this exterior beauty but an inner kind that seemed to make the outer one only glow more.

—You don't strike me as The Smiths sort of girl.

—And you don't strike me as *The Walking Dead* kind of guy.

I laugh. I have to.

—This is crazy. I'm dead in an Italian restaurant listening to The Smiths and talking to some . . .

—To some what?

—To an angel, I say.

"Handsome Devil" hovers over us like an airplane landing with its jolting, bouncy noise filling the space.

—I'm no angel, Spencer. Remember that.

—You look like one.

—And you look like a man full of want.

I think I blush. Maybe I do. Maybe it's the wine.
I don't know.

—Do I really look like that?

—Am I wrong? she asks.

—No.

—So there you go.

—I'm guessing you're not usually wrong, I say.

Her eyes linger over the table for a moment, then over the back of the restaurant.

—I was wrong many, *many* times in my life.

—Is this wrong, the two of us sitting here?

She shakes her head.

—You found me here, Spencer. There's nothing wrong with it. We're just two souls speaking and connecting.

—Am I supposed to do something? Anything? I mean, I'm not sure why and what this whole two souls thing means. I don't know how . . .

—Spencer?

—Yes?

—The album isn't over. Let's reminisce while the music plays.

—Reminisce about what?

—About all those things we never told anybody else we longed for.

I can only smile.

—Okay.

So we talk, and we share, and we tell, and I know that Morrissey will probably be right.

"And I'll probably never see you again. I'll probably never see you again."

Probably. But that doesn't keep me from continuing to talk.

IMDuhB

As I've grown older, I've realized my heart connects more with Johnny Marr's melodies on his black Rickenbacker 330 than Morrissey's brooding verses to a bucktoothed girl in Luxembourg. Combined, of course, the two changed the course of musical history. My heart will always hear those riffs and realized their timelessness. A guitar can age like a wonderful wine, much better than a voice and a personality like Morrissey. I hear the melodies of Manchester as the night swallows me.

I open my eyes and realize the truth.

Left alone feels familiar. Like the ocean washing over feet that are cut and stinging and needing to get away from the salt water.

All I know is I've seen Lissie before. Where, I'm not sure.

Of course, it takes a while to do the obvious.

But ghosts don't do the obvious, right? Or maybe they do and that's the point.

Maybe we assume the undead know so much more because they're in another place when in all reality they simply need to google like the rest of us. But somewhere and sometime it dawns on me to go ahead and try. So I do.

Lissie Hale

Suddenly I receive a big, fat F in the field of movies. I knew I knew her.

Lissie is an actress. Not a huge one, but big enough for me to have surely known her.

It turns out I've even done the trailer for one of her movies. No, wait . . .

Nope.

Make that two.

Yes, her hair color was different in one of them. And true, she looked quite different in another—fuller, more voluptuous—but both were because of the roles she played.

You had the biggest crush on her.

So how in the world did I not realize who she was? Or is? Or will always be?

Crap.

All that talk of movies and my job putting trailers together and being so knowledgeable of film and being such a connoisseur.

What a joke.

I want to reach out and apologize. But how?

Where do I call or text or email or connect?

She didn't leave me any number or anything. At least I can't remember if she did. And now I just want to tell her I'm an idiot and of course I'm a fan and look I actually made two of her trailers.

I used to blame things on the twins. Now I can blame it on death.

Look, I've been in a bit of a fog ever since . . . well, you know.

We are all connected in some form or another with the feel of a fingertip. Like some stranger touching our cheek, we resist the strange and the weird. Yet online, we allow anything to happen. Strangers and bastards and fellow freaks can all befriend us and communicate with us and suddenly become our best friends.

Where is she?

That's all I'm wondering. I don't want a best friend.

Maybe you want way more.

Slipped

She's there, across the street and past the sidewalk and on the driveway. These things taken for granted until all is taken away and we can only watch.

I see her slip out of the garage for the moment. The smoke from the exhaust of the minivan swirling up as she wheels the garbage can down the driveway. One of those many things I used to do. I look and wonder if she might possibly see me but she doesn't and I know it's because she can't. I want to run across the street and simply look and then tap and scratch and pound on the windows of the vehicle but I know I can't. I can watch Tamara but I can't bear to see the girls.

I look at her—so composed and put together, so beautiful. I miss Tamara and miss all the everything we once had. She slips back into the garage and then the minivan backs up and heads out. Missing me like one might miss the moon in the middle of the day. It's up there, of course, but nature just doesn't allow us to find it.

Can I slip inside for a moment?

I don't want to know. I think I can, but what good would it do? Slipping and sneaking does no good, does it? I should know.

Midmorning slipping back home through the garage door through the family room up the stairs. A mess nobody needed to see, so nobody would. Dirt-caked pants and a vomit-stained shirt I didn't bother to hide other than place in a pile on the tile floor of the bathroom before passing out in our bed. I just needed an hour of sleep but I didn't realize I was still drunk. You can throw up the contents of yesterday's hysteria but still feel the screaming inside your mind. So that's what happened.

And when Tamara and the girls came home, it wasn't Mommy who found me basically unconscious smelling worse than the Anheuser-Busch horses. It was M who tried to shake me awake until slipping under the covers next to her still-sloshed and hungover Daddy dearest.

It would be bad, not then but later. Then would consist of making sure the girls didn't know Daddy had majorly f'd up and then some. I'd slipped and fallen off the cliff and Mommy was trying to still act

61

like everything was okay but soon Daddy would be wide-awake and the girls would be fast asleep and the world would turn narrow and slow and haunting.

"I don't need any help to be breakable, believe me."

So sings Matt Berninger from The National.

Slipped and slipping further with these skeletons crackling like fireworks over the sidewalk on the Fourth of a failed July.

If we stop a yesterday scorching like a wildfire, sunset waits behind our shoulders. It's better to move ahead toward two moons and endless dreams.

Motivation

—I don't like any of them.

Six words with surprising results on my career. Sometimes you have to just have some guts to say exactly what you think and feel. Sometimes I struggle summing up the thinking part but I always get the feeling part. And this was that moment when suddenly for some reason I just had to share this with the man I was meeting with.

—You don't even like one of them?

I couldn't go back now and I knew it.

—No.

—Well, let's see you do something better than.

The truth can be a strange thing. Because sometimes you can do something bigger and better and have it produce absolutely nothing. Yet at the same time, it can open every door imaginable.

That's my story.

Of course, it always helps if your story involves the great director Martin Scorsese and if he happens to like your suggestion. My version of doing "something better" was never officially released nor seen by the public. This was before YouTube existed and before the internet was a bigger part of your life than your fingers typing to look something up. The only people who saw that trailer were Scorsese and the folks at Universal Pictures.

They all took notice and that's when I began to start getting calls to help studios craft unique trailers.

It was 1995. I was two years out of college and suddenly my life had begun. A career had blasted off without much of a touchdown. And all I could do was do the only thing I expected to be doing that year: to get married.

It's strange to think of that year. Just as one door blew open, another slammed shut. This juxtaposition could be felt even on our honeymoon. So imagine, twenty years later.

Twenty years.

Time can be a terrible animal if not treated properly. You can only keep it chained down for so long until it will break the shackles and run off into some sinking sunset.

The Grind

There were things I always wanted to share but couldn't. Whether it was telling Tamara and the girls or putting them online for the rest of the world to see. These were the things inside of me that I wanted to scrape off and burn but I never could. The things I wanted to exorcise but never would.

Expectations have been a noose I've knit carefully, tight enough to choke but always snapping from faulty wiring, leaving me on my rear in the dust under a door sliding shut above me.

Success can bring courage, which can then breed irresponsibility and a devil-may-care sort of belief. This can then lead you into a deep, dark wilderness you can't escape, a place where you're on your own and you get knocked down time and time again.

To stand back up is one thing, but it takes strength to actually walk up those steps and begin the whole process again. It takes pure grit to wrap that rope around the skin again, to tighten out the slack, to stand and wait for the bottom to drop once more.

They call it insanity. Yes, true, and I'm the *Gladiator* of it, suffering well, asking not the crowd but my soul if it's entertained.

The greatest ironies that happen in life are those you're too ashamed to admit. I was living the dream and it became my worst nightmare. Making trailers for a living and instead my life had become all about making trailers.

Yet I believed the work was the parachute after being pushed out of the propeller plane. I believed in time I'd land on some kind of solid ground.

This place, however, has no ground to stand on.

JACK AND JILL (Trailer #3)

An immaculate guitar begins to play and the man strumming is the talented Dominic Miller. Yet few will ever know he's behind these licks since it's for a Sting song. And it's Sting. One of those with one name, big enough to get rid of that bothersome last name. Heck, Sting got rid of the whole thing and thought of something that you think of with bees.

"I think I love you," the heroine says with a grin.

It's Lissie Hale as a blonde and still as beautiful as ever.

"I think I'm the luckiest man in the universe," the hero says with a smile.

"I think you're right," Lissie replies.

Cut to a myriad of images and scenes. All while the song is playing.

JACK AND JILL. This December in theaters everywhere.

Truth

I knew the trailer was artsy-fartsy. Some said it didn't do anything to tell the story of *Jack and Jill*. But even the title has a bit of irony and humor in it, right?

That smile. Lissie's wonderfully warm grin. I believed it could help sell a movie and get people to come in. And for such a small film like that one, it did. I had nothing to do with it except simply showing it off to the sound of a melancholy Sting.

The story told a love story about broken people doing messy things and finding themselves completely fragile.

How fragile we are.

Fragile. Like all those passing and all those you pass. Just because the window is down and the sunroof is open doesn't mean the wind won't be coming in with all its pain and noise and turbulence.

This Lissie Hall movie was painful to watch, especially near the end. But I painted it in elegant and beautiful strokes, because at the heart it still was a love story.

Love stories can often end in heartache. I know this all too well.

Of course, I didn't get it until it was done.

I thought I could wrap it around my heart and take it with me. Without help. Without hurts. Without anything but my love and my passion and me.

I'm this solitary figure and can do very little on my own. On my own, sailing, sinking, drowning.

I look now and see the wreckage and wonder what I could have done differently. Could I have brought anything more to you? Could I have tried to break those broken parts or at least allowed you to fill them in?

Between Waves

A trailer never tells the whole story. Sometimes it outright lies. And sometimes we live our lives that way, shaping some kind of narrative, fragmented and mostly false, to all those who watch.

How about that Christmas, or that Easter, or that birthday, or that f***ing Father's Day?

I painted many colors outside the lines. I reimagined stories that really weren't there.

So what if I did that to my own life? My own self? My own story?

Making the grays yellow. Making the blacks bright blue. Circling around the square blocks. Coloring outside every imaginable line.

Figuring out a formula to fit into everyone else's expectations.

What do they know and what do I expect?

Two minutes to show it all off just like everybody else. A greeting. A handshake. A smile. A nice comment about the world at large.

Pleasing and fine and friendly and fake.

This is the trailer for your life.

This is the trailer you've built time and time again.

—How are doing?

—I'm dying.

This is the conversation you always wanted to have.

—Congratulations.

—F*** that I'm drowning.

This is the response you always wanted to share.

—I have an idea for you.

—I will kill you in five minutes.

This is the answer you always hoped to be able to give.

They don't want your opinion. They want to give theirs. They don't want to be reasonable. They simply want to share the whole story.

Put the fascinating parts first. Put the intrigue second. Put the beautiful faces up front and center. Pipe in the dramatic music. And then press Play.

Somethings

I'm wondering if I can find something hidden or underwater or make-believe before I find something sun-sheltered.

So far, I haven't found anything except an hour of *Butch Cassidy and the Sundance Kid* that confirmed how much Matthew looks like a young Paul Newman.

Something sun-sheltered. Something hidden. Something underwater. Something make-believe. Something spinning round. Something without sorrow. Something not there. Something soaring in prayer.

I haven't found anything like that, not that I've been looking that hard.

I've found something sunny, something making my head spin around, something that's suddenly made my heart soar. But she feels as real as Matthew.

My "assignment" or whatever it might be still feels like I'm going to get a big, fat F for not figuring it out.

Then what?

I'm not sure I really want to find out.

Writing on the Wall

Curiosity. This gift from God that got us into so much trouble.

I'm full of it. Closed eyes, picturing her, picturing the lines, picturing the smile. It's a kerosene heater in a cabin in the middle of a winter full of broken power lines. I want to know more, want to find out something, want to fill my wonder with answers to these weird little questions.

But I can't find or see her.

Silence, this strange solace you want in the noise and hate in the echoes. The steps on the sidewalks you notice. The slide of the door to open up to strangers that don't see you in the first place. The wind blowing and making you cold even though you shouldn't feel the chill anymore. Right?

It's been—what?—two days or three since I realized Lissie was *the* Lissie I was talking to. I roam but keep thinking the chances of running into her again are quite remote.

I look and wait. Watch and stay. I glance and gaze and keep the stare scanning this place I never noticed.

We watch when there's something we want, don't we?

Stuck, staring out, these still lifes begging to be bought and set free.

Wanted and wishing to be found, arrived at, door opened and hugged with love. The always coming into your afternoon. With that smile. That smile that reflects the sky and tells you it won't ever leave.

I wonder if she was some kind of dream. A grim afterlife fantasy. Was it all imagined? Or simply too good to be true?

The streets and the stone and the sidewalks and the hanging lights surrounding us all hang like a painting on a wall staring you down day after day. Keeping you prisoner. Telling you—daring you to make that U-turn. But you just keep going keep walking keep breathing until the moment you turn and see a vague figure that might be and could be and possibly should be—

Her.

Stepping through. Opening then closing. And you stand and you stare and you wonder and then you go.

You go because there's nothing really you can do anymore.

There are no rules here and this is something you can and will and should do.

So you do.

OMG

I don't find her but I do find the back corner of the wine bar, so I make myself comfortably numb. Until the movie star appears and I know I'm imagining every single second of this encounter.

She smiles, so I stay seated.

—You don't have to be scared, she says.

Her eyes move, so mine stay put.

—You don't have to stare that way.

Her legs move but mine tighten up.

—You don't have to be afraid, she continues to tell me.

Her stride and her every little step she takes come toward me.

—It's okay, Spencer.

And I look up and open up and suddenly find her sitting across from me, leaning in as if to tell a secret, smiling. And I keep wondering if I'm dreaming.

—I'm really here, Spencer.

She keeps saying my name and I can't say a thing and I move up and finally silence her words with the words I've wanted to tell her ever since I saw her walking on that sidewalk toward my broken and beating soul.

—Am I having this conversation in my mind? I ask.

—Do you have conversations in your head often?

This isn't some sort of romantic comedy I've found myself in. This is more like *One Flew Over the Cuckoo's Nest*.

—I'm not always this . . .

I can't finish the sentence.

—Stilted? Confused?

Mesmerized.

That's what I want to say.

Can ghosts read your mind?

—Starstruck, I say.

—Oh, please, she says. You reach a point when all of that means very little in light of the big picture.

—What do you mean?

—The fantasy. The whole awe of meeting someone supposedly

famous.

—I'm just feeling rather stupid that I missed who you were. I'm just . . . I've been lost at what's been happening for the last few weeks.

—Roaming the streets looking for people to haunt, she says with a grin.

—Is that supposed to be sarcastic?

—Sorry, it's a bad habit of mine, she says. You look like you have a good sense of humor. And you look like a nice guy, a rare thing in Hollywood.

—Well, I guess that's good to hear.

—And you weren't operating on that whole "OMG I saw her in this film or that one," she says.

—I never say OMG, I tell her.

But I should've recognized you.

I just have to ask her something.

—Where'd you come from?

She only shrugs.

—Somewhere special, she answers with a smile.

—Heaven? I ask.

Lissie gently touches her neck as she continues to beam.

—Absolutely. It's a place called North Carolina.

I can only grin back, the best response for the best sort of answer.

—Do you know how brilliant you are? I ask.

—Of course I do. I ask myself that every day.

She's playing along, acting as if I'm completely high and drunk and out of my mind.

—I'm serious.

—I know you are, she says. And it's charming to see.

—You say that like I'm a preschooler and you're the teacher.

—Well . . . if the shoe fits . . .

Charm is a plastic ball, and I've dived right into a huge tank of it, like one of those play zones full of kids jumping into safe pits. I'm a child again, young and free and full of both of these.

—You really are a remarkable talent, I tell her.

—And you really are an earnest soul.

—I'm not twelve, you know.

—I know that, Spencer.

The way she says my name. Two syllables. Bah-bum. It's not like the sound at the end of a joke. It's like the opening of some kind of foreign gate. A fortress pounding two drumbeats and letting me in.

—I remember the trailer for *Starry Eyed*. I knew that I had seen you somewhere.

Lissie nods, a knowing look like a mother remembering a fond moment with her child.

—That was a special film, she says. And a special trailer.

—The music was from Hans Zimmer's *The Last Samurai*.

—Do you collect soundtracks?

I nod.

—Yes. But I also make trailers.

—For fun?

I laugh.

—I guess it's only fitting that the actress doesn't know the guy who made that trailer for her film. So now we both know each other.

—You make trailers? Seriously?

—Yes, I say. For a living. A career. A strange sort of career.

I tell her about the two trailers I made for her films and then I proceed to apologize again.

—If you apologize one more time, I'm going to ask that you get thrown out of here headfirst.

—Okay. Thanks for understanding.

—Don't thank me. You were looking so sad it was starting to make me feel something.

—Maybe that's a good a thing, I say.

Her smile. Her silence. Her something.

I can live with them.

—When did you start? Lissie asks. Have you done this sort of thing all the time?

I hold out a hand, not forceful or cutting but rather more of an *okay, we'll get to that* sort.

—I don't want to talk about me, I say.

—Why not?

—I want to talk about you.

—There's nothing to talk about.

My eyes feel pulled in by her glance. It's so intense. So deep. And saying this sounds like some kind of line. But there's this sort of world inside it and she wears it all with this giving, open kind of smile.

—I've seen the movies. Well, not *all* of them. But quite a few.

—I don't want to talk about my movies.

—I didn't say I wanted to talk about them.

—Then what are you saying?

—I'm saying . . . I'm saying I've spent quite a long time, half my life, working with the images of filmmakers and putting them into two-minute stories and sound bites. The movies no longer interest me. But the souls behind them, someone like you, that's what I'm fascinated about.

—What do you want to know?

My hand slips over the glass and then I drain the rest of the wine.

—Can I know everything? There's time, right?

—Everything? Everything about what?

—Everything about you, Lissie.

There's this glance. A bit of surprise, a bit embarrassment, a bit sweet shyness, and a bit of desire. I see it all. I'm not a fool, not now, not at this age. Or not at the age I used to be. The sixteen-year-old Spencer wouldn't have a clue. But I know. It's impossible not to see.

Surprised acclaim and sudden want are hard things to hide.

—Weren't you a typical guy? The kind who loves professional sports and light beer and unresolved emotions?

I nod.

—I'm so that guy. I have a Cubs logo tattooed somewhere.

—Where?

—Well, I can't say. But I'm sitting on it right now.

She laughs at my joke. A sound that feels like it can unlock some kind of treasure chest discovered in the deep waters of the Pacific.

—You're cute, Lissie tells me.

—There's nothing more I've wanted than to be called cute by a movie star.

—There's no movie star anywhere around here.

74

—Stars can't see themselves. Right?

—What? she asks.

—When I'm looking up at the constellations, they can't see the same sight I'm staring at. Right?

—I suppose.

—Well, I suppose too. I suppose it to be a fact.

—You're being a bit too kind. I'm blushing.

—I know, I say. And it's pretty beautiful.

So Young and So Old

—You carry regret around like a ragged piece of luggage, she says sometime much later.

—That sounds like a line from a movie.

—Nope, she says, shaking her head. Just a line from someone who knows.

—You don't seem to regret.

—I do. More than anybody will ever know. But I've dealt with them.

—How? I ask.

—That mystery is for you to answer.

—This isn't an Agatha Christie movie.

—Life—and death, too—are far better than anything ever imagined from Ms. Christie. No offense to our favorite mystery writer. But there are mysteries you'll have to solve, small and big.

—Like what?

—Like what you're doing here. Now. With me.

I only look at Lissie. *Good point.*

—Where should I be? I ask.

—I'm the last person who should you tell that.

—We're talking, so I wouldn't say the last.

—The first shall be last, Lissie says. Right?

—So you're the first?

—No. I'm the found.

—Then what am I?

She smiles.

—The lost.

The conversation shifts this way then that way like someone kitesurfing, fighting both the wind and the water to try to keep from falling.

Sometime later, maybe much later, maybe not that much later, and maybe with or without the help of wine, I just have to tell her this thing inside. A leak that's obviously filling and flooding the floor around us.

—There's something about you, I say.

—What's that?

—You make me feel young.

—Does that make me the same?

—That makes you the picture I just got in a packet of twenty-four where only one is worth the cost.

—Am I worth it?

—You're worth the invention of the camera.

Suddenly Lissie Hall, the actress and the confident and assured one on this side of the other side of life, blushes like some sophomore in high school.

—Stop it, she says.

—You want honesty.

—I don't want to be embarrassed.

I don't want to embarrass her, so I ease off, but I can't help feeling things that haven't been around for some time.

—You know something? I ask her.

—What?

—It's a weird thing to remember feeling so young at such an old age where you're nearly forgotten about.

—You're never forgotten, Spencer. Remember that. We're the ones that forget about God. But He's always there, searching our hearts.

I grin.

I want to lay my heart next to hers.

The Secret of Shadows

Strange. How the dead can keep their regrets. How the shadows seem to stay. How the light never seems to brighten.

Sometimes I wonder about these images soaring inside. I feel lost, yet still alive. I want to know it all and I want to bury everything.

A part of me wants to scream out but I don't have anybody to talk to. I can see and stand but I can't say a word. Frozen, standing still, I'm seeing all the things I need to try to be.

The bells in my heart wrinkle around, creating something I can see I can see, spinning softly like some kind of a tornado on a television screen. The sensations ripple and I walk right through them. Wet and weary. Worn down but continuing to keep on going.

Yet nobody sees me. Not a soul.

I'm not guessing I'm left on this planet to haunt. God knows I've got enough ghosts of the past haunting me. Why in the world would I want to do the same to someone else?

But the spaces on the sidewalks seem uneven. The markings on the building walls seem a bit ugly. I walk the same square lines in the day and wonder if I'm just going in circles that have a lot of ninety-degree turns.

Interesting. Ghosts don't have shadows, but they still hold secrets. Seems strange we should carry one while not being followed by the other.

Maybe those who know watch and get tired of waiting.

You Know

—Come back.

I hear her words and try to make sense of them. Surely I'm in a dream. Because, of course, ghosts have to sleep, right?

—You know where to find us.

Tamara tells me this, but I don't know where they ever went in the first place. Where to find them? Are they lost in the back of a Target?

—It'll be there, she says. It'll be on.

And I jerk awake but I'm actually already there. I just hear the sound of the train in the distance. The damn train. The one that would always greet me around midnight. The same sound, the same sort of recognition, like passing the same stranger every day in a liquor store, with him holding his and you holding yours. With a simple nod of an acknowledgment. Knowing you're both fueling up for the foolery that's to come.

"It'll be there."

What? The state of California? My morning brew? What's she mean?

Do you question the statements in a dream?

Maybe when they feel so real. It's like I'm reading a text or something.

I recall our song, that familiar one, the well-played and well-sung one. I think about it being played right there in front of us. So long ago.

A life and a universe away.

Do I really know? 'Cause I'm thinking I know nothing.

Fool's Gold

I'm sure there are a few out there that get this but I've never met them and don't think I ever will.

There are these things inside. This jerking sort of quake like the kind of thing you might feel in California.

Strangers. Sullen. Stupid. Standing there on the corner just watching, just staring, just sucking air and living some kind of life.

I want to wave at them while I accidentally drive my car into them.

I'm not a violent sort but for the love of mankind people need to get a pulse. Move. Do. React. Stop sitting there staring at your phones and trying to think of something interesting to post.

Live.

Do.

Breathe and go.

Think about it. I come from a generation that got fed up and decided to do a bit of *everything*. Generation X. The angry generation.

Now everything and everybody is PC. Politically Castrated.

Don't mock this.

Don't say a bad thing about that.

Gen Xers couldn't care less.

But maybe half of them are like me now. Broke, bruised, and trying to figure out what the f*** is going on with the world.

Fool's Gold.

Breakdown in the brilliance of the afternoon sun.

I find myself searching for liquor I don't have in my office.

Come on.

I'm better than his.

No, you're dead.

Hard to argue with that. Right.

So I turn it up louder and find some bad wine cooler in my fridge.

Yes.

This isn't supposed to be the story line.

I'm not twenty-four anymore.

But yeah, I'm standing alone. And yeah, I'm watching you all. A specific and very certain You.

Are you sinking? I sure am.

Weighing the gold sinking.

That's me.

What to do what am I supposed to do what the hell am I supposed to do?

So I finish my horrible-tasting cherry limeade while cranking up the tunes and I ponder and think and plan for a day that isn't going to come since I'm past all that.

My life's become fool's gold.

SCARLET WONDER (Trailer #4)

A hand writing in cursive on a letter. Simple and silent. Black ink on the white surface. Like oil on the surface of the ocean, floating, shivering almost. That's because the words are moving slightly, like some kind of trick of the eye. Then the camera begins to pan back and the words start to dissolve and you see a woman's long, blonde hair falling over her back and you see her hands crumple the page.

Then Adele begins to sing. And the blonde turns to look up at the birds passing in the sky and you see Gwyneth Paltrow. Looking beautiful and ordinary in the same way. The same actress we all fell in love with and yet older, wiser, and definitely more hurt.

"They say that time's supposed to heal ya, but I ain't done much healin'," Adele sings.

The woman on the screen begins to walk somewhere. Then as the chorus starts and swells, we see snapshots on the screen like ones being organized in a photo album. We see pictures of a young girl and a high school student and college graduate and summer vacation and a wedding and honeymoon. All shots of Gwyneth and we're still wondering what's going on.

Then as the figure begins to walk into the sunlight, we squint and can't see her anymore until the shadow shifts and a figure steps out into the frame. The same but different. And then you see what appears to be a man walking down a long dirt road. An average guy from the looks of it. He's wearing a jacket and the colors of autumn swirl around him and he reaches a wooden mailbox and opens it.

All we see is the empty box, a black hole lit for a second, then shut once again.

The figure turns and starts walking back where he came from, the fading sun encapsulating him and making it impossible to see who the actor happens to be. Then once again the camera moves back. He looks up and sees birds moving past.

SCARLET WONDER.

Coming soon to a theater near you.

No Ordinary Love

Passion can only fuel a car so long. But the ride you take . . . it will be a memorable one.

Perhaps that's why the inevitable slowing down and running out and stalling on the side of the road can feel so painful. You're left parked and abandoned and motionless, left with a pocket full of rainbows and a mind full of memories. Most of them racing with want and desire and need.

I think back and remember. The Goldmoor. I can close my eyes and remember and sometimes even get turned on by this simple exercise. Strange to think that something so disconnected and fragmented can still bring such an intensity to it. But longing and lust don't both equal love. I've learned that. Realized it. But we both did.

We had been told by Tamara's sister about the Goldmoor, booking it without even realizing we'd be in our own separate little house. With some fancy space rug stretched out over the carpet when you first walk in, almost begging to be messed around on. The fireplace, the large triangle tub overlooking the Mississippi River valley. This top-rated inn in Galena surprised us with its romance and its seclusion.

It felt sexy and secret. We were here, alone, without anybody else knowing. And it was there after being married a few years that Tamara and I found something we'd never found before. Something that would be hard to find ever since.

An openness. An acceptance. A vulnerability. Not just physically but emotionally.

I can still see her. So young and so rail-thin and so timid and so adorable. Standing before me and trying to cover herself. I can see myself, so young and so male-dumb and so eager and so overwhelmed. We had been married a few years and knew each other and knew what made us click but something about this weekend, something about this place, something about it all just felt right and raw and came into color like a tattoo.

Making love to my wife wasn't just that. Not this time. It felt like something more. It felt like pouring out water to someone thirsty and desperate for a taste and suddenly being overwhelmed. She would pour and then I would and it kept going.

Snow whipped outside and covered our house and we didn't leave the room for forty-eight hours. At one point we wondered if they were going to be able to deliver our dinner to our room/house/love shack in the middle of the unlikely hills of northwest Illinois. Food wasn't on our minds, however. Young and in love. Young without children. Young and hungry and finally free of the shackles life brings.

It was short-lived, of course. The fantasy and the dream always are. Just like the beauty of film. For two hours, you're transported away, then you leave and enter reality. You leave inspired and disappointed. The power of cinema. And the power of . . . well, love and romance and sex.

In my office, on the couch in the cold, this blanket really needing a major upgrade, I think of Tamara. I think of that weekend and then I think about her now—I imagine us meeting there again now. Her body no longer so tiny, her fears no longer so visible. The woman I know and I left coming before me with that same openness and vulnerability. With more curves and more character than before. Each fascinating line telling another story, physically or emotionally.

I want you.

Words I would give anything to hear. Ones that were missing, that had suddenly vanished like the green grass during a blizzard.

I don't want to stop.

Words I can only imagine now as the man I am or at least the man I used to be.

A candle flickering just like it was when we were just adult kids.

The jets bubbling in the whirlpool just like they were when we stumbled upon the place and discovered this little mecca away from the rest of the world.

I don't want to get out.

Words from a woman and a wife no longer bound by schedules and commitments and struggles and frustrations but simply by passion.

It's hard to imagine but I've spent my life imagining and that's what I'm doing.

The music in the background playing, always so important, this time chosen by someone else but doing the job. The music singing a chorus with the buzzing of the hot tub. The buzzing ignored by Tamara and me.

The right look and the right outfit and the right sound and the right everything was always my downfall. I could manipulate it with a trailer with constant edits and shades and sounds and sights. But in life, you can't control everything. And in a relationship and especially in a marriage, you can't control anything. You can only give. And I never gave and I only took.

"You took my love," Sade sings.

And that's what I did. Over and over and over again. And yet my perfectionistic tendencies and my desire to shape and control this desire proved to be my undoing.

Those vulnerable, open souls in the Goldmoor that weekend would soon be a thing of the past. Some distant memory that seemed to become more like an urban myth than truth. But now—right now—in this cold, dark room—I'm remembering it and I feel it. And all I know is the need and desire inside me.

Can a ghost feel lust? I don't know but this one does. And closed eyes and shadowed room around and only the sights and sounds of memory covering me, I remember. Every part of me remembers and reenacts and tries to receive a bit of the love poured over me back then.

But that's back then.

Imagination is wonderful for inspiration but not for insight. And with every inch of myself and my body giving way to being back there in that place, I'm left hollowed out and empty and reminded that I'll never be back in that place. I couldn't go back even if I tried.

The Long and Winding River

The others don't know and won't understand and can't ever see it. This flood. The water coughing over the cusp of the hilltop scattering into muddy downpour. The busy that once followed me. The busy that burrowed itself into my heart.

In my office, the four hushed walls with nothing moving except the images on the two monitors, I recall one of the last projects of mine. The endless trailer to the endless movie. A simple comedy that the actor/director everybody knows was suddenly turning into an epic, *Apocalypse Now* type of spectacle. I referred to that movie *a lot* since the dozen of trailers I had made still didn't work to his impossible-to-find satisfaction.

I would make changes and send them to him and wake up the next morning only to get some passive-aggressive comments with him remarking on the changes that I made to the trailer. Yet I reminded him that *he* was the one who made them and that this wasn't an actual movie I was working on but a f***ing trailer. Yet his charm and joking would win me back over, so I kept on.

—This is all I have, Spencer.

So he said, and so I kept on paddling downstream, wondering what kind of darkness I might find.

—This is my one and only shot, he said.

Unlike Lissie, this man's a household name, and once that name was good, but now not so much. The movie he was making . . . I take it back. It was initially supposed to be a comedy but it had gone from a dark comedy to now simply dark. There was drama and a bit of the supernatural and some indie-ness and also some wild artsy Kubrickian-out-there stuff.

—I do have other projects I have to work on, I told him.

In the two years of working with him on a trailer that hadn't yet seen the light of day, I had made a dozen others. I work fast, but I also work to support my family. To pay bills.

—This isn't just a "project" to me, Spencer.

What could I say to that? Yes, I understood. This wasn't just a work of art. This was his life poured into art. And if in the end, he stood before an audience accepting his Oscar, then his persistent dissection of every single aspect to the film would pay off. But I really and truly wondered if the movie was going to be released.

What happens to all the work I've done now that I'm gone?

Good question. He has everything I've done so far. Perhaps another company can take my ideas and work and do something with it.

Good luck with that is all I can tell them.

A one and only shot. Can an artist really end up down the line standing at a brick wall knowing there's only one more chance for the door to open?

You create out of need and desire and not out of fulfilling expectations.

Yet I wonder if that's what I've been doing for so long. That the last few years have been all operating on my one and only shot. That each project keeps me on this long and winding river going nowhere. But they give me a little more fuel to keep the boat moving. Floating along toward my inevitable doom.

With Friends like These . . .

A friend asks and you haven't had a question in years.

A friend knocks but all I've heard are your fingernails scratching on the windows.

Maybe you should be a little more interested in something other than yourself.

Maybe it would feel good to be asked about the family. The children.

Maybe my concessions have simply been padded envelopes full of nothing but bubble wrap ready to be flipped off some tall cliff.

You should know better but the better left you a long time ago.

You should know me but the me you once knew is a skeleton now.

There's a dictionary definition of a friend that you might decipher if you have a priest and a prophet beside you.

I'm persistent and stubborn and I've given you enough slack to let you slip out to the coast of the Netherlands.

You don't get it and I know now you never will.

A cactus can't comprehend a rain forest. It sits and stays under the sun and meanwhile there's this whole universe it cannot ever comprehend and never will.

So, friend—is that what I can call you? I'm not sure if an acquaintance even fits. The passing ripples of memory never seem to rattle your boat. You're asleep while I'm trying to figure out how to walk on water. But God knows you're no Christ figure. You're the one slipping up and telling me the tree isn't that deadly and that it's okay to take a simple bite.

I simply need to take a sip and I'm yours. And you have me. And I can't stand on any sort of solid ground because mine is so damn brittle and brutal.

So I let go and let you in again.

And again.

And again.

Come Talk to Me

I remember being so close and not talking.

Sitting across with the walls of headphones on one side of the cell bars, reality television on the other. So comfortable with barely anything worth comfort, with neither being able.

To go back to just wake us up.

That's what I'd want.

To shake and grab and see and hold and love.

All those jobs that meant so much seem so insignificant. Insufficient. Inward and idiotic. Insane, honestly.

I'm in my office drinking from that stash I had from people who sent me stuff. I always thought it'd be wrong to drink from my office. Home? Not so much. I was pretty good drinking the night away with wine. But never in my office. Never in the middle of the day. But now. Well, why not?

And I can't stop thinking of the two of us. Like ships passing in the night. Yeah, that's me trying to be funny. The ships are made of cloth and cushion, the anchors buried deep, the SOS alarms failing to work. Rising and falling and rising and then abandoning ship at different times.

Yeah. It wasn't the best of connections. I lost myself in my work in order to be the best of something. And she—well, I don't know, honestly. But she was lost. Maybe lost wondering why she'd married down.

I think of the settling. The complacency. The disconnect. So close but further away than the random Facebook friend liking some stupid post of mine.

Then sleeping above me while I work. And moving about me while I work. And parenting while I work. And running errands while I work. And living a life while I work.

Think there's a theme there. Yeah.

I've been playing music and it keeps getting louder and louder and now I feel the rumbling of tribal drums while Peter Gabriel sings the intro song to *Us*. Begging, imploring, inviting someone to come talk to him.

"I can imagine the moment, breaking out through the silence, all the things that we both might say."

I still find myself imagining it, even more so.

We never had that talk. And we never will.

Praying for Time

—Am I dreaming?

  —No, she says. This is real.

  —And you are real?

  —As real as I can possibly be.

She doesn't look real, however. She's a living and walking movie. A sit-down-in-your-seat-and-watch sort of woman, the kind only destined to be shot and captured and admired. The light seems to gently stroke her cheekbones and her long, sleek neck from every angle. I watch and keep watching and don't dare to blink or else I'll miss something.

  —Why are you looking at me that way?

I shrug and act like I have no idea what she's talking about.

Oh, you mean this face of complete and absolute obsessed desire raging right in front of you? That look?

  —What are you thinking? Lissie asks.

It's a combination of things. This blustery, hurricane of a beauty storming in front of me. This raging fire deep inside, one I'm trying to hold back, one that's saying, *Good Lord, what are you doing here with her?*

Then there's the whole *you're a ghost and dead so what the hell, Spencer* sort of thing.

  —I think you know what I'm thinking.

She smiles with a kindness I'm not looking for. It's a Maria from *The Sound of Music* sort of smile. Sweet and sisterly and soft and all wrong for this moment.

  —Those sort of things don't happen here, she says.

  —What? Are they forbidden? Or are they unable to happen because of . . . ?

  —I won't allow it.

Ah, okay. I finally find my fantasy woman and she refuses to "allow it," whatever "it" might be.

  —All righty then, I say.

For a moment she just looks at me. The song in the background plays and plays and keeps playing as if it's waiting for something and anything to happen so it can simply end.

—You have a sad, puppy-dog look on your face, Lissie says.

—No I don't.

—You do. Truly.

—I just . . . I feel like I just got rejected. And I didn't ask for anything.

—Oh, you didn't?

Her voice is startling in its power and passion. And she continues to talk.

—I swear I heard this voice of possibility, one which is asking without asking.

—I didn't ask anything.

—Your expression said everything you could have possibly said, and then some, she says.

—Maybe you don't know my *expressions*, I say.

—I'm not dumb, Spencer.

But I guess I am. I'm dumb and then some.

—I have all these . . . feelings . . . deep inside and I have no idea what I'm supposed to do.

—You're supposed to have dinner with me.

—We're ghosts having dinner. And wine. And salad. I mean, what the hell? I'm eating a salad. No ghost I've ever seen has eaten a salad.

Lissie smiles. Strong, knowing, wise. A smile that makes me want her even more.

—So you've dined with lots of ghosts? she asks.

—No. I've seen a lot of movies, though.

—So have I, she says. And I like to break the rules and push the envelope and bend the genre. Ghosts can have salad. Watch.

She puts her fork into the lettuce and then puts it to her mouth to swallow. She gives me a "ymmm."

I'm hungry, but not for salad. Or for any entrée.

—Why am I here? I ask her again.

—Because there is a way things work and a way things break. There are things that still need to be done. You saw Matthew, did you not?

—I had no what he meant.

—He was giving you more time, she says.

—I thought he was high on drugs.

—Yet you knew, did you not? You knew he was someone called by God.

I nod.

—Maybe he simply wanted to help push you.

—What? Over the cliff?

—Over the hurdle for bigger and brighter things.

I wait for something else, for something more, yet she doesn't say anything.

—Do you believe that's even possible? I ask.

—Yes. For you.

Now This Is Fun

Maybe it takes a cover to allow me the right to stamp a song onto my story. And that's okay because it's never about the original song and the musician or band who performed it. It's the core of the tune, the reason it connected, the shadow of memory it cast.

I'm twelve again walking into the mall with my dying grandfather who's allowing me to buy a cassette. Yes, an actual cassette.

I'm fifteen sneaking out onto the snow-covered golf course to meet the girl of my dreams even though my parents strictly forbid me to.

I'm seventeen waking up wondering where I am then realizing I'm under a blanket in my boxers in the house of the homecoming queen except never in the way I might have imagined I might be.

I'm eighteen driving up to somewhere in Michigan holding the love of my life in one arm on senior ditch day.

All while those songs, melodic imprints, follow like white clouds and thick coats and laughter from little ones.

This scattered biography can be built from those diverse songs signaling something.

I wait for this moving hand to scoop me up like the wave on a dance floor. But the chords and the chorus never seem to signify it all nor do they ever sum up these feelings inside.

When I turn off the music, the noise in the background remains. It's the train horns sounding off and playing their own familiar tune once again.

Shape of My Heart

—I've been working on this one particular trailer for some time.

Lissie waits there on the couch as if I'm going to play it for her.

—It's not finished, I say.

—Okay.

She still waits.

—I'm not going to show it to you.

—Why not?

—Because like I said, it's . . .

—Not ready?

—Yeah.

Her eyes grow wide in feigned shock.

—Heaven forbid you show something that's not *finished*.

—I've been working on it for some time.

—Is it a trailer for a movie you made? she asks.

—No, though . . . you might say the trailer has suddenly become a movie itself.

—Interesting. There's a concept.

—What?

—What if you made a trailer for a film that hasn't been made?

—That's sorta what I've done, I say with a grin.

—But your trailer is incomplete, right?

I nod.

—The story of my life, I say.

Creature Comfort

The number pops up. Why I'm carrying a phone, I don't know. Why someone's still calling me, I really don't know. And what the 616 area code happens to be, hell if I know.

Pick it up pick it up and realize the reality.

I'm kinda drunk. I'm listening to Arcade Fire.

Which album? God knows you've been living this life between becoming a Reflektor and wanting Everything Now.

The ring. And again. And once ringingly again and again.

Pick it up it will be painless.

But I don't. I let it ring.

"On and on, I don't know what I want."

On and on.

Ringing on and on.

It's been ringing before.

I turn up the music and set aside my phone and don't want to think anything about it.

Certain life seems so far away from me.

On and on and on and on and on . . .

I'm comfortable but not comforted. I'm feeling painless but still in pain.

The song comes on—a little new and little nuanced—and I turn it up and tune out.

Then I stare at the phone and see no message.

In the words of Genesis, there's "No Reply at All."

Another new song and another drink. They kinda go hand in hand.

What's with that number? Is it another one of those bill collectors wanting to collect something they'll never be able to bill?

The more I listen and listen like I do I find I like this album.

Did this just come out or has this been out?

In stories there's never a specific year, is there?

Keep it simple, stupid. Keep it vague, you vermin.

Turn it up and forget the rest.

Somehow and someway I swear I hear my phone going off again. It's gotta be someone who no longer matters.

96

Memories

I try to find Tamara, to see her pulling into the driveway or getting out of the car in the parking lot of the school. But I can't find her. I wonder if it's the real world blocking me out for some reason.

Perhaps my time around here is nearing its end.

Moments have been coming back to me. Not so pretty moments. The kind you want to forget. The sort you *have* to bury in order to keep moving. In order to simply survive.

The arguments. All the harsh words over insignificant matters. They seemed to come in force after the birth of our twins. The differences in our personalities were magnified exponentially as we daily tried to figure out how to parent. I walked around without a clue, feeling like I was drifting in the dark waters of an ocean trying to find some sort of dry land. And I began to feel as if I wasn't getting any help from Tamara. Instead, every single thing I did felt undermined and abandoned and neglected and disregarded.

The still and the silence of now know better.

I recall one of those last arguments after I had been on her time and time again.

—I'm glad you're leaving.

I was leaving on a short trip but she might as well have been talking about me leaving for good.

I try to remember the last words I said to her. Our last meaningful conversation. But like a childhood spent dealing with the trauma of moving and emotional abuse from my father, I have blocked out so many memories. I can't find them anymore.

And now, on the other side, they're starting to come back. And they hurt me even more.

They hurt because I let those memories happen. I chose to bury them.

I refused to change course and do anything about them.

In Dreams

The imagination of midnight prompts a thousand perhaps rolling around the ocean of sleep.

Perhaps you're a minor chord stuck in some major hit for someone to edit out.

Perhaps you're the drumbeat for some manufactured, manipulated mainstream tune.

Perhaps you're the chorus accepting every verse you find accompanying you on any given summer sunset.

Perhaps you wait for the night to shield you from the mistakes made during the day.

Perhaps your faith finds the beauty in the already gone.

Can you find the fault in all those stale formulas everybody else chooses to use?

Perhaps it's time to strip down to your single soul desire to show them all. But what if you're an emperor standing in his clothing?

Perhaps it's time to start to chime on some old grand and to let me love you like all those little boys you always seem to linger to.

The Shining

There's no arguing here in this place, only shadows on shadows where light can't be seen. I see the still and wonder if I'm in heaven or hell. But the smell of tacos and gasoline remind me I'm in neither because they're a combination of both.

It's strange because I feel half myself and half something else. Not quite here but not quite departed, either. I have the same feelings and same senses and the mirror tells me I have the same bags under my eyes and around my waist. I've still got tired eyes after dying. Can't a guy get a break?

My office remains with its desk and computer and love seat. This is where I rest. I guess ghosts sleep. Sometimes. Even though the middle of the night seems like the logical place for me to be. But nobody is around for me to haunt or watch or simply pass by.

The winter, so weary and so hell-bent for war. Snow piles and keeps me in. When I go outside, I don't see my tracks in the flakes, but I do feel the cold. The blizzard breathes and melts against my cheeks and tongue. Vehicles drive by as I search over the sidewalk but nobody waves or notices or knows. I'm a six-foot-tall snowflake.

My heart sometimes hurts but I think it's more from the loss than from pain. Can ghosts feel pain? I know the hurt swells inside.

I picture Tamara and me walking on a snowy sidewalk holding hands so I can keep her from falling. God—the notion of holding hands seems so foreign now. I want to hold it and squeeze it and never let it go. To drag her on into my world and place. But then I think of the girls and I know I'd never do that. I can't. I won't.

This world is a wonderful contradiction with its beauty blemished by weather.

It's so easy to hide in the snow. The streams facing north and south. Cutting into your core. I stay inside. In the dim light. The lone bed. The coffeemaker I only look at. The fridge that's empty.

This is *The Shining* turned into a novella. Everything is smaller. The place I'm in. The people I'm around. Everything's been edited to one solitary soul in a claustrophobic place.

Not sure how long the days and nights and weeks last. But they're long but they blink and they're gone.

Like life.

Like breathing, breathless life.

The river I pass daily, many times, still moves. Always.

Even in the ragged chill, I will stop and look down. The drop would take about two seconds. I stare at the endless, steady current of water below and I know. It'll always be there underneath this stone bridge.

Eyes circle and shift. I clench a fist. It's really not for effect. It really does make me feel a little better, this tight and angry squeeze. There's nothing loose or joyful about my soul right now.

Maybe I could simply dive into the river and be baptized and set free.

Thieves like Us

—Like New Order?

Lissie's question is silly.

—John Hughes introduced me to the band. And of course, I fell in love.

—Let me guess, she says. "Shellshock" in *Pretty in Pink*?

—Right movie but wrong song. For me it was when she was getting ready for prom and he used "Thieves Like Us." I had no idea that the same band who did "Shellshock" and the heartbreaking "Elegia" also did this one. That's when I knew.

—When you knew what?

—I'd heard a kindred soul. Or kindred souls, I should say.

Lissie smiles.

—What? I ask.

—You're cute when you're struck with passion.

—I think I'm far past the cute phase.

She shakes her head.

—No. You still have that young, boyish look about you.

—Could I be in a John Hughes film?

—Of course, she says.

—Really?

—Sure. As a daddy.

It stings and amuses at the same time.

—Low blow.

—Well . . .

I wait for her to say more and then ask her what she's talking about.

—Well, speaking of *low*.

—What? I ask.

—There's this particular band that's playing tonight in Chicago. *Low-Life*. Ever heard of that album?

This is so weird. Seeing her smile. The flicker in her eyes. Playful and far from death and haunting and doom and gloom. And I hear Bernard Sumner singing, "Let's go out and have some fun."

—Are you inviting me to a New Order concert?

Lissie gives me a mischievous grin.

—Yes. And we don't need tickets. Isn't that a beautiful thing?

I want to know lots of things but I don't ask. I'm learning that not asking is better. Because it seems I can blink and suddenly find myself somewhere else. Except in this case, that doesn't happen.

I don't just close my eyes and find myself at the Chicago Theatre. I find myself following Lissie and slipping onto a Metra train and sitting in the seat. And I swear . . . I can hear New Order playing as if it's the soundtrack. It's "Thieves like Us" once again. The B-side on *Substance*, the instrumental version, the John Hughes salutation to the world. This is playing in the background.

I'm sixteen again.

I'm stupid and sixteen. Not the stupid-fortyish-should-know-better but the dumb teen who also happens to be a male which makes me even more stupid. But I'm sitting in a seat next to someone who emotionally is twice my age. She gives me a confident, knowing grin that makes me feel like a turtle peering out of its shell.

—You seem uncertain.

I nod.

—Yeah. I've sorta been that way since . . . well, since I found out I was a DEAD MAN WALKING.

—Did you just go ALL CAPS on me?

—How could you tell?

—The dead can see typesetting.

—Really?

Lissie just laughs.

—No. But that's pretty funny.

Then later, after time passes—how much I can't say—I realize something.

—I see it, I tell her.

—See what?

—The darkness underneath the smile.

—I never said it wasn't there.

—Yet you glide like your feet aren't touching the ground.

—Isn't that what ghosts do?

I smile.

—But I felt your hand against me. Your touch is real.

—This is real. Don't you realize that?

—What? I ask.

—We connect in different ways. By sight and sound and touch. And sometimes even in our dreams.

—I like the touch part the best.

Lissie smiles.

—You like to think you do, but you don't, she says.

—Then what do I like the best?

—You like someone figuring out the mystery.

I shake my head.

—No.

—No? she asks.

—No. I like someone bothering to solve the mystery in the first place.

After the show when she's gone, I can't sleep. I'm lost in something, this thing I've been submerged inside.

I hear the outside noise. It's not a gust scattering paper across the lawn but a pelting of hail against the side of the window. This visible shaking, scattering thoughts, spilling out my soul and my secrets. Like the only place in a flat, endless field to hide out away from the lightning strikes. This slanted roof covering overhead and held up with a beam I cling to like the last dance of a prom night. Safe for the moment but wondering when the storm will shuffle away.

I tell myself my imagination is far better than the moment and the presence but then I'm proven wrong, so very wrong. You can't imagine the spirit behind a love like that. You can imagine the words and the embrace and the glance and the desire but you can't fathom the spark behind it. Not like that. Not like her.

Sky Blue

I recall an intimate getaway with Tamara not long ago. Something that became more and more rare the longer time passed and the older we got.

The bright hovering glow of the sun split between us in the snapshot. Restless water waving beneath us. A sky blue glory above. I breathe and am no longer tired.

I know.

The touch of a finger poking or nudging. The smile wavering toward mine. The laughter. And the lingering moments of just study.

After so many years, this is simple foreplay.

This is rare and it makes me giddy.

It makes me fifteen again.

I can't know and don't want to know the habits of others. Married or couples or two horny teens getting it on. All I know is this and I know tonight will end with a physical joy. But I also know it'll be more.

We walk on grass painted green. Near bubbling creek water. Over wooden docks toward the banquet hall. Bumping into one another. Smiling. Close.

These are things that I haven't known for a long time and they will be things I'll carry over to the other side.

I know that now.

There are moments in your life you remember past your grave. Not just moments of intimacy, of great sex, but ones where your heart is full. Where a heart rests at the surface of the lake like a full inner tube impossible to drown.

Where the smiles of older men and women know.

They know.

They know it's one of those moments. The cherished. The treasured. The kind you carry when it's dark and snowy and cold. Like now.

I take it out and polish it and I remember every moment. Every embrace. Every kiss. Every other thing.

When you're a teen, you dream of this. Not just the act but the intimacy. The closeness. The getting out of yourself and letting another fill you. The slow breath of resolution.

You find the twenties and you start to know. You start to feel. You start to get closer.

And every year and every decade and it's closer. The lines form along with a history of the highs and lows. Of knowing what works and when it works so when it comes, it's this release from the world you both know and no longer care about.

A hush over the rest of the noise. Just two voices. Just two bodies. Just two souls. Just two lovely days merging into one. Into a lifetime.

And I know.

I know it's what God wants and delights in.

I open my eyes and realize I've been imagining Tamara naked and real and relaxed and there.

The last time I can remember her being that way.

The last time.

The inner tube punctures and slowly starts to sink into the water while the snow outside taps at the window, desperate to come in and further sink my cold, dark soul.

Control

—I found myself sixteen again.

Lissie looks up, trying to understand what that means.

—In my early forties. I found myself repeating some of the same steps, feeling isolated just like I did thirty years earlier.

—How so? Lissie asks.

—It's easy to get lost in our own little worlds. Now more than ever. We slide through our portals into these bright and loud digital worlds where we're the hero and the god and meanwhile we don't realize we've all cocooned ourselves.

—I think you're right.

I stare out to the thick, colorless slate.

—Plus, that was my job, I add. That was my profession, my livelihood, my choice. To take others' creations and stories and then weave something out of them. To not only live in a fictitious story, but one that belonged to someone else. Even in the fantasy I was creating, I was censored and never in control.

—None of us are ever in control, Spencer. Don't you realize that?

The angles on her face seem jagged tonight, impossible to touch without slicing the skin, delicately defensive.

—I know I haven't been in control for a long time. A very long time.

Her bare face suddenly softens like dry feet on sand being washed over by a warm wave.

—And yet you're still fighting. You're still resisting. You're still refusing to just let go, aren't you?

—Let go of what? I ask.

—I can't see it all, and I have only heard a tiny fraction of things, but I can simply see it.

I shake my head.

—See what?

—This foundation set deep into the ground. A foundation of hurt, most buried in the dirt, unseen with an attempt to be forgotten.

—I guess there's no reason to carry the hurt anymore, right? Is that what you're saying?

—No. I'm saying now is the time to remember it. To recall and even rejoice in it. To embrace it.

Lissie must be drunk or mad because she's making no sense.

—So it's not enough to *die*? To physically just keel over and then wake up and have to be wandering and then—*oh yeah*, why don't we think about all the s***ty things that made life so bad and let's just *embrace* it?

—That's nothing like what I said, Lissie says.

—So what are you saying then?

I can hear the sharp crack of intensity in my voice, the kind I used to have without any hesitation with Tamara. It doesn't do a thing to Lissie. She's strong. She's very strong.

—I'm saying you can shut the life you had out and simply try to surround yourself in something else or you can settle the old score with yourself.

I love the way Lissie talks, especially when she says things like this. She sounds a little like I feel, and she manages to decipher my mood into something monumental and moving. Almost making me believe I came up with the words myself.

—Can I surround myself with you? I ask.

The smile on my face is larger than it's been for a long time.

—I'm too tall and skinny, she says with a laugh. I can't block out anything or anybody.

—But you can certainly be there when something comes to try to knock me down.

—Something already knocked you down, Spencer. I'm here to help you get back up.

—And when will that happen?

—You have to let me know that.

With those words, she slips back out the door and out of sight, just like the ghost she happens to be.

We Have All the Time in the World

I believed I'd find it. That I'd take it. That I'd conquer it.

I never knew it stood there on some mountaintop above me, simply watching and laughing. Seeing my futile attempts to climb the steep, sleek peak. Standing in silence, knowing how ill-equipped I happened to be, both inside and out.

So young and foolish and deluded. This would be me.

Am I the same stupid soul that I was as a twentysomething?

Passion and a belief that something could survive because of it.

How little did I know. How little my view could really be.

The snapshot of the intersection of two streets, giving a sigh, showing neither red or green but a blackout. I'm at a standstill, remembering. Regretting. Recoiling from the sheer stupidity of my teenage spirit. The belief that I could make it all work out.

How deluded could one guy be?

Like snowflakes in a storm, I know I'm simply one of the many. But I always believed I was unique and special and that this love inside could make anything—*anything*—work out. Differences and denials and depression and diversions. Yet I didn't know that I would be the one to ultimately destroy it all.

The end. A summary that sifts out the joy and simply shares the grains of what could have been. It's sad, being able to blow and watch it scatter in the air. Watching it and then knowing it's gone.

It's me—it has to be me. I'm the one.

I've always thought this. Believed this. But it's been a source of artistic, male, selfish, bulls*** pride.

It's my right, my prerogative, my issues, my fate.

I believed love could rescue anything, yet I never realized that contempt could drown all of that.

I never realized that the contempt wasn't for anyone else. It was held specifically for myself, this body I walked in, this spirit following me like some kind of set of battering cans in a wedding car full of one.

"We have all the time in the world," Louis Armstrong once said.

I believed him and I believed.

I just didn't know that time would disagree.

108

Hell to the Liars

Near the end, an end I didn't realize wouldn't just finish the chapter but would stop the story, I withdrew.

I withstood.

I withered away.

I waxed and waned. All while practicing bad alliteration.

I secluded and shut out and kept secrets and kept to myself and shut down and shut out.

Art can be a cup you pour yourself into. It's up to you if you want to offer it to others or to simply sip it for yourself.

In the end, all I could was cling on to this cup so tightly.

I didn't have to go out and live life to picture it. You no longer have to look it up or close your eyes or strain to imagine because it's instant in color and sound and simple beauty. The picture, the videos, the music, the history.

It's all there—the summary of a life—on Wikipedia and YouTube and Facebook, like the culmination of a Dickens novel in full vibrant 3-D Imax surround sound.

It's a bit scary because you can lose yourself in this place. Listening. Wondering. Staring. Knowing you're not being stared back at. Trying to figure out. Trying to know.

Blind, but never bored, and never belittled. Always forging on, knowing my efforts weren't understood or appreciated or even noticed. The worker bee. That was me. So that's what I did and when I had to do it, I kept doing it and kept doing more and kept on keeping on.

All unseen.

Perhaps if I could have had another heart, I would have held another profession. Perhaps if I could have had another mind, I would have lived another life. But fragments and pieces and confusion and shuffling have embodied my life, all making sense for me to do what I did for a living.

Is that what you call it? Living?

Truth spoken through the subconscious in a way only an artist can appreciate.

Every day with being unseen and unheard and unnoticed, I wanted to break this feeling of being undone. So I would work harder and go deeper and strive for the better and seek the brighter.

The brilliant glow of the computer screen will always pale to those grins being carried around by my girls.

Mistaken for Strangers

If I could sing and could be cool and could articulate my brooding, I'd be the lead singer of The National. I hear *Boxer* playing in the corner bar joint in the middle of nowhere on a closing midweek night while I'm marking time for Lissie. Someone here has got good taste because he or she doesn't just play one track off "Fake Empire" but lets it go and keep going.

I'm sitting there with a bottle all my own and I'm polishing it off song by song.

I brought this in myself, didn't I?

"Mistaken for Strangers." A theme song in many ways.

"Oh, you wouldn't want an angel watching over; surprise, surprise, they wouldn't wanna watch."

I've always loved that line. Makes me think of your guardian angel suddenly knocking on your door and handing you their contract and telling you they can't do it anymore.

—This is brutal, your angel says. I give up.

I can't help thinking about Matthew. My personal angel, I'm assuming.

Something make-believe. Something spinning round.

I guess I haven't gotten anywhere with his little puzzle. Maybe he'll come back and give me a few more clues.

Track three comes. Then track four. And they keep coming. And I have stories and ideas and emotions all wrapped inside each one.

I think of my friends in the city. The all-is-me hedonistic friends who'd let me act like a heathen and even take care of me while I did. "Slow Show" reminds me of them and that time. Concerts and craziness and singing in the cab while the caps of the Chicago skyscrapers race toward us.

And I hear this song bringing me back there and then I hear it once again.

"You know I dreamed about you for twenty-nine years before I saw you."

Boom.

"You know I dreamed about you. I missed you for, for twenty-

111

nine years."

And I rearrange the numbers but they still fit. I add just a few. Then I add a decade.

Did I dream of Lissie? Did I ever know her before we first met?

Music is a coat on a blustery winter morn. A cool drink on a record-setting summer day. A calm in the sanctuary of a chaotic home. A card with lyrics and sound and structure reminding you of life's important moments.

I love to drink wine while listening to The National. Maybe they go hand in hand. Like Morrissey and melancholy. But I feel the buzz and then hear the music.

I take a sip.

The last song of the album comes and Matt's singing straight at me.

"I don't worry anymore. 'Cause it's all right, all right to see a ghost."

THE REQUITAL (Trailer #5)

Blurry and black. Shuffling, out of focus, figuring out the shot. All to the scattering beats of Foals' "Stepson." And there we begin.

The use of the melancholy, heartbroken song isn't accidental, nor is the utterance of the title right away. The well-known Hollywood leading man begins to talk in a wounded and naked voice:

"I had an inheritance from my father. It was the moon and the sun."

The stairway and the stone steps moving, ascending, descending, confusing. Then feet moving. Running somewhere while the sun begins to rise. The light becomes brighter as the music becomes louder playing over a twentysomething arguing with his fiftysomething father.

"Step out, aching stepson," the song goes.

There is the kid running on the track and the bright burst of gunfire in the dusk and the outlined figure dragging another and the steady staccato of the song fading as we see the title and wonder what is happening.

"And though I roam all over the world, the spending of it's never done," our hero or antihero says, completing the Ernest Hemingway quote.

THE REQUITAL. In theaters everywhere Thanksgiving weekend.

Hostilities

Sometimes I wonder if my father is going to show up any moment. Knocking on my door, telling me I was supposed to meet him at 9:00 a.m. and now it's 9:07, inferring that I'm just as lazy and selfish as the rest of the whole damn country and culture and making sure I really, *really* feel s***ty about it.

My father died three years ago from cancer. He was seventy-one years old but still it felt too soon to lose him. He felt as old in the last year of his life as he felt when I was ten years old and frightened of him. The fear and discomfort of being around him never dissipated. It was always there like a second shadow. Instead of the familiar and always-there scent of Old Spice aftershave, I would always detect Dad's invisible malice covering his skin, ready to suddenly appear like some angry rash.

Professor Holloway. Sometimes it seemed my father wanted me to call him that, too. If only he could have been like the Professor from the X-Men films. My father didn't like films, however, unless they were some historical movie like *Schindler's List*. I stopped showing him the trailers I made because they not only didn't impress him but at times they confused him.

Even if he saw *The Requital* trailer, he wouldn't have any idea I was making a two-minute movie inspired by him.

I can't help watching that trailer. It came during a particularly rocky period in our relationship, a time where he had s***-shamed me (a term I coined only for me) after some stupid and insignificant thing made him utterly lose his cool. The older I became the more I realized how fathers and people in general shouldn't lose their tempers and shouldn't have impatience like my father. More than that, I began to realize the emotional abuse inflicted on me those first eighteen years of my life. It's no wonder at all why I loved to lose myself in films. Nor why I was so comfortable watching horror movies. I didn't want to think about the monster I was living with at the time.

When I made the trailer for *The Requital*, I didn't set out to create some sort of piece about my father. The film was a heavy indie film about an abused son eventually killing his father. The drama that unfolds comes in the why of the death. Did the son murder his father? Was it an act of self-defense? Could it have been an accident? Those questions, however, seemed less important to the director. The filmmaker seemed more intent on getting at the root of our lives, at exploring how our youth makes us who we are.

Working on that film created a toxic atmosphere inside myself, and that leaked out into every other aspect of my life. This was only a few years ago, so we had even younger girls and the financial strain was full throttle. My broken relationship with my father both influenced my work and my mood. I knew I wasn't easy to be around, though I never seemed to be able to change my own dark cloud surrounding me.

Eventually the project ended like they all did. So did my father's passive-aggressive distance, at least for a while. He would never change, however. The hostilities deep inside continued to resurface time and time again.

I wonder how many of them rubbed off on me.

Home Movies

You awake?

I only stare at my cell phone and the message from Lissie. I didn't even know if it was charged much less working. It's not as if I've been updating my Instagram on a daily basis.

Do ghosts sleep? I type back.

Obviously not unless you're sleep-texting.

I smile.

It's good to see ghosts still have senses of humor.

What are you doing? she asks.

I had been going through old trailers I'd made and hadn't watched for years.

Nothing.

You're lying, she writes back.

Fine. I'm watching old trailers I made.

Why?

I have to think about that for a moment before replying.

I guess I'm trying to grasp on to the parts of me I lost a long time before I died.

Having any luck? she asks.

Not really.

Want some company?

Absolutely.

Good. Then let me into your office. I'm by the door.

I laugh and shake my head and get up to let her in.

So another myth about ghosts. They can't just float in and out of buildings. At least I can't and Lissie seems like she can't either.

I discover her standing at the door to the building on the main level. I guess ghosts can stand at a doorstep with two wine bottles in one hand and two glasses in the other.

—Going to a party? I ask.

—I'm bringing the party to you.

—Come on in. You'll love my love seat.

I realize how that sounds as we're walking up the stairs to my office on the second floor.

116

—That's a song, you know.

—What? Lissie looks at me.

—"You'll love my love seat."

—Please don't ever say that sentence again, she jokes. Twice is more than enough in my lifetime.

Lissie enters my office and stares around, impressed.

—Very nice. Have you had this for a long time?

—I was in this building before the twins arrived. I've moved between offices a few times.

She's taking in everything: the walls covered with movie posters, the bookshelves full of things other than books, the framed photos. I watch her and note how tall she happens to be. Then I wonder if she's wearing heels.

—Let me try this out, she says, sitting on the leather love seat.

She sinks back into it.

—Okay, okay. I agree with you. I do love your love seat.

—Makes a pretty good bed, I tell her.

A quick, sad, knowing glance, then she's up again, looking around.

—A beautiful family, she says.

—Thank you.

She notices the three stacks of DVDs on the desk.

—Did you do movie trailers for these? Lissie asks.

—Yeah.

—Which ones?

—All of them.

Her eyes stare at them as if not believing me.

—Are you serious?

I nod. She pulls out the movie she starred in.

—You did *this* trailer?

Again, I nod.

—I'm quite embarrassed by the fact that I didn't immediately recognize you, I say.

She shows me the cover for the DVD.

—Look at me. I don't recognize myself. I filmed *Utmost* only a few months after giving birth to my second child.

I want to tell her just how incredible I thought she looked, but I

117

don't. I simply sidestep the whole discussion of that film.

—Do you know I had lost track of how many movies I had worked on? I had to count them up myself.

—And what's the number?

—Over 50. And that's just counting movies I've been contracted for. Not personal projects.

Lissie laughs.

—That's a lot of trailers.

—That's a lot of time.

—Time matters, doesn't it? she asks.

—It sure does. Especially now.

She scans the movies and makes comments on them. Ones like *Ooh, I loved this one* or *Didn't this one bomb?* or *I never heard of this one.*

—Can I watch some of the trailers you made?

I chuckle.

—Only if we can watch your movies.

—Trailers are two minutes. Films are two hours.

—You're the one who chose acting, I joke.

Sometime after showing her four or five or maybe fifteen, all while enjoying the wine she had brought, Lissie moves her body toward mine on the couch and seems more interested in me.

—What ever got you making trailers? she asks.

—I'm too impatient for making movies. I'm far better at creating something from something than something from nothing.

—Did you ever try to pursue making films?

—Who hasn't? Of course. But I couldn't move to LA.

—Why not?

—Tamara grew up here. Her whole family is here. I couldn't do that to her.

—Do you hold it against her?

I think about the question for a moment, staring at the ceiling in my office I haven't stared at often.

—That's an interesting way you put it.

—How?

—You said *do* I hold it against her. Not *did* I.

—Yes.

—You used present tense. When it's actually past.

—So you don't feel like you're living in the present right now?

—It's not about living in the present or past. My present simply got put on a permanent pause.

I see those dark eyes studying me.

—What?

—You didn't answer my question, she says.

—Do I hold the fact that I never moved out to LA against Tamara? Yeah. If I'm being honest, I do.

—I like honesty.

—I like being honest, I tell her. So I know you had children. Were you ever married?

—Yes.

—And how did he like you being in movies?

—Which husband are you talking about? she says with a grin.

—I didn't know there were two.

—I married my first as a mere child before my career happened. My second husband didn't like my career. So I had to choose.

—Really?

She nods, staring ahead, jaw so square, her gaze so somber. I know the path she chose.

—Some choices don't seem as big in the moment, she says. But in the end it was the right thing.

Lissie slips the wineglass in her hand, then slides up back to the movies and the computer as if to run away from talking about all that other stuff.

—So tell me something, she says, holding up one of the DVDs in her hand.

—I'm trying to.

—How do you start?

—Start what? I ask.

—Your process. I'm fascinated to know.

—Always depends, I say, standing and moving toward the control desk with glass and bottle in hand.

Ghosts can be a bit buzzed, something I'm continuing to learn from firsthand experience.

--Give me some details, Lissie says.

These are the sorts of things I never used to have. Questions about the process. At least not from someone I loved.

—I have to know the screenplay and see the footage in whatever shape it might be in.

—So the film might be finished? she asks.

—Or it might not even have begun. Usually it's being filmed in the process. It's never finished. It's rare to watch the whole movie before cutting a trailer.

—How do you do it?

—I know the *story* but usually don't have a full movie to help out. So I always start with that gem of a story, the heartbeat, the core. Then I go to music. Music. Always music.

—Give me an example, she says.

—You're inquisitive, aren't you?

—Always.

—Well. I can tell you about *Utmost*.

—Yes, she says. I'd love to hear about that. I thought that was quite a remarkable trailer.

—You say that to all the trailer-makers you talk to.

—Absolutely. She laughs.

—The scene where you're walking down the sidewalk at night crying. That's one of the earliest pieces of footage that I saw and I was a bit . . .

—A bit what? Lissie asks when I can't finish my sentence.

—I was a bit taken aback when I saw it. It was so lovely and heartbreaking.

—The music . . .

—Thomas Newman, I tell her. A piece from his early career. This lovely melody titled "Home Movies" from the film *Corrina, Corrina*. Ever seen it?

She shakes her head.

—I watched you walking down the sidewalk maybe a thousand times. I'm not joking. And I'd be watching with my MacBook at night while just listening and searching for songs on iTunes. Always

120

looking for that special something.

 —Looking for what?

 —Magic. And I'm not trying to be corny.

 —No, she says nodding at me. I get it.

I don't have to wonder, not for a second, whether or not she does. Some people just get it. And Lissie is one of those souls.

 —The truth? I start to say, unsure whether I'll keep going.

 —What?

 —That scene? It was already magical. It didn't need music to make it that way. It just . . . it just needed you.

What a Day

When she finally stands, I still sit. I'm demanded to.

—Thank you for tonight, Lissie says.

She sounds like she feels a bit more free due to the wine, but it's not taken her over. I know that much. And thankfully, it's not taken me, either.

—Thank you, I say.

Lissie waits by the office door. Standing, smiling, this glorious painting with its magnificent structure and lines and statement.

Waiting.

Watching.

Me.

—Can I give you hug before I go? Lissie asks.

—No.

I say it immediately, like I've been waiting to say it since the moment I first saw her.

—I should stay right here, I say. It's the safe place.

The knowing on her lips, her eyes, her wait.

—If you insist, she says.

The truth in her expression and glance is an eternity I will remember.

—You know, it's better if I just stay here.

—Of course, Lissie tells me.

As if it's harmless and simple and secure and nothing could ever happen and nothing will and she's safe and untouchable and unknowable and undesirable but I've never wanted to leap up and lunge at someone to simply scoop them into my arms and count the stars over the body.

—Well, good night, then, Lissie says.

No good night should ever begin with a *well*. And none should ever end with a *then*.

I think I say good night. Or maybe I black out. Or maybe I'm the astronaut at the end of *2001* taking it all in and freaking out just a bit. Or a whole lot.

Inspirations

In the right-hand drawer of the desk I've worked on for over twenty years—a wedding present from my parents which I find odd now since I'm the only one who ever used it—I pull out the folded article that is one of my pride and joys. I have a stack of meaningful things in this drawer, such as a signed photo from my best friend in third grade and a detention slip from tenth grade. This is an article featuring the top ten movie trailers according to the very legendary Spencer Holloway.

Two Glorious Minutes—My Favorite Trailers
     By Spencer Holloway, founder and CEO of The Creative Core

The music is the hook. And I believe for a movie trailer, it's always about the music. While I can't exactly give my "Top Ten Movie Trailers Ever Made," I can share the ones that have moved me the most and have had the biggest impact on my career.

CHILDHOOD INSPIRATIONS

ALIEN (1979)
     This one still feels unnerving to watch. The music doesn't just haunt; it inflicts. I can't imagine audiences seeing this first taste of *Alien* and wondering, *What the hell is going on here?* With the rocky landscape and the ominous cracking egg opening up to scenes from the film and all hell breaking loose. It builds and builds until its climax of horrific split-second images sends your mind reeling. *What's that squirting all over the place? Are those cat intestines I'm seeing? Why does everybody seem to be twitching and convulsing?*
     The best thing, however, is *that* tagline. Maybe the best ever made for a film:

"In space no one can hear you scream."

THE SHINING (1980)

In terms of pure artistic triumph, Kubrick's trailers for *Dr. Strangelove* and *A Clockwork Orange* probably rank higher than my favorite. This trailer terrified me, and it's nothing but a shot of red elevator doors with credits scrolling over the screen.

Ah, but the music.

There's nothing like Wendy Carlos's bizarre and truly unsettling music from *The Shining*. The ticking clocks and shivering, buzzing cacophony of voices building up in terror as blood begins to gush out of the still-closed doors.

You know this isn't going to be a comedy.

ST. ELMO'S FIRE (1985)

I was going into ninth grade when this movie came out, so even though I was starting high school, I wanted to know what it was like to have finished college like all these celebrated members of the brat pack. My parents didn't let me go see *St. Elmo's Fire*, so I could only see the trailer, which I did over and over again.

I love the opening, with David Foster's simple piano melody playing in the background as Ally Sheedy begins to talk in a wistful, melancholy tone:

"I can't remember who met who first, or who fell in love with who first. All I can remember is the seven of us always together."

The scenes all show these various personalities and how they're intersecting together. All the totally cool actors and actresses of the day. All ending with Rob Lowe, never looking more cool, saying, "You're not gonna believe how out of hand it's going to be." His tagline became mine later in college. (Which was not a good mantra to aspire to, but that's another story . . .)

TOP GUN (1986)

124

This is just cool fun. And just to make sure, The Cars's "Stranger Eyes" is in the background. Strangely, the song doesn't make it on the album, even though something like Miami Sound Machine's "Hot Summer Nights" does.

GAME CHANGER

PULP FICTION (1994)

Just as I was starting my career in the movie business after being fortunate to land a job with a media company specializing in movie trailers, this brilliant Tarantino gem was released. The film and its trailer are classics.

I already knew the power of music in trailers, and the dawn of the blockbuster movies had suddenly arrived. So had the demise of the voice-overs, with the same voice (usually Don LaFontaine) sounding dramatic and telling us what's happening.

For *Pulp Fiction*, the song that starts will now always make one think of the film. I had to look it up. It's "Misirlou" by Dick Dale & His Del-Tones. To me, it's just that *Pulp Fiction* song. And it does *everything*, showing the frenetic, exuberant thrill ride and vibe to the film.

THE FINCHER EFFECT

Since I love pretty much every trailer for David Fincher films, I'm just going to lump them all together. They've gone from dark and brooding to brilliant masterpieces.

For FIGHT CLUB in 1999, I COULD NOT WAIT to see this mind bender of a movie. Brad Pitt had never looked so cool. And since I've always been told I look like Edward Norton, I guess I could really live vicariously through these two (or spoiler alert: they're one and the same person!). "I want you to hit me as hard as you can," Brad tells Ed at the start. The Dust Brothers's incredible soundtrack backing them up. And then building to that ending where all f'ing hell is breaking loose while the Pixies scream out "Where Is My Mind?" I knew in the trailer that it was going to be a classic.

Then comes THE SOCIAL NETWORK more than ten years later in 2010. Again, it's the music. The song is perfect. It's Radiohead's "Creep." The song beloved by all and sending the band into superstardom. YET . . . we don't know it's this song at first since it's a cover by a Belgian women's choir called Scala and Kolacny Brothers. Very clever, Fincher and team. Because the words are perfect for this tale of how Facebook started. So many years later, the song and its title seem particularly perfect for Mark Zuckerberg.

THE GIRL WITH THE DRAGON TATTOO from 2011 might be better than the film itself. I don't know—it was ruined for me because I knew the book and it was utterly faithful to it. This trailer made everything look so dark and amazing and dark (did I say that?). Once again, they use a cover, this time a full-throttle cover of Led Zeppelin's "Immigrant Song." Leave it to only Trent Reznor to make a Zeppelin tune even more powerful. It builds and builds to its bloody ending with one of our favorite Bonds (Daniel Craig) looking absolutely haunted and gutted.

PERFECT SUMMARY

REQUIEM FOR A DREAM (2000)

It would have been a difficult task for a trailer to fully show the intensity and utter insanity of *Requiem for a Dream*, but they managed to pull it off. It's like a two-minute message to the viewer: "You've been warned."

PERSONAL FAVORITES

INCEPTION (2010)

Before every single trailer began to use this musical cue as often as the eighties used Don LaFontaine's voice, *Inception*'s trailer introduced the BBBWWWAAAAAMMMM sound to us. It's easy to assume this was music from the movie, but it was a track called "Mind Heist" by Zack Hemsey that seemed specifically written for this. The buildup is massive without giving anything away. All it offers are questions and riddles that force you to get to the film on opening day.

INTERSTELLAR (2014)

There were several trailers made for this, as there are for many of the big releases each year. This is the first long trailer that always makes me get teary-eyed. Matthew McConaughey's character is saying goodbye to his daughter while he goes off into space to save the earth. The world needs saving and he has to leave her. This trailer is all about the emotions.

As a huge Christopher Nolan fan (obviously), I dearly wanted to get this job. But instead of working on the film, I was able to fully enjoy it just like this trailer. I assumed at first the music was from Hans Zimmer, who was scoring it, yet later on I realized it's actually a perfect track from the film *V for Vendetta* by Dario Marianelli.

After the swelling surge, the screen goes to black, and all you hear is McConaughey saying, "I'm coming back."

MAD MAX: FURY ROAD (2015)

"My world is fire and blood." Oh yes, Mad Max is back, and he's Tom Hardy? Excellent. The trailer shows us the world we're going to be inhabiting, and it's utterly bonkers. Plus, it seems like the whole movie is one big epic car chase. Which it gloriously turns out to be.

BETTER THAN THE FILM

PROMETHEUS (2012)

An *Alien* prequel of sorts? By *the* Ridley Scott. Sign me up. This looked grand and epic and also terrifying. I went into the film expecting another bloody and terrifying ride. What I got was . . . a bit odd. I've come to appreciate the film, but it definitely didn't play out like this trailer.

MAN OF STEEL (2013)

Curse you, Hans Zimmer. You got me excited about this. So did you, Russell Crowe. Heck, everything got me excited. Then I saw the film and realized it was not, unfortunately, directed by Fincher or Nolan.

Day One

I'm the king of denial, the emperor of burying my feelings. My outward self seems incredibly open, and I honestly think that I always am. But open to a certain extent. There's a level that I am willing to share, a space I'm willing for others to venture into. Yet there's the Great Wall of China surrounding the deeper parts of me, the places that seem to only be truthfully told in my art.

Even now, I'm suppressing the truth. The reality of just how much I miss our girls.

Reading the *Rolling Stone* article reminds me of *Interstellar*, and that's just another reminder in a day full of thousands.

I can fully relate to Matthew McConaughey's character now, feeling as if he might never see his daughter again. Feeling the immense passage of time.

Those little things that would sometimes annoy the hell out of me now aren't only missed. They're splinters in the hands that spent so much time typing keys and using the mouse and working on the MacBook in order to perfect his wonderful trailers. I long to go back and try to wake the twins up out of bed. To hear our eldest singing in the morning. To hug them goodbye before venturing off with Mommy in the morning. To hear the raucous arriving in the afternoon. To feel the wave of emotion in one or two or three of them rushing toward me to tell a story about their day the moment I walk into the house.

I'd put up with their bad eating habits.

I'd gladly let them ignore Tamara and me while they play on their tablets or watch television.

I'd read more to them. I'd pray longer prayers at bedtime. I'd ask them more questions. I'd give them more answers.

I would do more.

I would take a boulder the size of the one in *Raiders of the Lost Ark* chasing Indy at the beginning and I would burst through my personal Great Wall of China. Then I would allow the emotions and sentiment to burst out and to *act*.

If only I could have one more day. So the cliché goes.

Just one more day . . .

Boom

Do ghosts have names other than their own? Nobody's coming around bothering to say "Spencer" out loud. Life is silent. Then again, half of my life used to be anyway. The rest has simply caught up with it.

The sidewalk cement still feels the same. Hard, winter-weary, and watchful. It remembers the routine, sunrise after sunset. Funny how you can be invisible yet still have footsteps that seem to echo.

Part of the mystery is how I died. I just don't know. I'm not disfigured nor do I wear a black suit. I'm not searching for my murderer nor am I waiting for something to amend. There's a hole in my heart but it's roughly the size of the one in my soul and in my head. I'm just not sure if they're new or have been there my whole life.

Christmas Eve finishing watching *It's a Wonderful Life* and feeling more connected with all those live souls on this night doing the same thing. I feel like I have a stuffed stomach because I ate too much today. Which is true because I did eat way too much. Age means the machinery inside operates slower. Like an older car engine that just doesn't fire up like it used to. Things are slower. Used to be I could eat anything I wanted and by midnight I'd still be hungry. Now I simply feel bloated.

And something else strange. My left arm feels . . . well, numb.

Nah. Come on.

The out-of-breath plus gut-burning might mean something. But add in the numb-left-arm.

Not cool.

At some point before eleven at night, I'm in bed but can't sleep. Heart racing.

Life can be like this.

You can just be going to bed and then—

Boom.

It can happen that fast.

The irony is painful.

Christmas Eve?

130

Really?

How cruel could God be?

But I never subscribed to that. Inflicting bad things on the feet of a God who allowed them to happen.

Life isn't fair and I've known this for some time.

Timing isn't fair either. You can't control it. You just try to stand in the path of success. But sometimes you can't see the storm sweeping over the surface of the damaged earth.

Sometimes there's nowhere to run or hide.

Sometimes you realize the end is there.

And so it comes.

One Man's Vision

I'll be honest. I'm sad my passing won't be mentioned in the way of someone like Anthony Goldschmidt.

Who's Anthony Goldschmidt? you might ask.

Oh, but you *know* Anthony.

The alien hand with the long finger touching a boy's hand over the lit title of *E.T.*

The black woman sitting next to the window. The tagline says, "It's about life. It's about love. It's about us."

Dustin Hoffman and Tom Cruise walking down the street.

The picture of the Arizona desert with a Polaroid shot of Susan Sarandon and Geena Davis.

Still wondering?

Really?

Oh, I can go on. And on.

The tiny boat riding up a massive wave.

The bat flying amidst falling debris from the buildings above it.

My favorite . . . the one I have in my office now. The one of the character with his shirt unbuttoned facing the pouring rain and stretching out his arms and seeming to swallow the piercing rain turning sideways on him. The tagline is still one of my favorites: "Fear can hold you prisoner. Hope can set you free."

The great *Shawshank Redemption*.

Like the musical scores of Thomas Newman, who composed many films that Anthony created posters for, Goldschmidt's work inspired my own. I couldn't put poster images in the trailer, of course, but I could see one man's vision of summing up the film in such a beautifully concise way.

Anthony passed away recently, and there were many articles that came out honoring his work. I go back and read them to see his work and to hear what people said about him.

Goldschmidt, a graphic designer whose firm created some of Hollywood's most memorable movie posters, died June 17 in a

Los Angeles hospital. He was 71. His wife, Cari Rachel, said he had cancer.

So said the *LA Times*.

I begin to scan his work and feel this wave of jealousy, not a bad kind but more of a respectful sort that used to drive me. *One day maybe I can do a trailer for this director and this film.*

Goldschmidt had put in his time.

He was over fifty when he designed the poster for Shawshank.

I used to think in these terms, telling myself I still had time.

Still had time.

The poster of *Chaplin* features the iconic actor at the doorway, with only his silhouette visible. It's beautiful and haunting and lonely. And it reminds me of me.

10,000 Hours

Here you go . . .

I'm sitting in that comfortable chair that my midcentury modern buddy gave me. Rocking back and forth staring at the screen. Like I've done ten thousand times for ten thousand hours. So tell me, Malcolm Gladwell, why haven't I achieved the greatness you talk about?

I've known guys who just started this and became masters. That whole 10K thing is bunk if you ask me.

Ten thousand hours of loving and living and yet a marriage still falls apart.

I'm not the Beatles in the love arena. I'm not even a one-hit wonder.

I sit here thinking that for all the hours I spent here—doing this, looking over this, creating this—I failed in all those other places. The projects built here only seemed to blow up other things in my life.

They didn't have to, I know that. But I *allowed* them to. Or maybe forced them to.

I'm working on a thing that doesn't exist. The trailer for a life that is no longer there. The soundtrack for a movie already put in the bargain DVD bin. No—a soundtrack for a film never green-lit and never funded and never fleshed out.

There's so much and yet I don't know what I'll do with all these random tangents of emotion once they're finished. Maybe simply send them out to space.

Or maybe get one more opportunity to do a *Sixth Sense* sort of send-off to her before I truly pass to that other place.

I don't know. But I keep working, keep trying, keep hoping, and keep dreaming.

The summary of my career and my calling and my collapse.

Guilty Partner

Far away and gone but not so far gone and away.

Remote and removed but not enough to remind me to follow suit.

I'm stuck and solid. Fireproof and soulproof.

Looking at my phone and trying to figure out a phone number to find and follow down a digital footpath. But the trail leads to a stone edge cliff she fell off.

I wonder if they're all sleeping.

Silent, into the shadows they fall.

I wonder what they're dreaming of.

Hopefully blow-up rafts and waffle cones full of ice cream.

I wish I could call them.

To hear the laughter and the levity and the mayhem that pictures can never broadcast.

I wish they could break this silence.

Instead, there's the clanking of the wine bottle dropping against the beer bottles. I can't help that everything I like comes in some form of glass.

I can see through it, see what I'm keeping in. Or what's on the outside, looking at me with my palms up waiting to be let in.

Freefall

So my story bores. What's really happening here?

I'm scared. There. There you go. How's that?

Say, *Boo,* why don't you? Ghosts can get spooked, too.

I fear the dark because it's another night of memory. I hate the sunrise because it's another day telling me I'm not free. The shadows shriek out and send a message of confinement.

God, do I just want to be free. To breathe and be all okay, all still.

Where will I be? The question I wonder.

Will I still be able to roam? Will I still be able to see? Will the reds and the blues ruin the day away for me?

There shouldn't be anything following the period at the end of a paragraph yet I still linger on like some run-on random fragment.

I thought it'd be different. When I thought about these things. But thinking wasn't a commodity I bartered in.

We rush and run and stare, full stare, at some strange place seen somewhere in sequence. The right place. The right person. The right everything smothered into your soulless smile. Grin and bear it till the night can bear no more and till your stomach can bear no more wine.

These were your days.

The beat would drum on droning, pretending, prying.

Then it would stop and leave you so silently curious.

Sometimes there's this cactus in the middle of the still, sharp and spiteful but fully ready to grant a little pleasure for its pain. So sometimes I try to seize it and run away knowing there's no way to hold and no way to steal it.

I'm so full of words now that they've left my life.

I see them streaming on the surface like swimming clowns grinning with their lips toward the sun. Afraid to pick them up. Afraid to look in but I can't look away.

The bridge so rocky and so rigid stands firm. I look down and see someone looking a lot like me. So melancholy. So young. So full of the *yet*s that so many others often outgrow.

I breathe in the night and exhale the morning. My hands stand out in shadows and my glance turns around in the windy sound. I walk similar streets and see the same shadows trying for familiarity but more than anything I can see something else breaking through.

There's this withering warmth deep inside. I want to drop and parachute down to the earth safe and secure. To close my eyes and hear it explode. To open them and see the glorious plume on the horizon.

So much genuine joy here and there and everywhere pulled and pushed together.

This is what it's like on the other side still looking in, still grinning, still somehow wondering. Questions still tap the fingertips.

The rest of revelation coming round the corner and still the darkness remains. Close-eyed heart-shut finger-clenched. Waiting to open a soul.

Oceans

I can still see her, this angel against the surf, this seagull ready to set sail. I can see proposing to her against the rocks and the hills of the Pacific. We were both twenty-five and so young and so naive and so in love. So unable to stop touching each other, to stop linking and locking and loving.

I never thought love could set like the sun. I thought the skies would always be clear, the waves always wild, the ocean always endless. I never expected storms. I never expected anything except the wind whipping against the soft wrinkles of our smiles.

But you grow up and you get with the program and you either sit still or you learn to fight.

I met Tamara in college. Familiar story, you can imagine. The parties and the classes and the long nights and the laughter. You're impatient in your youth only to find a temporary hiatus to adulthood during your college days. You've never felt so free. The possibilities seem endless. And then into all of that walks Tamara.

The sweet stories of yesterday that kiss your cheek like some kind of soft farewell. Wrapped around you and carried carefully. Hidden deep.

This is where it started. College. This is where it finally began to burst forward. The hillside on the Pacific. This is where the dream began.

But dreams end.

And sometimes, unfortunately, nightmares can sweep in with the tide.

Space

—I feel like I can keep talking forever when I'm with you.

Lissie pauses as if to let me continue, as if to let the shine on her stare hover like the morning sun.

—I'm talking too much, I say.

—It's okay.

So I keep talking. God knows what I'm talking about, but to be honest, I could see God tuning out simply because it's surely rambling. I've been blabbering about my inner feelings and the insecurities of being lost in this space. I've been wandering all over the place sharing memories of how I first met Tamara. Nobody should be tuning in to this drivel, but Lissie pays attention.

She watches and listens.

God knows it's been too long since a woman like that listened to me.

She's watches and laughs.

God knows my jokes have begun failing to produce laughs with others.

She never stops watching.

And I suddenly realize what God surely knows as well. That being listened to and laughed at and watched aren't just good things. For me, they're necessary. They're oxygen.

And I've been holding my breath underwater for a very long time.

—You seem surprised, Lissie tells me.

—Why? What do you mean?

—Your expression. Am I laughing too much?

—No, no. I'm just . . . I'm not used to it.

—Don't you think that it's much easier to put on a show for someone you don't really know? Not that I'm saying you're giving a performance or anything.

—I'm not the actor sitting here, I say.

—You know what I mean. How we put on our best appearance for others we just met?

—Well, if talking about—what was I talking about last? Fried pickles? If that's my best "appearance," then I'm in a lot of trouble.

—I'm still trying to figure out how your mind works. That's part of my amusement.

—Are you laughing with me or at me? I ask.

—How about I'm laughing *for* you?

I stare at her, the hard lines around the soft face.

—I like that. I've never heard it before. Not sure I know what it means.

—Me neither, Lissie says. But I agree—I think it's kinda cool.

Nice

—It's easy.

—What's easy? she asks.

Lissie's look lingers, waiting, so patient, so interested.

—To drift. To just drink and play songs by The National.

—You love to do that, right?

—What? Drink?

—No drift.

—I love to do both. Not sure which I love more.

—They're both easy to do, Lissie says.

—Yes.

—I always took walks. Shut off the volume. Simply spent time with myself.

—I spend enough time with myself, I say. And I sometimes hate it.

—Imagine those corporate meetings with endless corporate rhetoric all day long.

—We're lucky, I tell her.

Her look brings me back to reality.

—Yeah, okay, I reply. We *were* lucky. To have done this thing we loved and not have to sit in those meetings.

We're in the empty and softly lit art studio right across from my office. I guess someone left a door unlocked. Or something like that. The mocha of the red wine and the melancholy of The National is making me tired. So I put something else on. I'm about to tap my iPhone to play a song off the wireless speaker, and then I notice her waiting to see what I'm putting on. So I pause.

She waits.

—Close your eyes, I tell her.

—I'll still be able to hear the song.

—I don't want you to see my expression.

—What will it show?

Her eyes remain open, and I press Play. I see this marvelous sort of wonder cushion and frame her face, propping up her lips and eyelashes and the glow God gave her.

We listen to the song. We both know it so well. I've done my homework and I know how much she loves it.

I swear her eyes don't even blink. Like an anchor in sand, they remain on mine.

Three chords, shifting down, then building back up again. The first few words, they hover and never hurry and seem to hush every other thing in the world around us.

There's an intimacy in listening to a song with someone without sharing a single word. In allowing your eyes and your expression to share everything you could possibly say.

I swear she can read my mind.

It turns and begins down the road and then ends up at the dramatic cliffhanger and then it comes and she doesn't flinch or look away.

Lissie's so strong. She's stronger than I am.

In the glowing electronic world, we feel so free, yet sitting face-to-face and flesh to flesh, intimacy is real and raw. And when it comes freely, there's no comparison.

When the song is over and the silence starts to fan us back to reality, I want to just freeze this moment.

—That was nice, I tell her.

I say it as if we just made love.

—Very nice, she tells me.

As if we just made really, really good love.

Perhaps this special place I put art creates this common, kindred connection. But I believe it's more than that. These crevices I've carried my whole life can't be filled by her. They are simply recognized and acknowledged. Finally.

After all this time, in this very unlikely way.

PROVOCATEUR (Trailer #6)

Heels on carpet moving with a slow, determined urgency. Stopping at the door. Waiting as delicate taps rattle three times. Then stepping into the hotel room all while the distant, distorted piano plays its same few chords.

Long legs. A woman resembling Kim Basinger from the eighties. One of the various blatant attempts to make this another 9½ Weeks. To try. So the director wants.

The door shuts. She turns and grins. Beautiful and intoxicating. This has all been one long take.

As we finally get a cut, the face of the actor/hero/leading man shows desire. But the music changes. The droning, shifting, and brooding synth sounds of "Clean" by Depeche Mode plays.

A dozen images flash on the screen while the drums pound away. This isn't some sort of romance or hidden affair story. It goes from thriller straight to bonkers horror. Eyes filling up with blood and a heel (perhaps one of those we see at the beginning) piercing a palm and a woman screaming and a van bursting over lawns at eighty miles an hour . . .

Secrets can turn into nightmares. PROVOCATEUR. Coming this October.

Letting Go

I think of the lame line the studio forced me to put in *Provocateur*'s trailer. "Secrets can turn into nightmares." I remember telling them exactly what I thought of it.

"That sounds like a tagline from a fifth grader."

They, of course, didn't really like to hear that. I told them about the ridiculous line from the trailer for *White Sands* as spoken by Don LaFontaine.

"*White Sands*. The most dangerous place to be."

Then, just to double down on the cheese, a clip from the actress has her saying, "But you're not bored anymore, are you?"

Terrible stuff. Stuff I didn't want to do. But they made me.

At least I was able to get in my own version of what I thought was sexy.

I never should have taken the job and should have quit halfway. Diving into that world of debauchery on a film that went nowhere wasn't a good career move.

I remember this particularly haunting set of lines from the lead character to his forbidden desire at the start of *Provocateur*.

"So sing me a sweet love song. Just for me. Would that be okay? Would that be all right? For just this moment."

Wearing my late-night life-canceling headphones, I would find myself lost again in sensual and sexual images I tried to marry to appropriate melodies. These attractive strangers swimming in my head day after night after day.

Every beautiful thing I produced got sent back. Every inch I took on that film told me it was okay to let go.

Letting go.

This is what life is every day. A little letting go.

You reach a point of powerlessness and have to decide what choice you can take. You can fight or you can follow.

The colors aren't yours to pick but you can mix them up.

Afterlife

—What are you thinking?

Lissie's words come from nowhere, yet they're something I need to respond to. A thought or a text or a teasing question coming out of the dark.

—I'm wondering how in the world you found me.

She's there, somehow, someway.

—You're not that difficult to find, she says.

—Maybe my surprise is that someone's bothering to try.

—You didn't answer my question.

It doesn't take me long to answer.

—I'm stressed.

—About what?

—About my family. About my wife and the girls. About all of them.

—Even though you can't do anything for them?

I shake my head.

—I can do something, I say.

—But what?

—I don't know but something. I'll figure it out.

—Have you always been like that?

—Like what? I ask.

—Someone fixing some things. Someone figuring out exactly how to fix them.

—Why? Is that strange?

—Yes. For artists.

—Am I an artist?

—More than most I've seen, she tells me.

—I guess that's a compliment.

—It's the truth, Lissie says.

—Will it set me free?

—No, but it will point you in the right direction.

Again, I wonder where she came from. Not today, but in my life. Or . . . after that life. In this afterlife.

The Ghost

I'm no stranger to ghosts. This profession of mine has paid me to be haunted. I've felt their shadows replacing mine. Have seen their glances and heard their laughs. I've always seemed to have the need to grasp for stability, for daylight, for finding another soul to prove I'm simply alive.

Some people I used to meet sure didn't feel that way, staring at their phone screens and sharing their love and hate through fingertips instead of face-to-face. Behind windows, nameless and faceless and easily angered if you're as bad of a driver as they are. Awkward in the driveway or sidewalk or parking lot or shopping aisle but a rock star when haunting others online.

This place I'm at . . . Can I call it a condition? Are there antibiotics for the undead? I don't know really how this works because there's no manual and I wouldn't read it if I was holding it. It's strange because I find myself still acting the same. Breathing. Looking. Listening. I find myself walking around Appleton. I don't drive. But I do have a place I live in. Or should I say haunt? I never notice opening the door or using a key but I do sleep on the love seat with my legs either hanging over the side or perched on its thick arm. And I have two pillows. It's weird that way. I mean, really . . . do ghosts need pillows? This one does.

I notice things I've never seen. The tracks in the snow. The salt on the cars. The dark streaks on light pants of those hurrying along sidewalks. The slow, steady trickle of the ice melting under clear, blue skies.

Life is no longer how I remember it because it's not a life. It's a shadow of one. It's smoke signals that don't quite drift off to space. It's floating embers that don't glow. It's the air from a raging fire but it's cold and causes chills.

That's the only way I can describe it.

I know my mission. To get through to Tamara. But somedays my feet can't seem to find the way toward her. It's like they start heading that direction and then they meander off somewhere else. I see the tracks in the snow as if I'm hovering over them, following them,

146

studying them. But they always veer sideways for some reason I can't understand. And then I'm back alone, by myself, haunting some dimly lit pub where they still play halfway decent music. Some songs I remember and some I actually can recall putting on a jukebox. It's sad to think of a world where jukeboxes won't be waiting for drunken souls to slip their quarters into. But the world is sad and I'm refusing to go there. I won't. There's no need. Or maybe it's because I don't have the heart to since I no longer have one.

Sometimes I'll sit across from stranded souls and imagine I'm having a conversation with them.

"I love Foals," I'll say.

"This music sucks," he'll reply.

"There's always good music to put on, so who knows what's next."

"This jukebox is abysmal."

Sure, the conversations don't really mesh. It's better having a conversation with yourself. But I'm used to that. I'm used to splicing and splitting sentences. Where one character in a movie is saying something and then someone else answers even though it never ever happens that way. But that's the beauty in two-minute films that sell the movies.

I miss making them, to be honest.

I miss the art. Because it is an art.

Sometimes I tempt my plight and will stand in the middle of the street. Or will hover over the floating, freezing river. Or will think about guzzling a bottle of something bad and heavy. Just to prove I'm not here. But I don't know. Even now I'll get afraid. That somehow, I'll do something wrong and end in the wrong place.

Oh yeah—I think about that all the time.

Maybe I'm still around because . . . well, I don't know.

Sometimes I'll stumble upon a group and will just stare knowing they don't see me. I'll study them and this will be when I'm sad. I'll see the lack of wrinkles and body fat and will spot the exuberance in their eyes. They'll toast the night away, bottle after bottle. Having escaped their pasts, neglecting to focus on their futures, they remain squarely in the present. Laughing, loving, lusting, listening, living.

I want to go back.

I want to take back something and be one of them.

I didn't know those moments. But they're gone. They're silenced. They're a silent black-and-white movie stuck to my soul.

I love watching the young women. Putting on a show and knowing they're something to see. I don't stop looking. The way they brush back their hair. The long legs and toned muscles. The beauties. The babes.

God . . . isn't youth a blessing that we don't know? We wrap ourselves in it and forget this stage until we're older and we're no longer there and we're thinking of those times wondering why we didn't appreciate them in the first place.

Those divine moments with Tamara that feel more faint than any trailer I might make.

I want to go by that fireplace and make love to her once again.

I want to be in that car undressing and undoing and unloading and unleashing it all. Assuming and expecting that this is just life because it is.

Being a ghost isn't some weird, sad thing out of *It's a Wonderful Life* or *A Christmas Carol*. I can still find myself aroused. Can still find myself confused. Can still somehow even find myself drunk. It's lonely but life can be lonely, right? It's just in this state, I know what I must do.

The question is whether I'll be able to do it. In any sort of form.

Writing. On a napkin or in the sky. Drawing pictures on the wall or the chalkboard or a highway billboard.

It might seem easy but I can't. I physically can't.

But there are things I can do. And I keep trying. Every day and night.

BLOOD OF EDEN (Trailer #7)

The light leads, bridging the motion to the still. From the white to the golden pattern to the sun-streaked. The shot captures the slit in the sheer curtains revealing life, the magnificent creation from the great Maker. The water, no longer drowning but drifting, no long haunting but healing.

A figure looking at his reflection in the window, the shame coating it like yesterday's grime. The dark skies behind.

Contrasting with the figures in shadows. Two shapes becoming one silhouette. While the water flows.

Then the rain and the reports and the rain and the recession and the rain.

The late night and early morning prayers and screams.

Rushing and climaxing and outpouring.

To the still.

To rest.

Peace.

The glint and the gleam, flowing like a paintbrush, each stroke unique, the picture always changing but remaining the same.

There is no more dry land and no more standstill.

BLOOD OF EDEN. Coming soon to theaters.

Mercy Street

Watching my past work has gotten me to pull up that damn supernatural drama on my MacBook Pro and I'm tackling it again. As if I'm going to finish it and submit it to Sundance.

"And the Oscar goes to . . . Spencer Holloway? Wait—wasn't he just featured in the Oscars in Memoriam section?"

I realize so much of the film that I've been fiddling around with over the years has been the musical cues. Since, of course, that's what I've always specialized in. The drama features two actors I've filmed over a variety of years just living out their lives. Doing their own things. Over and over again. For this particular montage, I don't need some cool or creepy or funky tune. But I want—I *need* a song with vocals.

And I discover the perfect one while scrolling through the endless tunes on my computer.

I play it once and it's perfect. Then I play around inserting it into the footage. Different parts. The beginning, the middle, the end of the song.

Peter Gabriel is singing. But no, he's not singing *that* song. And no, my hero isn't standing outside of the heroine's house holding a boom box.

The rumble of the guitar sounds, then a tribal beat begins in the beautiful song. But I realize I can't use the beginning. I need the chorus.

I splice a series of shots. The husband, the wife, the husband, the wife.

"Won't you please talk to me? If you'd just talk to me, unblock this misery. If you'd only talk to me."

Peter Gabriel's song "Come Talk to Me" was supposedly written to his daughter after he had separated from his wife. But the song absolutely fits. Peter Gabriel is one of those artists who is timeless, who only needs his voice to convey emotion. I've used quite a bit of his music for my trailers. Once using his beloved and heartbreaking ballad "Here Comes the Flood." It's one of my favorites. I remember hearing people started to cry when they saw those two minutes.

150

Amazing. Another song I used was "Sky Blue" in an artsy, thought-provoking thriller I did a trailer for. And of course, when a film is called *Blood of Eden* based on a Gabriel song with the same name, I have to use it. I'd been waiting for the perfect film to try to use "Mercy Street" in. That film never came, however. I shouldn't have waited to use that tune.

I watch this four-minute montage I've been working on and end up feeling moved to tears myself. But that's just because this song and the album it came from used to belong to Tamara and me. We'd gone to see Peter Gabriel during this tour and we'd especially loved this album even though it was soaked in sadness.

The struggle. That's what a story needs to convey. A big, unsolvable problem our heroes need to figure out. Love or loss or war or death or something. I fiddle around with this film just for fun, just like I used to do.

I started making trailers before getting paid to do so. If you're lucky to do something you love to do, you usually slip into it like a surfer wading in the ocean suddenly realizing he's getting paid to ride the waves. Artists tend to create whether or not they get paid. Age complicates this. So does life. All the unnecessary things get added onto you and suddenly you realize something has to give. And for so many people, they have to let that one thing go. At least the giant dream of it.

I never had to let go of mine. But my big dream wasn't making trailers but rather making a film and having someone make a trailer out of it.

A director spends two years of his life that I will sum up in two minutes. It doesn't seem fair, but life's not. And, oh yeah, then you die, just like I did.

Very few people knew I was making this film. My wife did. Batman had his Bane and my wife had hers. It was the bane of her existence, and it happened to be my little film that I kept trying to figure out how to make work. I think I had maybe a thousand hours of footage on it. Of course, that's an exaggeration. Perhaps Tamara was the one who said that. It was just an indie flick that was supposed to be intimate. Over the years, I'd sometimes acted like I believed I was

Kubrick.

But I'm no Kubrick, young or old.

I can say that now. But back when I took real breaths and still had an opportunity to believe, I clung to this hope and desire. I wanted to do something small and intimate that would make a lot of noise. I had all these plans and all these dreams.

Yet the thing I would learn and learn fast is that creating is difficult. It's easy to critique and easy to cut and splice but it's hard to fill up that white screen or page.

More than that, it's difficult to build a masterpiece over a series of moments and montages. You can have others help, whether it's songs or actors or colors of cuts. But ultimately, the story has to be one you write. And it either works or it doesn't.

When I'm finally done working, I look at the time and see it's around 3:30 a.m. I used to do that all the time, working until very late. Getting some IPAs or a bottle of wine and working. Then working more. Cranking music at the office and eventually falling asleep on my couch.

Am I working now?

Yes. That must be it. I'm not a ghost but I'm working and I'm going to wake up and find out that it's all been a dream or something like that.

In the morning, however, I wake up and still feel and hear and see the truth. But sorry, Martin Gore. I don't enjoy this silence. Not anymore.

Don't Give Up

—How are you doing? Have you discovered any answers to the riddle?

I'm standing under an awning outside a closed restaurant while the sleet batters the sidewalk and street. My angel friend, if that's what I can call him, has shown up and this is what he asks me.

—I've found lots of those *something*s. But the biggest something has been my own brain that's spinning around.

—The answers aren't in objects, Matthew tells me in a loud voice above the tapping in front of us. It's more of an apprehension. A belief.

I nod but don't have a clue what he's talking about.

—Can you give me a clue? I ask.

—I've been giving you them on a daily basis.

—You have? What? Have you been hiding and lurking around the corners?

—Most people don't see me when I show up in their lives.

—Well, I feel your pain. Nobody's seeing me these days.

He just smiles.

—Don't give up, Matthew says. 'Cause you have friends.

Then once again, he starts walking down the sidewalk, under the little icy pellets. I watch and wonder if he's going to vanish or slowly dissipate but he keeps walking, crossing a street, then finally turning to go down another side street.

I'm still as lost as I was before.

Father's Child

God, I know You see me.

I say the name not as an exclamation but more as a declaration.

Hanging high overhead, You see me, so can You share a little of Your glorious shadow and walk with me?

I want to step in the silence and the still and hide away and get away from the endless noise. The endless drain. The endless everything siphoning every single nerve.

God, where are You? Every inch seems to be sucked up by every mile. These brief moments of joy are thin rocks skipping out over the Pacific Ocean.

Can't You walk with me?

Won't You walk with me?

I know a man's worth is not summed up in numbers. But, God, You're supposed to be the provider. I look and see the negatives and wonder how and why and when and who? I'm angry and yes I'm angry when I know I shouldn't be and I'm defiant and I'm stubborn and I'm stupid and I'm a sinner but God help me, help me now, help me 'cause I'm looking for a shadow to walk inside of.

Walk with me.

Please, Lord, walk with me.

Take my hand and guide me over the street with the busy, bewildering vehicles coming by.

Doubt.

All of it.

I don't know what to say anymore.

I pray and then I stop because I wonder why.

I know You hear me and I know You know me.

God, You see me. This heart. Angry, frustrating, fighting back, drunk and lustful and stubborn and stupid.

I already said that, right, but I'll say it again and again.

Can't You at least lend me a few more moments to walk alongside me?

Just a few steps?

Can I see the footprints in the sand? Or perhaps a few in the snow?

Can I see Your shadow standing between me and the blistering sun?

God, You know this road.

God, You know this mess.

God, I ask that You please just come down and walk a few miles with me.

Just a few.

Please, Lord, please.

Real Words

—You've been broken.

—Hasn't everyone?

I nod at Lissie. It's taken me hours of conversation and the past weeks (months?) to realize what I've been seeing on her and in her.

—Yes, but you look . . . Your wounds still look fresh, I say.

—They are.

—I can relate.

—I know.

—I just wish . . .

—I know.

—All I want—I just want to smother the pain, you know? To just try . . .

—*I know.*

I look at her. She knows.

Mortal, made of flesh and bone, these tiny and frail hearts that used to pump to keep us alive, somewhere carrying a soul nearby. We are who we are and the more we know the less we seem to be.

—Maybe it's best that we don't . . . , I start to say.

—It's best.

So I don't push anymore.

I see someone like me, strong and insecure and fiery and forgotten.

—I get it, more than most, I tell her.

—Get what?

—All of it. Every little bit of your perfect mess.

—That's just the truth.

—What? I ask.

—All of it. Most of the lines I've said come from others, from brilliant screenwriters, but not those.

—I thought they sounded different.

—Really?

—They sound real. They sound like you.

Dance Yrself Clean

In another trailer for my life, I would have selected LCD Soundsystem's "Dance Yrself Clean." Go ahead, check it out. Like now. Dial it up on your phone or laptop or iPad.

The low, minimal drumbeats start along with the lead singer's talking more than singing. A low, old-school synth playing simple keys.

"Talking like a jerk except you are an actual jerk and living proof that sometimes friends are mean."

The line that describes Steve, one of my best buddies. To call him a friend is exaggerating because—well, that line above sums it all up. He's not just a jerk, but Steve's a dick, and he is happy to admit it.

So the tune is slowly building, slowly, slowly . . .

Then.

Three minutes in, the drop. The kick. The soaring synth, beautifully rolling along.

This would show my former life, all the insanity.

I'd show a guy running in his neighborhood in his boxers (true story).

Then I'd show a guy running out of gas with three little girls screaming in the back of his really sad white rusted-out minivan.

I'd show drinking wine. And beer. And laughing. And more wine.

Then I'd show meticulous, marvelous, minuscule cutting at the computer.

Then more wine.

Then more whining from the girls.

Then dancing in boxers.

Then wandering in the narrow alley behind Steve's town home in downtown Chicago.

People would look and be like *What the hell is this?* and surely they'd be intrigued enough to buy a ticket.

Maybe.

I'd show some sweet moments too.

I'd show the meaning of life thing.

I'd make it about them. Because the essence of every trailer is that this movie is about you and for you and will CHANGE you. Even with Vin Diesel.

Yeah.

It always starts with music. At least for me.

But then it's about visuals. Striking. Strange.

Then it's about the start of a story. Just the start. Just the tiny pinprick of a start.

Because at the end of the day you want to get people intrigued to go pay money and sit down and watch.

The beauty.

The reality of my trailer is that nobody is going to pay jack to watch any of it. With or without LCD Soundsystem.

Truth.

But maybe. Maybe possibly. Well, yeah.

All My Friends

There comes a point in your life when you grow up and realize time is precious. When you realize some of those closest to you haven't grown up and still treat life with a flippant, f-off mentality.

If you're lucky, you finally come to a realization that you have to move on. You need to seize this current day because the last few dozen or hundred or more have been surrendered. It's time to put up a fight, and this fight simply means disconnecting.

It's easy but so damn hard. Because unfriending someone still doesn't mean you don't see their friends' or family's or spouse's posts. Blocking their annoying texts still doesn't mean you can't get others from all those in this someone's life. Dates you've done something together and moments when you've congregated and life's events all end up putting a mirror in your face and causing you to question your decision.

I made the decision far too late. And I look at a life with so much I left undone. With so little actually put into the well.

There was this unlikely young sorry sap I once met who loved films as much as I did. I discovered him one drunken night in Columbia College after some Kubrick fest in Chicago. I was high on delusions of grandeur and dark obsessive desires when Steve suddenly showed up wearing a David Lynch T-shirt. I gave him props and high-fived him or something stupid like that. But then I saw him the next day in one of my classes, a dorky, dark-haired kid I'd never seen before. And we became friends.

"That's how it starts," LCD Soundsystem sings.

Twenty-five years, you still hang out. But it's been different for a long time.

You've known for some time you should have let go. Too much wasted time.

Just Like Heaven

The pub is dark and crowded but we sit in the back in silence unnoticed. Because, well, we're dead and we're ghosts and we also like our privacy.

—Did you like making trailers? Lissie asks.

—Yes. Absolutely. I still do.

—Your face lit up when I asked that.

—Despite everything—the egos I needed to deal with and the frustrations with the finances—I loved it. I still loved it before I . . . before I got to this state.

—*To this state,* she repeats with a laugh.

—You know what I mean.

—I do. I know what *state* you mean.

—I was working on a couple of really big trailers before I died, I say. Among other things.

—And you can't keep working on them?

I look at her, the shadows covering her, the lines so smooth and rich, her smile so endless.

—Sure. But I keep wondering why I should.

—Well, if you liked working on them so much.

—Good point, I say.

I hadn't thought that way.

—What were the movies about? Lissie asks.

—One was about a husband and wife separating. A really fascinating film. A study of contrasts, these two lonely souls, a family trying to make its way through turbulent times.

—How did it end?

—I don't know. Really. They had filmed two different endings. I talked to the director and he wouldn't say. He liked ambiguity. I was like, "Okay, that's fine, so what do you want the trailer to convey?" And guess what he said?

—Ambiguity.

I nodded and took a sip of my beer.

—Exactly. Smart gal.

—So what was the trailer like?

I think about explaining it, then decide to offer up the obvious.

—I can show it to you sometime.

Normally to any other attractive woman my age, this might sound a bit like an invitation to something. But I don't worry about this with Lissie.

—I'd love to see it.

—What's the other trailer about?

I laugh.

—What? Lissie asks.

—This one was like a twin brother to the other film. It was zany, a comedy of sorts, about this Cubs fan whose life is falling apart while his favorite team is winning. He's a workaholic and everything's going down the drain but he finds this crazy solace in his team.

—What happens?

—You really like spoilers, don't you?

The golden grin comes again.

—When you come across life's great big spoiler called death, knowing a film's outcome doesn't exactly carry the same weight.

—I'm glad you're here to enlighten me about our world and perspective.

—It's my pleasure, Lissie says.

—Well, *that* particular film wasn't finished. They still had some scenes to film. And they wanted to know if the Cubs would win the World Series. The movie would be much more relevant if they did.

—The Cubs are never winning the World Series, are they? she says.

—Never say never. I said that about minivans and country music and I blinked and found myself driving one while working on a country music video.

—For who? Lissie asked.

I tell her and her eyebrows make a "wow" sort of gesture.

—Are you mocking me?

—Of course not.

—I cannot tell.

—I used to have a crush on him when I was younger, she says.

—You know he's like ninety-five years old? I say with a laugh.

—Well, he was certainly handsome when he was seventy-seven.

We keep talking. And talking more. And never stopping.

I think heaven will be like this. A place with no interruptions. No distractions. No deadlines. No needing to get to the next thing and forgetting this golden moment you've found yourself in.

Lissie keeps asking me questions, always sounding and seeming interested, always an audience of one I wanted to have by my side. I can't tell her the truth and don't want to tell myself this but it's the truth I've lived with so long. I've wanted this sort of interest, any kind of interest, with the woman facing me day after day.

But when was the last time you were that interested in her?

I have to agree with my other better half. The kind that talks sense in my brain when I'm talking stupid.

Lissie and I close the pub down. The bartender calls out for everybody to leave and we're the only ones left inside but then they just shut down and leave us alone. We slip out eventually and go outside to the summer night.

But wait a minute, it's been winter, so how in the hell can it be summertime?

Perhaps seasons are different when you're dead. I don't know. I'm not interested in asking tonight.

—How much of yourself would you put into your trailers? Lissie asks as we walk on the sidewalk over the bridge.

—As much as I could. Always.

—That's good.

—What about you? I ask. What about the characters you played? Some of them . . .

—Yes. I know. Some are nothing like me. Hence the *acting*. But every character I've ever played always had some part of me inside of them. Humans are complex creatures, aren't we?

—Yes, we are.

I see her hair blowing in the wind as the moon lights our path.

—It was nice to chat with you tonight, Lissie says as we arrive at her building.

Is this her apartment or her office or a place she's just hiding inside?

162

Again I'm not going to ask. Not now.

—You too.

I'm wondering if she's going to invite me in or if I should ask or if this is still all kind of a crazy fever dream.

—I enjoy hearing your thoughts, she says.

I laugh.

—I guess I like sharing them. With you.

—Good night. Talk with you later.

—Good night, I tell her.

Yes, I'm sure we'll be talking later.

I'm sure.

Soul Mate

Where would you meet your soul mate? Where would you choose to meet the one who could envelop your spirit and summon your energy?

There are sidewalks but the wind blows and the weather can grow a little wearisome. I don't believe people even talk on sidewalks, at least not in the Chicago area. People pass you by on the sidewalk and if you follow them, you don't find yourself in a sweet Nicholas Sparks movie but on the end of a stalker suit.

I first imagine an elevator. So close you can't help but smell someone else. Perhaps gaze closely in the eyes even for a cliff dive of a second. Stand there so close almost touching you warmth and your life so close to them. Then they might be gone. Elevators have electricity and that potential of getting stuck and changing your life forever.

There's the crowded, dismal dread of the party you hate to be at. Where you're bored and irritated and wanting to get the hell out of there when suddenly the spotlight shines on this other sweet soul. Perhaps you share a drink. Perhaps you tell a story. Perhaps you make a connection that both of you will remember for a long time. Perhaps you both realize you're different from the rest of the schmucks around you and really all you want to do is take off and drive in a convertible and feel the night air stroke your skin and mess your hair. Maybe you can park somewhere and share songs you love and share stories only your closest friends know and the night can become day again and you realize you have found someone who actually finally fully GETS it.

Yeah.

There are other places, too. I don't know.

A bus you're riding during the day or a train you're riding in the night. A bike ride on a lonely trail or a bridge you're crossing over an empty river.

But those don't really necessarily fit.

There are the loud places of life. But I don't see them working simply because you don't have the luxury of awkward new talk.

164

I could imagine many places but I don't think I could imagine this one that was about to happen.

Present tense can always be put on hold and made to go into past tense. That's the beauty of suddenly finding yourself lost in someone else. You time travel in your spirit and your soul. You figure out that you're telling a story about this even while it's happening.

Simply because it seems so damn unreal.

Brittle and Chipped

This feeling and these echoes of echoes of feelings bring me back to yourself. To your doorstep. To step up and step out. Can you let me? Can you swallow all these hollow places? The kind that nobody knows about. The kind the world discards. The kind I'm uncomfortable talking about. But heaven forbid I'm ever forbidden to utter these heavenly sensations.

I'm pontificating nonsense.

So let me come inside.

So let me know how you feel.

Let me see. Tell me, Tamara. Write it out. Share and show. See me and let me know.

Want never used to hesitate. It walked over the walkway through the door and into the room to hold the hand and take it away. To sneak out and then suffocate the day's noise. To clutch and claw in the center of quotations marks called "love."

What did our sweat and those steamed-up windows know about this mysterious word, this blind notion hovering in the imagination?

Whispered words so delicate and so precise. Amidst the music and the emotions. And the hands clasped every single thing they could. But you can't touch the unconditional.

I want to knock but know the shell is already cracked, the insides already released, leaving brittle and chipped remains.

Anjunabeats

I remember the insanity, the adrenaline, the late nights and early mornings and endless clipping and cutting and shifting and connecting in order to make some kind of magical two-minute mystery. It sometimes felt like being in the middle of a club with a thousand bodies moving and pressing and hovering and shifting around you while you're unable to control any of them but simply hope to maintain your balance in the crowd and the lights and the sounds.

A club metaphor. Good Lord, what am I, twenty-four again?

The spirit never dies.

And maybe not and maybe I still long to be out there.

Maybe I still long to be in the middle of something like that.

Blink and see it again for a moment.

Blink and I'm back there. The madness that found me.

The spirit of letting go, of being free, of believing that everything's going to be okay.

Age and life never seemed to support this freedom. Bills and pressures and deadlines and children and loves and resistance and struggles.

I want to go dance somewhere. To be lost in the middle once again.

And somewhere as I'm walking, looking for Lissie, I wonder why those times and moments still have this meaning inside of me.

You were finally free, Spence. You were finally surrounded.

After spending a life without roots and without stability or consistency or figuring out any-f***ing-thing, the lost-on-the-dance-floor feeling feels like home. Surrounded by strangers just like I had been for twenty years. Moving just like I always seemed to do year after year. Yet knowing nobody cares and nobody watches and nobody is concerned with me. Lost in a crowd like everybody else and found in the sanctuary of a song. Sweating and twisting and catching glimpses of beauty while catching my breath.

The beat of the drum goes on and on and on.

I wish I could find one, but Appleton's not exactly a club-hopping sort of town. No Chicago suburb happens to be.

If I could find a club, what exactly would I do? Drift through the crowd unseen and unheard and dance without sweating? The fun came in the intoxicating rush of the bodies all around, being set adrift and rescued at the same time.

Now I feel like I'm simply adrift. Foolishly I think Lissie's going to come and rescue me.

I wouldn't even know how one would rescue me in the first place. Not anymore.

Cherry-Coloured Funk

I searched for something, for some wading wonderful thing over the surface of the blue. I wanted to jet by and pick it up. A relief, a respite, a remedy. A rock sunken down in the surface keeping me from floating away. A dock pointing directly toward a sanctuary to hide out in.

I wanted something more. My spirit and soul. Singing over and over tunes nobody knows.

Sometimes salt water can find itself drifting in a lake.

Midnight

The lights on the garage glow like some tablet left on in a black cell, ready to be touched, ready to be opened. I sit in the shadows of my car and stare at the same thing I've been staring at for the last hour. Something I never really noticed when I lived there. The four-bedroom, two-and-a-half bathroom two-story house. The one I took for granted. The one I never said goodbye to.

I dream of knocking on the door and opening it up and seeing one of my girls. Any of my girls. Smiling and welcoming me.

It's hard to be in the moment living it out and celebrating it too. NFL teams don't do that. When they're playing, they're focused and they're deadly. Eventually they celebrate, but not in the moments. They're machines. Animals. Readying themselves for anything.

I never got to fully embrace the moments. Some, but selective. So quickly gone. So quickly forgotten.

In the silence of this car, I remember.

The warmth. The laughter. The love. Amidst confusion and exhaustion and frustration.

This is parenthood. This is life.

I imagine going off on some grand adventure only to stagger home to those glowing lights. Welcoming me back with warmth.

To not have to knock. To know.

To be able to say *yes*.

To be able to share *finally*.

To be able to see *all*.

The little feet skipping away from yours during the day. The little smiles cracking one on your frustrated face in the evening. The little hands gripping yours in the darkness.

These beautiful moments.

Leave a light on.

I want to go back and love and listen and laugh more.

I want to know. To remember. To be.

I want to dance during bath time. I want to play during breakfast. I want run during lunch. And I want to break out the songs during dinnertime.

God, to get it all back. Just a few moments. Just a tiny bit of memories.

The darkness cloaks and conceals and ultimately chokes.

But the light is on and it's there and it's so close to touch. So close.

MAKE ME STRONGER (Trailer #8)

There's no starting with one musical cue only to cut seconds later to a surprising other piece of music. No.

When you have the rights to "Burning Down the House" by Talking Heads, you use every single second you can.

The guitar intro plays as the camera hovers over a typical suburban house and comes up to a typical suburban door.

Suddenly you're entering the door and into chaos.

A little furball is running for what reason you don't know but the sweeping Steadicam follows it like some kind of ambitious Kubrick prot g . Then it veers off and follows another set of feet. A youngster running. Then it jerks and tilts and then finds another set of short legs, these a bit more chunky, running up the steps.

The camera is fluid and flows and you see the ten-year-old daughter in her room on her iPad ignoring her parents in every way possible.

Hovering, zooming, floating all to the iconic song, we finally see the suburban mother. Overwhelmed and overtired and overwrought. Yelling even though we can't hear anything. Then just as we think something will change, we see the suburban daddy. At first he looks like a nice guy. A lovable loser. With his hands washing the dishes and a beer nearby that he drains in a few gulps. He seems a bit pissed off and searching for some set of matches. Of course, maybe it's just the song. Or maybe he's two steps away from opening up shop with a meth lab in his basement.

The music gets louder and louder and we see the Steadicam continuing in crazy, dizzying motion with kids crying and laughing and the parents screaming and the chaos until some gigantic fourth-wall push comes over the screen as if Tyler Durden is setting this trailer straight. Suddenly all you can see is darkness. You hear heavy breathing.

"This has got to end," the woman says.

"Enough," the man says. "This ends . . . today."

172

A pause. Complete silence can work to your favor.

"I'm so tired," she says.

"Yeah? Well, I'm tired of this sh—"

Before the curse finishes, Kanye West blasts over the speakers.

"N-n-now th-th-that that don't kill me can only make me stronger."

Suddenly we see Daddy and Mommy turning into Olympic champions of parenting. Working and disciplining and cleaning and ordering and taking stuff away and jogging and driving and standing strong and high-fiving.

Is this a dream? Or a motivational video?

Then another chaotic montage. A food fight, a car exploding, the husband and wife trying to strangle one another. Then finally we see the ten-year-old daughter, dancing on her bed with headphones while Kanye's words gets bleeped.

"So go ahead, go nuts, go apes***, 'specially on my Pastel, on my Bape s***. Act like you can't tell who made this new gospel, homey. Take six, and take this, haters."

The music screeches to a halt. The screen shows the parents, petrified and alarmed, staring at each other. Then screaming . . .

MAKE ME STRONGER. Coming soon.

Firework

I see a trailer of the better man I wished I could be.

There's this passionate fella fighting for truth on the screen while all I could see was this impatient husband and father failing time and time again.

I never felt my age nor did I ever act like it.

I never felt any semblance of stability even though I was supposed to be the one showing it.

Sometimes I just wanted to dance with our five-year-olds and their nine-year-old sister. And sometimes I wanted to get into my SUV and get away. Far, far, *far* away. But I wouldn't. I couldn't.

I felt like a man unable to be free who actually found freedom from the first moment of the day when one of the twins sprinted across the carpet to crash into our bed and snuggle with me.

I was always armed with a hundred more words than anybody else. Sentences unfinished and thoughts abandoned. There was a reason I'm a filmmaker. My brain and my mouth didn't communicate much, and sometimes when they did, it would be a disaster. My insecurities might have sounded out like some kind of miserable song by The Smiths song when I began to talk. So I stayed more secure on the screen. A place I knew better. A place where I didn't have to worry. I could simply dump it all off and leave it behind. For better or worse.

So I thought.

The day would find fault in the friends I never connected with. The simple tasks I never seemed to do. That damn Comcast bill I swore I paid that was three months behind. I'd be lost in these lyrical worlds, these stories belonging to someone else. These dreams and these desires simply to figure out how to pay bills.

I watched what I said publicly online so I didn't get some stranger from afar reading some strange entry and deciding not to work with this strange trailer-maker. God knows I'm strange but I've met far more stranger artists out there.

For those who didn't know me, I promised to keep my heart in check. For family and friends, well . . . they already knew me too well.

174

Far too well.

Youth is wasted on the young. So they say. Familiarity breeds contempt. So they say. And all those who say these things were exactly right.

I miss being young and free. And I miss being known, at least for a few handful of folks.

I wish I could have held back all of it. All of these clouds and these blood clots and these covered wounds I showed. But when I met fellow kindred souls, I suddenly assumed they were like me. They *got* me. They understood.

Yet the older I became, the more I thought they were passengers in other cars, watching me waving them down and shouting out my car window. They heard me but that's all they did. Then they drove on by in the lane next to mine while I was stuck behind some semi.

So a song would come on and tell me the truth. The same kind God asked every single day. He waited and watched and surely wondered why this Spencer Holloway must meander in the way he did.

I hated to. I didn't want to. I lived a whole life refusing to accept any kind of help. Any kind of hope.

The kind I clung on.

So I chose to block it out, to break the hurt, to battle through. Perhaps others didn't understand and perhaps they were never meant to. This was for me and by me and all for me.

I wondered if someone would notice.

I wondered if anybody would care.

I often found myself on this freeway without anybody on it.

I took some kind of special way to my destination.

So be it.

I was driving and heading somewhere and didn't have to wave to you while I passed.

So I'm letting it go. Letting it all go. Letting the noise and the buzz and the pictures go.

I'm letting you go.

Get it?

You're gone and I'm driving on.

Driving and speeding and realizing nobody is in front of or behind me to give me a ticket. Nobody is paying any attention to me. Just like you. Everybody is on some other freeway. So let them drive.

Drive on, all of you. Drive on.

I'm still here, still pushing the pedal, amused by how surprised you'll be when you realize how far and fast this vehicle can take me.

Then again, maybe you won't even notice. The world won't listen.

Steer This Ship

—I used to keep track of the hours and the footage. Like each one brought some kind of great validation all across me.

—Did your wife feel that way?

I want to laugh at Lissie but instead I just smile and shake my head. We sit on the bench enjoying the afternoon sun on the cold winter's day.

—Nobody ever doubted my work ethic. But life isn't about living out the best work ethic, is it?

—I've always loved my naps myself.

I laugh at her half joke.

—I used to try so hard, I say.

—Try so hard to do what?

This time I shake my head, not knowing, not realizing the half joke is filled by my past actions.

—To find the silver bullet. To try to find that absolute classic, incredible oh-my-gosh moment.

—Did you?

—We all try, and we all fail when we're trying on our own.

—Did you ever ask her for help?

I look at the ground and know the truth in the question.

—I didn't believe she could help. I didn't think *anybody* could help.

—What about now?

—Now? Like, right now, right here? Yeah. I would ask. I would beg for help. I'd beg for someone to take my hand and help out and let me not have to try to steer this ship by myself.

—You don't have to steer anymore, Spencer.

—Yeah.

—And you're not by yourself.

Yeah.

The words that I wish I could let go and let others give and let it lie and let it be and let out and let simply linger.

Cover Me

Others don't know but I see it.

I feel it and I can breathe.

I can be.

It's stale and stands firm and stays away the day after day after day. So we do everything we can do to make it to the end, to make it to some kind of distant shore.

But I know.

God, I know.

I know what you're feeling right now and the reckless abandonment that follows you.

You're a true artist.

You want to run.

You want to rail against the system.

So let's go . . .

Let's try.

Hold my hand as we dive.

Clutch my fist as we dig out.

Hold your breath 'cause you'll need to save it.

The smoke and the wind and the water and the weather.

Hush. For a moment.

Hold it for one more second.

Then.

Breathe. God, breathe it in.

Breathe it in with me.

Let me be your oxygen.

Let me be your heart rate and your heartbeat and your heartache and let me be able be mend every single break.

So Green and Lonely

I've always wanted to get the rights to use a Radiohead song in a trailer. They're very hard to get. I still can remember those first few minutes of *Vanilla Sky*, the trippy remake by Cameron Crowe that not everybody got. I always thought they should simply show *that* as a trailer since it felt so intriguing. A seductive woman with a Spanish accent saying, *"Abre los ojos"* and then the English translation, "Open your eyes" just as "Everything in Its Right Place" starts to play. Soon Tom Cruise heads to work and finds Times Square in New York completely empty.

Ah, yes. What a way to start a mind-blowing film.

I'll admit the trailer was pretty magnificent. If I could, I'd edit my *Rolling Stone* article and add this one to the list. Tom Cruise's character has everything. Cameron Diaz as a casual "girlfriend" with benefits. Wealth, fame. But . . . "You Dream of Something More" the trailer says just as Penélope Cruz walks into the frame. For the first minute and a half, the trailer reminds you that the director behind *Jerry Maguire* is giving us another love story of sorts. Until . . . Cameron's character shows up, quite jealous and angry, and suddenly their car veers off the side of a bridge and then this romance turns into a psychological drama, completely throwing viewers for a loop.

As far as Radiohead goes, I can see using "Planet Telex" off *The Bends*. Go ahead, google it. You can switch screens for a second. I'd use the buildup to the final end. It could be used for so many different movies.

For the movie of my life? Ah, good question.

I think it'd be "There There." There's something raw about that song, something righteous. Something a bit hypnotic. Yeah, I know, a lot of Radiohead songs are hypnotic. But I'm thinking of the effect of the images on the screen and the rocking song waking people up.

I'd use the end of the song once again. Song ends are always the best in my mind.

I'd show a man walking with things falling apart around him.

"Why so green and lonely (and lonely and lonely) . . ."

Oh, it'd be beautiful.

Then things would get tense.

A child screaming and another laughing. The messes and the disasters. The endless information.

"We are accidents waiting, waiting to happen."

Then the car would slam against something. The nose would be bloody. The main character would be running now. A Tom Cruise movie, running into the fog, into the night, into the scene again, into your lap.

Boom. Coming to a theater near you sometime.

Illuminate

In love is not the same as love. The first floats down the river while the other swims upstream against every current imaginable. An idea is quite another thing in action. But love is quite that something, isn't it?

I think the idea of being in something still entrances. At this age I can still be entranced. It's feeling the blood circling over my bones. Like the mist of my breath on a beautiful January morning. Like a song I stumble upon and hear for the first time. Entering something, somewhere, some passage away from everything and everyone and into a place of safety and beauty.

Trailers used to do that. My own magical little worlds. Startling, epic, entrancing in two minutes. Colors, motion, music, and the beautiful people can truly do that.

Watching Lissie can do that, too. And I can't help it. I watch her every movement, her every mumble, every single moment she's on-screen, even if it's for no other reason except to be a part of the ensemble. I watch hypnotized.

Should I feel guilty for these feelings? Am I still tied down, not that I'm not longer alive?

I keep going back to that one thing, the sort of center-of-the-universe as far as Lissie is concerned.

Her smile.

I compare the impact to Julia Roberts's smile. Tough thing to compare, of course, since Julia is the actress who hit it big. But those wide billboard grins from *Pretty Woman* and their impact are the same kind that I'm watching now. They're real, first off. They're everything on her face. And they're bright and blinding. Yet unlike shining stars that dull everything else around them, Lissie's smile is the kind that make the others around her more colorful and animated, as if they've finally been found.

I study her every move. There's a clumsy sort of sensuality about her. Not knowing how sexy she could be if she tried, thus making her even more sexy than she could ever be.

Have you ever been moved by a motion picture? Can you

remember what film did it to you? Can you visualize that moment?

I'm seeing this woman I met in passing, in the dim-lit restaurant, in the bar, in the sanctuary of my life, and now I'm seeing her on-screen walking on a sidewalk after a romantic encounter and she's smiling. But it's not a smile. It's a Pixar movie. It makes you feel up and inside out at the same time, along with shrugging off the obvious puns that description might bring.

Fears and Trepidation

There's always been a noise deep down. The crackling burn of a campfire. The never-ending hum of a nearby highway. The crashing bottom of a waterfall. And all your life the volume has gone up, and all your life you've been fighting to silence them.

Enter the world of film and editing and moviemaking in the form of a two-minute trailer.

I reimagine life with the pieces of another's work, shading it the way I want to with a soundtrack of my own choosing. This was my gift and my interest and my means to an end until the end brought no meaning.

Do you hear it too?

I wonder if Lissie does. Or did at one time.

Do you feel the restless winds around your heels?

I wonder if she can. Or if she used to.

Movies would allow me to find relief. Brief, of course, but also brilliant. Two hours of bliss. Of imagining myself on an adventure or terrified or falling in love or figuring out the mystery.

I want to ask Lissie if she ever felt like this. If this makes any sense. So I do the next time I see her. Her and that sweet smile.

—Did the world ever feel too busy, too overwhelming?

—Every day, Lissie says.

—So how did you cope?

—Do you believe in God?

I nod.

—Yes. But so far I haven't seen Him show up, I say.

—I put the tension before Him. That's all I could do.

—So did it work?

Lissie nods.

—But? I ask.

—But? she asks back.

—I'm waiting for the inevitable *but*.

—There is no *but*. It did work. The only times it didn't were the times I didn't believe they wouldn't.

—Really?

—Why would I lie? Lissie asks. What point would I prove?

I shake my head. I just wish she understood.

—Tell me what you're thinking, she says.

—Can you read my mind? I ask.

—No.

—So how'd you know what I was thinking?

—I could have understood your expression back when I was ten.

—Ouch.

—Yes, ouch indeed, she says.

—I love how you never hesitate to say what's on your mind.

—I spent too many years doing exactly that. Time is not a luxury for the living.

—So what about the dead? I ask.

—Should the dead have any luxuries?

—Yes, I say. They shouldn't have to worry.

—You look consumed with it.

—I know. What's that about?

—Perhaps this is what you're meant to find. How not to burn with fears and trepidation.

I nod.

—Can you tell me how? I ask.

—No. I'm not your guide here.

—So what part of the movie trailer do you play?

Lissie smiles.

—Do you need to ask? I'm the pretty, underpaid actress.

—Yes, you are. I wish I could make another trailer with you starring in it.

—So imagine you could right now. How would you start it?

I glance at her and feel strangely normal and also quite strange.

—I'd begin the trailer with silence. And with you staring at the screen, smiling.

—Boring, Lissie says.

—No. Absolutely not.

Still, with the lock finally feeling the turn of the right key, until moved enough to allow someone in. But can't ghosts float between walls?

Comfort

The daily would beat me down with swallowed hours and a sinking heart. I clawed and tapped and scratched and played but no amount of keys pressed ever seemed sufficient when midnight finally arrived.
Creativity paled in comparison to compassion.
The brilliant pale in comparison to the belittled.
I know this stark bit of truth:

A simple word of encouragement pales in comparison to an entire stanza from some meaningful song.

So there right next to you is comfort.
The real, standing there in front of you, is the right thing. The beautiful thing.

Wake Up

I used to wear my Arcade Fire T-shirt with defiance. As if the white words scrawled onto black showed my fist up to the sky. Sure, *The Suburbs* said little to those suburbanites passing by in their minivans and SUVs. Certainly they didn't need to be reminded where they lived. But I still used to take a certain pride knowing that a lot of the folks in Appleton had no clue what "The Suburbs" actually stood for. It made me feel a bit better about living west of the city.

Chicago, this massive, beating heart pumped so close by. I could pop onto I-88 and then head east. Toward the city. The skyscrapers. The endless sea called Lake Michigan. The traffic would swell, so it would feel even better to finally park and get a parking permit from my buddy Steve and then know that I have freedom. For an evening. A night. Twelve-plus hours.

I remember the last show I took in before the twins were born. It was a Sunday at Lollapalooza, where they had fifty-plus acts to choose from in a single day after a three-day binge. So I did a final combo of The National and Arcade Fire.

I remember leaving listening to the final song of Arcade Fire playing. My buddy and his wife wanted to get a jump on the crowd and I was tired. I was tired from working and from worrying and from wondering. And I thought they'd played their last song. But I forgot they still had "Wake Up" to launch out to the world.

So I'm walking down this major street in this major city feeling like some kind of minor fool. The tug pulled and it pulled because I felt like I was going to give up something. This was a finale in a certain stage of my life. I had to let go. I had to give it up because I was going to go from a father of one to a father of three. I had to get serious. I had to be studious. I had to be someone.

The glow of the night laughing their lights off at me. The big beating pulse of the midnight moon. The sighing wind chuckling. Three people walking down an empty street with the echoes of their time surrounding them.

Don't think I didn't remember these minutes and moments.

I still think of them now.

I would soon awake and life wouldn't be over.

I'd walk more streets like those.

I'd listen to more acts like those.

I'd see the moon in a bigger and brighter way.

But we all think the worst, don't we?

Eventually we all start to run and hide. But running and hiding sometimes doesn't work.

Clever

—So you showed back up, Lissie says.

  —I'm the king of pain.

  —A Police fan?

  —No, it just sounded kinda cool.

  —You're halfway there.

I sit across from her like we're just patrons of the store. *Fill my coffee cup one more time. She'd like a bagel, too. Thanks so much.*

  —You look tired.

  —How do the dead look tired?

My question is a good one because seriously—can we be dead and *still* look dog-tired?

  —Life is full of mysteries.

I smile.

  —I had a dream about you.

  —A good one? she asks.

  —You can't see dreams?

  —I'm not omniscient.

  —And I'm not an oxymoron.

I'm trying to be funny but I guess I'm not that clever.

To the Wonder

I'm suddenly in the middle of a Terrence Malick movie. Not pulling the pieces I've been given for the final trailer I was working on but living out the life of a character inside it. The beauty is in front of me. Lissie. So alive and carefree with a shadow of sadness seeming to follow her from behind.

We sit on the bench in the park staring at children. It's warmer and brighter. It feels as if it's springtime now.

—Do you remember your childhood? she asks.

—More and more every day, I tell her.

—I had a wonderful youth. Becoming an adult only made it feel more and more incredible.

We hear laughter and see energy and feel the life on full display right there in front of us.

—I remember only uncertainty, I say. Only questions. Only instability.

—I only moved a few times, but I understand those feelings.

—Every year, I'd spend so much time trying to figure out my surroundings. Only to suddenly see them disappear again. Kids I'd tried so hard to get to know suddenly gone. Restarting again and again.

—I'm sorry.

I look at Lissie and know she is sorry. She understands.

There's no anger, no regret, just realization. I wish I could have known more and been more ready for the giant shift from being a child to becoming an adult. I would have made mistakes, but maybe not as many.

A father pushes his daughter in a swing. She looks to be maybe two years old.

—We are formed in those precious moments, Lissie says as she watches them.

—Yes, we are. As a child and a parent.

She looks at me, an expression on a painting except moving and caring and penetrating.

—You miss them.

—Of course.

—They are not far, she says. You can still see them.

—Seeing is not enough.

Seeing is never enough.

I've stood and watched so many things from the sideline. Entire lives and thrills and treasures and promises and mysteries all seen but not touched or opened or carried.

—Love can't be seen. It can only be shown. Lived out.

—Yes, I say.

She waits for more, then lets the moment settle, as the kids play and the father pushes his daughter and the sky stares down below.

Soon I breathe in and blink and then I'm sitting on a train next to Lissie. We're talking about film and music scores but I'm really just hovering over us watching. The suburbs pass and little by little the landscape changes until the urban sprawl is upon us. The hour trip feels like a moment, a pebble tapping the surface of a still pond, disappearing but leaving memories floating away.

There's a skyscraper and the sand of the beach and the smell of beef from the Portillo's we pass. Hunger tears through me, for all the things I want and can't have.

Hours pass. Days, even. Weeks? Months?

A kindred soul and a kind heart break down the barriers of time and space. Being heard overcomes being hurt. Being known replaces becoming old.

—I know.

I hear this again and again.

—I understand.

—Yes.

To not just talk but to talk freely. To share without hesitation. To finish sentences and to finish them with strength. To not doubt. To never be uncertain.

These have been the dreams and desires I've held and never quite caught up with. Now I'm here and I'm not having to try to get my point across or even struggling to be heard.

A dream. Yes.

—Does she know this? Lissie eventually asks.

I shake my head, knowing the "she" in her question.

—She would understand, she says.

—Not anymore. Not now. Now that it's too late.

In front of me, stopping me, looking at me, so tall and strong, Lissie sweeps me into her stare.

—My mother used to always say, "It's never too late, Lissie. As long as the sun shows up in the morning, it's never too late."

—What would you say to that now?

—Did you see the sunset this morning?

—I was still asleep.

—But when you awoke, was it there? Hanging in the sky, waiting for you to open your eyes?

—Yes.

She turns and continues walking down the street. And I follow.

I've been good at that. Following. For my whole life.

Leading is the thing I never learned. Leading by loving. By allowing. By waiting. By simply being.

The city I knew only in the dark, blurry night opens up its arms and reveals a softer, gentler side. Ornate structures and overhanging spirals all whirl around my head. I'm lost in a bit of a tornado but I keep thinking of Lissie's comment.

Was it there? Hanging in the sky, waiting for you to open your eyes?

My eyes feel open for the first time in a long time. I don't like the me I see, yet the striking warmth and glow of the sun still shines on me.

"Maybe it's time."

I hear Lissie talking to me but she seems ahead of me. This really is a Malick film where there's a narrator talking over images.

"Maybe you just need to go."

The words sound familiar, haunting, strange.

"Maybe there's nothing else I can do. Nothing else we can do."

I see tears smeared across my palm. Do they belong to me? To someone else?

"I'm tired of living in a state of maybe. In a state of someday."

This voice doesn't belong to Lissie. I realize it belongs to someone else. Someone who spoke them not too long ago.

"I don't want this but I need it. I can't think of anything else."

They belong to Tamara. They're thick masses of fog crossing my path.

"We never did and we never will. That's the truth."

I want to hear my words but I can't. They're behind those dark clouds, unable to be spelled out.

"You have to go."

"You need to leave."

"You can't stay here."

"You don't belong here anymore."

The sky suddenly looks blue and I can feel the wind blowing and then I hear my words brushing up against my sides.

"Okay."

That's all. One simple word. But instead of a pebble popping into the still water, this is a bomb shattering the center of the ocean.

Okay.

A life shouldn't have too many *okay*s surfacing inside it. They are the easy things to utter, the easy way out.

I was okay. It was okay. Everything was okay.

I heard my footsteps and then the door and then the engine and then suddenly felt gone. Very gone. Very gone and very not okay. With anything.

The Start of It All

Words can crash upon rocky shores like salty waves tearing apart since we all know that's what love can do. I'm hearing and listening and remembering.

"This has never happened before," Tamara tells me.

I can see it in her teenage eyes, too. This never-happened sort of look. I smile and she smiles even more.

"Thank you."

She's thanking me even though I should be thanking and praising God and celebrating the very opening of her parents' front door. But I don't answer except with a kiss long and hard and full of a lot more.

"I love you."

And that's this moment, this piece of fabric forever torn off another's chest and slipped into my side pocket. I've smothered another and she's leaving me with this stunning declaration.

"I love you too."

I say this with all sincerity, with all heart, with all my everything. But I don't know anything about love. I know that now, so many years later. And anytime you declare your first *I love you* and have to add a *too* is always a deadly thing.

The center of the universe rests in this entryway where falling stars land and black holes avoid. Where I hold the sun and the moon in my arms.

"This has been the best night of my life," she says.

And how can I not think of the utter *whaaaaaaa* of her words? I'm not worthy of them, not even worthy of a *One of the best nights of my life* sort of statements. But it's here and it's real and it's thrown out to me like the opening pitch of the first World Series game in a way that is absolutely and positively unavoidable not to catch and then celebrate.

"Me too."

I say that because . . . because I'm stupid.

I mean it. Yes, absolutely.

I also have no idea what else to say. How to respond to those words and those eyes and that expression.

I'm also a guy responding in a very typical guy-like way.

More could and should be said but instead we both respond with a kiss. Even more wanting, more needing, more to leave with. I enter midnight in the cool dark all warm and bright, full of the need and desire to have more.

Passion offers promise, but there is so much more that exists beyond those starry-eyed sparks. It only took me twenty-five years to discover this.

Single, Solitary Look

So I remember.

How you chased me.

How I fell.

How it seemed so easy. Even though I could be so difficult.

Passing in those halls. Watching in those rooms. Smiling by those corners. Stealing moments away in those shadows.

High school is an echo. A heartbeat. Some distant laugh echoing in the walls of some grand canyon.

You spotted me and searched me out.

I didn't know. How could I?

So soft and sweet and smiley-faced . . . How could I know I couldn't stand up to you?

I wasn't strong enough.

The strength and stubbornness in your soul rises high above the earth like some gliding, glowing balloon blowing in the wind.

So strong.

So determined.

And me . . . so clueless. And so smitten.

So there. Somewhere it clicked.

I know the moment.

The rush of the water. Sure. The rapture of the midnight sky. Of course.

But something about standing by that doorway and looking in your eyes and seeing this look that destroyed an eighteen-year-old.

I'd never seen that look before.

It wasn't a look of longing or puppy love.

It was the look of completion.

This single, solitary look that singled that I was taken. That I couldn't do anything else because I finally found that someone.

So different and yet so utterly divine. Mine. The look that says, *You're mine and you're not going anywhere.*

I stood and kissed her but it wasn't the kiss that spoke words.

It was the look afterward.

Yes.

It sang.

I've found you.

It whispered.

You're not going anywhere.

It told me.

You know I love you and you know you're sorta loving me, too.

It said.

And yes.

And of course.

And naturally.

And so it began.

And so . . .

These pieces of the puzzle all start to form. Put in their places. Colored and melted away. Stuck and solid.

Then life starts to happen. And with it comes the breaks and the bright lies.

Life singles you out. Target practice for the afternoon.

It peels away at the saint you used to be and at the soldier you thought you could be.

The big, bold sun seems to smother you with confidence, but the cold, cool moon only shrugs with indifference.

You want to stand back out on a lawn and cry out to God above. But you wonder if He's stopped listening, if He finally put the Mute button on your mouth.

You wouldn't blame Him if He did.

If you created all of this, you wouldn't want a character like you.

Whiny, weary, full of woe, you'd want to delete and start over.

Thank God that yes, He didn't actually do that.

So breathless, so bold, you begin to wonder anew. Questioning and contemplating. The chords of life. The major moments and the minor ones.

You want to fly on. Right through.

Breathless and breathing and so bold.

Beautiful you are and you will always be.

Please one day let me please.

I want to fly with you again. One day.

196

Clair de Lune

Playlists paid for many a meal in my life. Yet they continue to haunt my soul when I decide to listen without watching out. Without caring.

Like tonight.

Ah, "Clair de Lune."

You, monster, you.

You sweet temptress gliding over those notes like some sweet swan tapping the tips of the water.

I find myself one night, alone, as always, listening to music, like I used to do. To remind myself. To feel alive. And the sweet song nudges up beside me.

Like a dog needing to be petted.

Like a dog you've owned for ten years slipping beside you to fall asleep.

The melodies of yesterday never wrinkle. They never fade away.

They simply grow stronger because they carry the lines of memory with them.

The Rigid and the Ragged

I see the glass. Half-full. The half-full glass. The f***ing half-full glass. A billboard of a cliché staring at me with a dim, quarter-dark glow. Staring shockingly like some kind of missile. I'm standing, waiting for the explosion, secretly knowing I'm ignited inside.

And maybe I like it like this, like this bit of sensation, this bit of raggedness. The day so rigid, so regimented, so routine. So what's not to love about breaking it all down and suddenly swimming out to sea and finally being able to not only breathe but to see and to be? To really, truly *be*. Awake, staring up, face surrounded by the sea, floating on air and water, to be gliding along and loving and light, and to just finally fully being everything I can ever dream of trying to be.

Up and down. The waves. The wonder. And this little bit of trying to know my worth. Trying and hoping and feeling and finding but never quite knowing.

Reckless Is He

Creating is as easy as tearing down. You compose a song on the same phone you destroy a brand with. You edit that selfie to make yourself look more beautiful, then you meme that snapshot of the president to make yourself feel better. It's never been easier to make art. Capturing someone's attention, however, has never been more difficult.

She never had your attention, did she?

Inner monologue hangs over my head like some kind of broken halo, letting hot air seep out and dissipate into silence before ever being seen. Seeing the world in cinematic terms can sometimes make you feel like a character yourself. Yet I've never quite found that screen I'm looking for.

Did you ever try looking somewhere else?

Sometimes.

Sometimes I managed to.

Sometimes I got the balance right.

Few times.

The few and the far between, staring at each other on opposite sides of the Grand Canyon.

It became too grand after all.

I grew up dreaming about the Hollywood stars. The bright lights and the golden statues and the rolling reels flickering and clicking. The glorious sights and sounds all set to some magnificent story.

This was the obsession, the goal, the desire, the destination.

The stars fell and the lights turned off and the reels turned to files and the magic in all of it turned to mercurial, mechanical toil.

A toil I was damn good at toiling away at.

I close my eyes. I'm in my office/apartment/space and I can see her.

Tamara tired and tepid. I've sucked the energy out of her. I've driven over her happiness and replaced it with treads of disappointment.

I see her talking, explaining, suggesting, planning.

What is she talking about?

I can't see. The room is spinning around. It's strange how ghosts can still get as drunk as humans. What would I blow in a Breathalyzer?

Those thoughts of the uncertain, changing tides of the terrible industry only make me think of Tamara. But why?

I can picture the desperation in her eyes.

Why can't I remember this moment?

I'm trying to picture the where and the when. Having kids can erase the moments or at least blur the memories. They can resemble the drawing held on the fridge with magnets starting to bleed its colors from the ice machine above it.

That happened and K was so upset.

The tears and wailing can tarnish those precious moments if there have been any stolen moments between the madness. The bliss is overshadowed by the bombs exploding and spreading shrapnel and blood everywhere.

God, we were so not ready.

But God blessed us anyway. Again and again and again.

Life isn't a movie and it's sure as hell not a movie trailer. It's not a song nor a story. It's not tidy nor is it edited. It's not linear nor does it follow a predestined arc.

Life lingers and loses. Life drops and breaks. Life rushes and riots. Life leaves you stuck. Life never looks over its shoulder.

Life always, always, *always* leaves you behind.

But there's one who doesn't, Spencer. And you know this and always have.

Ah, yes.

Spoken like Yoda talking to Obi-Wan Kenobi.

"Told you I did. Reckless is he. Now matters are worse."

Well, yeah, Yoda. I'm dead.

"That boy is our last hope."

Well, sorry, Obi-Wan. I'm dead.

"No. There is another."

Not another me. God help me if I had another me out there.

Another.

The other.

I look at the ceiling and know I'm heard.

—God, help me.

I'm not sure what kind of help the deceased can have except to finally be truly laid to rest. That's all I want now. To be let go of all of this.

Yet I'm still here moments later, and I'm still here hours later.

And somehow the sun splinters through the blinds the next morning.

THE MORE I DIE (Trailer #9)

Haunting, romantic, melancholy music begins. To be specific, it's a song that's been used before in trailers. "Nara" by E.S. Posthumus.

Antwone Fisher in 2002.

The Clearing in 2004.

The Other Boleyn Girl in 2008.

Vanity Fair in 2004.

But the most known trailer was for 2002's Unfaithful.

It's an odd choice for this 2005 film. But everything about this film is odd. It's unsettling. And naturally, they wanted something a little bit different.

The exotic locations begin to show as the music plays. A beach. A tropical sunset. A grand hotel lobby. A four-poster bed. After a minute of elaborate, erotic shots of beautiful things including a man and a woman, we hear this bit of disturbing dialogue.

"You can't kill something you love. But I chose to anyway."

There's a shot of a body in the water, floating up to the beach, the color of blood washing up alongside it. And that's when the wonderfully horrible cue of the next song comes. It starts 1:53 minutes into the Nine Inch Nails song "We're in This Together" and suddenly all this wonderful romantic sexy foreplay has turned horrific.

Leave it to Trent Reznor to allow his voice and anger and synthetic symphony of dread to put us not in Nicholas Sparks territory but rather David Fincher land.

The cuts are vicious and fast and confusing and brutal.

Until the mayhem and violence and terrifying scenes reveal the title.

THE MORE I DIE. A Little Love Story. Coming Valentine's Day 2005.

Irony is a wonderful thing when you have the visuals and the music to back it

202

up. And you lead the viewer onto one road until they drop off a cliff and discover they're in a whole other section of the country.

It's always a fun thing to have happen. Unless, of course, it's to you.

Really There

—Are you there?

   —Of course I am, she says.

   —But you're not real.

   —Of course I am.

   —Are you really talking to me?

   —Of course I am.

And over and over again comes the words. Four of them. Spoken, as if rehearsed, as if they're a sound bite.

She hovers overhead, a persona, a projection, a *Pretty in Pink* picture in my mind. Gone when the spark of my earnest imagination finally gets unplugged.

I suddenly realize the truth.

Sometimes we fill in the white spaces, and sometimes we color over entire sections to imagine a painting never even imagined.

   —Have I imagined all of this?

   —Of course you have, she says.

This one hurts.

   —Am I really standing here?

   —Of course you are.

I wait. Pause for a moment.

   —Are you really standing there?

   —Of course I'm not.

This one really hurts.

All of this. All of her. All of us. Imagined.

I can create a reality as massive as the *Titanic* and forget about all those submerged icebergs floating out there.

So all of this, every little bit, filling my poor insecure little soul?

Maybe it's the thin cries sticking thick in those long, dark hallways.

Unconnected

And so you drift somewhere else . . .

It's easy to let the space claim this clay piece in your hands. To claw it apart until a tiny piece remains and hardens. To awaken and become painfully aware that it's china and it's chipped and it's nothing like you ever imagined it could be. To knock back on the door of the art studio and then realize it's closed for repairs indefinitely.

There's no sort of memo or email that alerts you. It's the silent night staring at the side belly of your shih tzu. Working again, studying, searching, mind wandering, separated again naturally.

And so the vices tend to tempt and comfort. The beer has become wine in order not to grow the belly. And lust becomes a necessity you try to take care of before it becomes a nuisance. Buzzing and exploring and being alone. Not the greatest thing but you're on your own in this world and you do what you have to do.

You love looking at moving images that shape the imagination. You love listening to moving melodies that shape the emotion. You love listing out all the many ideas produced by late-night creative binges.

So you can file them away for the moment they're needed.

So you can keep them in storage until the moment you have to shine.

So you can refrigerate these hot, wild, easily spoiled delicacies.

Yet love remains hovering asleep and loyalty remains sitting alive. And the two barely manage to pass in the night except for the bed the two reside in sleeping and dreaming but never resting in one another.

Connected

—Don't drift off.

—I won't, I say, coming back to reality.

I shift in my seat so I fulfill my promise. The days of being a teen or twentysomething seem so far off. When sleep was this strange thing people forced on us. Now it's somewhere between air and water. A precious necessity that suddenly doesn't seem like either.

—Tell me something about yourself.

—Like what?

—Like what are you like.

I'm not following her question. I'm safe over here on this chair, safe far away from her gaze and her touch. Safe, safe. And I'll tell myself that again and again and again.

—With what?

—With your wife.

—Ah.

—Are you kind?

—Sometimes. Impatient a lot.

—Really?

—There are so few connections. So few common interests.

—Really?

Maybe this is difficult for her to realize but not for me.

I just stand still and watch the world open its mouth wide. I can see her. Can see it. Can feel myself falling like always.

—Tell me, I say.

—What?

—Tell me the things that move you.

—I don't know.

—Anything.

—It's always in the moment.

I nod and look at her and feel like she's in the moment. This moment is mine and it's a bubble floating and I refuse to pop it.

—Tell me, I say.

—Tell you what?

—Tell me what moves you.

—I told you it's hard to say.

—I want some ammunition.

—You have plenty.

—I need more.

—You need to stop looking at me that way.

—Is it that obvious?

—Oh, it's obvious.

—How does this work in the ghost world?

—I don't know but I know I'm feeling the same as I used to feel.

—Meaning . . .

—Meaning I'm still feeling pretty horny if you want to know the truth.

I laugh.

--I love the honesty, I tell her.

—I'm being serious.

She nods as if to confirm her words.

—There's nothing but serious talk here. So just tell me what moves you.

—Why?

—I want a road map.

—I don't think you know where you're headed, she says.

—I know where I want to go.

—Not sure if you can get to that land, my friend.

—"My friend" seems so fake. So artificial.

—So does your GPS.

—Talk Talk says that life is what you make it, I say.

—What happens when you're on the other side of that phrase?

Such a great question. I've never thought of it.

—I don't know.

—I knew you wouldn't.

—Don't be smug in ghost knowledge.

—Just saying.

About Yesterday

I make the choice when I awake. To worry and to want. To watch and to wish. When everything ever wanted and wished for surrounds me.

To pass and stumble and repeat and poke and dismiss and then to depart with the crumbles of a life left in my hand like the crumbs of a half-eaten breakfast remaining on the kitchen table.

More to say but of course unable to. When opening and coming in and staying and passing and stumbling again.

Without trying because I'm so damn tired.

Without explaining because I'm so damn heavy.

Without waiting because I'm so damn busy.

Without help because I'm so damn me.

And then later the sun slips and stumbles with me and I'm here in the noise and the violence and the stir and the crackle and the creases and I melt and I stumble again and I'm lost and I'm moving and all I can do is try to make it better little by little and sip by sip. To turn down the noise and to try to do something, anything, everything but not ever listening or even trying.

And this is my today. With the hope of tomorrow to be better. But today always shows up. Again and again and again.

Until it's finally tomorrow, and I'm looking back longing for the yesterday I can no longer have.

Suffer Well

Sleeping, unknowing, unwatching, unwaiting, unhearing, unseeing, uncomprehending, unaware at all.

Am I some hero or a prisoner of my own making?

I fight and I take flight and I strive and I suffer and I sure don't "Suffer Well."

Eyes drooping and dropping. Too much too often too again.

Again.

And again.

And I wonder when the midnight will crack its bat and allow me to stop suffocating?

Let me go?

Let me get rid of these midnight demons?

Make A Smile For Me

—Listen.

 —What's this?

 —Just hush.

I'm telling a ghost to be quiet. I love these strange ironies.

I play the song and Bill Withers wraps his arms around Lissie and me.

 "Make a smile for me," Bill says and Lissie does exactly that.

It's pretty wonderful.

 "Stay awhile with me. Can't you tell I've been lonely?"

Her smile grows like an orchestra filling in string by glorious string. It might be one of the most stirring things I've ever seen.

Slow, personal, real. God, do I love this song.

They don't make music like they used to, do they?

Sleek and sophisticated sure isn't as sexy of some of those wonderful tunes from the seventies.

This is the kind of tune you put on a playlist in the background while you're away and lost and alone and ready to make love for a long time.

I don't look at Lissie and imagine that, however. She's different, special, off-limits, untouchable in ways. This smile of hers is different. There's a sacred quality about it. I don't ruin it or taint it or retouch it.

 —I love this, she says.

 —It's so romantic, right?

 —Yes.

As it drifts away, Lissie seems lost for a bit.

 —Play it again, she asks.

So I do. And so we continue to do as the song asks.

A sweet moment in this lost solace we're living in.

Avalon

She waits in the corner like the last candle left in an abandoned world. I try not to rush to her table and her smile and her world. She already knows me but I'm still trying to convince her that she doesn't. That there's more to me. That I'm as deep as she happens to be. But we both know who the little kid is and we both accept it. It's better to admit these things late at night when adults are present. When the facade of games evaporates like last glow of exploding fireworks.

—I was beginning to think you weren't coming, she says with eyes that put my head in a choke hold.

—I have so many other things to do, I say, trying to sound brave and all James Bond like.

But I'm not Sean Connery or Roger Moore. I'm that one lone Bond named George Lazenby who never quite fit the role. I try but still. Who am I kidding?

This is a dream I'm having. A ghost having a dream.

—You can sit, you know, she says.

—I'm just looking at you.

—Do you like what you see?

—I've liked what I see since the first time I saw you. But tonight . . .

—Tonight what? she asks.

—Tonight it's a little more than like.

She grins. She knows. She doesn't need to hear my words to confirm this.

God, she looks hot in this dream of mine in her white blouse that's holding on to her as tight as possible.

—Sit. I need someone to help with this bread.

I look and see her eating but the bread barely looks touched. I sit down and break off a piece, then pour some olive oil on the plate, drizzling parmesan cheese over it and a bit of pepper to give it some bite.

—Sorry you were waiting, I tell her.

—It's okay.

That smile. Again. It's just not right. It's like turning the dial on

211

your shower when you need just a bit more heat.

—You look nervous.

—I am, I say.

It's not like I've had anything like this in a long time. A date? With another woman? It's been years. *Decades.*

But why am I nervous if this is a dream?

—I won't bite, she says. Unless you want me to.

I probably give her a look because she starts to laugh.

—I'm just teasing, she says. Man, you are tense.

—I'm not sure what to make of this.

She dips a piece of bread into the cheese.

—It's called dinner. Conversation. Soon, hopefully, wine.

—Yeah, I need a little of that. Can ghosts get tipsy?

I already know the answer to that.

—Let's see, she says. I know I will.

—Good thing 'cause I'll finally know what you *really* think.

The look is stone. Cement. Unmovable. Unbreakable. All over me. She just stares with a serious look, a kind I recognize. I might be nervous but I'm not stupid.

—Do you need to ask? she asks.

The small, round, soft curve of those lips grip the bread and move with such grace.

—Maybe not?

She laughs. And right then, a server comes to ask what we'd like to drink.

—Shiraz? I say.

Then I find a bottle to order.The waiter doesn't seem particularly in the mood for romance. He nods and leaves.

—I hope you want some, I say.

—Of course.

—He seemed very unpleasant.

—He seems bored, she says.

—He sees us, I realize.

—You're dreaming all of this, she says just as it all disappears.

Spying

I see her in a way I've never seen her. In the parking lot. Then the store. And then looking through the hanging clothes for sale.

She's not just content. Not just so calmly beautiful. But she's alive in herself. Her soul. Her person.

She lost that somehow. I lost it. We both just lost it. But I see it like the stalker I am.

It's a sexy kind of glorious. And it brings back all those intimate times.

Life likes to throw a blanket on beautiful things. The thankful moments that it suddenly deems too dull to celebrate.

So you forget.

So you wander off.

But I can't help. Can't help but fall back into it all.

All with a simple grace of her gaze at the fellow strangers around her.

I find myself behind the steering wheel secretly watching with the biggest smile I've had in some time.

It feels pretty good.

The Message

Here's a typical day in my former life of working full-time for myself and trying to make it work.

I want to forget but I can't because it's forged inside like the reinforced concrete of a skyscraper. Another day. Just one more day. Groundhog Day, again and again and again.

Asking when. Wondering when. How about when. Let me know when. Until finally hearing it and knowing it's still not tomorrow and not the next day and not next week and maybe not half a month away.

F***.

I just look at the computer and then the walls around me.

Yes, nobody's dying. But this is getting really old.

Ten years of this. This s***. This frustration. All these idiotic bastards.

I do my job. I fulfill my obligations. But it's nobody else's job to try to fulfill their obligations because they don't have many or any.

If this was just me like it used to be when everything got handed to me, I'd be fine. If this was just Tamara and me who got everything handed to us, then we'd be fine. But the fortune ran out when a greater fortune trumped it all.

Those three little ladies.

God must have said, *Okay, Spencer. That's enough. I've given you far too much anyway and that's more than enough. You figure the rest out.*

Figure the rest out.

I never had anything figured out in the first place.

Five years old and I was floundering just trying to figure out where the hell I was supposed to walk to.

Fifteen years old and I was already a forgotten figure, lost in a myriad of moves. Never finding my space or my life or myself.

I've had to do this on my own crippled with self-doubt and self-ignorance. And all those games and all that fuss and all the lavish praise and all the promise . . .

Gone.

I don't know what to do.

Gone.

I have no idea what I'm going to do anymore.

I'm terrified. And weak. The tears in my eyes and the lightness in my head and the inability to breathe don't scare me. It's the look from Tamara, the disappointment. The inevitable denial. Walking away. Back turned. Silent. Suggesting using coupons when there's no cash in our hand. Inferring it's my fault when yeah, it's pretty much my fault.

The words remain close.

They remain close and they call out.

"Take a good, hard look at your life. Think it over."

I've been thinking it over and I don't like what I see.

"You have spent a lot of money, but you haven't much to show for it."

Nothing but debt and regret and Banana Republic calling me up to ask why I haven't paid for the pants I bought fifteen f'ing years ago.

"You keep filling your plates, but you never get filled up."

That's because I'm walking around empty. Trying to find something. Trying to *make* something out of nothing. That's what I do but it's nothing and never meaningful. Ever.

"You keep drinking and drinking and drinking, but you're always thirsty."

And I just want more. And more.

"You put on layer after layer of clothes, but you can't get warm. And the people who work for you, what are they getting out of it? Not much—a leaky, rusted-out bucket, that's what."

The words.

Words from the book of Haggai from *The Message.*

I turn to those in my time of fear and frustration and only find rebuke.

Because you've rebuked Me.

But I never had anything and never had anybody and I've been on my own all this time forty f***ing years and more without some kind of gentle loving father figure to give me something or anything besides a shadow of doubt and failure falling all over me like a blanket trying to smother not cover.

"You keep drinking and drinking and drinking, but you're always thirsty."

And vacant. And empty. And absent. And irritated. And self-absorbed. And self-medicated. And selfish. And self-centered.

And that's what I'll be doing later. Where I'll find myself. Drinking and drinking. Saying I'm working. Actually working, of course, but really just working on getting away.

But I'm still thirsty.

Every night and every morning.

My Rituals

Work awaits. Wrapped around fingertips, words flow. The never-ending wonders. The never ceasing summations.

Sigh.

So many things probably pass you by.

You're in the most boring Choose Your Own Adventure ever written. There are no choices, only answers, only blank pages left to fill.

It's not a Do You sort of world but rather it's a Do sort of world.

Busy and buried.

Beyond.

Out there, beyond the window, the sky, the howling world watches.

Those endless pages. The word count. The tired, tossed-about, tattered soul.

An afternoon grin. You keep going.

An evening cocktail. You keep plugging away.

A nightly ritual. Planted, creating. Directed, crafting.

February starts to go away. Slipping down and stalling.

While you count the hours in the day. The minutes. The moments. The words.

Page counts and word counts and summaries and story lines.

Who are you?

Someone take over the wheel and drive.

Someone keep typing and keep summarizing.

Spelling it out.

Saying something. Anything.

Give It All

I live in a world of my own making, surrounded by the sounds I choose, immersed in the images I envision. A universe of one, full of imagination and full of ideas and full of himself.

The world arrives each morning like the ashes of a bonfire in your backyard. It shivers throughout the day like aftershocks. Then blows a gust of a good-night kiss while the wildfires still rage on. All the while, I feel helpless, confused, angry, and singed.

Burning everywhere inside with a need to let out something. To unleash. To release this heavy load somehow and someway. To unwind with liquor and to imagine with the internet. The vices of the late-night souls. Of the dreamers. Of the passionate. Of the smoke-filled souls.

The voices sing in the background to your cries. Soothing harmonies all while you slowly lose your voice screaming and howling and beckoning for more. For sorting through this mess. For making sense of it all. But sense self-destructs near midnight and remains AWOL near sunrise.

The ticks and the tocks and tension awake you without a single sound. They pulse like a high-definition heartbeat throughout the hours of the day. They tap you on the back when you're busy and they knock on your door when you're focused and they ping and pong away all day. They howl and bluster and then when you have had enough, they suddenly shut off like the computer battery running down, leaving you alone and quiet and cut off and very light.

The habits became heavy. The impatience to get back to work, the restlessness to go back down into the dark waters full of red wine and wasted energy. Midnight would offer the mirage of solace and relief, yet it would be blurry and empty. I'd drown in some kind of story, some kind of creation, some kind of dead end I'd understand the next morning.

These embers I carry inside are familiar. They glow the brightest around midnight, when they shine on the tales I strive to tell. The pieces I stumble upon—fragments, messy and haphazard—can only be scooped up and sorted out with the limited tools I have. Ten fingers, striving to work hard to organize and arrange and cut and splice and present something beautiful.

I wait for the moment I'm moved. And with each passing day, each passing assortment of heartbeats pounding away, it takes more and more for my heart to be moved. I search for songs and signs and colors and pictures and film and footage and any sort of source. Yet more and more I long and need and desire more. More of the kind of more I shouldn't want.

And every now and then I stop and stumble and stare at this snapshot of being moved right in front of me. It can be anything. Something I see or someone I meet or some kind of experience. It lights a spark and strips off the flames and soon I'm exploding with some kind of burst of passion and excitement and love for you name it. I love to love something with a lost-love sort of longing. I long as if I've been marooned, as if I'm a prisoner. Yet I'm simply a drunk, jealous glutton, wanting the more and more. And more and more.

What remains? Good question. And a good song by Foals.

The night has silent ripples over its surface. Sometimes I feel them in my seat. Unsure and shaken, I wonder what's next. I always wonder what's next. Something I haven't seen. The red light turning green. The words not the page.

Echoes of the way it could have been. A ghost on the screen. The way but not the means. So I try and I try. To give it all.

Give it all.

Why not and why?

The questions that swell and that we try to sequester.

I wonder where. But. I wonder when. But. I wonder when and where the *but*s will ever end. I wonder this and wonder that and wonder if I've even gotten all the facts right.

The Brilliant Bits

—Shhh.

I do what Lissie says.

—Look. Over there.

So I do what she says again. I see the leaf floating down the river. Gentle, unknowing, peaceful, beautiful. Yet I find myself thinking of all those things while watching her watch the leaf.

—There, in the water, look over there, Lissie tells me.

—I see it.

—It looks like it's floating above the water, doesn't it?

But I'm still looking at her, and yes, she looks like she's floating above the water.

—Stop giving me that look, she tells me.

—What look is that?

—*That* look. The one you're giving me now.

—I'm just looking at you.

—No, you're smiling. Like that. Like, that smile—stop it.

—What?

—You know what. Are you trying to be Ryan Gosling or something?

—What's wrong with this smile? Do I look goofy "or something"?

—You don't look goofy, Lissie says.

—Then what?

Her look tells me exactly what I already know, but this is all part of the game, isn't it?

—You look familiar and trustworthy, and you look like you know what comes next.

I suddenly feel stilted, her words a bit too frank for me to continue that *look*.

—I'm sorry.

Now she's lost, knowing how real she must have just been.

—I'm sorry.

We're both sorry for different reasons but feeling the same way.

This moment—magical, floating downstream like a leaf on the water—suddenly gone.

220

Drive 1

—I want you to watch a favorite with me.

Lissie doesn't seem rushed or anxious or bored or even curious as she watches me riffling through my DVDs as she's comfortable on my couch. She smiles, waiting for me to continue.

—You already told me you haven't seen this.

—Are you going to say *The English Patient*?

I stop and open my mouth and appear shocked. Of course it's obvious I'm *not* talking about *The English Patient*.

—Yes, I joke. We're definitely watching *The English Patient*.

—Have you ever seen the episode of—?

—*Seinfeld*? I interrupt. With Elaine? Right?

We both laugh.

—We're sounding a little like twins or something, Lissie says.

—How about BFFs?

—Did you just say *BFFs*?

I nod.

—Terrible to use acronyms, huh? I'm picking up your habit, I tell her.

—I love when Elaine is in the movie theater dying after having to watch the movie. And I haven't even seen it.

—I actually really loved *The English Patient*, I say. But no—have you ever seen *Drive*?

She shakes her head.

—Do you even *watch* movies? Come on. You're a movie star.

—Hardly.

—You have to like Ryan Gosling, right?

Her mentioning the actor's name earlier this afternoon made me think of this.

—Well, of course. *Hey, girl.* I love that meme.

—You know he never even said those words, right?

Lissie looks surprised.

—Seriously, I continue. Some major fan started it and then it became this *thing*.

—Did it go *viral*?

She says that last word as if she might have been saying, "It's like totally tubular" or some kind of dumb catchphrase from some different era.

—Okay, so *Drive* is a Ryan Gosling flick?

—One of his best. You sure you haven't seen it?

—No.

Oh yeah.

—Tonight's the night, my fair lady.

Drive 2

I have everything set up. The monitor on my desk, the speakers, the dim light, the love seat moved to face it perfectly. We just need some popcorn.

Lissie can probably see that I'm giddy.

—So is this a favorite? she asks.

—Yeah. I adore this movie.

—But why?

—I don't know. It's just got this thing . . . It's like it sums me up.

—How so? Is it because of the visuals or the music or the story line?

She can create grins merely by blinking.

—Well, you have to just watch, I say.

The opening credits begin with this synth-heavy, eighties *Blade Runner* vibe.

—I love this music, I say.

The song that plays is "Nightcall" and it seriously could have been so absolutely corny with the muffled, distorted voice saying how he's giving someone a nightcall. But it works, and when the artist named Lovefoxxx starts to sing the chorus, it swells into something magnificent.

"There's something inside you. It's hard to explain. They're talking about you, boy, but you're still the same," she sings.

The song is simply the backdrop to Ryan Gosling's character— dark and shadowy and mysterious—doing what the movie says he does: drive.

I'm sitting on the armrest of the sofa, as if I'm not allowed on it because it's a love seat and that's a little too intimate. I have to sum up my feelings about this movie, so I do the cardinal sin of talking.

—The first time I saw this movie, I went by myself. It was a late-night showing, I think. We had just had our twins and they were like really young. Only months old. I remember when these opening credits came I was like *What is this? This is awesome.* It was the soundtrack of *Miami Vice* meeting *Blade Runner.*

I hadn't paid much attention to the director, Nicolas Winding

Refn, up to that point, but suddenly I was in. From the opening heist, where Gosling's character proved he was the best driver out there, to this mysterious vibe and the whole question of what's his character's backstory? They would never give him a name, either. He was always "Driver."

As the movie plays, Lissie taps on the seat beside her for me to sit. So I do.

Yet suddenly the film becomes a teenage John Hughes picture. Gosling sees his neighbor, played by the sublime Carey Mulligan, and her young son at the apartment complex, and he's all mushy and dreamy even though she's got a not-so-nice backstory, too.

There's the sweet desire of "Under Your Spell," which has the same sort of vibe that a New Order song in *Pretty in Pink* might. You almost can see Duckie riding his bike to "Shell Shock."

Then there's the totally eighties fantastic song called "A Real Hero," where Gosling's character drives (there you go again, Gos) the woman and her son around Los Angeles and so far he's done nothing heroic but by God you will swear for the rest of your life that this driver is a "real hero" because the song says it and the sun glows off the water and Carey Mulligan is just so damn cute.

Of course there's this *thing* beating in the film. You know it's got a darkness about it. The score by Cliff Martinez echoes this. There's melancholy and there's brooding and there's something coming. The longer the movie goes where nothing but sweet things happen, like Gosling watching TV with the kid, the more you realize something really bad is going to erupt.

Suddenly the woman's husband, who's been in jail, shows up and things get darker. He looks mysterious and he—*wait a minute. It's Oscar Isaac in an early role!* A robbery turns into a setup and a shoot-out and a bloody carnage where we learn the Driver isn't just an expert at driving. He's also excellent in surviving and punishing and he seems to have this trigger-thin switch that unleashes something not so good that's deep down inside him.

I don't say all this meandering nonsense to Lissie. But I comment here and there.

We still don't quite know the Driver until the motel scene after the

224

botched robbery, where we see this other guy. This monster that's somehow been kept at bay inside Gosling.

Just like I was when I first saw the scene, Lissie is first in shock and then starts to slowly reassess the Driver just like everybody else does the first time they see his bloody face staring at the dead bodies.

—The rage in his character, Lissie says. It's scary.

It's not just that.

—It's his silence, I tell her. We never quite know what he's thinking. We do but it's all through his looks and body expressions.

Then there's the elevator scene.

I almost want to tell Lissie not to look. But she has to. The same way Tamara did. Watching a scene where a killer threatens Gosling and Mulligan, and it's tense and then suddenly . . . it's glowing light and ethereal and Cliff Martinez dreamlike and we see Gosling kissing Mulligan passionately. Their first kiss that also feels like their last. The Driver knows. It's his last moment being *that* guy she thinks she knows. His last moment where she trusts him and feels safe with him. He has to protect her and he knows this but it's not going to be good in any sort of way.

She's going to discover who this Driver really happens to be.

Then the scene in the elevator becomes brutal and beyond violent. A rage inside Gosling is unleashed again. He doesn't just fend off an attacker. He unleashes hell. And as the assailant is on the floor wounded, Gosling begins to kick his head in, crushing it over and over with his boot, the sickly sound effect giving us more than we want to know until that slight image shows the audience the grisly results.

Mulligan's character doesn't see it for a split second, however. She's mortified. And when the elevator door opens, she slips out in shock, staring at the blood-drenched face of Gosling.

Who is this monster?

That's the look she has as she stares at him.

It's not a goodbye. It's a judgment.

Gosling's face has fading rage that's turning into horror at himself.

I can't help myself.

That's the look he has as the elevator doors shut.

Lissie has to sit there for a moment and try to decompress. Try to pick herself up from the awfulness she just saw.

—Okay . . . what just happened? she finally says.

—Something very bad.

—Did that really happen? What did I just see?

I pause for a moment.

—You saw him. His true colors.

—That was terrible.

—I know. And he knows, too.

Drive 3

Drive is not a feel-good date movie. It becomes grisly and unrelenting and there's no happy ending. There's hope, which I admire. But there's not happiness. The two don't always have to equal one another.

With the end credits playing, Lissie looks over at me, her body and head sunk down on the sofa, now staring up at me as if from a dream.

—So that sums you up? Lissie asks. How? Do you step people to death on elevator rides?

I laugh.

—I love the dichotomy of *Drive*. You have this sweet, almost-corny love story happening that's suddenly mixed with brutal violence.

—You don't strike me as violent.

—Gosling doesn't strike you as violent, either. Right? Not at first.

—So what's the film trying to say? *Stay away from Drivers?*

—I think it's about a guy who's almost gotten out of a bad life. A bad situation. He's trying to make a new life but he can't. And the demons keep following him and taunting him and finally they unleash all the awful things inside him.

Lissie looks at me, studying me.

—And again I'll ask: how does this sum you up?

—I've had my share of demons seeming to follow me around. Seeming to stir the pot inside my soul.

—I can't see that, Lissie says.

—It's because I'm a chameleon. Nobody ever sees it. Nobody except Tamara. You know what she said to me after this film? And after she scolded me for taking her to something so violent?

—What? Lissie asks.

—She said that Gosling reminded her of me. To which I initially said, "Wow, I'll take that." But then Tamara said it wasn't just the overall look or even his sometimes-mischievous smile that Gosling has mastered. She said it was his intensity. That look about him.

Lissie didn't look surprised or didn't seem to want to say anything.

—She said his *intensity*. This inspired by a man who uses a hammer on a guy and stomps another's head in.

—What'd you say to your wife? How did you respond?

—I didn't. I probably made a stupid joke. But I knew . . . I knew she meant it. And I knew she was right. Sometimes the anger and frustration can swell and resemble something as awful as that elevator scene. Sometimes there doesn't have to be bloodshed for someone to receive a piercing wound. There doesn't have to be broken bones and there doesn't have to be a fallen corpse. Sometimes the death can be inside, and it can be invisible but it can still have the same sort of feeling that a brutal beating might take on.

—I'm sorry, Lissie says.

—For what?

—For pressing. For prying.

—I invited you into this dialogue. Probably deep down, I wanted it.

—You're not a bad guy, Spencer.

—You don't know all the things about this guy.

—And vice versa.

—I'm just saying—there's always more.

—There is. My only problem is with the mother in the film. She's too much of a fantasy. There has to be more there, too.

—Sure. But the point of view is from the Driver's standpoint. Remember—Mulligan's character married the guy who went to prison. There's definitely more to her.

—There always is, Lissie says.

—I was going to say that.

228

Somebody

Just a nice memory in the dark in the parked car in the distant day where no one can disturb us. Wrapped around without the weight of history untangling us. This all-now feeling with a maybe-then hope for the future in front of us.

Rain fell yet Tamara and I held one another without a care. Not worried about tomorrow or the others or later tonight or anything except this hold and embrace and heat under the thunderstorm.

Exhaling in surprise and wonder. These moments—soft and surreal and wanted like hunger and thirst. Full and then saying goodbye and thinking of those next moments without worrying about a future or a past or a cyclone of hurt surrounding us.

Youth isn't always wasted on the young. We didn't waste it. We grabbed what we wanted and it happened to be each other. So we snuck out and then let it happen.

Scared or Selfish

My earlier memory of young love and lust ends up leaving when the more recent memory of adult loathing and letdown invades my mind.

I'm right back at that place I knew so well. Back at the place where I'm saying the same thing once again.

—I don't have anything left to say.

When you stand there not looking at someone and carrying several manuscripts' worth of notes full of statements and sayings that you suddenly don't want to say, then you know something is very, very wrong.

—I know you're tired, Tamara says.

—I'm tired of talking about this.

She doesn't understand and never will. Of course I could help. Of course I could be a little more loving and a little less of a douchebag. But there's something about these walls that peel the skin off of me. That get underneath and start scraping, cutting up and sucking out. I'm carved into a different creation every night.

—I don't know what to do anymore.

I shake my head but I know what I want her to do. Shut up and shut down. Which is exactly what she does. Every time.

I hate myself for being this way. I know how awful I can be. But I have no more emotional anything. It's not that I'm looking for something because there's nothing there to give. It's obvious that she's been on land too long when I've been far out to sea. I don't even know what those firm foundations even feel like anymore. I know she can't begin to feel the restless, relentless waves of the deep blue sea suddenly underneath her.

—It'll get better, I tell her.

She nods. But I've said this a long time.

Time and money can be brutal, bickering bedside companions.

They can pick at you all night long—11:30 and 12:15 and 1:34 and 2:17 and 3:00ish when one of the girls wakes up and the 4:20 drop and the 5:40 float up and the 6:30 realization. Picking. Peck peck pecking away.

There's a moment, a chance, an opportunity, but then it folds. The failure so obvious that seems so natural. Time and time again. A chance to say more, to say, *Let's don't do this*, an opportunity to hold one another and just try. Just try to connect. And we sometimes still do connect but maybe that's just out of primal, human need. The need for the body to release itself and the longing to just get it over with. To be close for a brief little moment and then to go back to the winds of failure.

I blame myself, of course. Always have. I have mastered the art of self-loathing. This allows me an out, too.

My personality is one of stubborn discontent. Like a dog that will never decide to give up, that will continue to chase and bite and bark off the mailman day after day even though the US postal service will always keep coming. Doesn't matter. I continue to look and wait and watch until I see the familiar.

I can be such an asshole.

Which is ironic. Truly. Because people know me as the world's nicest guy. One of them. Funny and laid-back. But I can act. And I can be artful in presentation.

But Tamara knows.

She knows only so well. She's got the bite marks in her heels. Permanent punctures in feet that refuse to leave me.

Guess that makes me a lucky guy, right?

I guess I should feel so.

Maybe

Maybe you did this.

Maybe the misery you used to see simply mirrored that ache deep inside.

Maybe it's not your fault or her fault or your parents' fault or fate's fault but maybe it just happens to be. This fault that ruptured and turned into some kind of earthquake.

Maybe you crawled out only to find yourself a dead man walking.

Maybe you're supposed to discover something here but you have no idea, no notion, no memory, no nothing.

Daughters

That silver square block with wheels pulls into the driveway. For a second, the garage door stays open and allows me to see.

I hold my breath as if I need to, as if it matters. Then I see her holding one. Then another climbing out, then another.

Say their names, you turd.

But I can't. I won't. I refuse to.

Three fingernails cutting into my heart while the thumb can't touch me. This sorta sums it all up.

I close my eyes and open them again. I want to run and want to rush in but I see the door closing and see their little legs disappearing and soon they're gone and I'm shut out. Waiting and watching. But there will be no glimpses again. Not today.

It's too cold outside. To secure inside.

I miss them but can't admit how much. I won't because I know it won't get me anywhere. Even if I could talk to them, what words would I say? And what possible outcome would I want those statements to produce?

Then later, after dusk and darkness and curtains drawn, I see them again. This time inside the space that I used to be allowed to occupy.

In the silence, heart pumping at half-time, head slowing down its topspin, I settle in to glance over the sleeping seas. They're still. Dreaming. Waiting for their restless storms to surprise meteorologists. To send me into hiding again. The watery, wintry ebb and flow at the end of summertime. Fatherhood never ceases to amaze.

I can retreat and refresh and restore my sanity. Well, I used to try. I had my ways. I had my struggles. But I remember the moments when all would be silent and it would just be me and I would actually feel thankful. Sometimes I didn't feel this way. That's a sad fact but it's true. But these moments—they were special. Just thinking in the middle of night, usually listening to something good and drinking something good.

I miss those moments. I miss that life. I miss it so much.

Something in the Shadows

You can stay the same. Stay stuck inside. Shut down encased in the ruts of your own making. And every sad song and every stormy sunrise can remind you and reinforce your own misery.

The music fuels. Pours it all over the fire. Desire, boom. Pain, boom. Mystery. Adventure.

The right song always fits. And we see so many two-minute movies that we begin to see ourselves as the hero. The soundtrack playing as we tweet and take selfies and describe our lives and share to nobody watching or listening.

Did you do the same, Spence? Did you fill in the trailer with the images and the tunes you wanted your tale to tell?

I'm stuck, standing, curious as I stare.

Did I create it? To subtract that and add to this?

Those love songs with those lyrics lining the walls like new crown molding. The minor synths making the mood so melancholy. When life—when *your* life—doesn't require them.

But you grab a piece to slide into place with the others. Wondering what picture it will form. The puzzle remains, however, hovering away, still invisible even though all the portions have been used.

Have I made a trailer for my own life, yet lied to the consumer and to the ticket holder?

The melodrama. Memories on display like train tracks, simply there to be run over and overshadowed and swallowed.

There's something in the shadows but it's not necessarily good.

The rustling until the ground shakes and rocks and sends nervous waves over you.

Made up most of this—the struggle, the curse, the craziness all made up.

Love and loss and living and lingering on is all part of the drama that we sell, that I sell.

I'm not a movie and I can't be summed up.

But somehow I keep trying. Making it up as I go. Filling in details that aren't and weren't there. Making it better or worse. Far, far worse.

234

Glass Eyes

—You go places, Lissie says.

    —Yes, I do.

    —Where?

    —Back home.

    —Do you miss it?

    —Like the broken glass of a pressed fire alarm.

She waits for more but doesn't get it.

    —Did you get out alive?

I shake my head.

    —I didn't. But those who needed to did.

    —That's bleak, she says.

    —We're dead, aren't we?

    —Were you alive before the broken glass?

I can only smile. Ghosts can not only haunt, but they can also be pretty damn smart.

    —I wanted every single cut and every bit of pain.

    —Why do you go back there, then? she asks.

    —I have to. I do. But it just makes me sad.

    —Lots of things make you sad.

I stare back.

Why fight it? She knows—maybe everybody knows in this new reality.

    —I work hard to act like they don't.

    —You don't have to work so hard here.

    —I want, I *need*, to go back. Not just to see. But to live.

    —And if you could, Lissie asks, what would you do?

    —More. The more I could've done but refused to. Every single more I can no longer choose.

Here Comes The Night Time

We stand in the stream and somehow it seems to work out well. The songs they stir your heart. And sometimes the little footsteps in the house slow down and stop. Then you find yourself on a couch restless and needing rest and wanting to just wrestle something down with your lazy comfort. A scream of noise and you take off the headphones but it's not the kids, it's the music. You think, at least.

There is a reality but it's not on this television. These people look strangely familiar. All of them. One after another. Faces smiling. Faces talking. Faces showing off. Faces all of them. Ridiculous and scripted and utterly not real. But we watch anyway.

The number of channels is redundant. There are too many to choose from. Not just the remote for the television but the remote to your life. But we sit and try to choose. We settle on one and settle down and settle our hearts. Then the still comes over and the soul goes and then suddenly I'm left in the dark with my songs and my subtitles.

Breathe.

That's what I do when I want more.

Breath.

That's what I take when I want to hold it.

Be.

I can't do anything else, so I just sit and wait and want and want a little more.

Is this life? Locked in some kind of turnover style subconscious?

Is this the life you wanted? The life you wanted to lead? The life you really thought you could have?

I don't know.

Too tired to connect anymore. Too full to ask any more questions. But I swear there's got to be more. There needs to be more than these fake people fooling us. There's got to be more than noise-canceling headphones and pillows that pull down your eyelids. There has to be more.

I use the dog as an armrest. A big ball of fur, this little Ewok that's escaped from *Return of the Jedi*. She sleeps while I wander.

236

Sometimes there's more to say and sometimes you try.

Enjoy the Silence, Spencer.

Indeed.

Voices speak in each speaker on your ear. A boy on the left and a girl on the right. The boy is wide-awake and the girl sleeps soundly. And you wonder. And the Ewok forgets about Darth Vader.

This is your night and it's not just about suburbia. It's the suburbs of your soul and you've let the grass grow too long. The backyard is a mess and the front door is full of cobwebs. The siding needs painting and the gutters need cleaning. The windows stare out through eyes that need glasses. A decade passes too quickly. A short breath in the shot of the night. Take it but don't drive home. God forbid you drive home.

Breathe.

You see someone talking on the television.

Breath.

You see her drifting to slumberland.

Be.

You study the motions and the simplicity in two-minute stories. These tales you tell and sell and feel.

None of them are real. Nothing is real. This isn't real. This is just a copy of a copy of a copy. This is a reflection of a reflection. This is window dressing. This is some kind of fake in the face of reality.

Soon she goes to sleep, groggy and swaying. She goes upstairs and leaves you alone and you just wonder. Sometimes you wait. But most of the time you just don't worry anymore. The moment is gone. It's always gone.

That's the reality and those are the breaths and that's the story and that's the nighttime.

Really, Truly Yours

Maybe I said too much. Maybe too much was too real. Too raw. Too much reality for you. Too much of me.

I can scrape back the scabs already there, but I can't cut the splinters already in place.

I can't patch up the wounds. I have no more Band-Aids to hand out.

An angry, arrogant soul I used to be. Silly, stupid, and soul-leaking. I never knew how much I spilled out walking down the sidewalk of life.

I hated the things I couldn't control. So naturally life became something I was pretty damn bitter about.

Like salt thrown over the ice on a sidewalk, I spread out my pellets. Yet instead of melting, all they did was freeze and stick to the surface.

Once upon a time, I loved the lovely things I discovered. So eventually I tried to make them my own. But few things are really, truly yours to own. Ever.

Albatross

Maybe this time.

Maybe this month.

Maybe this moment.

Maybe the mystery will be over and will dissipate like the morning fog. Soft, sudden, and sweeping with a brilliant gust of light and color and form.

Maybe.

And maybe the mention of all those possibilities will stir and sweep you up into something more.

Maybe you'll think about it.

Maybe you'll remember me.

Maybe I'll never be forgotten.

And possibly all these maybes drifting toward you with their uncertainties will stop and be scooped up and be set all right.

Hover

We smile and act sympathetic to the world's sadness but it's all about us, all about ourselves.

We paddle forward.

We carry our load.

We move in the deep waters alone.

The sun setting has forgotten us and the moon ignores our floundering souls searching for some kind of a spotlight.

Do we dare close our eyes to dream of those bright dauntless things?

Hover instead. Hover and lead me out of the bed. Toward the dawn, toward the light, toward the night's promise of another day dawning.

Would you want to know this little enclosed, encapsulated endeavor?

Hover.

Lover.

Try and try again.

Breathe.

I'll hear you. And I'll dive again.

Sweep and sweat and searching and everything letting out.

Surrender to the edge of the sand, this beach of fortitude.

Where I sit and wait.

I sit and wait.

And wait.

Wait.

Things I Don't Understand

The feelings. Still there. Still ripe. Still raw. Still real.

I thought I'd be free of them.

But then again, Marley's ghost sure wasn't free, was he?

Yeah.

I'm looking for Marley but I can't seem to find him.

I feel like I'm a ghost of Christmas past, present, and future all tied into one.

Heroes

The lead singer of Depeche Mode battles with self-hatred and loathing that drove him to debauchery. Even sober he's full of contempt.

Brad Pitt wrestles with demons he's had all his life even though he rejects the Christianity of his youth that set all sorts of rules.

Heroes, so unhappy.

I look in the mirror.

I've got to ask.

I stare.

Sometimes I can't believe it, I'm moving past the feeling.

Again.

And again.

And again.

Another's Arms

Tamara talks to the dark-haired man again. He looks younger. He's way better than me in every outward thing I see. Looks, muscles, conversations, grin, coolness, awesomeness.

S***.

Strange to see it staring back at me so obvious. I see the car in the driveway. I see them walking down the sidewalk. I see the car picking up the girls from school.

I sound like a stalker but the cool thing is ghosts can stalk. They just watch. They really just be.

The pieces can just pull themselves off the pavement, can they? Don't they at least need sweeping? Can't they at least be stepped on? Just for a few moments?

I feel strange things. Jealousy, sort of. But also a bit of wonder. And fascination. I'm seeing something I haven't seen in a long time.

Tamara's smile.

Not just a smile but joy. Genuine. The kind of air that helium produces. That lifts you up and keeps you up just like your voice when you suck it in.

I find things I wish. I find things I want to go back to. And then I seriously wonder why I'm still here.

What reason is there? Why? What for?

Something sun-sheltered. Something hidden. Something underwater. Something make-believe. Something spinning round. Something without sorrow. Something not there. Something soaring in prayer.

Ugh. I don't want to think about the stranger's cryptic poem. Something make-believe? This is *all* make-believe.

Maybe I need to save someone. Or perhaps I need to secretly haunt someone.I can do that to that square-faced, big-shouldered, dark-haired thug slinging his arm around Tamara. I can wake him up in the middle of the night like a freaky Dennis Shore. I can make him think he's reached the threshold of hell even though he's only on the outskirts of Appleton near the quarry.

Instead I have to just grit it and bear it and suck it in. Sort of like I

243

did my entire life. Staggered, a face haggard, I feel like a picture tacked on, then forgotten about.

Why is the first, *when* is the second, *how* comes around third, and *who* is the approach to home.

I don't get it and can't figure out the timing or the situation or the person who did this.

But I am still here. In a small way. Watching. Whittling away. Weary and wondering.

Yeah.

That's me.

When I'm not in a puddle full of pity, I'm floating on a helium balloon full of it.

That Smile on the Screen

You there?

Yes.

What are you doing?

Staring at a text from a ghost, I type.

Funny.

Not as funny as the truth.

Nobody would believe you.

Why can't you just float over to here?

Afterlife humor. Clever.

Can I see you? I ask.

Do you want to?

You know the answer to that.

Things are complicated, she writes.

Really? You think so?

Yes.

They seem pretty black-and-white to me.

Have you ever done a trailer for a black-and-white film?

Good question, I write. **No.**

Why not?

Not too many black-and-white films are being made. Color is too hard to compete with.

Life isn't black-and-white, right? Lissie writes.

Sometimes it is. Sometimes the black is darker than you ever thought it'd be and the white is blinding with its light.

I like how you put that.

And I like how you asked me about that.

Seems we're a pretty good communication team, huh?

I can only laugh. I love laughing like this. It feels so absolutely freeing.

Yes, I'd say we are a good team. In lots of ways.

And I'd say you like seeing stories that aren't quite in the narrative. That's why you're good at making movie trailers.

If you showed up in them, they'd be beautiful every single time.

I wish I could see what she looks like by my text. By her text. But I can close my eyes and see that smile on the screen and hope that maybe she's wearing the very same one.

I think she is.

Many Beautiful Things

I realize my sanctuary and my self have been on that silver screen far too many times, trying to find some kind of peace that my normal soul never seems to sustain. Yet for all my tweaks and transitions and taking all the best parts I can to sum up some kind of brilliant story, I'm always left on the side looking in. Staring at the waves I can never surf down. I only take snapshots of the ocean in motion yet never seem to wade deep inside it.

Perhaps this is thinking about my profession far too much, far too deeply. But I can't help it. Not now, not seeing her filling the screen. Lissie doesn't simply envelop her character with strength and intrigue and long legs. She steps onto the stage and suddenly gives the film *life*. The way only those few, gifted select can do. Any beautiful woman can smile and laugh, but Julia Roberts perfected it. Right? The list could be long, but not that long. Seeing a beating heart you want to run away with on the big screen is truly a treasure.

That's what I'm seeing now on my laptop. And I can't help thinking the obvious insanity.

I just met her.

But even more—

She died a few months ago.

And even more so—

How can I be falling for a ghost?

Maybe I'm still locked in my office creating some kind of epic trailer and I'm delusional and sleep-deprived. But no . . . that's not the case. I have all my wits and sanity with me. And I've been getting plenty of sleep. There's no one around to keep me awake.

Well, almost no one.

When I'm not seeing her come and go, I'm seeing her come and go. Pressing Play and pausing and playing and passing out next to her. Sometimes you can feel more connected to that oval glowing monitor in front of you than the sleeping, silent life.

It's a life you chose a life, you made a life, you desired.

But God, I was young and stupid and didn't know a single thing about her and even less about my f***ing stupid self.

247

Cursing doesn't make it more important.

But maybe sometimes I want to curse because some people never wanted me to. F*** it all.

A romantic moment can suddenly evaporate with f-bombs, right? Yet I know a fact to this thing we called life. Life isn't a genre, because f-bombs can show up in G-rated films and love stories don't have to get to first base. Life—messy, unorganized and unexpected and unwritten—happens. They say other things *happen* too, but I'll choose to keep the topic on life since it can certainly be crappy enough on its own.

I turn on the movie again. I have to. I need to.

I must see her smile.

And boom, there she goes.

And wow, there she goes again.

And yes, there it shows up again. It's lovely and endless. It reminds me of a summer day in the middle of my youth surrounded by my cousins when I thought I was the center of the universe without a single care in the world.

A smile can do that. Especially to an impressionable sap like myself.

She's given that same smile to you.

Do grins from ghosts count the way normal ones do?

I don't know and right now I don't care. I just watch with a bit of amazement.

Where were you twenty years ago?

But of course I can ask the same thing of myself.

Overthinking

One day flips into another. A story untold, one I'm listening to, one I'm trying to tell, one I'm engaging with.

—How are you?

Three simple words so left behind so long ago.

Nobody ever wonders how I am anymore. But a ghost does. Or a mirage. Or a dream.

—Stuck, I reply.

Am I speaking? I'm not sure. Texting? Messaging? Posting? Pleading? Pontificating?

Doesn't matter in this era and this arena.

—Want to talk? she asks.

—Yes.

So we do.

Time and time again.

Time is a strange thing. Sometimes it melts away, dripping hours that fall by the wayside, turning to hard wax enclosing my legs. Making it impossible to run or walk or leave.

Then time can evaporate like drops on leaves in the morning sun. To simply and softly disappear.

—What are you thinking? she asks, which makes me want to be stay and simply tell her everything. And strangely, incredibly, unbelievably, I find myself doing just that.

Time here somehow doesn't have the boxes of hours and minutes and seconds. It floats above all that. Words drift like bubbles that won't break. I can see them anytime I want and remember how they lifted my spirit, making me want to fly.

—What do you think about?

The question is asked about so many things. Her movies. My trailers. The world at large. Specific colors. Words choices and strange voices.

—How'd you feel?

Something she add to the beginning of the sentence time and time again.

And she waits.

And she watches.

And wonders, letting me talk and ramble and blabber and back up and break off and not make any f***ing sense whatsoever, and being absolutely okay with it. Even smiling at me like some third-grade crush.

It's nice being noticed.

That's the thing I missed, I longed for, I feared: being noticed. When you're unknown, and suddenly stuck somewhere you don't want to be, you're noticed, but for all the wrong reasons.

Notice the real me for the real reasons.

She looks into me and seems to hear me and somehow gets me.

We talk about the small things, like blackberries. An hour talking about blackberries. An hour passing in the time it would take to swallow a blackberry. So easy and simple and effortless.

We talk about the big things, like God and eternity and our place in it.

We laugh—of course we do. There's this glint she seems to always have, as if slightly mocking me, as if wondering what she's supposed to do with me. As if she's going, *This is the only ghost You could send my way, God?* But that grin is good. The grin gets me.

So we talk a little more and the conversation like that is the kind that seems so repetitive and nonmemorable except that you're talking this way to someone like her and you're open and she's paying attention and she actually seems to be enjoying listening to you and you're wondering how in the hell she ever came your way. Of course, hell probably doesn't have a thing to do with it.

—You can say it, Lissie tells me.

And so I say it.

—Just tell me, Lissie says.

So I just tell her.

—Go ahead, you know you want to answer my question, Lissie suggests.

So I do. And I do more. And I find myself saying things I don't think I've ever uttered out loud. As if she's my beautiful, artistic shrink, looking on as if she likes hearing my voice and likes looking at my smile.

250

I might be imagining this. All of this.

Is this some kind of acid trip of a purgatory I'm in?

—Are you real?

I've asked this a dozen or a hundred times.

—Do you think I'm real? Lissie asks.

I shake my head. She smiles, then nods. And this answers nothing and I completely don't care. I'm fine with ambivalence.

—What are your dreams? she asks me.

—Back then or now?

—Now?

—I dream of you, I tell her.

—What if all of this is a dream?

—I keep asking myself that.

—So what makes you believe this is real? Lissie asks.

—Because the things you say are better than anything I might imagine.

—You don't give yourself enough credit.

—Neither do you, I say.

Smiling. Grinning. Wanting.

We talk more on this day, and we'll talk more tomorrow.

Is this some kind of settling place where I'm supposed to learn something special before moving on?

—Don't overthink all of this, Lissie tells me.

—You don't know me. That's what I do.

—Do others know this?

—No. I disguise it.

—Did your wife know?

—Oh yeah, she knew the moving train of my mind. She just hopped off long ago and has always resisted getting on and taking a ride again.

Riding the Horses

Someone to know you. To recognize your shadows. To sense your energy with a simple smile. This is the goal and the grand idea.

Somehow, in some way, I got stuck.

I don't know how. 'Cause sometimes it could feel so good I didn't know what to do with myself.

Overflowing and over myself and overcome with emotion, I would do anything and say anything just for more. Just for more of it all.

But sometimes I'd feel stale and depleted. The world defeated. And the more would feel so less and I'd look elsewhere.

I don't know of others because I can only view through my own eyes.

We would ride the horses until they'd tire and then we'd put them in stables and forget wherever they might be.

Barely

The bad news is the bad all comes from you. The shift in the morning moods, the aggressive ticking clock, the unawareness and absentmindedness and utterly gone state of mind. Hungover in one way or another. Off meds and back on. Sluggish or wanting to riot. Racing and demanding and hating the pauses and the uncertainty and the slow. Hating the slow. The slow.

Yet you don't stop.

World-weary with a brain that can't function, you still have to pour it on after all that.

Barely getting by and barely stepping with one foot after another.

Yet you want more.

You need more.

Needing more and more.

Until tomorrow tells you otherwise.

Until you tell yourself something else.

Never again.

Stop this now.

Get a grip.

It's about time, isn't it?

You know and you know better and these shadows have stung and sucked out and sunk in your sides for so long and yet . . .

That's the problem, isn't it?

Maybe you like second person because it feels a bit more safe than admitting something in the first place.

Maybe you like hovering over yourself instead of evaluating everything from afar. Hovering but never in your own two shoes, never willing to walk in them, never willing to accept they belong to you.

I gotta tonight.

Pleasure and ease.

I need it deserve it demand it.

While someone else watches without saying a word.

While someone else walks past.

While someone has to see.

While someone has to suffer.

So maybe you did the whole world a favor but in particular this very one person a favor in leaving. In going bye-bye.

This someone is Tamara.

This you is me.

And I realize it and realize everything I never wanted to become.

Conjured-Up Half Stories

Two-minute memories. That's what I'm creating.

One hundred twenty seconds of majesty.

Can you see it? The melodies and the movement and the suggestion and the scenery and the beauty, so much beauty, even in the darkness.

A story but not telling one.

The enticement of something spectacular, then holding back and becoming secretive.

The word *trailer* has never really captivated me. A trailer is something a truck hauls cross-country. I make mysteries needing to be solved. And the only way to solve them is to purchase a ticket in order to figure them out.

I love the prospect of teasing, of tempting, of telling something that's not really there.

This is what I've always done, to be honest. Conjured up half stories and almost tales and inviting others to stay tuned.

Stay tuned, there will be more.

But on this cold night—*God, it's cold, the wind feeling so stripping real against my skin*—I wonder if there will be more. If there will ever be more.

Sea Of Love

So let's do a little National riff. Let's put a hashtag on it for this supernatural online space: Music#

The National. It's the sort of songwriting you turn on when you're tipping over glasses of wine. The sort that have the swirl and the smell of a just-poured glass. Yeah. At least, that's the way it is with me.

And crazy that a ghost can get tipsy. But really, truthfully, that term—that silly little five-letter word—doesn't do justice. No, I'm not talking about the last name of Casper. I'm talking about intoxication, yet I call it drunk with a capital *D*. And the *D* can be for *dumb* or *dufus* or *delirious* or a nice, simply *duh*. It's all the same. But still. I'm feeling the ascent and listening to a little The National and I'm wondering how and why. How and why this can be. And yet they say it would be painless—needle in the dark. Oh wait—that's a lyric. My thoughts and these echoes are the same.

It's funny. Some songs and some singers make me want to just open up and reveal everything. It's that college-streaking sort of thing. Some, maybe most, don't get it. They won't get it. And that's okay. But there are some that just get it. They get me. They understand this crazy urge to hear a sound and a song and to suddenly want to abandon a little bit of everything and go darting and daring into the night. We're all toddlers at the core, longing to go sprinting off somewhere completely stark naked. Laughing while we do so. Laughing like we're Adam, who's suddenly discovered Eve across the garden walking toward him.

I could go ahead with the idea but nobody would see me. Maybe that means I should. But instead, I simply listen to the songs and drink the syrup.

"If I stay here, trouble will find me. I believe."

And no lyric could sum up the truth more than this.

Trouble didn't find me. Right?

Right, Spencer?

It's crazy for an album to haunt you. For a whole band to simply stalk you with shadows and specters.

256

I'm drunk. What do I know?

But I'm not *really*. To me, by now, at this point, up to this moment, *drunk* means staggering over sidewalks barely able to make it back home to my buddy's condo in order to pass out cold. That's drunk with a capital *D*. Yeah, sure, that might also be *COMATOSE* with a capital everything. But drunk isn't sitting still watching a video or working or writing or wondering.

To be drunk is to be completely obliterated. Right?

Right?

"Hey, Jo, sorry I hurt you, but they say love is a virtue, don't they?"

All I have to do is substitute Tam for Jo.

"I see you rushing now. Tell me how to reach you."

But the only people speaking to ghosts are the songs that haunt them.

Ghost Story

Hearing The National's "Anyone's Ghost" makes me start to do one of my random, ADD-driven musical searches. This time it's for songs that have the word "ghost" in the title. There are lots.

I play "The Ghost Inside" by Broken Bells. Then keep going. Scanning and skimming on my own personal iTunes list. The B-side "Ghost" by Depeche Mode. "A Ghost Beneath the Tower" by The Winston Jazz Routine. "Ghost Town" by Cary Brothers.

Ah, yes . . . the classic. "The Ghost in You." My youth as played by the Psychedelic Furs. I listen and remember being a teen again.

"Ghost of the Year" by Max Q. The long-lost Michael Hutchence album he made apart from INXS that had people worried he was leaving the band. "Ghosts" by UNKLE and "A Life as a Ghost" by Editors and "Ghosts" by The Presets.

Two great tracks from Thomas Newman come from *Fried Green Tomatoes* and *Road to Perdition*, respectively titled "Ghost Train" and "Ghosts." The latter in the brilliant Tom Hanks film is a cue I always wanted to use, one so amazing and haunting. Yes, that's so cliché to use the *haunting* word, but it's true.

I get stuck on "Ghost Story" by Sting off *Brand New Day*. It's a poem set to music. I listen to the song and then replay it, then replay it again after looking up the lyrics to listen alongside me.

Why was I missing then
That whole December?
I give my usual line,
I don't remember

I wonder who Sting is singing this song to. Or who he's singing about. Perhaps his wife, Trudie. Maybe someone else. Or maybe just painting a fictitious picture. But I imagine me singing it to Tamara.

"It's time that I confessed. I must have loved you."

258

SHE'S HAVING A BABY (Trailer #10)

It begins with a couple laughing. Midthirties maybe.

"Wait a minute, are you—?" he asks.

"Wait a minute, can you read minds?" she says.

Then the music starting and the montage and the Love and Rockets sing "Haunted When the Minutes Drag." A nod to the original movie that inspired this film.

The modern remake of She's Having a Baby is a moving portrait of a marriage in the fast-moving all-connected world with temptations and distractions and big letdowns. But the trailer is a love letter of persistence. You see tears and a baby being born and struggles and failure and love.

The second half of the trailer uses a James Horner cue. Yes, shameless, I know, but the late, great Horner, who became a household name with his Titanic score, had an amazingly diverse career. This cut is from The New World, one of Terrence Malick's films that always uses scores in interesting ways.

SHE'S HAVING A BABY. This March in theaters everywhere.

The Girls

I see them running around and my heart breaks just a bit.

This breathless energy inside.

Laughter doubled over with tears. Wailing with sudden watching. A spiral of do-it-myself with a dose of help-me-now.

These are the toddlers.

And then there's the seven-year-old smiling and directing and showing off and carefully dissecting everything.

God, I love her. God, I love them. And, God, why did You take me away from them?

I want to suffer in this insanity once more between dinner and bedtime.

I want to have to shuffle through the madness again. The kind I wanted to run away from. The kind I wanted to get in a car and drive far, far from. To turn up the music and go and get out.

Now I want the silence disrupted by their noisy chaos. Now I want to stay still and get rolled over with their love.

I finally see Tamara again. She's really more beautiful than when I met her. Those slight little lines under her eyes are like stripes on a general's chest. They are deserved and they give her character. And she doesn't seem stressed even though I know she's tugged and tossed about enough.

Maybe life is easier without me.

But that's a load of bunk because it can't be easier.

Easy is sitting and thinking about yourself.

Easy is looking at the sunset.

Easy is laughing and loving life.

Easy is not taking care of three girls on your own.

A heart can be big but not that big. You need help. A heart can't be an air balloon. It needs to reside inside, where it pumps and where it helps you.

The routine is the same. And the same things that used to annoy the hell out of me now find a way to strangely be alluring.

This isn't the greener grass. It's like I'm standing on volcanic ash and I'll take anything softer and brighter and better.

That white beautiful blonde. Those curly locks. The strawberry fields forever. Three heads and hearts so different but all ours.

Being an underpaid performer brings resentment. But being an unlikely spectator brings sadness and regret.

I hear the giggles and the grunts and feel the pangs of regret.

Oh, to get back yesterday.

Oh, to have the promise of tomorrow.

Daydreaming

Let go of the balloons at your shins. The helium no longer works.

Don't worry about closing the screen door. It doesn't matter what we let in or out.

Those packed bags . . . are they for a family picnic or for my predicted departure?

I'm not at a loss for words. I'm just at a loss, wading inside it, like plunging under salt water only to find myself drifting upwards in the sludge of an oil spill. I can burst through the surface, yet anything I might say sounds suffocating, distant, nonsensical.

All sounds you've heard from the beginning, becoming louder and louder and louder and lingering on and on and on.

I stand outside the house I used to never fit inside. Knocking on the door with the reversed peephole. Trying to find a home key I never duplicated. Climbing up the back tree only to see the limbs that once caressed the house have been cut.

The lawn is my soccer field but I've shown up on the wrong day. I can't see anybody in the windows. No tiny waving hand through the glass. No sneaky little smile showing up by the back door. No cackle of laughter just beyond.

Just beyond.

What's just about anything and what's beyond all of this? Have I stepped inside the just beyond? Because there's nothing just about this empty, hollow hole.

I'm not daydreaming, not anymore, not here and now. This is a full-fledged nightmare. Waging war with the only person it can find.

Me.

Wash the Pain Away

—You first.

—Me first? I ask.

—Yeah. You first in sharing the forest fires.

—I don't have any forest fires to talk about. Mine's one giant inferno.

She only laughs.

I've told Lissie about my latest trip back home, to spy on the girls and Tamara and to linger like some dog let out in the rain. Regret and pain are all I bring back from this visit.

—This is a safe place, you know. Perhaps the safest place you'll ever find, Spencer.

—Maybe I'm not looking for a safe place.

—Then what are you looking for?

—A similar spirit to share everything with.

The eyes curl up as if lining my arm to my shoulder to my neck and cheek until they reach my own gaze.

—It's no accident that you're here, she says.

I know you're a ghost but were you like this when you were real? Did you capture others' hearts the way you've captured my breath?

We stand and look out at the lake and listen to the music and somehow I don't believe you can be real.

Calm and composed, some soft creature smiling, all angular and alive. Looking my way. Looking and never looking away.

A calm tapping breath of a hug in the afternoon.

A sweet soul hug of a midnight good night.

The Traveler

She talks about a painting she's working on. And instead of seeing it, I want to watch her describe it. I want to see the joy reflecting on her face as she speaks about it using words like *ugly* and *amateurish*. She doesn't diminish the actual work, however. Lissie loves the process.

I tell her about the songs I used to try to write on my keyboard. Ridiculous sad songs I'd at least not try to sing on.

She talks about wallpaper and I talk about grocery shopping and she mentions traffic jams and I'm suddenly talking about Ted talks. It's one of those conversations. The kind that goes off like a pack of fireworks. One pop leading to another and another and seemingly never wanting to end. Each subject leads to another verb. Each sentence seems to lead with a question.

It's been a long time since I've had a conversation like this.

—It's late, Lissie says.

—Is it?

—Yes.

—It doesn't feel like it.

She smiles.

—No, it doesn't, she says.

—Is this all a dream?

—That's so cliché, she says.

—This feels like a dream.

She pinches me hard enough to get me to howl.

—Why'd you do that? I ask.

—Did that feel like a dream?

—Yeah, the wrong kind.

—This is real.

—Okay. Whatever "real" might mean.

—This is real, she says again.

—Okay, I say again. I'll try to accept that.

—Reality seems to have been a hard thing for you to accept, right? In your previous life?

A good question.

—I made movie trailers, I remind her.

264

—And I starred in those movies. Or . . . well, at least costarred in movies. Or maybe just showed up.

I just shake my head. Shaking in absolute marvel of her.

Marvelous

So I watch. Her graceful entrance in the picture and her electric smile and her smooth voice and her soul on the screen feeling like a hand holding yours while crossing the street. The story suddenly plays second fiddle to this shining actress.

Why aren't you bigger? Why doesn't the world really know?

But this unseen star is an even brighter one to watch in the darkness of my office. Glowing and going and giving and gracious. So damn lovely.

I watch with surprise. I watch with wonder. I watch with excitement.

And I'm scared. Terrified, to be honest. Because I still don't know what I'm doing and why I'm still here and what this all means and how it's all supposed to be.

Didn't you feel the same way when your breaths actually helped you stay alive?

You realize so much when you find yourself with so little to spare.

A spotlight can shine so long that it starts to dull your soul. But the dark—the dark can make it start to sparkle again.

A song begins to play and you feel this pain since it's a song that's meant so much to you.

Flickers of the past floating overhead, filling the screen.

The sound feels like someone pressing their palm against your heart, then twisting inward. It hurts. I close my eyes and remember and stop this dream academy of a viewing. I'm now mourning. I'm now regretting and wanting out.

Some songs need to be bottled up and sent out to the sea for someone else to listen to. Maybe the memories they carry will float along with them.

Art Exhibit

The scenes play like dancers starting to sway. Moving arms and legs in rhythm and routine and then suddenly surprising with a break in their motion. Stopping. Allowing me to focus and find something more. Something else. Something much deeper and richer and better.

Better.

Looking at something better.

Stopped.

Seeing her move to slow motion to being still.

I pause and go back and go forward and stop it again and find some kind of feeling just seeing her. Just seeing this someone I know doing this thing I know but doing it so well. So beautifully. So bright. So blissful.

The world lost such a gem when Lissie died.

This still and this study makes me wonder something else. Something haunting.

How many times did I put life on pause to stop and study and stare? To mute the sound and to dim the screen? To just be? And to be still?

Every distraction distracting, an ensemble of actors acting in front of you, the movie never stopping, the mysteries never relenting.

For once, for this time, a time I've lost count with, I've slowed down and have been still. I've been silent. Not verbally since that's never been a problem but emotionally. The tempest of thoughts has occasionally drifted off like a patch of storm clouds.

I never stopped anymore. Not with Tamara.

So consumed. So concentrated. So concerned with projects and getting out of debt and providing and persisting in a tough and bitter business.

I never bothered to study anybody anymore. I blinked and they were getting older and changing and I was still the same and then I blinked again and now I'm here.

Lost in a world of lonesome study.

The movie gets turned off and I suddenly find myself looking through pictures. Far-off shots and recent ones. And I start to see a face I fell in love with. A friend I used to know. One I remember. One I never really knew. One I began to know more and sometimes resent and sometimes disrespect and sometimes outright loathe.

The more differences I would learn, the more I would neglect to study. Soon I began flunking the tests. And then I no longer was tested.

I used to wonder if there would ever come a time when I'd stop and study all those pictures we'd take on our cameras and cell phones. Digital memories are never as clear as real ones. And sometimes when we look back, all we can remember is capturing snapshots. Ones that now keep us imprisoned.

I want to see Tamara again. The real, breathing Tamara. I want to see her move. To do something simple around the house. To sit there at the table and take her time like she always used to do whenever eating a meal. Her deliberate manner and methods.

I want to see you laugh.

More than anything else that's what I want. The smile in so many pictures is the photo shot. Except . . . except when it comes to the girls. Occasionally there's the genuine smile. Something funny making her laugh. It's wonderful. Lovely. Stunning, in fact.

I've missed that. I miss her. I've missed her for a long time. And I've missed even knowing how much I've missed her.

God, have I messed up and missed so many things.

If only I could try one more time.

Dialogue

Those rides to church so loud and so silent. Dissention amidst the complete disintegration. Riding with the bubble in my throat and the stone in my gut. Full of failure and fear and hate. Regretting a bit of everything except the little souls in the back. Yet the wheels turned and the pilgrimage toward our so-called faith beckoned.

I never knew what Tamara felt. She was a line, a polygraph never lying, a heartbeat never dropping. But I felt like I was parasailing over the Pacific, like I was gliding over the Grand Canyon. I'd feel every pound of my heart with every foot of our ride. The silence seizing and suffocating and sucking every little bit of good out of me.

I didn't know when it got to this point. I just knew I'd arrived and the destination was burning all around me. I couldn't get out either. I was choking on the flames and soon I'd be seeped in flames myself.

Call me dramatic but put yourself in a deteriorating marriage. Plummeting. Pillaging. Those desperate, pious moments, praying that you can somehow find common ground, wondering how in the world you got to this point of such utter despair.

The silence.

That's the thing I hated the most.

The silence.

And it only seemed elevated in the midst of the chaos brought on by the girls.

My mind would ravage all over the place. Telling me so many things.

You're a failure.

Yep.

She should've married someone else.

Absolutely.

Your creative mind creates only messes.

Sure.

Your moody s***ty little halfhearted temper cracking at the very breath of anything just shuts everything down.

Whatever—shut up.

I don't like the truth and I hated looking in the mirror.

But the rage inside me just wanted to claw and tear and beg for some kind of thing. Some kind of dialogue. But all I got was a soul-sucking silence. Staring ahead. Shut down. Shipped out. Emotions spent.

I wanted dialogue but I just got the grand hand of wiping-it-all-away.

So we enter the world. The crowd and the nursery and the seats and the songs and the prayers and the burning deep inside me just raged away.

This wasn't any kind of good place but I didn't know where to go.

I couldn't go anywhere.

Eventually they had to go on without me.

Hold On . . .

The year. Did I forget, or did it pass me by?

The digit trembles like the passing of time. I question the number like my age and like the time and like the amount in my account.

I have to think for a moment.

Where am I? Right here and right now?

Am I still stuck somewhere, haunting those who can't hear me? Am I drifting through time and space without the wind worrying about moving around me?

Would you, could you, should you, over and over again, be good for me and you?

I wonder.

Crash the car into the curb lining the cliff.

Carve out some hollow hole inside the tree you used to hang on as a kid.

Climb the wall wrapped around the building you once worked in.

Clip the stems sticking out that always seemed so selfish.

Con the smug man at the counter just one time.

Then run and keep running and run a little more.

Feel like you're fourteen and not forty-six. Or forty-seven.

Forget the time and the year and the obligations and the fears.

Tell me you remember so I can tell you to forget.

Tell me you mind so I can tell you not to get upset.

Maybe time knows all but if you don't know it by name, how can you keep track anyway?

Perhaps is sometimes the most definitive thing you can say.

5

I open this door and let the warmth out in the winter night only to realize I don't want to see my breath, not tonight, not at this moment. I'm not ready for a gust of laughing wind. I'm not really wanting to see the endless brilliance above. I'm stuck in this comfort and want to stay here for a moment, before letting the rest of the world in.

You there?

Halfway, I type back on my iPhone.

I'm eating this remarkable cheesecake.

I'm stuck soul-searching. I don't want to hear about cheesecake.

It's like when you're at the party with a girl you just want to take home. You're playing the game but inside you're dying because you want this one thing and you want to keep her from the rest of the world. You want to laugh with her and only her when she's in your arms and you don't want to laugh at lame anecdotes about nothing and no one.

You're starting to seriously sound postal, buddy.

Yes. But these thoughts are deep down. Like layers, the lower ones, the late-night ones nobody will ever see.

I'd like to get out of this place, she writes.

If I could drive and pick her up, I would. In a heartbeat. But I don't know where she is.

Social networks will never see the contexts and can never connect the dots. They're snapshots of the sky from the place you're standing.

Me too.

Meet you halfway?

I laugh. I'm standing in a square backyard and she's a falling star. I'm a stamp of suburbia and she's a brilliant shift in the sky. It's unfair, but then again it's reality.

Funny that I should be the lucky one.

Again

A black figure moving in the gray, spotted only by my car's two lights before shutting off and leaving us alone. Creaking open, the car door lets the humid night rush over me. I stand to hear the still. Complete, solemn still. Then Lissie says my name.

I greet her. And then we embrace. A friendly, familiar, family sort of kind. We are suddenly the sole survivors of a war nobody else made it through.

She missed me. That I know. What she feels and wants and needs and dreams about, I don't know. I won't know. But this, this moment, this now, is something I do know.

Maybe it's been one day. Or one month. I don't know. But we're here again for another few moments.

The eyes open and wipe away twenty-one years. Half a self, half a life. The twenty-one-year-old, falling and failing and figuring himself and his world out with each mistake. Running to stand still, never wanting or worrying. Running headfirst into the other side of his self, the fortysomething-year old.

Then she surprises you out of the blue.

—Let's go dancing . . .

Dance Hall Days

You feel like a fool or maybe just a fraud. Being in here around all of this . . . youth.

You're forty-two and suddenly you're feeling it. Or forty-seven—what is it? You're feeling a little like you're double the twenty-one. Double the weight. Double the stress. Doubling down on every single thing here. But nobody notices or cares. It's dark and the lights throb and thank God you still have hair to make you kinda sorta blend into the crowd.

You're here, looking for her.

But the music speaks and you remember.

Third grade dancing to the Bee Gees in a disco in Italy open for the youngsters on your school ski trip.

The junior high school dance standing on the side waiting and watching and wondering what to do. Who to ask and how to dance and what to say and how to move.

The senior in high school moving amidst the dark eyeliner in the darker club where goth lives and industrial music throbs.

The college party of throwing everything to the wind and then throwing a few things against the wall or outside the sliding-glass doors onto the apartment lawn below. Dancing deliriously to Prince and Nirvana.

The twentysomething still trying to reclaim some of his youth even though he's feeling conflicted and feeling out of place and feeling like he doesn't quite belong (familiar feeling, huh).

The thirtysomething surrounded by three beautiful ladies, all friends and colleagues, all celebrating a victory and a work outing and blowing off steam and feeling dizzy and delirious and eighteen all over again.

You drink. It helps. Always.

The bass and the driving droning synths and the simple melodies and the even simpler lyrics.

You scan the Chicago-hotshot-club dance floor looking for her. Surely she's not here. Surely you're going to stand in the corner watching and waiting and wondering.

But then you do something that surprises even you.

You step out there on the wood floor.

You don't really care anymore.

Who is going to judge you and your love handles?

So what that you might be wearing an Arcade Fire T-shirt? Maybe that's even too old.

Does it really matter that you're not one of the beautiful ones? You never have been and at this point, buddy, you never will be.

You've never met one of them before. Before, well, *now*.

Is she one of them?

You don't know. Of course, you think so, but then again, maybe she's not. Maybe *they* might claim her but maybe she's just like you. Just a lot more, well, beautiful.

You move and keep up with the beat and nobody is watching. There is no dark-haired stranger watching you. No golden-haired princess looking over at you. But there never has been. Not really. Those few, finite moments when someone actually saw you and came over and called your bluff. Those are forever gone. Now you're alone and you feel a little okay.

You close your eyes while you move on the dance floor. There is no small little soul tugging at your leg. No whining or complaining. No baby talk with no end. No fussy chatter. No demanding directive.

Just the music.

Just the sound and your soul dancing to it.

You never thought that you'd leave this—all of it—behind. People say you grow old and you grow out of it but the thing is it's not the pickup lines and the mysterious looks that made you love this in the first place. It's the solitary place in the middle of this energetic, satisfying crowd. It's a place you can be whoever you want to be. Raising your hands and moving your hips and not giving one damn what the rest of the world thinks. The others around you feel the same. They are similar souls moving to the music and lost in the moment.

You dance for one minute or five or ten or twenty. You really have no idea. It might be one song or seven. But the feeling you feel is like the breath you take after being outside on a subzero day. It's that first glorious warm rush into your lungs. Opening, giving, graceful, gushing.

Lost.

So alone.

Yet surrounded.

And then you see Lissie.

The smile hanging on her lips like the crest of the moon shining down on you.

And suddenly the song and the strobe lights and the scene all exist for the two of you.

Suddenly you throw your age and your reality and your angst all out the window in this car you're driving.

Then you roll it up and head toward her wearing the same sort of smile she still carries.

It's a bit glorious. The smile. The feeling. All of it.

This Is What You Came For

I think I can see. Those young souls so naive. Bouncing, trouncing out the doubts. The stars feel like they can be scooped in raised hands. Then unleashed like a million electronic disco balls. Strobe lights set out like tiny fireflies.

I'm not old not yet, not now, not ever.

Death does not designate an age. That's what I've learned.

I want to tell these people to keep it up. Moving, shaking, living, and loving.

I laugh and nobody hears me.

I cling on to shoulders but nobody notices.

It's kinda cool, I gotta admit. But then again, maybe I'm just an old guy in a young crowd. Keeping up with the beat and keeping his hair but still. Old.

The brilliance and the beauty is being here as some anonymous soul. Another moving body. Sweaty, out-of-breath. Breathing.

It's good to sweat and breathe and yes, that's exactly what I do.

I thought I'd never do that again but I do.

This is why fifty-year-olds dance at weddings like they do.

This is why retired people take dance lessons.

There is something freeing in dancing like a fool. It's a get-out-of-jail-free card. One you wear on your belt and your forehead.

Doesn't matter what you dance to. It doesn't matter what you look like. What matters is how you feel. Are you immersed and isolated? Are you some dancing fool? 'Cause you should be. That's the freedom it brings. The music cocoons you and the floor props you up and for several glorious moments you are John Travolta and Patrick Swayze and you're electric and energized and everything you never thought you could be.

Youth isn't wasted on the young when they're yelling and screaming out their age.

And in the middle here I am and it's glorious.

Take Me By the Hand

The sun sneaks in through twisty limbs. The breath of leaves falling. The ground hard without a heartbeat.

There, somewhere, standing, waiting, wondering.

Dreaming.

Like always.

Picturing something. Imagining someone. Closing eyes and becoming someone else somewhere else some other time in some other place.

Blink and beat.

Eyes and heart.

Blink and beat.

A smile trembling across the lips.

A sax stirring trouble.

Black and red and wanting and needing.

Blink and beat.

Wanting to run off to somewhere in the sand and somewhere in the snow. Footprints in both. Trails that time will wear off until tomorrow.

And in the meantime the dreams of the night come . . .

The jingle awakes you. You're waiting for your dog as you daydream over lunch.

You sigh and find the spot she did her business.

You love the dreaming.

You don't always like the waking.

Awful Sound

So I sit around and stare and do the things I used to do before I . . . died? Went into neutral? Got stuck? I'm not sure. But I'm back to old habits because old habits don't . . .

Yeah.

Maybe some things *should* die. Just move on out. Get outta town.

The night reminds me of those lonely times and the work that used to get done during the silent fogs. I'm not sure if my work brought on the loneliness or if the loneliness brought on more work. It sometimes felt like a big tire spinning down a massive hill, picking up speed with no stop in sight.

I find myself going back to recent and older films. All featuring Lissie Hale in some way.

She laughs and it pricks a bit. She kisses someone and I imagine her kissing me. She runs on a beach and I'm jealous of the sand. She brushes back her hair and I want to do the same with my hand and my head and heart.

These are documents of desire. Minutes where I'm lost.

So I start to do a video montage.

I start to build a trailer to her. I know I shouldn't, but then again, why not? Why can't I fully and completely lose myself to the melancholy midnight?

I want to make a trailer that tells the world what it missed. Not that it didn't know but I don't think it fully comprehended. I forgot her name when I first saw her, and I'm *in* the business.

Of course, this business of making a trailer begins to suddenly become an obsession. I think an index finger is a passion while your middle finger becomes the obsession. (And if you carry out that metaphor, well, obviously you're losing the pinkie).

I'm not sure what kind of music I could put to these images. Maybe I can have several trailers.

I can start out with the 9½ weeks trailer. Yeah, I know I've already mentioned it. I know I'm showing my age, too, but that's still a sexy movie with a sultry soundtrack. Then I'd put Bryan Ferry's "Slave to Love" on the trailer. I know that song played in the movie but not sure if it was on the trailer, too.

There's a shot of her walking where the director seemed particularly interested in getting a shot of her long legs. She's wearing heels and they seem to be a mountain you just are dying to climb. I know how that sounds, how tacky and not even mildly clever. But it's true. God, those legs are lovely. And hearing Bryan Ferry say "slave to love" over and over just seems to give it a nice, long exclamation point.

Suddenly I start listening to Roxy Music while looking at pictures and images. It's a bad idea but a good way to get lost a little. Ten trillion distractions keeping your eyes down on something that's not life and that's not moving.

A motion picture. What irony. Such a lifeless thing is supposedly in motion. And yes, with the images and the sound and the art all on full display, it certainly does *look* in motion. But it's still not life. The life I miss. The life I can't have back.

I want to hold a hand. Touch lips. I want to laugh and be laughed at. I want to tickle the top of someone's feet. I want to run in a field after a tiny little set of feet. I want to hear squeaking, giggling guffaws.

I'm in tears. No longer immersed in my obsession with a dead actress but now thinking of a live child. Thinking of live children. Living and breathing and blinking all while I'm gone.

All the things I missed staring at static images.

All the moving creatures I ignored studying supposed motion pictures.

A job is one thing, yes, but . . .

Time to change the track. Bryan Ferry went into BT's "Good Morning, Kaia," and of course I'm thinking of the girls.

I put my computer in shuffle mode and it goes into a remix of "Shake the Disease" by Depeche Mode. Yep. That's what I need.

Now. What other kind of trailer could I make? I have the sexy, sultry one.

Well, I need musical inspiration. So I continue to shuffle.

Jan Hammer from *Miami Vice*? Wow. Another eighties icon. Nope.

Michael Brook. Instrumental and composer. Good moody stuff. But no.

Arcade Fire's "Awful Sound" off their *Reflektor*. Ah. Yes. Very interesting.

I listen to it and shuffle around images and pieces.

Ooh, yes. Very good.

This will be the complex, indie drama I-shoulda-been-an-Oscar-contender sorta trailer that makes you cry in the sheer brilliance.

This is the trailer showing the torture of being an artist. Showing the loss. The agony. The amazing awful sort of ache that it feels like now that she's gone.

Oh yes.

A song can do everything.

Should I contact Arcade Fire's people for permission?

Maybe the dead don't need permission. But then again, lawyers can sure haunt you bad like demon dogs.

I play around and then I try for the shuffle again. And boom. A random pick.

I listen.

Ooh. Totally different vibe.

It's the second version of the love theme for *The Saint* circa 1997 by the wonderful and magnificent Graeme Revell. And it's something else. So sad. So poignant. So sweeping.

This would be the she's-lost-and-gone-forever trailer I'm putting together like pieces from different jigsaw puzzles.

I keep working and know that I could keep doing this all night. I used to do this for pay. And I was always great at it. They didn't have to tell me over and over again. No. I knew. I had the knack. I'd never be Spielberg or Scorsese but I could take what they made and have two minutes that would truly shine.

I eventually stop because I know there's no point. Except for distraction. Except for depression. Except for dissolution.

Fine Time

"We're like crystal. We break easy."

I guess ghosts still get to go to concerts. I'm standing on the edge of the crowd and can feel the heat and the sweat from everybody. And I'm moving. Hell yeah, am I moving.

Wait, you've been here before with her. Is this your second concert with Lissie or your first?

The passage of time is strange. I honestly can't tell if this is the first or second New Order concert. But I'm not enjoying it any less.

I still remember first hearing New Order in a John Hughes film. It was *Pretty in Pink* and I had no idea the songs unfolding before me. Such glorious tunes. In modern day times I would've simply googled it from my iPhone. But back then, stuck in a Carolina sand trap, I simply had to wonder and hope somehow I'd discover who it might be.

New Order.

Bernard Sumner and Peter Hook.

The ghosts of a band that should've folded.

When a lead singer kills himself, well . . . you only can go down. But that didn't stop the foursome that ended up becoming New Order and helped influence my teenage and twentysomething and thirtysomething years.

And yeah. They're still influencing me now.

It's amazing how songs come back and remind you.

That first kiss.

That first more-than-a-kiss.

The first time you got wasted.

The first time you woke up wondering where you were.

The smiles and the scents and the secrets and all those many shout-outs that songs can bring.

Like a great bass, there's this propeller full of soul pushing you forward. You just gotta hang on.

I'm listening and wondering how in the world I can still be here. I look around but don't see anybody I know. But then again, that's not a first. Sometimes I'd find myself alone for concerts. Sometimes buying expensive seats only for myself. Sometimes trying to get into the action a little more. It's been a pattern but right now I think it has a little something to with the fact that I'm, uh, *dead.*

Hello. Ticket for one. Don't mind the cold hand or the expired ticket. I'm good for half a seat or even less.

But I'm not being bothered by anybody as I stand and watch the show. It's general admission and the crowd is thick with both old-timers and youngsters. But the band performs and impresses and I dance and somehow even break a sweat.

This is the thing. I'm plunged into teenage territory again. I'm skinny and naive and thinking these songs might possibly save me.

I'm there to press the button on the cassette. To balance the nob over the record player. To get the song going and to listen. To listen to the whole song, not just to sample a portion.

I'm here to stay and I'm listening and I know I love New Order. They were always one of the four. The Smiths, The Cure, Depeche Mode, and New Order.

So long afterward and I'm seeing them.

So I'm dead. Leave me alone. Let me enjoy something before I head to wherever it is I need to go next.

Let me just jump in a little bit of eighties love.

It's not the same since Peter Hook isn't here. Oh, they try to substitute. But it's not as good as the real thing. I feel this thing missing. A little like the soul of the band that's suddenly MIA. Yet I still enjoy them because I know they're like me. Not all of the parts but still trying to sing the same tunes of yesterday.

I can still bounce and keep the bad things at bay. The synths and the sound all feel good in my soul for some reason. Maybe because they're twenty-five years old. Maybe because I need to remember.

I seriously wonder if heaven could feel this way. Where a song reminds us of a hundred different emotions. Feelings, decisions, actions. Can it be grandiose and great?

I don't know.

I just know I'm feeling so much. Ten fingers full of grappling with the sentiment.

Minor chords that mean so much.

Messing with my heart in a way a heart attack never could.

I celebrate and I stand tall and I try to see the reality of being here.

I'm thankful for life. The life I had. The life that could have been. All those moments. All those sounds.

I'm in the shadow of these grooves, sung by people I never met, structured by souls I never knew. But I can still see further than the darkness. I can see the bright lights. I just have to look up.

Faithfully

We embrace, strangers holding one another so close, there on the gym floor, with the disco lights from assorted balls on each side of us playing some kind of strange game of Pong. I guess I'm old enough to know what that even means.

It's the slow and sweet Journey ballad we know well. The one which will forever remind me of this moment. Our first moment. I'm holding and moving alongside this tall and slender girl with the biggest blue eyes staring up at me. Just looking and waiting and wondering. Just taking my lead and letting me do whatever.

So I pull her closer and move my hands lower and realize she fits me perfectly like a glove. She's not only worth using an adverb on but also a cliché. When love comes quickly, you have to resort to basic, primitive needs.

It turns out we'll dance again. And again.

To a Bruce Springsteen song during a pom-pom routine for homecoming. One I'll have to leave due to my uncle dying and having to attend the funeral.

Could this be eerie foreshadowing?

Then came the high school musical.

Then there's prom. Ah, prom. The night that built up and built up and then suddenly appeared. The girl you kind of liked and then started to really like and then suddenly fell head over heels in love with. A girl going with someone else, some complete douche bag, some guy completely and absolutely wrong for her. A group you used to be a part of, the party guys, the bad guys, the complete asses. Let's be honest. They're complete asses. They're the jerks in a John Hughes film, the haters you see coming ten million miles away. There's even the one with the thick locks of blonde hair à la major douche James Spader. And she's with one of the guys from this clique. The big and tall and everything-is-wrong-with-this-picture sort of guy.

And the moment I see her with him, I also see she's inebriated. Maybe not soused but she's giggling and tipsy. And she's so damn cute and so damn happy and suddenly I find myself so damn miserable with longing and need and desire.

Suddenly this fun little fling has become more.

Suddenly she might not be a forgone conclusion.

Suddenly I'm wondering if those big blue eyes will ever be looking up at me like they once did.

I have to and must have and have to try and must have every little chance. So I completely wreck prom for my date and for my love's date.

My date is this absolutely beautiful and charismatic girl two years younger. The sort kings would go to war over in medieval times. The sort of girl who is truly a diamond in the middle of a sandy beach. She's stunning and startling with her charm and she really means nothing to me.

This is a sign. So's the jealousy burning a hole in my tux.

I can't think of anything else once I set foot on that damn cruise ship and see Tamara.

I see those glazed, giddy eyes and I can only feel this deep rage inside. My date doesn't realize what's happening with me at first, my crumbling everything, my distance, my desire to plunge into Lake Michigan or plant my fist onto Frankenstein's face. But eventually I stand at the railing way out into the lake and I tell my date everything. I tell her I'm in love but it's not with her.

Oops.

It's not like this angel is heartbroken. She wanted to come to this event. A sophomore attending senior prom is part of the résumé. She likes me and is interested in me, but I know I might go a hundred years without seeing her look at me the way Tamara looked at me when we first danced.

People might be nothing alike but might fall in love with this nothing just because of it.

And so, after the anger and jealously, and after the truth with my date and searching out Tamara, we finally came together. I couldn't take it and I could tell she still felt the same, maybe even more so. So I asked her to dance the last song with me.

Amazing how a night full of Bon Jovi and Metallica and George Michael can suddenly open its door and become me.

"Somebody" by Depeche Mode plays and we dance and we spin

around the dance floor, just the two of us with nobody else.

So it's been. On so many floors. In so many ways.

There's no video footage but simply a random shot featuring the two of us in the background. Her tall, sleek form with her arms around mine and my back to the camera. This little image but one I remember and one that suddenly fits.

That was the fantasy, the young love, the "Faithfully" as a soundtrack.

The reality of adult life, however, was a whole other thing.

Oh Yeah!

—Talk to me.

I'm no longer asking. This is begging. A late-night, desperate plea for something.

—We are talking, Tamara says.

—Not the way some people talk. Not the way some couples talk.

—I'm not Vanessa.

—What the f***? What's that supposed to mean?

—I hate it when you use that word.

—And I hate it when you suddenly bring up someone who has nothing to do with this, I tell her.

—I see how you talk to her, she says.

—That's because she *talks*.

I'm trying to make a point but of course I'm ignoring the fact that Vanessa is easy to talk to because she's easy to look at and then imagine hours later when I'm by myself in the imagining sort of mood.

Tamara doesn't look like she wants to imagine anything. She's stating the very obvious in a very easy way.

—I've never talked a lot.

This is my wife's way of saying, *You knew what you were getting.*

—Yeah, well, I happen to like to talk a lot, I say.

—You like to drink a lot, too, she says.

My forced smile feels like a clenched fist.

—You used to not mind that, I say.

—You're not twenty-one anymore, she says.

No. Multiply two and then add a few more for good measure.

—You're not fun anymore, I say.

—And you're not single anymore, she says. No, you're over forty and you have children and *what are you thinking?*

I shake my head. The longer I'm here sitting on this couch facing her on the love seat, the more in trouble I'll be. With every word I say, her fears are confirmed.

Yep, he's drunk.

Yep, it's two forty-five—no, just make that three in the morning.

288

Yep, he's coming from the party at Vanessa's house and I don't even have to ask if she was awake when he left because I know she was.

I half expect her to ask something. Anything. If I'm attracted to Vanessa. What we talked about. If I ever fantasize about her. If I wish she had the same personality. Or maybe just a few ingredients of her personality. But she doesn't. Probably because she already knows the answer and she knows I'd never be honest in answering her anyway.

—I'm tired, she says. I want to go to bed.

"Sing me to sleep."

I hear The Smiths in my drunken, stupid, and wretched head while watching my wife walk back up the stairs. I could follow. I could have said something or anything. But instead I'm hearing Morrissey crooning.

Sure enough, I have to listen to the song before bedtime. What's another half hour when it's the middle of night?

The song is depressing. Of course. Of course it's depressing because that's what The Smiths are. They depress. They take your misery and then stretch it out and make you wait. And wait. And wait. All while the music keeps playing.

"Deep in the cell of my heart I will feel so glad to go."

But I don't feel glad and I want this s***ty cell to be cracked open.

"I don't want to wake up on my own anymore."

A body sleeping beside you doesn't mean you're not alone.

"There is another world."

I believe it but I don't belong there.

"There is a better world."

But God knows I'm not ready.

"WELLLL, THERE MUST BE . . ."

Will I go? Am I ready?

I listen to this sad song and I just wonder. Is there really and truly some other place? And if I suddenly am ready to go, will I head there? Will I be *allowed* to go there?

Will I hear a children's music box playing "Auld Lang Syne"?

On this night, I can't dwell on the morbid. I have to snap out of it before I pass out halfway unconsciousness for the night/morning.

I need another song.

Just one more.

I don't think the rest of the world is like this. Obsessed with trying to spotlight and score these moments. But somehow I like to imagine this to be some kind of wretched trailer. Or maybe a hilarious one.

So I start to search. And I search. And I search more.

I realize we no longer have theme songs. We don't have any more soundtracks to score our trailers.

Someone stopped making them years ago.

What you have are lots and lots of other songs for other movies and memories. But Tamara isn't a part of them. For whatever reason.

So I start to search. The soft and the melancholy and the rocking and the rebellious. Hoping to find something to spark some bit of meaning that will alleviate all the nothingness I feel inside.

Then I discover this little song.

Oh yeah.

Actually, that's its title.

This little ode. This surprising little bird that came and sat at my window just like she did.

It feels young and free and spells out freedom in bright Magic Markers.

I'm back. Right there. Right next to her.

There's a band playing on the radio
With a rhythm of rhyming guitars
They're playing "Oh Yeah" on the radio

And yes. We had "Oh Yeah" playing on the radio while we drove and while we loved and longed.

Summers and winters and day and night drifting into love. Like the song would say. Like we said to the song.

And we drove and loved and thought that we might be twentysomething forever with these feelings and emotions and raging desire. It could only scrape a surface we would never get past.

And now time has gone and time has passed and suddenly I'm in the back of the song.

It's some time since we said goodbye
And now we lead our separate lives
But where am I, where can I go?
Driving alone to a movie show

So I guess I have one option now. Will I continue to drive alone?
Will I let the song drown the sound of my tears? Will I stop and get
out of the car and tell her to get back in? To *ask* her if she'd like to get
back in? To take a moonlit drive? To possibly remember and to
suddenly be thinking . . .
   Oh yeah.
   Yeah. That's my late-night drunken answer.
   Yeah and yeah and yeah a little more.

Times So Rare

We sit or stand mostly but I love it when we skip.

That occasional let-out laugh I get from you when I least expect it.

A look of knowing someone so well you don't even have to look at them to know what they're thinking.

Those times, so rare, of cracking the surface, of lighting to fireworks, and letting go, letting go, God, letting go.

This still so silent blowing in our ears a nighttime story with no words.

Dreams await but sometimes I fear them, living in this other world where I'm a hero and a saint and someone without a worry in the world.

Waiting for the Night to Fall

Confusion come over me and give comfort. These sounds and these beeps and these syncopated beats and these melodies.

Waiting.

Knowing.

Wanting to be safe and saved and spared the stark reality.

God, being alone is a terrible thing.

God, do You know this?

Do You hear my solitary heart speaking when I hear these songs?

Do You see through me when I try to see through Your stars?

Can I ever cast such a glow as the kind the moon gives?

Can I ever know I'll be okay and be fine and be all right?

I'm waiting and waiting and waiting a little more.

In the dark and the stark I don't feel like anything is real. Not anymore.

But it's quiet and it's still and it's okay. It's bearable and delightful.

The calm can comfort but can cover the harm about to come.

So I cover up my eyes and my ears, not wanting to see nor wanting to hear.

But I stay silent until half opening my eyes and seeing some sort of supernatural life out there. Saving us all.

"The stark reality."

I'm scared because I'm not young anymore. Nothing is bearable anymore.

"All that you feel . . . is tranquility."

But I just feel the beat continue. A tapping on my head and my heart. On. And on. And on. And on. And on. And on. And on. And on. And on. And on. And on. And on.

And on.

And on.

And on.

On.

And on.

On.

And on.

On.
On.
On.
On.
And yeah . . .
On.

And Then . . .

Then later . . .

—You're like listening to a new album, I tell Lissie.

—With headphones or on a computer? She smiles.

—Only you'd ask that.

—Well?

—Maybe in my car on the stereo since there's no better sound than that.

—How's it sound? she asks.

—Magnificent, I tell her.

—Good.

—I love your lovely confidence, I tell Lissie.

—I try to allow the loveliness to overshadow my insecurities.

—Job well done.

Then much later . . .

—You look like you have something to say, Lissie tells me.

—There's nothing more to say.

—But you're still talking.

—Because you're still asking me questions like you always do.

—I just care about my friend.

—Cut the friend fallacy, I say.

—There's no fallacy about it.

—You are as imaginary as the love existing in my marriage. Both are vapors, vanishing.

—I like that description, she says.

—Don't smile like that.

—You're smiling too.

—It's kinda hard not to when I'm looking at you.

—That's a good thing, isn't it?

—Yeah, sure, if you weren't *a ghost*. And if I wasn't a ghost, too, only I'm one crushed by the failure of his marriage.

Silence.

—I finally shut you up, I say.

—I chose not to respond.

—There's a first.

—Don't be mean.

—I'm being honest.

—You can be honest and still be nice.

Lissie looks away.

—What happens when you realize the spark for the fireworks is just a box of empty matches you're holding in your hand?

—There's nothing empty here, Lissie tells me.

—There's a whole lot of emptiness and it starts here, right here, in this space, in this place where I can begin to fill.

More silence.

—I need this to end, I say.

—Okay.

—No, do you understand? I mean—end. Gone. Bye-bye.

—I don't want that.

—Yeah, well, there's a lot about life I don't want either. But can't do a thing about that, can I?

My anger has come out of nowhere. I think because this is going nowhere, because I'm going nowhere, because my passions are finding nothing.

—I don't want you to be mad, Lissie says.

—And I don't want you talking in metaphors and putting a mirror in front of my face and making me feel like crap again and again.

—I do that?

—Yeah, pretty much, I lie.

—I'm sorry.

—I am too. But there's no catching that fish and pulling it out of the deep, is there?

Silence again.

—This is the thing I need, I tell her. You being quiet. You just being like this.

—You don't have to hurt me.

—You hurt me the moment you smiled at me. 'Cause I suddenly wanted something I could never, ever have.

—That smile was innocent.

—Yeah. But the heart it was aimed at sure wasn't. You didn't know that. But you know that now.

And then . . . finally and suddenly . . .

—I love you, Spencer. And I'm not ashamed to tell you that.

A Sky Full

The stars suddenly got a little closer. And they sound exquisite.

Her

Stick to the stuff you're good at, they say, and meanwhile they let the whole damn thing pass by over your head, over toward some other gray, empty-barrel day while you're sitting there simply trying to get some sun. Others will come up and say it's not fair, but you see the waters out there and know what awaits underneath and you're just glad on your dry land. You might be on a deserted island without the treasure the map promised you, but you're not ten feet under swallowing salt water and seeing your whole life pass you by like plankton.

Good God, Spence, when did you get so ramblingly poetic with your melancholy?

It's the silence that I'm trying to fill with these words. I know that. I wish that other words could fill them. That I could hear a few of them. Perhaps just a few simple messages.

Can you share love the way you fill a wineglass full of smiles and toasts until a bottle is empty and you're left with red stains on your white shirt? Or maybe I mistook the whole thing. Maybe I was the one pouring the bottle and the one spilling and the one—

—Spencer.

The voice. The reality right now.

—Can you hear me?

I wait for a moment.

—Yes, I tell Lissie.

Can I hear it or read it? Is it spoken or written? I'm not sure.

—Are you busy? I ask.

—What do you think?

—I don't know what to think.

And I don't know if she's talking in another room or if I have a phone chip in my head.

—I'm here, she says.

—Can you come over? Can you come be with me tonight?

—It's thirty minutes past midnight, she says.

—Is that your curfew?

—Funny, funny guy.

—I'm here.

—So you are.

Are these words typed or talked out? I'm seriously not sure. This feels like the movie *Her*.

—I want to talk, I type/tell her.

—So talk.

—I want to see you.

—You weirdo.

—Be nice, I say.

—Okay.

—And be near. Okay?

—Okay.

Honest

—Tell me a story, Lissie says.

She's sitting on a couch next to me. So comfortable this family room. Warm and cozy and blue.

—About what? I ask.

—About yourself.

—I'm a remainder book waiting to happen.

—There are some pretty great tales inside. I know there are. You've told me them.

—You have the only signed copy of my life's greatest work.

—Can I have a sequel? she asks.

Oh, that smile.

—I'll sign it in blood, I tell her.

—Epic.

—Disaster.

—You're funny when you smirk like that.

—It's half a halo, my smirk. It's half a noose.

—You're more bleak that usual tonight, Lissie says.

—You're the knot to the noose scratching my neck. You're the kick to the chair I'm balancing on.

—You're the Edgar Allan Poe to my *Fifty Shades of Grey*.

—You didn't just reference that work, did you? I joke.

—Somewhere you just called me your noose.

—Pretty Smiths-like.

—I can use whatever metaphor I'm in the mood for, Lissie says.

—I like your feisty spirit.

—Even though I'm your death.

—I'm your ghost, I say.

—Bill Murray's coming to *bust* you out.

—You're a cross between *Groundhog Day* and *The Exorcist*.

—I like pea soup.

—I like you.

—You don't sound like it, Lissie says.

—I breathe and think and feel like it even though the words are just camo in the woods.

The Beautiful Ones

—This room . . . it's very blue.

—It's purple.

—Seriously? I ask.

I have to laugh.

—I'm color-blind, I say.

—I know, Lissie says. I'm just teasing.

—I never realized how much purple exists until having the girls. They *loved* purple.

—I did too.

I shift just a bit on the couch. Just a tiny bit, not wanting it to mean anything or to signal anything or for it to be anything except me trying desperately to get closer. Lissie doesn't flinch. Of course not.

—Why'd you love purple? I ask.

—I loved Prince. Right? Who didn't?

—I can't believe he died.

—Me neither.

—So does that mean we'll see him soon?

My question is a bit of a joke but also a bit serious. She only looks at me with a serious case of *Come on, man.*

—It doesn't quite work out like that, she says.

I'm sure it doesn't even though I haven't quite figured out how it does work.

—So what about Prince do you like? I ask.

So she tells me. About this talented artist and this strange soulful and religious man combining his sexuality with his faith. She loves it and at the same time knows he's about the most brilliant artist out there.

—Why do you say that? I ask.

I've heard this and maybe believe it myself but I'm wondering why *Lissie* thinks this.

—He knew how to play everything. How to do everything. How to *be* everything. He was the whole package and he lived it to until the very end.

—Is this the very end?

302

She laughs. Her soft skin reflects in the light and I can't help thinking how much I want and need right now. I look at her and keep looking.

—You look like you're thinking about something, she tells me.

Yeah, you and a hundred times in a hundred different ways.

—Not really, I tell her, clearly lying.

—No really. Tell me.

She's moved closer, and she looks like she's leaning against me. Nudging in close to a loved one on a cold winter's day. She's close but not that close but it's all about the vibe and I'm sensing it's very, *very* intimate.

Spoken Out Loud

—Why do you always seem to say half of what you feel? she asks me.

—Maybe half is safer than the whole.

—Yes. That's why you spend your time crafting two-minute spots to be shown in the dark.

—Are you mocking me? I say with my smile floating off my face.

—That's a whole thought there.

—Maybe we should go back to the halfsies.

I know exactly what she's talking about because sometimes I'm unable to hold back what I'm thinking yet my mouth seems to slam shut midway through a thought I don't quite want to reveal.

—You have a dangerous spirit, Spencer.

—Why's that?

—Because you're curious and you care. A deadly combination.

—Aren't we past deadly?

—Perhaps, she says with a similar smile. Maybe halfway past.

These are the fun little deviations we take amidst our conversations. Flirtatious and fun. That's what I'll call them. They're safe and harmless. Yet I'm wondering why they wouldn't be. Am I still married? Still spoken for? And what about her?

I'm not rushed, not ready to jump at someone's beck and call. I've been wishing I could, except I'm comfortable now. Just talking. Just listening and being listened to.

And sometime in the middle of our chat/conversation/talk, Lissie just stops. Looking overcome by emotion for some reason. And we weren't really talking about something super deep.

—What is it? I ask.

She just shakes her head.

—What? You look . . . surprised. Sad, almost.

—I'm not sad. Definitely not sad.

—Then what is it?

—It's nothing, she says with a kind look.

When a woman says those two words, there's about a 99 percent chance it is indeed something.

—Tell me, I say.

—No.

—Tell me. . . . Look at me, Lissie.

She smiles again, shaking her head.

—The sound, she says.

—Of what?

—My name.

—Lissie?

—Spoken by you. In that way.

Startled, the seconds seem to hold their breath, stopped by her simple smile. Amazing how peace can suddenly pause the world's violent laments. I envy—no, love—her lovely calm.

—In what way? Be more specific.

—I've already said enough, Lissie tells me.

—But you haven't *said* it.

—Do you need to hear the truth spoken?

—Sometimes, yeah. Like now. Yes.

—Why?

—Because I do. Because I'm weak and fragile and stupid and moronic and mostly because I'm just a dumb man.

—You're getting far too emotional for a man, Lissie says.

—That's been my plight in life. Too much aggression for someone so emotional.

—I love that word, *plight*. It takes the *light* and shoves a *p* on it to pop it out.

—Are you saying I'm the *p*?

—I'm saying I love the words you say. And how you say them. Especially my name.

—Lissie.

—Yes.

—I said your name.

—And I replied with a statement, not a question.

That look says more than any sort of two-minute montage could ever do. Ablaze and aglow and anew, the smile on her lips circles around my head like a halo. I just wish they would plant a big, wet kiss on mine.

I'm

sometimes still sixteen watching a red blue world confused and needing to be known for four minutes in a song sung by someone so young.

Twisted Logic

I dream about her. Not Lissie, but Tamara. I picture scenes, not made-up but real. Remembering the rolling into sunshine and daydream and light and favor and fearlessness and the rush.

The rush of letting go of fears. Letting go of resistance. Letting go of constraints. Letting go of reasons.

And every reason I've never seen I want to hold back, want to get back, want to capture one more time in my head and my heart to redo, to regain, to recover one more time.

But I hear it knocking, hear it saying, swearing, stating the facts and their case, telling me their sentence, sharing their verdict, and cursing down the door to find me shivering and hiding.

Fear can be a bigot and a bitch. It can smile as it cuts. It can drip as it bleeds. It can stain as you run.

I hear the midnight trains sounding and I still them in my dreams.

The daydreams and nightmares and stony eyes and stony stares.

I still remember. The light of day, lighter over there, the wind watching, the wind sharing its stare.

I can remember it now and want to let it go. But it won't drop or won't float away. It hovers nearby, circling me, gliding with the current, coasting with the fair winds. This moving patch of regret that can't be punctured or shot down. It can't be cut in two or obliterated but rather hangs there like a sports blimp broadcasting for only me.

It was once so easy.

The music allowed it to be.

The volume allowed me to drown out reason.

The emotions and the passions killed the good inside.

So I fell and drifted and wandered and lingered.

I waited for the voices to stop encouraging and guiding me, but they kept singing and talking and encouraging. So I believed.

Now, in the instrumental portion of my life, I hear the timbre and the shiver and wait for some kind of description, some kind of recipe, some bit of instruction.

I'd like to know what I'm supposed to do and how to get out of here.

Ful Stop

If you could go back and change it, you would but you can't, so you're stuck, so now what? So now what do you want to do and can you ever try to wrap your mind around it, and if you do, where will you go with your decision? Do you see the forest or the trees? Do you see the road or its signs? Do you want to turn around or will you try to discover a simple road stop to go and breathe and find a bit of respite?

Can you stop? Tell me, can you?

They sit sunglassed and unsmiling and staring and you feel judged and swamped and weighted in the sludge. Not one of them. Never one of them. And you gotta battle one against the world, you against them all. It angers and fires the flicker of a spark of the *back off* inside of you.

So different and so not the same. So is the course falling down some kind of dried-up spicket already forgotten about. It's not pretty but it's functional. And when it's not even functional, it's pretty ugly.

They want clarity. They want an absolute. *Look over there at the pretty orange spruce sprouting in the hard clay.* And you look over there to simply see a bush in some crumbling ground and already you've wasted too much time trying to describe it.

Hang on, hang on, hang on.

The truth hurts but the other side hurts a bit more, doesn't it?

Hang on.

The reality can really bite. This real life, real love, real living can bring you down, can't it?

You're behind the wheel alongside the curb away from the streetlamp glow in the cul-de-sac watching the unmoving garage door and the simmering yellow-orange skylight above it. Watching and waiting until the simmer shuts off and the darkness comes.

The switch to turn it off used to come from your fingers. So errant, so routine, so unnoticed. Until Someone far greater flicks another switch. Not to a light but to a life.

What I Do . . . Or Did

I get to see the whole picture. And yes, pun intended.

So many times I'm seeing the final, "final" film. But I see enough.

And what I do—I guess the reason I'm paid well and the reason I have developed this reputation—is that I take the best nuggets and make it into an alluring story.

I don't simply take the best moments and tell the story in two minutes. No no no no no no no.

No.

Instead my goal is create interest. Sometimes intrigue if it's a smaller movie, a sense of *What's that all about?* If it's a bigger movie, then I try to do a whole *This is why you need to see this.*

See—everything's been done. Every story's been told. Every effect rendered. Every single everything has been shown. So why go pay ten bucks to see this film? Why not stay home and watch reality television?

That's where I come in.

It's amazing what I can do with such little time. I don't need to know the whole story. I don't have to watch the whole film. I scan through and know enough. I do the work necessary. I usually watch a film multiple times, but I don't have to.

I guess I can say that now because I'm sorta unemployed. Right?

But the dead don't make movie trailers. Do they?

Way Back When

"Do something beautiful."

That's my assignment.

"What do you mean?" I ask.

I'm talking to Heidi. One of those rigid souls. Not an ounce of flab on her body or her sentences or her leadership style. It's all hard-edged and cutting.

"You're the most talented person in this building. But that's when you're working with film. The things you're able to do with movies—especially the really awful ones—is nothing short of brilliant."

"Thank you," I tell her.

"This isn't a bragging session."

"Okay."

"I sometimes think you store up all your energy to do those amazing things. Then you're left depleted. Then you're left . . . well, you're left to become an exhausted mess. Like today."

"I take back my 'thanks,'" I tell her.

She laughs.

"I'm giving you some time off."

"I can't take time off," I say.

"Yes, you can. If I say so, you sure as hell can."

"But why?"

"Because if you don't, your marriage might not make it. Just like mine didn't."

I just sit there, a bit in disbelief. It's not like Tamara and I have been married that long.

"You don't have children, so you're lucky," she says.

"I am?"

"It's bad enough to ignore one in your family. You need to right the ship, Spencer."

"How do you suggest doing that?"

"You need to figure that out on your own," she says.

Lonely Hunter

So I did. I guess. For a short while, at least.

Figuring this out ended up being my ticket out of the corporate life. It wasn't a simple "See ya!" but the seeds were planted.

Soon I found myself on my own, building something, trying things out. The business came and so did the family.

I often think of what Heidi said. The encouragement in my craft and warning in the rest of my life.

I don't think I listened to the second half of that.

I'm still lost, still trying to pursue something amazing, still trying and trying.

Sometimes it's as simple as a song that makes me take off. Like some siren, a song can make you turn around and wince, wondering what's coming your way.

I hear it and wonder how I can use it and what way it will make me feel.

I've always made music about me, choosing to let certain songs dictate my mood, speak my secrets, and define the undefinable inside. Perhaps they say more than I feel, and they sound more powerful than my thoughts might be inside. Or maybe, just maybe, they're still simply glimmers of the raging fire inside.

Replicas can never match the real thing.

I plunge and I pursue and I try to perceive these things deep down, deeper than others ever know and ever see and ever try to imagine. I go down and then I resurface and find myself babbling and rambling with the breathless uncertainty I just found.

I wonder if they all know where my mind goes. Somewhere far away. With ideas for images matched with songs and sound. Telling a spark of a story.

A movie trailer is that first crack in the sky on a July 4 when you see just a taste of things to come. Sometimes it overwhelms and flattens your emotions. Other times, it simply teases and taunts, luring you closer and closer to the edge.

I love the edge. Teetering on it, looking over it, playing with the idea of suddenly falling down, plunging to my demise.

Creatives are exactly that way, even in imagining their own deaths.

I hear songs and can picture just how they might unfold if I'm helping sum up a love story or a drama or a supernatural thriller or whatever the hell I might be doing.

Sometimes in the middle of the night the passion on the project I have suddenly overwhelms me like some kind of tsunami and I know that nobody else can ever understand or comprehend or ever try to mix or match.

Life. Press Play and run. Pause. Breathe. Try to rewind or fast-forward, then realize it's not some simple cassette tape.

I think I know more but maybe I don't. Maybe I can't know any more right now. But maybe I didn't learn so much from thirty-five to forty-five or from twenty-five to forty-five or maybe just a whole lot of damn years I was pretty ignorant.

Why must I wait in line?

Yes.

I know these things, these bugs, these corruptions to the system. And so many others show me so much more and so many tell me and share with me and bless me and I find myself turning my back.

At least I used to.

And yes. Yes.

It's 3 a.m. I got held up.

In times of the tortured unknown, you can simply go and sit and wait and hold a hand.

And sometimes, the mountain you imagined turns out to be made-up. It's flat and fixed and completely fictitious. Yet you still wonder.

Will I see you? I've got lost in foreign lands.

You're trying to get back. But somehow you can't.

Just remember, that love is a gun in your hand.

Stagger or Shuffle or Step

The door, this rectangular invitation, creaking and cutting, grins and taunts. At midnight sometimes I long to get away. At noon sometimes I wish I could never get in.

The noisy silence we suffocate in. The conversations never really held. Separated with each of us standing on the other side.

I know better but fall back into the ruts of life.

Every day versus every night.

One bouncing off the other.

Striving and hurting and breaking only to wake up to some kind of pink suburban reality.

I'm stuck in another world, mired in Hollywood reality, and yet wake up with real life standing by my bed asking me for a password for Animal Jam. Hungover but not really, but definitely saying, "Wait a minute," ticked off with cotton mouth only to stagger and wonder what day/time/month/year it might be. Then back to reality, knowing. Then back to reality, going, *S***, Spencer, seriously.*

I love creating and I love feeling well and I love losing myself and I hate coming back out of that particular well. Crawling, crying, coughing.

"You were up late," Tamara says.

I can say something. Creatives can always pull out their creative card about creating late at night and feeling creative and all those creative lies.

"Did you hear M last night?" Tamara asks.

I can only shake my head since I was six feet under for the six hours I managed to sleep. I get a story about our dog getting scared and needing and wanting and yeah. And I just have to give a big fat yeah to her story. What else can I do? Might as well be a check in the mail, a fairy tale with no end in sight.

Lock the door, Spencer, and check all the remaining locks.

Yeah. Safety. Priority number one.

Heading upstairs and sometimes sneaking into the twins' double-size room to see them stretched out with their bodies intertwined with their blankets. Passing our firstborn's room and wondering what she's dreaming about. Sneaking and silent and stepping on that blasted creaking spot before getting to the bathroom.

Hello, Spencer boy. Having a good night?

I'm never in the mood for conversations with myself.

Wow, you're looking like s***, Spencer.

I never really like looking at myself in the first place.

And then I stagger or shuffle or step or do whatever the hell it is I do because God knows I will wake up with bright-eyed wonders looking at me and will have no idea of what I was doing the night before.

Sights

Lissie's there. Up on the screen. Talking, crying, as if I'm in front of her. As if I'm the one breaking her heart.

I know it's a part, just a character, with lines given to her and movements suggested to make. She's enticing the world to love her. And they do. Everybody does. She should've been the next Julia Roberts. She's got every bit of it inside of her. Her talent and her abilities and her raw beauty. Maybe it shouldn't be so important, but for Lissie it's her everything and I'm sorry, but I just think she's every bit as glorious as her character and the movie she's playing in.

I watch better, closer, deeper. Studying and trying to see the things others might not see. Do I know more and do I have some hidden talent for deeper meanings? Or maybe do I simply spot things that aren't meant to be highlighted?

This statuesque stalemate that sweeps into the room is unfolded with her simple smile. A calm interest and an interesting calm. Worthy of confessions you'd never imagine you'd ever give.

I feel this buzz and see my phone lighting up.

What are you doing?

I can only smile.

I'm watching you.

How do I look?

You look like the Christmas present asked for a thousand times.

There's a pause before she answers.

I've never heard something like that.

Really? I type.

Really.

Rereading it makes me sound a bit corny and clichéd.

It's very kind.

You're very remarkable.

Not really.

Just then I hear her say a joke and laugh and I just shake my head. *Yes, it's a real you don't and can't ever realize.*

Yes, really. Honestly—it's surreal, too. Just seeing you

315

and then realizing that only a day or so ago, we were talking in person. Whatever this kind of "person" means now.

It's still real. Still in person.

If you find a kindred soul, does it matter if you can't touch their skin in person?

Maybe you can.

Is she saying this in terms of talking about being a ghost? Or about being appropriate?

Losing your mind, Spence.

I go back and see her on the screen, smiling, being followed by our hero, her eyes following his, and she stops and asks him.

—Can I move you? she says.

—Move me to do what? the hero asks.

—To move this mountain.

—What sort?

—The highest of high, the kind you feel you can't ever get over, the peak that passes all understanding, unshakable and unmovable.

—Yes, he tells her.

—Yes what?

—Yes, you can move it. You could probably shift around time and space if you set your head and heart to it.

—That's ludicrous.

She laughs on-screen and I study it and shake my head.

So's that. That smile. That heart. That genuine generosity.

I love everything about you, I want to text her. But I don't.

This whole thing reeks of insanity. So why not embrace it fully? Why not just go ahead and give in?

But I'm still here for a reason and it's not for this. It's not to suddenly be texting some ghost on the screen.

You still there?

I almost want to not answer. Because I want to not be honest. I want to lie to her. To tell her everything is warm and wonderful and worked out. That I'm here with all the answers instead of over there raising a hand with questions.

Yeah.

Obviously I'm not doing a good job moving away from the banter.

316

My Truth

I don't imagine those lips on mine. I imagine them moving to inspire.

I don't imagine those hands touching my body. I imagine them holding my own, for safety, for security.

I don't imagine the voice wanting and pleading and desiring. I imagine it saying my name and asking me questions and being there and laughing.

Imagination can suit a profession, but it can spoil a friendship. The buildings it can build can be made out of paper, the beams made out of words and expressions. Delicate and often deleted and sometimes so delirious.

I've always imagined but I couldn't have imagined you and I wish you could know this and accept this and understand.

But you don't.

You run.

You hide behind the pines. You run through the forest. You hover by the hillside. And I sprint and fall and tumble into the passing river, all while you remain hiding.

I imagine I'm smart, but that's a fantasy I cannot make sense of.

Skipping Over Cement

It's a picture tagged and highlighted on my page.

It should have a halo around your head and an asterisk around your name.

I find myself at a wall. Then as I turn, I'm in a box. Every stone has your image, each block something I could have held if only I'd gotten there in time. Now it's sealed and unmovable, so smooth to touch. I stare and want to grab it and take it and own it. I want to make it mine.

This is desire wrapped up around my heart. Desire for you. Desire to have that picture I'm seeing. Every inch of it and more.

It's a strange feeling. I am breathless, a word so surely overused these days. I ache a bit, knowing the longing can't go anywhere. Knowing it shouldn't go anywhere. Knowing but not knowing at the same time. Not having an idea where to take all of this. I'm falling out of a plane, dropping without a chute, spinning without a destination, yet I refuse to have it any other way.

Your smile is a lot like that. Free, racing, effortless, weightless.

I know it'd be better if I just stopped glancing like some stalker. But I keep going back there. It makes me happy and sad at the same moment. Someone I know and someone I care for. Someone I can't have and someone I can never fully embrace. Someone who is a friend but someone I can't love and make love to. Someone, this someone, the someone making me feel like this falling, foolish fan.

I move my arms over my desk and almost spill my coffee mug. I'm shaking. Surely I'm just tired and a bit sick and a bit more hungover.

Surely.

I've memorized your smile.

I wonder what you'd do if you knew that.

I've imagined your body wrapped around mine.

I wouldn't want you to know I was thinking that.

Delicate, distant, these drops of connection that fall so fast, so deliberately. They can draw doubt and desire from the same place. A place that flows like a waterfall. A little more every day.

I wonder—worry—wait to see how to stop it.

318

Sometimes I ache wondering what if and realizing this is it.

I've spent a whole lifetime longing for more. And the longing gets long. Endless and listless.

Skipping over cement trying to capture your shadow. Trying to outrun your shape. Trying to be someone else.

The fear isn't slowing down and realizing. It's stopping and finally seeing for the first time.

Conversation

—You showed up.

   —So did you.

   —I thought you were busy.

   —I'm not the one working.

   —I thought I'd scared you away.

   —I'm still a little scared. Or a lot.

   —You don't have to be.

   —I know.

   —You looked pretty good out there.

   —If it wasn't so dark, you'd see me blushing.

   —I'm being serious.

   —I am too.

   —Do you want to dance?

   —I want to do anything.

   —I like the sound of that.

   —I can see. Well, maybe just a drink for starters.

   —I've got a nice head start.

   —Let me catch up to you.

   —Take your time.

   —I like doing that. Don't you?

   —When I can.

   —You're smiling like a schoolboy.

   —I'm sorta feeling like one, too.

   —The music always makes me feel young.

   —You are young.

   —I'm two years younger than you.

   —So you're twenty-five.

   —Exactly.

   —You're beautiful, you know that.

   —I've been told that before.

   —I need to be more creative.

   —I've never been told by someone with that look.

   —Sheer desperation.

   —Sheer delight.

—I like the sound of that.
—Are you gonna buy me a drink or what?
—What do you want?
—Be creative and choose.
—Okay.
—And, Spencer?
—Yeah?
—Stop smiling like that. It's ridiculous.
—It's for you.
—Then I'll keep it safe with me.

More

The night doesn't allow me to see you, but you take my hand anyway. Off and away we go yet my feet don't start to float, do they?

Where? I wonder though don't stop to ask out loud. I'm free, more free than I think I've ever felt. So light, so young, so curious, so unstuck.

Age cements. Adulthood suffocates. So wise, so pristine, so calm, so damn old. I can finally run and breathe and laugh again.

That smile like the moon with its simply there quality you cannot change. Unmovable. Understanding all you can do is stare up and wonder.

—Where are you taking me?

—Do you need to know?

Of course I don't. So of course I shake my head. Because I'm an of course always staying on it.

I suddenly realize adults should run on sidewalks more than they do. Then skip off curbs into the street and sprint down its center. Age only slows us down and keeps us in our individual lanes.

A Painting to Admire

Sometimes I don't know if it would be better to hear from her or not. But that's a little like a junkie saying he doesn't know if it would be better to just take one more hit.

You never get enough. And with Lissie, I never get enough. I never seem to even start. I only share and listen, then later I imagine.

Being able to watch someone on-screen after spending time with them is an intoxicating and dangerous thing.

Sometimes it seems like she's talking to me from her movies.

Am I losing it?

I question my mind about a lot of things lately.

Silence can be a heavy comforter when the voices begin to pile up. Yet words can be like bombs, blasting and ripping and opening holes you didn't know were there.

You there?

Like that.

Through my computer. Through a social network. Through one device to another. Suddenly after silent days comes a stealth bomb.

Yeah.

Because of course I'm here. Because do you really think I'd be somewhere else? I'm a ghost that can't haunt anybody but myself.

I miss you.

I shake my head.

She misses *me*.

How can that even possibly be?

You can't imagine the smart-ass things I want to say.

Because I'm suddenly swimming in them.

Be nice.

She tells me to be nice while throwing down her little grenades.

I will.

Because I want whatever she will give. Whenever. And whatever way.

Drops to a parched soul. That's what words can do. Especially the right ones.

I gotta go. Just telling you the truth.

Again the thoughts I have. Oh, the ghostly irony I could come up with. But I don't.

Thanks for saying that.

I could be mean or block her out but I don't want to. There's no need. She's not mine anyway. And how can I block her anyway?

She's a painting I can go visit and look at and admire. I can even stand very close up. But I can never take it off the wall. I can never touch it. I don't know—the metaphor can begin to be stupid if I keep it up.

Metaphors are nice but life is nicer. Comparing is fun but you know what's more fun? Wrapping my arms and legs around a woman and not going anywhere. Yeah.

Good night.

My thoughts are fireworks on a bright, busy day. Unseen in the sunshine. Unheard in the crowds.

But they're always there.

Always.

Midnight 2

I long for the surprise of love finding me in my midnight.

To meet and mingle and wrap myself around you in some kind of myriad of a dream.

Without words or worries or wondering anything. Just giving. Then more. Then a little more.

Pale in Comparison

The images and the music can't equate a memory. I try to make them emote a feeling, yet they don't compare to the real thing. The twins insisting at bedtime to be danced into their room and delivered by arms into their beds. The giddy, raucous laughter of your ten-year-old by the simple, random mannerisms you provoke by a simple, random comment.

The most brilliant concept ever created will ever compare to the reality of being close to someone.

You've pillaged every emotion and memory from your well, yet you're the thirstiest man you'll ever meet. In need of drops of reality, of human touch, of the actual.

Stay thirsty, my friend.

You wish you could see the Most Interesting Man in the World. Because if you could, you'd punch him in his big, grinning face.

3

The fondness of my children and the folly of my career. So were the days of my life.

The calendar and the clock playing their chess match on my chest every day, the dates daring the hours to keep up. Their draw always drifts across midnight.

Finding me where I stand.

Finding me where I sit.

Finding me in the shelter of my own making, out of the sun's reach and far away from any sort of moonlight.

I'm trying, though. I'm trying—baby steps, I'm trying.

But the voice, the darkness, the depth whispers with a laugh that I won't succeed.

I feel the soul's surge and yet I try to keep it at bay.

I try to keep from dabbling in clichés like that s***ty keep-it-at-bay sort of thing.

Yet I fail and fall. I dribble out the weakest of doubts and verbiage. A vegetable. That's me and my brain.

Bollocks

And then, this. Already there, thus. The longing and the leaving. It's a bit crazy and I want to seize this moment for all it is.

I stand there on concrete crushing me, reminding me, ruining me. I used to walk the same sidewalk alive and alone and always looking around for something else. Something other. Something new and something, anything, everything.

Things can be nothing what they seem on the other side.

—Stop.

I hear her. She's talking to me. So I stop and turn.

—Hold on.

So I do. And when she nears, she doesn't stop but she holds on herself, wrapping arms around me and then moving and kissing me. I taste hunger and fear and this clenching, clawing soul finally telling me to stop and hold on and to be. To be here and now and right on this sort of thing, so I kiss back and I'm lost like some spiraling spirit. Breathless with closed eyes, floating like the wind swirling, we're suddenly this sort of one that U2 once sang about.

—What was that?

—Sometimes you have to run down the things you desire.

—And what do you do with them?

—You run away before you actually keep going.

So this is exactly what she does.

Footsteps light as a four-year-old's weave their way down this sidewalk lit by shadows and my failure to adequately say goodbye.

I want to wrap my lips up in some kind of tinfoil memory. I realize the beginning of the kiss is the start of the end, yet I'm still struggling to adjust to the opening credits. The logo came on the screen and then suddenly the end credits scrolled across the picture.

She kissed me and why?

It's also one of those *That's not just a kiss* sort of moments. I've had several of those in my life. Okay, I've had two. Two, so just bug off. Or do you say bugger off? What's the cool British term for that, you wanker? Just tell me, bollocks.

What happened here and what do I want to happen next?

328

The Me I Used to Know

This song, splitting through my senses, waking me up to the wonder of four years past. I listen and think back to that guy and his thoughts and his heart and his reckless stupidity. Tracks found the further and further back you go. Messy, uneven, wandering and circling, tracks backtracking, then sprinting forward.

I turn the track. I don't want to think about the me from a few years ago. He's a distant friend, an odd family member, a figure I can't figure out. He's infuriating in his fearlessness.

Sometimes a cloud spots a star and tries to run after it, dissipating under a glow too bright to look back.

King's Cross

—What is wrong with you? Tamara asks.

But there's nothing wrong with me.

—Why? I don't get it.

But why do you have to *get* everything?

—Talk to me.

But I don't.

—Say something, Spence. Say something because this is ending.

But I can't.

Broken and lost but I don't say anything.

Now on the other side there are ten thousand things I want to say. I've been good and I've been bad and I've been guilty of hanging around.

Yeah.

I've been guilty of many things except of overtalking and overtelling and overanything.

My trailers were always lessons in cutting, in simplicity, in less is more. I guess that carried over into my life. Or maybe my life carried into those summaries.

God, I wish I could do it over again.

God, I wish I could just gush.

Tell and talk and tell more and share tales and share everything I need to desperately tell.

But there's never a guarantee. Is there?

There's absolutely no guarantee. For tomorrow. Or even for the corner of the rest of this day.

There's this moment, and what are you going to do with it?

—Talk to me, Spence.

I would if I could.

—You can tell me what you're feeling. You can say anything—you really can.

Yeah. But I didn't believe her then.

I wonder if I believe her now.

This place hovers like a hot-air balloon, slowly moving, seen from all directions, serene and a bit scary.

330

It stays right over me like some bad rain cloud.

Will it go? I don't know. I didn't know then and I don't know now.

—You'll never change.

So she said.

But I can change, Tamara. I can change. I can be a little different. I can be a little better. I can be that bell inside that muted ordinary song. I can bounce in that unmoving house. I can be better, Tamara.

I know I can.

—Talk to me.

Okay.

I'll try. Somehow and someway. I'll try for the first time.

I will, Tamara.

Midnight Memory

Fingers pointing to the sky, reminding me, recommending the right thing in the middle of the night. I stare, watching our shih tzu scamper onto the grass with the gray-black of the night in the background. My eyes wander up to see the top of the pine tree with those bristling branches and I can't help but think God is telling me not to forget.

It's time and I know it's time but I'm scared at the pause that's presenting itself.

Change comes tapping at the glass door, visible and waving and inviting you to simply slide it open. So seen, you have to decide whether to rip it open or simply run in self-defense.

Life isn't about capturing the conquest in order to wrap your hands around the dream. It's sneaking outside and staring up at the sky and believing God is watching you, knowing you, loving you.

Forty-five and still figuring it out. With CliffsNotes from God capturing my mind. Juggling the maladjusted. And loving the joyful-minded.

15

I find a sheet filled with my handwriting from a notebook in my desk drawer. It's from a couple of years ago. I start to read, hearing my own voice talking back to me.

I feel overwhelmed. With debt and doubt and demons strangling me. Tightening this noose around my neck, tighter, tighter, my eyes blackening and my skin turning blue and the blood starting to spit out. All while I'm supposed to be standing there acting strong and acting like I know what I'm doing. Acting like someone.

This world makes me weary. This position makes me feel unworthy. Husband and father. Husband and father. Weary and unworthy. Weary and unworthy.

Sometimes I struggle to breathe. It's pathetic, really, these thoughts and feelings. Get over it and come on now. I get it more than anybody else and I try to get and I try to come on. But I'm sucked back to that sickening, suffocating place. Ripped and rotten. Hovering over my face with hot, brittle breath. Laughing. Laughing.

I believe in my heart if I suddenly became a better man, a better person, a better Christian, then I'd be altogether better. I'd be more happy, more hearty, less disheartened, less hungry. But I refuse to go there. I refuse to let go of these ugly vices.

Everything's an anthem while I stare back in apathy. The masses begin to march but I'm not even on the sideline. I need smiles and songs and dancing and motion to jostle my soul. I need something real, something raw, something like me.

I feel like I'm living somewhere else, in some other time, longing and wondering what kind of person I used to be thirty years ago. 1986. Thirty years ago I spent breakfast and lunchtime washing dishes while making small talk with the girls who served the food. We'd spend the rest of the day playing foosball and flirting. I was fifteen but finally felt this invisible touch of freedom. I would share a kiss on a cliff overlooking our campus that summer. I'd fall in love with this beautiful Burmese girl. I'd believe that life could and would always be this carefree, this laid-back, this fun. We worked hard and played hard and I'd go back home to life in the middle of nowhere, but I'd be okay because I knew I'd be coming back. The next day. And the one after that.

I miss fifteen. First albums and first loves and firsts of many kind.

I miss movies like Top Gun. I remember taking three—or maybe four—girls to that film. And making out with at least two of them. Not because I was some kind of player, but because of the power of Berlin's "Take My Breath Away."

You have no idea of the power of "Take My Breath Away" combined with the images of Tom Cruise and Kelly McGillis.

I miss those simple, naive days. Lovely, lively, and so long.

Sunburnt

The summer knows.

It's like a child waiting on the curb knowing the school bus is almost there. Seconds tick off before the chugging, sighing sound of those brakes. Then the door opening to an internal chaos. Then school and fall and life anew.

I look around at these people. This life. Families. Every sort imaginable. Busy bodies. Restless faces. But mainly content in their place.

I always wondered if I could be like them and I still wonder now.

I never was one to waste time. For me there was always something deeper. Something brighter. Something more important.

Seriously, can you see David Fincher at a water park? I'm not saying he's never been at one. Maybe he's got a summer pass at his local water park (no, he doesn't).

But I've always been so not like them. So not like the others. So not like the rest of the world.

Has that made me fail at seeing and breathing and being?

Today I just watch. So many stuffed inside this place full of pools and slides and sprinklers and screaming. I watch because I can't remember the last time I ever came here.

Maybe another life called. But this one was still here.

It's funny because I'm not sure if I'll ever feel at peace here. Not because I'm above these people or because I should be doing something else but because . . . I don't know. I just feel like there's more than bare skin and bathing in the sun.

But there are kids and they don't understand my viewpoint.

Yeah.

So yeah. I should learn.

If only I could.

If only I could get sunburnt and really, truly feel the thrill of an inner tube coasting in circles down a slide.

Yeah.

Another life. The only one I had.

Lights

So you don't have a clue how heavy the night sounds seem to be.

The fog and fatigue and free fall all wrap themselves around in some similar facade.

Echoes of every single soul you've ever been inspired by become etched out on some easel.

The words and the rhythms and the patterns sown in skin and soaked in a soul.

Too long. Too leery. Too lasting. Too limited.

So it goes and so they say and so they come and so they go.

You breathe out and you turn on the light and you try to find yourself amidst this haze. These days and these nights that somehow merge into one.

Where were you at the forefront and could you find yourself at the end?

Do you hear those echoes longing for this when you see yourself falling and floating so freely?

The work is there. Late at night. In the middle of midnight and midmorning. At the rush of the start of the day. At high noon. At afternoon doldrums. At evening psychopaths.

The sound and the fury. Loud and vibrant.

You fall and you get up again. Then plummet, then stand. Then crumble, then crawl back.

Again.

And so it goes.

Again.

So it goes.

Again and again and again.

Patterns in the snow and in the mud and in the mulch and in the afternoon haze.

A gasp and you wonder how and when and why.

A frown and you wonder where and what.

These questions claw. They corrupt. They condemn.

336

Everything You Never Had

Shuffling in adequate space yet feeling squashed. Running while there's still plenty of time until departing without a goodbye.

A brief stated text stating the state of something or other.

Passing by and rushing and wolfing down food and saying an abbreviated hello and an exaggerated goodbye with the girls all while you're sitting.

The noise welcomes me. Screaming and shouting. Or silent indifference. Either one takes a while to get used to.

A head scrambled and a soul empty and skin covered with creative blood and it's so damn hard to try. It's so easy to just drink down a little joy even though I'm staring it right in the face.

Right in the face.

That's right, Spencer. It was right in front of your f'ing face all along but you did nothing, you did nothing but try to drain the bottles of barrels to try to help brace the impact of the work. Pour it out all day and then pour it down all night.

No, no, no, you don't have a problem—you're functioning and you're functioning quite fine.

Some games maybe. Some stories maybe. Some running around. Some yelling to do something. Many, many interruptions. Bath time perhaps. Vitamins and then the *Did they get their vitamins?* and then shows and then *Five minutes till bedtime*. The conversations that you want to abbreviate. The questions and the laughter and the complaining and the confusion and the arguing and the delaying and the cuddling and crying all while we simply want to do our own thing.

I gotta work on projects.

So I believe.

I'm exhausted.

So she states and acts like and clearly happens to be.

Then as the crickets lament and the moons gushes, we end up departing with a simple good night. Preparing to do it all over again the following day.

Wake Up 2

—How long have we been here?

For a moment, Lissie only looks back at me, more like a painting than a person.

—Time can start to turn around on itself.

—What's that mean? I ask, because I have no clue.

—You're impatient.

—I'm just wondering.

—Why?

—Because it seems like a long time.

—What's long to you?

—Months. Years. Seasons. Birthdays.

—Perhaps that's the case, she tells me.

—And all the while, it's just been this... This. Nothing much of this.

—Do you see the most valuable moments of your life in large chunks or individual scenes?

—Those individual scenes.

—Okay, then. So why can't you make every single moment the best scene you could possibly make it?

—I'm not a leading actor.

—And that's your problem. You've made a living creating dozens of leading actors being at their height of their leading manness.

—I'll never be the star in a leading role.

—But that's *exactly* what you've been. The only problem is you've been wanting to be in an entirely different movie. And stupid you—sweet, adorable moron that you are—you've been searching for the movie you think you need to be in. You haven't even landed on a false reality. Instead, you just wander, back and forth and back and forth like some kind of zombie stuck in a romantic comedy.

—That's encouraging.

—That's reality. Look at me. Right? Am I wrong?

—No.

—So then wake up, Spencer. Wake up. Because you're not part of the walking dead. And there's no better motion picture you're ever going to be able to find in your life than the one you're living now.

338

Throughout the Dark Months of April and May

Tiny glimpses like yellow-and-orange streaks from a sparkler zip through my mind.

It's in the dark because that's all those days were. Dark and brutal and buried.

The final argument. Then the one after that. Then the truths. Then more.

It's no fun remembering these. But they happened.

You still see her, standing there, unshackling those cuffs of courtesy, tearing open her soul to give you a glimpse of the lit fuse and the flaming fire inside.

—I hate . . .

But you are no longer there, you are just an imprint on a page.

—I wish we . . .

But we are no longer here, we have suddenly disappeared.

You stand. You listen. You don't respond. You don't react. You don't defend or detract. You don't dare try to retaliate. You simply stand and breathe and feel the half of you cut and wonder where the other half will finally disappear to.

—I should've known . . .

But she didn't know everything and she didn't realize and she didn't stop and didn't hold back.

The damage is done.

This is the scene, the moment, the time, the picture you're so looking for, the moment to figure out in a scene, a pirouette on the big screen.

Beyond me, beyond me.

The look. That look. That glimpse. So void and so empty and so not what that look and glimpse looked like years ago. The glance up with hope and desire and trust and longing.

This glance is down without hope or desire or trust or longing.

More said but you can't hear anything, you can just feel ripples across your skin like molten lava. More promised. More uttered. But you just stand, numb, acting dumb.

She's no longer yours and never will be again.

Foreign Hands

Echoes sound louder in this cavern I crouch in. Lighting a small fuse, the glow bouncing all around, I hover and wait.

And I wait and I hear nothing more than a sigh steeping sideways down from the heavens. A gust in a desert awaiting the rain.

Maybe.

The other side knows why.

I guess it's time, right?

Right?

And maybe there's nothing more that I want and need and desire than this feeling of letting go and getting out and trying to let it out with the bleeding and the needing and all these desires deep down.

God, You see me deep down.

You saw Moses deep down, too, didn't You?

And am I in any sort of company?

Have I been waiting for so long for something more and if so, then how can I start again?

How can I see a way out?

How can the sun surface to see me straightway toward some kind of conclusion that I feel will let me somehow survive?

I'm lost, hovering and humored to the noise and the odd places I've always wanted to avoid.

Cynical

Shiny posts of people and places and portraits occupying the ashes of this planet assault me near midnight. The vacation never taken and the dinner party never attended and the group of friends never found and the bliss never blossoming. Empty scrolls and empty hands. Discovering more and more and more of the endless other.

Even those not cynical can turn.

I was once guilty of oversharing and overcaring and overdoing it all. A star in my own little world, with five who might care and five hundred who didn't. Politics and parenting advice and party selfies and patronizing posts. Echoing off rubber souls. Fibers in the carpet, trampled and worn, while the rest of the world walked on wood.

Shouting in the circus, screaming on the highway home, then sighing our secrets while the tornado siren blares in the background. Our social network, neither enjoyable nor involving any true communication.

I eventually had to stop and let it go and let it all drift away down the river of my discontent since God knows Facebook wasn't going anywhere. People would still be tweeting and coming up with hashtags and providing personal portraits for Instagram and doing #TheNextBigApp sort of thing.

I had to stop.

I had to have a little peace of mind and soul.

My life didn't stop. And strangely, others' lives didn't stop either.

We just stopped crisscrossing in annoying, uncertain ways.

I lost no "connections." But I did lose the cynicism.

Well . . . most of it.

Abandoned

My fingers move up and down, counting seconds that aren't numbered, typing imaginary keys that don't spell anything out. The shadow of a dark room waits.

Where are you?

I can only imagine. Floating in sleep or in another world. Or maybe lost in other words or in song.

I haven't seen or heard from Lissie in days. Weeks.

Will you come around?

The frustration is pointless and excused and silly away.

But I still feel it and swallow it like a nightly pill.

What makes you tremble and will you call out for me to rescue you?

Will you hear the minor chords and move them up the scale?

Will we meet in a dream, a place we call our own, only to awake wanting and needing and asking for more?

A call away. A message for a single moment.

Late-Night Cinema

Here in this place, all I have is music and wine and words. This place, this warmth, this clear cloud I find myself in with Lissie . . . nobody can see us and nobody knows and nobody pays attention except for the two of us and this articulate connection.

We're left alone to simply be.

Of course, I'm only watching her on-screen.

It doesn't substitute. Of course not. But when the other option is simply not there, then this works. This must work or mean something, anything. Because I find myself lost in this world.

I wonder what it would be like to be next to her, to hold her hand freely, to hold more. To slide against her and feel her shift closer. To feel her near me, against me, on me, over me.

Perhaps there wouldn't be as many words. Then again, maybe there would be more.

Maybe the stories would finally never slow down or pause or awkwardly end. Maybe they would swim toward a shore I've dreamed about. Where the sand is silk and the water is warm and I close my eyes and feel her rush into me.

Something inside builds, swells, sings. And each little comment and praise has this crazy power. It's a drug, something more than desire. It's cement, smoothed over and hardened. Stuck and unmoving. Staying with me.

I don't want to think about how to get out of this place. To go to that "next place." The songs are still going and the wineglass is still half-full.

This beautiful world, a place dreamt about, touched with quivering hands, slipping away so fast. So soon.

I'm a teenager again, but then again I'm not. The silence and curiosity of those years are exactly opposite of this. I hear more and know more and feel more, so much more. Technology brings hope and both stifles and stirs the desire.

Then the movie is over.

It ends and it must. Reality reaches in.

They're a snowstorm around me, these images and moving stories, falling and surrounding and smothering. But they're glorious and I want to feel them against my face and skin. I want to catch them in my open hands. But before I realize it, they melt away.

Myth

I cover the glow with ten fingers, blocking my view and the light slipping out. I dare the smile to leak through my curled knuckles, so ready to hit something I can't touch. The movie with its mystery, with its majesty, begging you to begin once again. I don't want to see the opening or the end credits and I don't want to hear the soundtrack.

Maybe I'm the only one seeing the chasm hovering all around me. But does that mean I should take a leap of faith over the edge?

Kindred souls.

So she said.

Maybe we aren't.

Maybe that was some kind of teaser for a film you eventually see and end up hating. The kind where the best statements were summed up like the words on a simple note.

So very nice to meet another kindred soul.

Yes, maybe. Cut the word in half and you have kind and red. In the end, it's very fitting, isn't it?

Kind love and red anger.

Some roads you stumble down are simply no good. You forget about the barricades you drove around miles back. In fact, you forget how you got here in the first place.

Yet here you are, still watching, still looking at the screen, still studying every single movement and word and smile. God, the smile. Can it ever end? Can it ever go away? You certainly hope not.

Pieces of the Past

Reminders ruin.

The silence of this place slowly simmering.

I recall trying to talk to Tamara but her refusing to. I wish I could try now.

How are you?

The inevitable irritation.

I wish we could talk.

And I wish I could go back. To a place and a time when I could focus on Tamara and her alone. I know more now. I'm better now. I'm figuring it out now. And yet.

That crutch is so much easier to hobble along with. That oxygen tank is so much better to breathe a little better. That river flowing is a lot better than that trickling creek hidden under the branches.

Covered in love and regret by the same source is a rare thing. We peel back the leaves and see the fresh, wet dirt and then we put our print on it.

Can we talk?

I wish I can ask Tamara that.

I hope you're okay.

But really I wonder if I'll ever be okay. Anymore.

I wonder if—the almighty *if*—I finally figure out how to move on, whether this glowing sun hanging on my hood will finally be loosened and left behind.

The river heads one way, but I'm driving by, heading the other way.

And parts of me float in that water under the sun. I see them, pieces of the past, particles of the present. But I'm driving to patch tomorrow.

Whisper of a Thrill

She's more beautiful now than ever before. Standing before you. Somehow. In some spectacular way. This is like the first time all over again.

She slides her hand to cover her belly but you move it away. It's not ugly. *Comparison* and *critique* are synonyms to that word. You see a work of art in front of you. Then you move to kiss her soft skin and those slight lines that show proof of your girls.

Men always feel like they know but women know exactly how they feel. God made it this way, complicating already-complicated creatures.

I don't know anything anymore except for this. Before me stands this love, this life, and my legacy. And she's giving herself to me again even though I don't deserve it. Even though I don't have a right to take it. But she's standing there opening herself up again and wanting me to accept it. So I do. I move my hands around her hips and pull her toward me with the slightest nudge, not wanting her to take any sort of step she doesn't want to take.

But she's over me with her own choosing.

—Are you really there? I ask her.

—I don't know. This feels like a dream.

I don't breathe but rather inhale Tamara. I don't embrace her but rather fasten myself against her. Covered and clutched and clasped together. For who knows how long. But long enough for us to not wonder if this means something. Long enough to know there's enough left over to last. And it's not in the touch but in the faith found inside her eyes. And in every little thing said.

—I'm sorry.

—I thought I'd lost you.

—I felt like I'd died.

—I can't imagine life without you.

—I'm sorry.

—I was stupid.

—I've missed you.

—I need you.

—I'm right here.

—I want you so bad.

—I can't believe we're here again.

—I love you.

Sometimes it doesn't matter who says the words when they're uttered in a safe place. Love is a space full of interchangeable statements.

—Did you play Sade?

—Did you put all these bubbles in here?

—Do you want another sip of this?

—Do you want to head over to the bed?

Our conversation resembles all the conversations before and we know each answer before asking. She's managed to shift my point of view from second to first. Somehow I've gone from the you over there to the me right here. And I don't want to move from this place. I want to stay in this warmth and never leave.

Blame

I can imagine the us in my mind. A parade and a picnic in the grass. Blue or gray skies above and winter or summertime come what may. The sudden pause of the button of life while we simply be. While we simply see. We stay and remain still and listen and look and long and love.

We live.

Then go back to life.

We stay still, then succumb to the noise.

I wonder what you'd say right about now. And I wonder how I'd answer.

That marvelous, wonderful, awe-filled glory inside of me would dissipate. Days turning to years can do that.

The shy-turning shell I'd find myself shoving into would leave.

Perhaps I'd be amazing.

Perhaps I'd be articulate.

Maybe I'd make the most of the moments instead of worrying them into a distant May.

I'd listen and know and I'd be okay and I'd be fine and I'd be safe and I'd be okay and God knows I'd be okay and I'd be normal and I'd be fine and I'd be just this normal guy, normal, so normal, so normal it's okay to be fine and normal and safe and fine near me, so please love me.

Maybe, though, however it goes, I wouldn't be fine, and I'd be far from normal.

I wonder if I made the right decision or if you did.

I wonder how it went from there to here.

I wonder how you can stand on a curb and see the daylight and suddenly find one September turn into another and then turn into this sudden sunset.

Love surpasses time, and memories survive the moments. A heart bursting like a torch will always still be lit tomorrow.

Hi, God, It's Me, Spencer

I look up and wonder as flakes tap and melt against my face. The black endless sky. Vast. So utterly endless.

God, what do You want with me?

Is that the question to ask?

God, do You want anything from me?

Maybe that's a little better.

God, are You paying attention?

But you know and believe He is.

God, are You angry for my actions?

And if You are, then is this what I get?

Breathe out. Breathe in. The cold blanket sucking in.

Echoes of the Deceased

—I need to go.

Lissie's stare isn't straight ahead but surrounding, like a squad filing in around me before commencing to shoot. I'd look away but have nowhere to hide. She's come back to talk to me but I don't want to talk to her anymore.

It's been no big deal for her to have been gone. She didn't miss me and obviously doesn't care. So I'm telling *her* I need to go.

—Where are you going? Lissie asks.

—Anywhere. I just have to get away . . .

—From me.

I can only nod because we both know she's right.

Stepping out on this tightwire, we bumped into each other. I'm just the one with the lack of balance. The one with the fear of heights. The one clawing his way back to solid ground.

—I understand.

But I wish she wouldn't. I wish she'd fight. I wish she'd claw her way on top of me.

—I don't think you do.

—I understand as much as I should.

A sandstorm can't compete with the serene surface of a lake. Even if both hold the same weight deep underneath. Worried winds only help to scatter and can't touch what's below.

—I wish you'd help educate me on some of your understanding.

She only smiles.

—Why?

—Why? Because . . . because I'm this insipid, insecure man standing here wanting to be loved. Wanting to be wanted. F***.

She pauses for a moment.

—Did you say wanting to be . . . ?

I can only shake my head.

—I said wanting to be *wanted*. Then I added the obligatory curse word. But yeah, I want that too, and I want it pretty bad.

—I told you that can't happen here.

—Of course it can't. I mean—this is like the dream-nightmare PG-rated version of my love-dream fantasy.

—Are you drunk?

—Yeah. Pretty much so. I think. I don't know. I'm not even alive but hey, look, Spencer can be drunk and yet can't get laid.

—You don't have to shout.

I take a sip of my wine and curse again.

—Will anyone hear?

She laughs in a not-sure-if-that's-a-yes-or-a-no sort of chuckle.

—I love your passion.

This stare, cutting and sawing me in half once again, keeps slicing.

God, is she beautiful, this beauty. I love her.

—I love you.

She doesn't give me the same reply. Always careful, always so thoughtful with her words.

Maybe I don't mean my words. Maybe I don't, I can't, I won't understand what unconditional love happens to be. I sure didn't know what it looked like with Tamara. But here and now I believe I feel it but the passion that she loves so much is bubbling over and foaming, so I can't see anything else.

—You can't say the same words, can you?

—I've already told you that, she says. Several times, in fact.

I nod.

But . . .

—I was hoping for this raging, wanting sort of "I love you" chant before you hurl yourself at me.

—That sounds violent.

—Well, yeah . . . and now it sounds even better.

—You're impossible.

I smile.

—We're ghosts talking in the shadows of life.

—Have you ever considered something, Spencer?

—What?

—That a life can hear the echoes of the deceased?

I think about that for a moment.

—So which one am I?

—You'll never be an echo. You're much too loud to be one.

Strawberry Swing

The moon beats tonight just behind a rib cage of clouds. The sun has lasted as long as it possibly can, so this is just payback now. It's a light switch left on in the sky. It's a flashlight waking you up in the middle of the night, aimed directly at you.

I stand on the edge of the patio and stare up and know it has to be something special. Something exciting. A rare blood moon or dawn of the dead meteor coming down to the earth or something interesting like that the media can cover. Then I remember something I heard today.

It's the first day of summer, the longest day of the year. It's also a full moon. It has to be. I'm sure it's a rarity on a summer solstice.

Standing on this patio—there's a rarity. I've spent more darkened nights on my friends' rooftop in Wicker Park than I have outside on this small, square concrete slab that's been chipped away by ignorance. The stupidity of someone throwing melting salt over it to get rid of the ice. Who knew it would also scrape away the surface of concrete? Well, actually, a lot of people, but not those who spend many hours of the day in the circle of cinema.

I stand here not because of the beauty of the sky but because of the beware sign hanging over the locked, sliding-glass door. A sign only I can see. A sign that's been there for a long time. A sign I want to rip apart and throw into a bonfire.

Instead, the only thing being ripped apart is the very beating thing keeping me alive, the very same thing thrown to the flames.

They're all surely sleeping, aren't they?

I just want to hover over each of them and watch with wonder.

I want to hear each breath. Each rustle. Each motion in the room. I want to see blankets bundled to one side of the bed. To see mouths half-open. To watch arms and legs shifting with the slightest semblance of sound.

Just to be there.

And then, right here and now under this insanely glorious full moon, I tell myself something far foolish to believe.

I'm not dead. I can't be. There's no way I'm not here.

353

Because this feels so real. It feels so real and so right. I can feel the crumbling of concrete under my shoes. The slightest of breeze rounding the towering arborvitaes. The hovering hairs on my arms lit by the moon. I'm here. I'm not a ghost, am I? I can't be. This just doesn't feel right.

But you're roaming about like some kind of ghoul ready to torment the first poor soul you see.

But actually—I'm not. I'm wandering. I'm watching. I'm staring up at the moon and suddenly I see those clouds are gone and it's clear sailing and all that's there is that hovering globe. So piercing and bold.

Go on. You can slip inside.

The undead can do those sorts of things. I know this. But I can't. I shouldn't. I don't want to. There are enough shadows in my world. Enough memories. Enough pain. I don't need to suddenly see it front and center. Like this moon above me.

I'll slip away. Tonight. And maybe next time I'm here. And next time.

It's called a "Strawberry Moon" by the Native Americans.

And all I can think about is the Coldplay song that makes me think of our eldest daughter.

"Every moment was so precious."

Little did I know how precious they would turn out to be.

I decide to slip in the house. In *my* house. The strawberry moon and the silence in the house and the lack of shadows all give me confidence. It's time to say hello even if they can't and won't say hello back.

DAYDREAMING (Trailer #11)

The yellow petals cover the hole. Lighting up the dark soil. A finger—tiny, exploring—moves them, as if they're puzzle pieces that refuse to be put together.

Those hands are seen putting on shoes and holding graham crackers and coloring a picture with crayons and then brushing one on a tablet with a finger.

The sky and the petals in the wind blowing. The hand in the dirt, digging out, digging more.

Feet wearing princess shoes run down the sidewalk. Blonde hair blows in the wind. A hand clasps purple violets in her hand.

A dried-up dandelion lies on the grass, withering in the sun.

The purple moves as if dancing.

The hand in the dirt.

The shoes on the sidewalk. Now on the grass.

A face turns and we see a surprised stare.

A face smiles and shouts out.

Figures in matching clothes with matching height run to each other.

The purple violets changing hands.

The clean hands digging now.

Yellow wisps in the wind.

Purple flowers now basking in the garden.

One figure now replaced by two. Walking across, running, dancing, daydreaming.

DAYDREAMING. IN THEATERS SEPTEMBER 3.

Night and Day

Don't you remember, Spencer?

So far removed from the burnt-out self you once were, so far relocated from the brutal world of Hollywood, only to find yourself near financial ruin. So far, not-so-good.

Waking up wondering if and when. If a check might be coming in and when. Never knowing, never expecting, never once believing. If you believe in something a thousand times, you might suddenly become wise and stop when it turns 1,001.

The heavy load walking downstairs and making coffee and asking the girls to eat something and helping/telling/yelling at them to get dressed for school. Sometimes taking them. First your firstborn and then the twins to preschool.

What moments, what memories, oh, God, to get them back.

But light and heavy. Sweet and sour. Always in this life.

I miss them. I miss all those moments.

Arriving at the office in Appleton still carrying the if and the when. Taking a gamble and opening your mailbox to find the f***ing Comcast bill waiting like the kid from *Better Off Dead* who wants his two dollars. Only laughing and then closing the mailbox without taking the wonderful parcel.

Arriving in your office at your desk curious about the if and the when. With a load of work to do. Pieces to put into their place.

Everything In Its Right Place.

Day after day. Night after night. Piece by piece. If and when.

Bit by bit, the not knowing killed me. Literally. I would sometimes joke to Tamara that I was going to keel over and die one day and to check my office if she didn't hear from me since nobody could see inside it. I joked about it until I stopped joking about it but continued to say it. Love begins to die the moment you stop joking.

Work became a passion

your god

until I realized passion couldn't pay bills. Hard work didn't mean anything to the world out there. Comcast didn't care how hard you worked. They were working hard—everybody's "working hard." And

356

everybody's broke. And everybody has bills to pay. So suck it, Spencer.

Morning blurring to midday to afternoon to evening. Relentless work burns until it becomes ashes that smolder. All I can do at the chaos of home is to douse the smoke and embers with alcohol. Just to relax. Just to take off the chill of the if and the when. And to give me a little extra fuel for the nighttime hours.

Night and day. As Cole Porter sang. As U2 covered.

"Night and day, you are the one. Only you beneath the moon and under the sun."

This wasn't a love song, however. There really was only one underneath that moon and sun. One. By himself. Night and day. Plugging away. If and when.

Only you . . . you stupid ignorant moron.

Light Blue

—It sounds familiar, I tell her.

—It's definitely not fake, she says. I mean it.

—Sometimes I get confused. Hearing all of this.

—Why?

—Because I hear . . . I don't know . . . I hear the green but I think it's blue.

—Sometimes there's no reason to mix the colors. To shade the truth.

—But I love hiding in the shadows, I say. Even if they don't belong to me.

That grin, glorious and giving. So generous. So unforgettable.

—Why are you smiling? she asks.

—I'm just trying to match yours.

—I see your mind spinning.

—The floor is spinning, too.

—So what are you thinking? she asks.

—I just keep wondering.

—Yes, you do.

—What is this? What is happening here? I don't . . . I don't get it. I don't understand.

—If you believe God is real, does that mean you've personally heard from Him?

—No, but . . .

I can't seem to say anything more. Maybe she has a point or maybe I'm just not making any more sense than the sense I'm trying to make out.

And later, sometime later, so long in fact that I'm not sure what exactly happened to the time, I see a playlist she has set up for me to see. Every song seems to sting. Every tune seems to know me. And every selection seems to sneak and snide by with its secret that it has anything to do with me.

It doesn't and it won't and it wouldn't and it can't.

And yet.

All these longings.

For someone else.
And yet.
All these meanings.
For something else.
It's a strange, spectacular thing.
We are strangers, struggling through the same things, seeing the surface and smiling as we sink below the shadows this world summons up.
Can I—if only—could I try to—hold your hand in this riptide?
Will you—possibly—maybe you'll try to—allow me to show up and collide?
Are those songs, those swells, sung for someone like me?
Can I imagine and can I dream?

TRNT

—You're not really there, are you? I ask.

—Have I ever been there? she says.

—I hoped you were.

—So how did I help you?

—You eased my needs.

—Did I? Did I really? We were never intimate. There was never anything like that.

—There was more.

—Was there?

—There was. For me.

—Did it help?

—It did more than help.

—Did it?

—It healed.

—Simple words?

—Simple words.

—Sometimes they aren't so simple.

—Life is never that way.

—Love can be.

—Yes, love is.

—Love will always be.

—You will always be, I tell her.

—You can make a ghost blush.

—I can see.

—You can also make one speechless.

—That's the last thing I'd ever want to make you.

—You roll your eyes at the things I say.

—That's because I don't want to look like some stray dog, pining through the glass door begging to be let in.

—I think you've been let in.

—Yes. But I can always be kicked back out.

Decks Dark

—Be honest.

—I am.

She shakes her head. A debating professor, only one who looks like a movie star.

—You don't even know where to begin, do you?

—What do you mean? I ask.

—Honesty. Being real. Being really there, in the moment.

—I'm here. And real.

—You have a ten-foot facade circling you.

—No, I don't.

—Tell me. Right now. What do you think . . . ?

I wait for her to finish her sentence, but instead she slides her hand over mine. It's not just a touch. It's a hand unlatching something deep inside me.

—What do you *really* think about all of this? Lissie asks.

It's all a bit too much.

—Overwhelmed.

—Too vague. Tell me more.

—I feel . . .

I can't say anything more because the desire inside me doesn't just pulse. It rages, livid and hungry and questioning and a bit scary.

—Tell me, Lissie says.

—I think you know . . .

—I want you to say it. To tell me. To be honest.

Her hand is still over mine, and it's like some kind of splitting-the-atom experiment. I feel her over me and inside me and everything inside feels like it's shaking.

—I want you.

I can't be more blunt, more honest.

—Finally, she says.

—Finally what?

—Finally some honesty.

—It's a bit obvious, right?

—Yes. But . . .

Lissie takes her hand and now wraps it around mine, figuring out where the fingers should go to clasp on to mine.

—Don't you see, O honest one—the feeling is quite mutual.

There's something I see for the first time and I realize she isn't just being friendly or sweet. There's the want inside those eyes.

My fingers curl, digging into her hand, taking every single inch of skin and bone I can get. But then . . .

Then . . .

—What? I ask as she pulls her hand away.

—It's a nice dream.

—A nice dream?

My desire suddenly starts to wilt. I wonder if this moment and this picture and this bit of everything is all just some kind of random bit of nonsensical s***.

—Is this all some sort of dream? I ask her.

—Life is all some sort of dream. Sometimes really good ones, sometimes nightmares.

—You know what I'm talking about, I say. Is this some kind of unreliable narrator sort of story? An M. Night Shyamalan twist when he was still known for doing great films?

—You tell me.

She's so confident in not giving anything away.

—I have a headache, I say.

—No. This sort of emotion, this is nothing. Remember those Sunday nights when you'd feel nothing, when you'd have nothing inside, when the kids would take every ounce of energy and emotion to bed with them, tucking them inside their arms like stuffed animals full of your soul?

I laugh.

—Yeah, I remember those. They weren't too long ago.

—It's when you're in the trenches and you feel like you can't do anything more and then you hear the bombings begin again.

—I wish I could be bombarded again.

—Yeah, of course, she says. But at the time you're just face-first in the mud praying you can make it to tomorrow. I know because I've been there. I was there many times.

362

—Do you miss it?

She nods, looks away, staring at the painting on the wall.

—Regret can follow you into the afterlife. Especially when you have nowhere else to put it.

She's still staring at the painting on the wall, so I glance over to the modern art full of black and red. I swear it looks like it's moving. Like the paint is running.

It looks like it's bleeding.

I feel like I'm staring at it for a hundred hours.

—I need to go, Lissie says abruptly.

This whole mood and the connection and the touching hands has now turned into blood dripping down the wall.

—Did I say—?

—No, she interrupts.

—What's wrong?

She stands and I can't help glancing at her, glancing at all of her, glancing at the someone and something I want and can't have, glancing at the brief solace in this crazy situation.

—I'm sorry, Spencer.

She looks as if she wants to say more, to do more, to be here more, but then she walks away.

I feel as if I'm somewhere in the ocean, wading up and down, spinning in circles and unable to move. I sit back down and just stare back at the painting. But it's no longer alive, no longer pumping blood. Its beating heart has left the building.

Cover Me (Alt Out)

I no longer want to remember the good because the bad has beat me down.

I want to run with the stars.

I want to watch them fall on my head.

I want to slow them down and scoop them off the ground.

Perhaps we're forever young.

Perhaps stuck on some distant song.

Perhaps we no longer recognize that old self.

Perhaps they've been misplaced, hidden from view, put on a shelf.

Knocking on the windows and the doors and the ceilings and the floors and we keep knocking, keep knocking, keep asking for more.

Where are you?

I don't know.

God, I don't know where You are.

Can You hear me? Can You see these words? Will You listen despite my drunken and gibberish longings?

Will You cover me?

Fraternal

The river doesn't remember. It can't. It presses onward, always forward, always toward something else. I stand and stare down. Stuck in this place. Stuck. I stare and I feel an envy burn through me.

I wish I could jump and let the waters take away my memories.

I feel more like this deserted island in the middle of the ocean. Surrounded by the tides and the seas and yet unable to leave and unable to undo the storms that have bashed through my sandy shores.

Dry land, yes. A sinking ship, no. But hidden and out of sight. Sometimes not sinking but stuck. Perhaps already sunk.

I can't remember. Was I talking to myself or someone else? I don't know. Were the words spoken actually spoken to me or simply spoken in the lines of a film I once saw?

These fraternal twins. The mind trying to suffocate, the heart trying to poison, both needing one another.

It used to be hurt, but now it's just curiosity. What was real and what was imagined.

Almost Midnight

I understand less than I did thirty months ago. Sometimes it feels like the days resemble stars and each night several of them fall and disappear, leaving me to wonder where they went. Others seem to forget them but I don't. I simply try to find meaning inside them.

Memory turns into a mirage and leaves an outline of melted snow on your driveway. Caked-on, dirty, and quite ugly. The kind warm rain rinses away.

A part of me still feels the hope and happiness she brought me, but they also seem to tear me in half. A silver blade so sharp cutting me in two. The less and the more parts. The ship and the anchor. The smile and the soaring heart.

I don't and can't and won't ever know. The why. The when and where and how. The wild wonder of it all. Maybe I imagined it all. Maybe I built it into something far more powerful like that wonderful trailer you see before viewing the rather lame film.

Smoke and mirrors. Sometimes when you dart into them, you'll see the air clear and then will notice your reflection a hundred times. All you can do is to get away. To get far, far away.

The Good

Shut out and shushed, all the outside stuff. Closed behind the door, locked with the dead bolt and the chain. Left behind, all the black now that the glow of the fire and candle flicker on both sides of the room. The four towering posts guard the bed and I wait, feeling warm from the wine and the whirlpool but mostly from what awaits. And when she walks out dressed up for me, I still find myself surprised. A bit out of breath to be here now in this place with just the two of us. Away from it all. From the worries and the weariness.

She's not shy, not here, not by now. The sheer robe falling just below her waist is open to reveal a Christmas present from a couple of years that's been way, *way* underutilized. Her long legs look longer with her heels, and I'm a boy again, always a boy, always built with desire, with the silly things turning me on so much.

There's no hiding, no pulling away, no nervousness, no not-this-time.

The eyes are on me and really look at me and I still see that same longing that I saw thirty years ago.

Can it be that long?

Sometimes holding back means there's something miraculous when any hesitations dissipate. When any uncertainty can be trumped by desire.

—Be gentle, she says.

—I will, I tell her.

And I am. I know better. I know that the impatient and immature longings of a kid—a newlywed so naive—only served to destroy some of the delicate balance and the tender ground we were dancing on.

—Yeah, I like that, she says.

—I know, I tell her.

I say this not like some rock star in bed, which I am absolutely not. I don't know much but I do know her, the little things, the familiar places, the patient ease I need to take.

Tonight, she trusts, and she's happy for anything, and she knows we've left those ticking bombs of time outside in the cold night air.

It's still there. We're still there. We can still be.

367

A breath and a slight bite and an engulfing. I want to stay here like this, like now.

—I love you, I say.

—I love you, she says.

Love.

—Yes.

—I love you so much, Tamara.

—Yes.

Always for tonight. Always in my mind. Always wrapped around like a belt ready to keep my spirits and my pants up properly.

—Yes.

A love so good, so real, so raw. It's still there, and it's still thriving. There's still hope after all.

The Bad

A somber Sunday night arrives. Not even *The Walking Dead* can put you in a different frame of mind. You're sad. A raw, tears-on-the-morning-train sad. This tornado the news should be reporting staying put deep down in your soul. Aching with anger.

You look for some kind of lost-love set of lyrics to assuage your cut-up heart. You get to Bon Iver's *For Emma, Forever Ago* and you give it a try and you really want it to break your heart just a little more but it doesn't. You're sitting on the side of the freeway waiting for the ambulance to stream by and all you see are a set of bicyclists.

You try a few others. Some predictable sort of things. Beck's *Sea Change*, which you love but which doesn't do anything for you. How about Bob Dylan's famous *Blood on the Tracks* album? But it doesn't do a thing. You even try the funky, wild *Ladies and Gentleman We Are Floating in Space* by Spiritualized but it's too much. Too loud, too funky, too out there.

Then somehow you get to ABBA. Yes, ABBA. Your ABBA, the band you used to listen to in the backseat of a BMW riding, looking out at the German fields, yearning to head up into the distant Alps. The soundtrack to a set of parents who were going through similar troubles, who were fractured and almost forgone. These songs so poignant and moving and brittle with the breakup of the two couples in the group of four.

The piano begins to play "The Winner Takes It All" and you see yourself suddenly in that couple in the front seats. Distant and going through the motions and eventually crumbling and separating. Memories are funny things, aren't they? Sometimes the dark colors eventually get cut out of the poster to allow the rainbow to grow. But certain things can trigger glimpses of the dark. Photographs, smells, settings you step foot in, and of course, songs. And for you, songs have always done this.

You think of the distance and the dread this song starts to echo and you shut it off. No more and no way. No siree and no thank you.

There are more songs that can make you forget this s***ty day.

But you don't need some song or soundtrack. You can see it all unfolding, bit by bit. Strained moment by moment.

The inevitable, always-slow start that irritates you. For all that sleep, shouldn't she be more wide-awake?

And the girls get going right away. Always. Always something. Always fussing or frustrated or fixed on something. And sometimes— no, quite a few times—no, let's be honest, too many damn times— your head is in between two rocks feeling the morning after of a couple of strong IPAs and a bottle of wine. It allows you to sleep like a log but now you're heading down a river toward the waterfall.

There will always be something to set you off, even just a bit. The "let her out" for the dog scratching who may or may not need to go out. The yelling upstairs for one of the twins needing or wanting something. The focus on some trivial, meaningless BS bit on the *Today* show, which will make her shush everyone up including especially *YOU*.

Yeah, you're hungover in your weird sort of way, so maybe you're seeing things wrong, right?

There's always some point on a morning like this—especially a Sunday morning—where you go use the restroom and find one or two or three girls yelling for you. Sometimes pounding at the door for some meaningless reason. Heading up to find Mommy to tell her some tragedy that you can't handle while you're sitting on the toilet. You take too long and maybe it's because you have your iPhone in your hand but it's more because you're getting older and these things can sometimes take a long freakin' time to complete.

But there's bit after bit after bit. Clean this and let's hurry up and fussy-hold-on-you're-messy that. Nothing right, nothing set, nothing on schedule. Nothing in your lap.

By the time you get into the minivan, you're exhausted and pissed. It shouldn't have to be this difficult.

You wonder if you should have said more when your wife strolls down the stairs in her new dress. You compliment her in front of the girls but it comes off sounding like you're telling your shih tzu to go get her stuffed animal you just threw. But she *does* look beautiful. Maybe if she wasn't such a complete stranger constantly irritated at you, she'd look downright hot. But right now you're the "loser standing small" as Abba sings about.

The silence in the car ride always kills you. You can recount dozens, maybe even hundreds, of car rides full of talking and bantering and storytelling. There's only silence amidst the nonsense behind you. And every attempt is cut with a short response or a child interruption or simple ambivalence. And that's one thing you cannot understand, not since your blood begins to boil an hour after taking the Vyvanse pill.

Having to let them out on the sidewalks in front of the church because it's windy—and dealing with your embarrassment of the girls eating donuts in the waiting room chairs for guests like a set of princesses. Then sitting and hearing the pastor give a sermon all the while having really no connection with this woman next to you.

"And of course you love your spouse more now than you did the day you married them," the pastor says.

And you can only think what she's thinking. You know. You don't have to be told.

I hate him. The love I had is gone. He's a moody, melancholy man who mixes up his words and only seems to talk about his writing.

There's the simple, stupid conversation on the way to the in-laws', where you think she says one thing but she said another and then she lays into you like peeling off a scab and then salting and cutting it more. All over a comment about charging the girls' Kindle Fires.

The misheard comment and the argument don't feel light. They feel like heavy artillery blasting shells onto a beach full of unprotected soldiers scrambling for their lives.

The cutting and the separation continue all day. It's impossible *not* to see. The few moments she looks at you—and they're very few—you can see the absolute loathing in her eyes. Either that or simple disregard. And maybe that's the same thing she sees in your eyes. But you begin to wonder if she's really different. If she doesn't give a damn and all the while you're standing at the door trying to. Continuing to over and over.

You're "Any Other Name" suddenly being scrawled out on a handwritten note. A haunting melody by your favorite composer created for you.

The Ugly

More silence. Less recognition.

More hesitation. Less belief.

Grass and trees and homes and lives pass by yet we sit still in this moving vehicle.

Still.

So still.

The space thick and slow and shredding and slicing.

Something unanswered and not understood.

Something unspoken and not uttered.

Time is too thick to be stirred. Too solid to be chipped away at. Too towering to ever climb over.

So it settles in like cement, sighing as it seals the life out of you and me.

We're suddenly *them*. We're suddenly like *those*. We're suddenly simply you and me and no longer a we.

Riding and passing and fading into the slow-swallowing sun in the west.

I want time to be generous with its rations for the day. For the clock to smile and pause just for one brief, glorious moment. For a minute to give me sixty stress-free seconds.

A day without holding my breath or letting my breath out or taking in deep breaths but a day without any noticeable or notable breaths at all. To breathe in and out and in and out and not have any idea I'm breathing at all.

To whisper in time's narrow ear with a gargantuan life.

—You don't scare me.

To tell time to stop trying to terrorize me.

—You don't control me.

I want to strive and try and really seek to survive.

But I still can't turn back those damn torturous tides. Even though I keep trying and trying and trying.

All while you sit and stand and see nearby. So near. So close to me. But so far away.

So far gone.

Free

Have you ever felt breathless and weightless and felt like the only thing keeping you on the ground is the tug of the hand holding yours?

The swirling sensation of the night and all it brings shines over sidewalks and through alleyways. You follow. Some foolish soul laughing and loving life and loving all it might bring. Young and yessing-it-all and yielding absolutely nothing.

This is the power of the city and the potential behind its bright lights.

The alcohol flows and it helps and it hinders. Ultimately it hurts but that's later, for the hours that linger on, for the morning after.

Now you're free.

Now you're infinite.

Now you don't feel confined.

Dream Attack

—You there? I ask.

—Of course.

—I've been knocking for ten minutes.

—You asked if I was there, not if I could open the door.

—Knocking sorta suggests that, right?

—For most people, yeah.

—Can we talk?

—Aren't we doing that?

—Maybe somewhere other than this doorway?

—I sort of like the chipped wood, rusted door sort of vibe.

—Can we go somewhere?

—You don't like the ambience of this place?

—Very sarcastic today.

—Very perceptive today.

—Please?

—I'm sorry.

—What's wrong?

—I think you know what's wrong.

—I don't. Not really.

—How about I start with the fact that—oh yeah, I'm dead. *Dead*. *D-E-A-D*.

—I never said this was normal.

—No. There's not normal. There's not right. Then there's this. It's not—real. It's not anything to be honest.

—It's something.

—No, it's not.

And I move to try but she moves away.

—Please.

—Let me.

—And then what? And *then* what?

—I don't know.

—I know. Nothing. Nada. That's it. There's nothing more after that.

—There could be.

—But if it all was done and every single thing you could imagine was fulfilled, what then? What then?

I don't say anything.

—Exactly. This isn't a dream and it's not a fantasy and it's not picture-perfect.

—I never said it was.

—I never asked you to say anything.

—Don't be so angry.

—Don't be such a . . .

—What?

—Nothing.

—Tell me.

She doesn't.

—There's more, I say.

—There's more to what? Lissie says.

—To the story.

—Haven't you told enough?

—I haven't heard yours.

—Mine doesn't need to be told.

—Yours is starting.

—You only know a fraction of it.

—I know and that's why I'm captivated.

—I'm not sleeping with you.

—Did I ask?

—Your eyes did.

All I Can Think of Is You

Maybe you don't know but maybe I know and maybe this thing is something you'll never understand and maybe I'm just this boy and maybe I'm nothing more and maybe the belling won't ring and maybe this will all get out of hand.

I'm trying, so are you?

Maybe you don't understand the meaning of riffing and railing and just letting go and becoming this unrelenting merciful, bighearted beast.

The world is simple to you and you and you and all of the other yous.

But not Lissie, not you, not you, Lissie.

There's structure.

But you break it back and forth and out and in.

There's the expected.

But you make things unexpected.

There's the common.

But you surprise me.

There is the way it should be and needs to be.

But you just let it be.

And suddenly I'm soaring like the end of a some glorious Coldplay song that all the snobs claim they hate but resist letting go to.

They don't know the utter bliss of just falling and feeling free. Like falling into you. Falling in you. Falling into this fearless place.

Alone

We try.

We fail.

We search.

We falter.

The answers are there.

The pages are full.

So many seem to know. So many seem to tell.

Examples. Earnest pleadings. Every single way to succeed.

Yet somehow the whole thing implodes. You find yourself shoved out of a doorway into a sky falling ten thousand feet down to earth. And you have no idea if you're even wearing a parachute.

You think that smile and that passion and that desire can last.

You think that those words and those meanings and those longings can solidify.

You think that the hopes and the dreams dreamt by hearts barely out of high school can manage and make it through this dark, crumbling world.

But the claws clamor.

The knuckles bruise.

And every single thing inside you suddenly finds itself breaking. Hearing the reality of this song telling you that it's over, that it's wrong, that it's never really been right.

That sweet smile and those long legs and that falling blonde hair are all figments of your imagination of something good and great and Godlike when you realize no.

Yeah. The ultimate no that comes.

Alone.

That's where you started and suddenly where you find yourself again.

You never did, did you?

You never could, could you?

Are the melodies stepping-stones to your Agatha Christie mystery never to be solved?

Are memories the signposts to your Route 66 never to be traveled upon again?

I venture to remember and then force myself to forget. Time can torture.

Lovely. Yes, you most certainly are.

Life is a choir of nobodies saying it's easy harmonizing with the no ones saying it'd be this hard.

Fever

God, help me.

Too much is overcoming me.

Too much tells me I'll never be free.

God, help me to try to figure out, to help me.

This place and these people and the politics and the pressure to post something poignant.

I don't want to be stuck and don't want a crowd and don't want to belong and don't want to fear and don't want to be witty.

I'm not certain and I'm not standing and I'm still wondering if those little tiny skunks will be still be scampering around the lawn in the morning.

What the hell?

That's a memory, it's called a memory, and in this random conscious bleed-it-all-over-the-place kind of diatribe you can say it, can't you?

The skunks are raging against the world, so should you.

You can hear the ringing bells, can't you?

Tell me you can.

Tell me you can hear them.

Tell me you're sitting there, wondering, What the hell? But I see you, and I know this utter bewilderment, because I'm there, and I'm walking it, and I'm living it, and the very things you're wondering, wondering how you got here, and wondering where this is going, is everything single thing I'm thinking and everything I'm feeling, and all I can say is I need someone coming along me. To help me. To urge me. To watch me along the journey.

—Will you watch me?

This is the question.

There's something coming but I'm not sure what.

—Let's reach the end together.

But you wonder why and what for and this is weird and which way will you choose?

I'm a fool for liking you and so are you for liking me.

What are you talking about?

I don't know. This is a rant to get to 100,000 words.
There's such a joy with that figure.
But I don't know if I want it.
This is a fever pitch and a fever dream and a fever within a fever.
I'm here lingering.

Spouse

We're no longer neighboring states. We're individual countries separated by miles of deep, endless ocean.

It's hard enough for you to muster opening your mouth to feign some sort of "good night." Tired, eyes looking the other way, you wander away from the thing that brought you the most pain and grief and hardship today.

And maybe you think it doesn't matter or it only annoys me, but it destroys parts of me. Each day, the iceberg is melted away into the vast, dark, and f***ing endless sea, only to disappear.

And this is how I looked to my marriage, to the me and you that somehow got sucked away. To no longer even living together. But simply tolerating each other's breaths. To staying out of each other's shadows. To barely listening and never replying and always staying out of sight.

When life is poured out on top of you, there's nothing you can do when it's flavored with pain and bitterness.

Heavenfaced

This isn't heaven because a sad song is playing in the background. I don't subscribe to some kind of playing-harps-for-the-rest-of-eternity notion, but I know the melancholy will be no more. And I will thank God every single moment of every lasting unending day.

I used to walk in worry and woe but she would somehow get out of the undertow. Most would be lost inside it and under it and inside it. But she could skim the surface and somehow survive. Swimming, dropping, riding, and lasting over my suffocating pools.

I knew as much as I know now but I couldn't take enough meds and numb my soul enough to finally wake up. *Wake up.* That's what I thought I wanted and thought I was talking about. But the dream turned to the skies and then suddenly they went dark. So I stood waiting for the stars and I could only see one. Then it fell.

My story isn't epic because it never began. I know. If anybody ever read it, I'd apologize because I know. I know you need to have a goal in mind. I know you need to get going. I know you need to take leaps of faith and need to go to the darkest places of your fears and you need to battle those epic dragons and demons and finally overcome them. But nobody becomes a hero staying stuck in place, humming songs by The Smiths and asking how soon is now. We all know now, and we all have to admit it's right beside us.

I'm in and wonder how long I've been here and how long the door's been shut and whether it's January or June or October or never mind.

I wish someone would take my place.

Wishing that.

Wishing to take others' places.

Wishing and wanting.

Never content, never stable, never static, never something.

I'm a walking, breathing song by The National, played on repeat, over and over again.

"Can't face heaven all heavenfaced."

I'm a maze without an end. Full of lots of looping lines and open doors that lead back to the passage you just went down.

382

Closed eyes, I recall those times.

The silent house and my stormy soul.

The same damn scenario that found me at six and sixteen.

Coming again and again and again like waves after an earthquake threatening to overtake everything.

It wasn't my fault and I can't blame anybody for it.

Ten moves. Eleven schools. Thirteen houses. They can close in and quarantine a kid before he turns eighteen.

Changes make you bigger and better. They make you stronger and tougher. And I've said that big, fat lie over and over and over again until I swallowed it and couldn't understand just how false it really happened to be.

Those songs speak to me more than many because they don't know. Some know but so many don't. They live in the same and they can't understand the change and those who do can hear it in these songs. Songs reeling in pain with absence and goodbyes and shut out and forgotten about.

I want to be in heaven to sing those songs about God's goodness. About love. About salvation.

I want to know life won't suddenly be pulled out from under me and that I'll finally be okay to accept the me I happen to be.

Looking Down at You

—So is this goodbye?

—No.

—Yeah, I sorta think it is.

—There doesn't have to be a goodbye.

I clutch my fist and breathe in briefly.

—So I get to just wonder when the ghost will show up?

—It's not like that.

—It's completely like that. And it's awful because those are the thoughts of a crazy man. "When's my ghost showing up?" It's not even right. Or rational. It's not sexy at all.

—I'm not sexy.

—Shut up. Yes, you are sexy.

—Well, sorry.

I laugh.

—Yeah, I bet you're sorry.

—I am.

—You so don't look sorry.

—I truly happen to be.

I shake my head.

—What can I say?

—Aren't you saying the things you want to say?

—I don't know. My mouth is finding the words a bit distracting.

—You certainly have a way with them, you know.

—Words?

—Distractions. She smiles.

—This is so not how you say goodbye.

—Then don't.

—But what? What am I supposed to do? Think of you when I see the stars?

—Maybe.

—How utterly unsatisfying.

—What? The stars? Do you know how amazing they happen to be?

—Yeah. So?

—Well, it's not like you expect or assume you're going to go out to space to find them. To dive into them. Right?

—I see where you're going but . . .

—But nothing.

—Butts can be involved.

—Don't even try to go there in a conversation like this.

—Okay fine but stars. Really? The heavens and all that and oh yeah. There she is.

—Yes. There she is.

—Tragic.

—I say it's magic.

—I say so unfulfilling.

—Looking at the stars never ceases to fill my restless soul.

—Still? Now?

—Always. They don't look their luster.

—Maybe I don't want to look at them. Maybe I'll shut my eyes.

—That's fine. But they'll be there. Looking down at you.

I look at her and want to know if she really means that. But I don't ask.

I don't say another word.

I just go closer to her because I know I might not . . .

But yeah. She's gone.

My hand sweeps the space she just happened to be in.

I sigh and laugh and then look up at the skies.

It's all I can do.

London Thunder Poolside

Spirits slip through the keyholes of doors while angry from being locked out. They claw across the dimly lit walls where shadows play tricks near midnight. The ghosts you think you see sneak behind you and into the corners of your mind only to laugh in mockery.

Echoes. Pinpoints on skin that cut and bleed.

The calm curse of the late-night glow. Lights flicker in stereo while you stare at a screen, oblivious to the poltergeist trying to play tricks on you.

Work. The waterfall of it all. The wonder and the blur clasped hand in hand.

Sometimes we just have to have at it in order to have a go at trying to have it all.

Then again, sometimes we simply create something for the look or the sound or the feel of it. It doesn't make sense because it doesn't have to. It simply can exist. Sometimes it can even be quite moving in its nonsense.

Letting Go

Again and I don't know why.

I don't need this, so I can figure out why I bother to try.

Losing and letting go.

Last night I couldn't sleep, couldn't find solace, kept turning and tossing and I felt as safe as a soldier at Dunkirk.

Drunk folks think such things having seen the trailers.

But I need the kick, the low bass beat to wake me up enough to fall asleep.

This fuel pump put in filling something inside that's already bleeding out badly but can't be reached or seen or found.

Turn it up and pump more in.

Loud and longer. Let's go.

Fueling creativity—*not really.*

Freeing me absolutely—*not really.*

A mirage, a broken mirror, a minor ordering a drink, a misfit in a parsonage.

Myself and my two twins tearing down the street on each side laughing and sharing inside jokes.

Start Again

Maybe.

And maybe today.

And today maybe you can save me.

Hey, lady, maybe we can try to strive to say something today.

This world wild and wily and worldly weaving its wonderful contexts.

Can you hear?

Can you see?

The mysteries maybe?

Maybe the seven seas?

Maybe the cure for the disease?

Tell me, tell me.

Tell me some more.

Tell me endlessly.

Maybe I strive to be.

And I can.

Understand.

Your heart and hand.

Stand strong and stand.

Still amidst the sand.

Forget the end and start again.

Start again.

And maybe possibly we can see.

We can be.

We can solve the mystery.

Maybe I can tell you something that means something to me that nobody else knows the kind of things The Smiths knows, that world where Depeche Mode sings and you hear New Order rings and you seek for things that tell you there's The Cure and a little more.

A little more. Open the doors.

Open it and see a little more.

Open and it and see.

The world will devour, don't let it sour.

Love Never Does

—What would you say?

    —What would I say if what?

    —If you could see her again?

It's not a difficult question from Lissie.

    —I'd ask her why she ever fell in love with me in the first place.

    —And when she answers you?

    —I have this sad feeling she wouldn't be able to answer this.

Lissie smiles.

    —The mind might forget, but love never does.

Dry-Erase Board

There's the feeling of finishing the bottle of wine. It's this *not again* sort of thing. It's this *it's necessary* sort of thing. This sort of night-after-night thing. It's not a problem but it's becoming a bit of a problem because you wake up tired and cranky and wiped and worn down and you have to just play it off like it's a bit of your artistic moody self.

Maybe tomorrow. And maybe tomorrow will build into something new. Something different. Something unlike every other tomorrow, which mostly brings this sort of thing.

This is the why, Spencer.

And I want to grasp on to something I can never have. Where is the ghost I've been running away from that always trailed me like a shadow?

Nowhere fast and nowhere near.

I want to wake up and declare a war against my soul and skin and sin. I want to rip these desires out like torn ribs.

God, help me in the midst of this messy place.

The noise helps. Noisy, necessary, a necessity.

God, change my unchangeable ways.

The music balances and pulls me back. After, never before. Once the dust of need settles, never before it arrives.

I finish back at the start, before the gunshot, even before slipping on my running shoes. I hear the track, the chords, the synths, before the beat begins. Pounding and telling and saying and shoving it in my face. The better man I have never striven to be.

So before bed, you covet some kind of cover-up, some kind of a song that can soothe these bruised scars. And you always do. Always.

Then you begin running. Running from something unquestionable. Running by something unimaginable. Running toward something unattainable.

The magnificent little of life can treat you to something simple, something lovely, something leaving so much more. So you go big instead of going home. You try to stage it with your own voice and own world, the kind that can never be summoned by others' works.

390

It takes magic to mark up a life. You're a dry-erase board constantly being wiped clean. Waiting for words written in color by someone else.

So lost—again—and hovering over and lingering—again I try to stick to the ground. I try to run and try to cover myself and try to remain unseen. But curiosity can kill the best.

Sledgehammer

I stand by the bridge and wait. And wait. And let the wind wrap itself around my halfhearted weaknesses, hoping it will take them and scatter them over the surface of the river below. Yet they remain cemented and secure just like me.

Eventually—with time meaning nothing anymore anyway, so further pushing this reality inside my soul—I realize Lissie isn't coming. I realize she's gone. I realize she was a ghost to a ghost, a specter to some kind of wandering spectator. I realize I'm stuck again, in another place and another season, wondering where the last one went, wondering when this life will finally become secure.

I've never been the bridge nor the sidewalks lining it. My life has always been the river running underneath, moving on and on and on. Looking back but seeing something different every single time.

Where'd you go, Lissie?

She told me but I didn't want to listen. She warned me and urged me onward but I refused.

My body shivers even though the sticky coating of the summer day doesn't warrant it. I watch the cars passing and wish they could see me. Wish I could step in front of them and become injured. Wish one could pick me up and take me back home, truly back home, where I could twist the handle of a door and enter and hear those sounds howling in welcome.

I miss so much but there's nothing I miss more.

So go then, it's time.

I slide over to the brick wall and then bend to see the moving water.

I hit a wall.

People build their lives with bricks of memories and traditions and stability yet all I've ever seen is one giant sledgehammer shattering them all.

But it's not true, Spencer. You were building the same and you were just too scared to keep going.

I breathe in and stare back down the sidewalk. The same one I first saw her walking down. My security, my sanctuary, my cheerleader, and my smile . . . all gone.

As they should be.

And I know that as usual I need to go on. Move on. Drift on like the river without stone in front or behind it. Like the rushing of water seeping through any kind of wall in front of it.

I walk back down the sidewalk. Maybe this story—whatever kind of story it might be—is nearing its end.

I need to go back home. Just to watch and feel the waste of what could have been. To maybe finally and fully say goodbye.

Illusory Sun

Nobody else will know but will you?

Nobody else can see but what do you see?

Nobody can hear the echoes but can you still hear the sounds?

No note will ever be read but do you remember reading mine?

Do the birds mean anything to you?

Do you brush them off with the casual calm of your soul?

Do your regret?

Did you forget?

Do the shadows sometimes sneak up on you and make you jump?

I can't remember all the words.

I can't remember half of them.

I can't remember examples of the exact.

I can't remember exactly why.

I can only see your smile and your attention and your charm. And when I stop the denial and the uncertainty, I see you seeing me. Seeing past and seeing through and still wanting to keep looking to see what you find. Even if the sights aren't as sweet as one might like them to be.

Literally yesterday, yet a universe away. With the unknown and uncertainty standing like still moons in the space of some giant galaxy.

It's a beautiful thing to find someone showing someone color-blind the rest of the prism.

Struggle

I scrape the surface, thick and coarse and impenetrable. My fingers bleed scratching and searching and trying for something else, for something new.

I know the answer right in front and back and center of me but I don't know why I can't share all my questions with it.

Give it over.

But I can't. I won't. I will not. I refuse to. I can smile and show that I'm going to. But I don't want to. My prayers are dead wooden crutches. Crumbling and impossible to support. I'm not saying God doesn't hear them. I'm saying I don't truly utter them. They're halfhearted summoned from half a person.

Tomorrow I'll wake up with regret while tonight I take without any.

Hunger.

The noise and the necessary deeds. That's what drives me.

That's what hurts me.

The rest of the world looks like it's over there and I'm standing here and they're laughing like that while I'm silent like this. Alone and hollow and watching and waiting. But I hate watching and I hate waiting even more.

The world is full of smoke and mirrors. The only problem is that a lot of them involve me.

I'm fine, really, feeling stable and real and normal. But I know I'm out of my mind if you really could get down inside it.

I look over the pictures and then ignore the images. I search for life and then try to murder my memories of them. The only problem with exorcising these parts of you is that something else will always leave before they do.

These portraits I portray. And the snapshots. And the musical melodies. And the images which might become iconic. I paint and piece together and portray something the public cannot ignore. If only a life could be so easily manipulated.

Searching for the right song and right album and finding it half-adrift near midnight and listening and rubbing my feet together as my laptop glows and I make notes and I figure out how and when and where can I use this tune.

Even in the break I think about the work. Even when I'm standing without a clock, I still gladly feel like I'm part of lesson. So I keep listening and learning and loving the buzzed empty void I'm always leaning toward.

Solitary Confinement

When the work is done alone, there's only one of you to meet with. To celebrate with. To lift up and to banter around with.

Even if there are a thousand voices in your head, it still only feels like you've got one beating heart inside the confines of your solitary office.

Little by little, week by week, month by month, the years drained and that flimsy little sense of self-worth withered up. It didn't matter how many trailers you had. It didn't matter what sort of accolades you might have received (few). The movie people are busy and preoccupied and nobody is waiting to give you a pat on the back. You're not doing this for any pats. Those who want them can go look somewhere else.

Those who can't take this solitary confinement will have to go back to the corporate world, where their souls are slowly sucked away.

I wonder if somehow I've managed to do that to myself. After so many years and so many miles, I wasn't just tired. I felt like paper set out to the side and dried up under the blaring sun.

So brittle, that the slightest touch might disintegrate me.

Yesterday

So loud these walls bouncing off the blistering screams. We try to talk, then try to speak through Morse code but nothing works. Scattered thoughts and sentences say little to nothing. We reserve articulation for our children, who don't listen.

I sit in the dark, waiting, breathing, fuming. I step down stairs and feel numb, unable to speak, unable to think.

Failed again. A failure as a father, unable to figure it out. Furious with discipline, fumbling at guidance. I'm afraid, more afraid than I've ever been. So helpless. So utterly f***ing helpless. These precious souls we prayed for and waited for now suddenly bringing us to our knees in some kind of strange Disney sequel to *Deliverance*. I need some words, some guidance, someone telling me I'm doing a halfway decent job. But Tamara isn't about to say anything because she needs the same thing and God forbid that I'm able to comfort her.

Breathe in, breathe out.

The words of *Karate Kid* have been burned in my soul and either I'm going to get busy waxing on or waxing off.

You just combined Karate Kid *and* The Shawshank Redemption. *What kind of soul does that?*

Come Alive

I see the picture. The smug smile masking all that soft strength coming apart at the seams.

Wanting something and needing something and trying something and hiding everything.

Drown it out and drink it in. That's right, Foo Fighters.

I tried. And I failed. And I ran and I stopped. I left but I came back around. Every single thing pointed to this moment. To that moment.

Sitting. Holding a sleeping ten-month-old.

Come alive, Spencer.

The dead shall rise.

I needed to live and to breathe and to hope and to give and to break and to stop.

I breathed in air and wept and prayed and cried out.

God, help me, please bring me through this, please help me, I don't want to lose her, I don't want to lose them.

Stopping breathing and breathing and rocking and crying and wincing and clenching and sweating and searching and hating and trying so very trying to just believe God will take care of this.

This mess I'd made.

A mess I still remember.

A mess that still mars the person I look at in the mirror every morning and night.

But God heard that prayer from that messy man. And He answered it.

There was a plan, even though I wouldn't have believed it or wanted it if I could have seen it in the first place.

Some Kind of Tourniquet

Maybe I should try.

Maybe I should cry out.

Let me take something that's my own and tell me if it's going to be undone.

This sorrow and this sorry-I'm-gonna-keep-going-on.

I don't know. Maybe I should try.

The ticking bomb of time telling me tales and lying through every single one of them.

Can you hear it?

Can you see it?

The night pulses with the trains in the background and the haunting sounds they make. Serenading me to sleep, reminding me in the darkness, stamped out into the light.

So tell me and yell at me and spell it out for me, all over me.

The sunlight is spilling out over me like a gunshot wound.

Sunrise is gonna come like some kind of tourniquet.

Some trauma can't be treated, and some loss can't be lessened.

But you let go by holding on fast to a faith that's beyond you.

Watching

I see you.

I see you in the picture on the screen held in the touch of my hand far away.

I hear you like yesterday.

I watch you smile and laugh and think and linger there like a lily hovering over the surface of a gentle lake. Floating, so fond of life.

I see you and it's not a distant memory. It's not an afterthought from a long time ago.

It's from yesterday.

It's from less than twenty-four hours ago.

And I realize something especially amazing in this moment.

Not only am I alive, but so are you.

Not only do I breathe, but so do you.

I'm still striving and surviving and struggling and swimming upstream. And I guess, in so many ways, so are you.

So are you.

The memories sneak inside at midnight, making me wonder if they're made-up or real. A writer can wreak havoc with his own history.

Yet there she is.

And here am I.

And I wonder how much I've made up. How many images were never meant to be mine to begin with? How many smiles were spent for the screen? How many subversive longings were simply props and lighting and lines from some other screenwriter?

She was real and she said all that and she happened the same way I happened.

But the truth is a pebble dropped from the top of a bridge, a solid and smooth stone slipping through the waters without a care. Away from the flow and down to the bottom. To sleep and be stolen away and to be forever silenced.

Forever hushed.

Forever gone.

Delilah

I don't hear it anymore. The voice, the knock, the thunder.

I don't awaken to wonder if the sun will rise.

I don't fall asleep wondering if the dark will suffocate.

An imaginary lifeline on a fictitious mountain slope. Every day I used to head up to the summit but would feel the oxygen failing.

The world makes a little more sense when you're viewing it from a flat, safe plateau where you can breathe.

I'm not sure the why and I can't say the what-if. I just know where I am now.

Your sky is coated with more clouds than I can count. They look pretty but the forecast will always be thunderstorms.

I'm still standing behind a door. Maybe it'll open again.

Father's Child 2

Waiting. Around the corner, over the headway, side by side the siding.

Waiting and wondering.

I can hear but can't see. I can walk but can't run. I can feel but can't think.

The words and the staircases and the steps and the songs. I'm wondering how many I can use and in what way.

I look through the playlists trying to find the right one. Imagery and music. The tune and the tone and the attitude.

The majors are fine but I'm staring at the minors.

The minor moments in the songs where I can lift up a little emotion.

I scan and search. Then I add a little more. Waiting on the call. Waiting on input.

Give us a day. A number. A time.

The days of waiting for a muse can barely be remembered.

This road turning to an avenue, into a sidewalk, over a bridge, onto a path, and then becoming a trail finds two feet traveling too far and too wide and too alone.

Walk with me.

My prayer every moment of every day.

Walk with me.

Hold on to My Hand

We stand by the river, watching it move beneath us. It seems like I've had that same motion inside me from the first time I met Lissie. Now I realize this might be the last time I see her.

—I think it's for the best, she says.

—When someone says for the best, it usually is far from that.

—All I seem to be doing is confuse you. To make you more frustrated. I never meant to do any of that. All I wanted to do was help.

—Help what? Lead me to the gates of heaven? Save me from the gates of hell?

She sighs, staring out. Lissie is brighter than the sun's reflection off the water below. I'd say this, but it sounds like a bad line from a Hallmark film.

I realize something.

The world moves a bit faster, the horizon stretches out a bit farther, and your imagination feels a bit more familiar when you're with her. That high-school-crush sort of ache inside your soul. That twentysomething devilish delight of doing anything you want. The invincibility of a stupid thirtysomething who still hasn't figured things out. She embodies them and more. Yet of course she can't and won't ever know this. No. Of course not.

—Should we say goodbye? I ask.

—Haven't we been saying it since we first said hello?

—Maybe people shouldn't have greeting and farewells. Maybe they should remain connected like a bookmark stuck in between the pages of some grand story.

—When you're not stammering, you can be pretty poetic, she says to me as her gaze rushes over me.

—I don't stammer when I want something.

—No, you don't. So what is it you want, Spencer?

I want to tell her but I can't. I shouldn't. She already knows what I might say, but then again, this might just be my flesh talking. My empty soul needing.

A part of me also wants to beg her to escape with me.

Let's stay and watch the world blow up with all these words.
Hold my hand before it explodes. Just clutch on to me beforehand.
And if we have to hurl over the cliff into the ravine, let's go together.

Like so many thoughts and feelings, I don't say those things.

I tell her the one truth I do know.

—I just want to go home.

She smiles and nods.

Lissie knows.

—Just wait, she says.

Vitamin C

So this is how it ends. Not with a bang but with a complete

Yeah. An incomplete sentence. Imagine how I feel.

Soft-spoken and still cuts deep.

I wonder what she thinks and what she feels and really what she was thinking anyway.

Maybe she was a demon instead of a ghost.

I'm joking if you can read these thoughts put on metaphoric paper 'cause I don't want to upset a ghost.

That's called internal voice humor. Get it?

So I wait, doing what she told me to do.

And I don't know what I wait for.

An embrace. A sign. A sound.

I close my eyes and see her eyes. And I hear her voice. And I suddenly feel overcome with her spirit.

And I wonder why.

I wonder why I met her. Why I could see this spirit. Why I could hold on to this soul.

Why she offered a little. When she knew I wanted—when I needed so much.

And the night falls and I find myself yearning and burning.

I hold my breath. Hoping. Waiting. Needing.

Smiling.

Seeing.

And on film, there you are. This sweet cloud of sunlight moving in order to give me some much needed love and vitamin C.

And I know I love you. I know I need you.

And I also realize that these realizations are suddenly as terrifying as the world around me.

In the still.

All that you feel.

Is it truly tranquility?

I don't know.

I really don't know.

I'm afraid for the answer.

Runaway

So if you could, you would . . .

   —Maybe I don't know but I know you.

You'd say something.

   —I know you're hiding away. Where've you been?

You'd confront.

   —I'm tired of the silence.

You'd confound.

   —I realize you're running away.

You'd not let go.

   —Why are you doing this?

You'd stay until she answers. So you do. You wait. Watching.

   —Why won't you say anything?

But the door remains shut and you're not sure if there's anyone behind it. You knock and knock and knock. But nothing.

   —I'm not leaving you.

But maybe the reality you're knocking on right now is that she's left you.

Ripped Off

You and I. Like a stamp stuck on some rough surface. The kind you have to pry to get off. It's better to simply stay and look at it instead of peeling away like skin. Like a soul. Nobody likes anything being ripped off. Ever. Unless you're the part to go.

And then you're gone.

Wait

The water goes, glowing and grinning down its merry away, away from me. I wait on the hill, my feet stamped in place, fitting in the prints I made before when I wasn't the only one here. But those other prints remain empty.

The surface is tricky. You see shifting colors and strange shapes on the outside. You can also see yourself, twisted and distorted but still you, still standing, still breathing, still there. But you're only partially there. Not a ghost and not a human, but something in between.

Told you so.

Yes, but still, this stings. It felt real and made you feel alive and you can't figure out if it was your imagination or some simple lie.

—I stood here, I know it, and I know she was standing next to me.

Speaking it out loud doesn't mean it happened, just like standing here. The fox is sly and its river only slides away. The flowing water has moving amnesia, never beginning and ending but only disappearing, so its story isn't fully formed or even known.

—I'd just love to know what this all meant.

The words seem to echo, maybe bounce off the glassy top, then disintegrate in front of me.

I wait a little longer.

Then a little more.

Then a little.

Maybe

The past is more present now, more poking, more precarious. I see it so real, so now.

I see us.

The sparrow flying freely so far beyond but always coming back, always seeming to smile while it soars by.

I hit a wall.

I didn't know what to do anymore.

I didn't know what to say anymore.

I didn't know what to try to feign or fool anymore.

Tamara knew my personas and my performances and had seen every one and she no longer wanted to watch them. And God bless her, I didn't want her to, either.

Tell me something. Tell me now.

Tell me my biggest weakness. Tell me one thing you'd change right now in this instant, in a single blink. Tell me without hesitating because maybe possibly I'll change. I might listen. I might evolve.

I might be the man you wanted me to be, the man you thought you were marrying, the man who might melt your morning and midway and your midnight.

Maybe I still can. Maybe I still want to. Maybe I still might be that mighty man you wanted me to be.

These maybes are branches to pile upon your bonfire and light to let us see the dark night ahead. God maybe will show us the way. God might let us see some little bits of light.

Anniversary

Every couple needs a song. And if that song gets old, replace it. Quickly.

Ours for this day . . . it remains ours. It remains known to only two. It's special and special things should remain unknown to others.

I remember one of those first songs that belonged to us. "Cherish the Day" by Sade. Which surely inspires love and sex on a daily basis. I remember falling in love again and again to this song.

"If you were mine, if you were mine, I wouldn't want to go to heaven."

But we would try. Again and again.

Cherishing the day would forever become a synonym to becoming intertwined in desire and passion.

So many years later, the song does somehow remain the same. It's a different song for different people, but the sentiment stays the same.

We're no longer kids.

I can't help this as we ask strangers to take our picture on the bridge. Or as we try to figure out which way to go to get to our dinner reservation. We're not two silly, sappy teens laughing with insecurities. We have an full Wikipedia page detailing our relationship, from the unlikely falling in love to the passionate marriage to the fun days to the crumbles in the bridge. We're veterans but we're still fighting, still waging the war, still trying for some kind of victory.

A selfie with Chicago in the background is a victory. We're both here. That's enough.

We arrive to the hotel and wait in the lobby bar for my meeting. All I want is to get a room and to figure out things and to try to remember being newlyweds again. But instead we share a drink overlooking the sprawling, windy city.

—Think he'll come? she asks.

—Yeah, I think so.

I see someone coming and can't tell exactly who it is because I'm not wearing my glasses. Eventually I discover he's some Korean guy

411

in his fifties. I tell Tamara of the confusion and she can't help but laugh. I follow and soon we're both laughing.

I realize it's been a long time since we've done such a simple thing. Even the sex during those dark, last days still worked. We were always both satisfied, brief and short in the few times we'd go there. But laughter? Genuine laughter? It's way better than sex because it's the best kind of foreplay out there.

My meeting never happens because the guy never shows up but Tamara and I still have a good time. Simple touches of talking. Chuckling. Me telling a joke and her laughing. God, what a difference being able to talk in silence can be. Surrounded only by adults.

Memory

The head-turning things aren't the memories that ultimately reside in your heart. It's smaller, softer moments, often unseen, sometimes unspoken.

You settle down and glance at the stars and see them waving back at you. Smiling. And you wonder what you did to deserve such an audience.

Still

Those moments. Simple, straightforward.

The dim lights shadowing our still.

Facing different directions and remaining.

It's easy looking back to connect the dots. But when you're there, round and solid and still, you have no idea where to go.

Stars cease to shine and Septembers come and go and still you're there. Sitting. Waiting. For one singular moment.

Where your hand is taken and held and gripped hard and shoved against your heart. Where your pulse paces. Where your mind no longer meanders.

Still.

The word wrapped around your waist. Still.

Unmovable. Unshakable. Unlivable.

Still.

Waiting. Wondering. Watching.

Still.

Paused. Perched. Pent-up.

Still sideways. Still backward. Still longing. Still forgotten.

And those breaths you can still feel against your ear. Close your eyes and smile.

Still sitting. Still maybe. Still possibly. Still me.

And in this still, this distracted and fragmented photograph, you watch and wait for some kind motion.

This is called life wrapped in ordinary paper and sealed with invisible tape.

This is solitary confinement so close and so near to escape. But the still smothers and breaks.

Wondering

I see the curved smile and the long, lean figure and the balloon let go and soaring up into the sky. These films are no longer stories to me. They're love letters never written but signed with her name and her lips. Personal invitations to walk through that door for two hours or more and just spend time with her at home.

To wrap myself around her eyes and her voice and her soul and to see her watching me. Loving me. Leaving me. Losing me.

I see the personality I know and yet see different colors and shades and personas. I love it. Each moment and scene feels like I'm living it. Yet all I'm doing is watching, often without breathing, wondering how in the world, wondering how she could have seen so much in this man watching these videos.

Then I have to remind myself that she's gone. She was always gone to begin with. She simply allowed me to step inside and . . .

And what?

That's what I'm wondering. Still wondering.

What I might always be wondering.

HERE COMES THE FLOOD (Trailer #12)

"Maybe I want something else, something more."

The narrator speaks above the melancholy, minimal piano chords as a couple stands on a patio watching girls playing.

"Maybe I want to hear some voice—something—telling me that I'm something more."

The couple is now at a restaurant and then in a car and then in a church and then lounging in their family room.

Peter Gabriel begins to sing "Here Comes the Flood."

"Maybe I want to get some kind of something, something tiny, minuscule but, God, can it be at least something, maybe something more?"

The silhouette of the man looking at the stars. The portrait of the woman staring down at the sand.

"I don't know. I don't go and I don't show anything anymore."

The man continues to talk, his voice weak and haunting and lost.

"I don't feel 'cause feeling is fearing the inevitable disappointment. So I stay away far away from the something more. Something else, something free, something different, something more."

The actor looks suburbanized, stressed and stretched out.

"I see it in your eyes every morning, noon, and night. Your desire for that something too."

The beautiful actress looks normal in this role, her gaze striking and real.

"I know you wish but you've pressed pause on those wishes. Staying on the obvious less while you long for something more."

The couple in tears. Then arguing. Then making love.

416

"I can hear your song singing if you were to do so. Love and longing and freedom in some kind of fine finish. But instead the frame is broken and the picture half-done."

The family portrait is on the floor, the glass on top of it cracked.

"We're neither half-full nor half-empty because we both find each other on the other side."

The screen fades to black.

HERE COMES THE FLOOD on screens this fall.

One Big Messy Mixtape

On the screen, I see you. It's the only place I can tell you goodbye.

In a box, with a sound capable of muting or rewinding, I hear your laugh. I wince because it sounds so glorious. I want it back. I want you back. I'm not sure where you've gone, nor am I sure why I'm still here, but I hate hearing it. I hate seeing it.

You're a sun that's not too bright to stare into. Yet like it always does, the sun disappears, leaving me gazing around, wondering where it went.

Maybe—no, I know—that the importance I've given you is far too much. You have the same size footprints just like anybody else. But I've spent far too long following them. Now I'm standing on rocky cliffs where the sun's melted the snow away.

Maybe I'm mixing metaphors but let's be honest. Life is one big messy mixtape of metaphors that sometimes doesn't quite make sense.

Seasons

I think of the conversations and time spent with Lissie while I'm alone. Those moments seem long forgotten. Words wrapped from shadows and fog. Gifts drifting throughout, cutting the seams and dispelling the dreams.

I've not forgotten but have you?

Springtime's a million sunsets away. Summer's a message in a bottle tossed out into the ocean long ago. Fall is brittle with piles of suffocating leaves. Winter is settling into this heart.

And I'm not sure and I don't know and I can't really hear any of it anymore.

Ragged and torn, the sails clutch the air in their grip, demanding today. Demanding every little bit. Until tomorrow reminds them it's okay to let go.

Time

Something's beating. This pounding cursor that waits for you to fill the white. To say something and to utter some kind of sorry. But some apologies will never come.

The words are nails on some faded circus poster with a date from twenty-seven months ago.

Could you know or feel or find something you've never known and never seen and never believed but rather have tried to follow with every fiber of your heart and your wandering eyes so clutteringly close to the abyss they look over?

Time tells you.

Time knows.

Time stitches.

Time goes.

Time feels.

Time finds you where you are.

Time stares.

And time falls like some star.

Boil over with time.

Time can falter fine.

In your heart and your mind.

So heat it up and find.

Everything you have to find.

Take and heal and hold it in your hand.

Hold it and find.

Hold it and do everything you can.

Again.

Again.

And again.

The burning in your hand and your heart again and again.

Echoes in the dust.

Again and again.

Strangelove

Time slices like scissors being wielded by a six-year-old. When I see the results, the cuts make odd shapes and the scissors make bloody cuts. I see the wrinkles under my eyes and the stains on my jeans.

Still I search. Always searching.

Sometimes I would become obsessed.

"So when we have another showing, maybe we should try to . . ."

So Tamara says and so I nod, not really listening to her.

I'm trying to capture this moment, this time, this era, this aura from thirty years ago.

"Uh-huh."

But yeah. F*** the whole uh-huh. 'Cause that's not working and never has worked.

I'm so absorbed, so enthralled, so inspired, so obsessed, so unbridled.

I'm not unbridled, but damn, I needed to add a *U* to complete my *A-E-I-O-U* sort of summary.

I'm not there for her SO DO YOU THINK THAT WE SHOULD because I don't know and mostly I don't care.

"When they come tomorrow, we should . . ."

But I'm back on the songs and suddenly I'm thinking there's a Heartbreak Beat.

Life is a little like "Lips like Sugar."

"What do you think?" Tamara asks.

I'm searching the web and my iTunes for songs for the trailer for the job for the fix, for the fix.

"I don't know," I say. It sounds strange.

Or maybe it's because I'm thinking about "Strangelove, strange highs and strange lows."

She talks and I nod and think I might appear to be possibly out of reach.

I give in to sin . . .
I'm not trying to say . . .

I'm always willing to learn
Oh, and I'll make it all worthwhile
Pain . . .
I'll say it again
Pain . . .
I'll say it again
Pain . . .
I'll say it again.

Tamara is wondering what the hell I'm doing

I won't say it again.
That's how my love goes.

She should know by now.
She should know me.
She should realize this is how my love goes.

Will you give it to me?

Losing My Mind

Hell comes to find you. Knocking. More. Then breaking. Then backing off until it comes barging in with its steel-plated BMW.

This is the world we live in.

This is hell happy to see you and sell you some cookies.

You don't look like a Girl Scout.

But the hand seizes your throat.

Maybe I'll take some Thin Mints.

Shoot the messenger.

And okay, I can't breathe, I'll take some Samoas. Oh, wait, they're called Caramel deLites? Since when?

The threat is just outside. Just within breathing range. Just within every thought and everything summed up.

We know where you live.

You try to lock the door and try to spy out the blinds but they're out there somewhere and they're feeding and they're hungry and they're limitless and they do not care.

This was my world. My stresses. My exhaustion. My coming undone.

Bones of Ribbon

The truth is the real always betters the reverie. Cut into a magnificent assortment of pieces, a trailer still pales to a marvelous film. No image or quip or footage ever compares to a real person, to a breathing soul. I've spent a lifetime trying to capture—no, trying to remake—hell, trying to better—the magnificent and the beautiful and the breathing, but I still have never been able to come close to the real presence of love. Flawed fingers and hands try to make it perfect, and a faulty imagination and heart try to make it profound. Yet the trailers I've made and continue to make are pretty postcards from an exotic land I never visited.

So someone comes in to shatter my stronghold of safety, the thick and stubborn walls built to protect that ten-year-old residing inside. And so I battle back and wonder if I've been the one to create this enemy, or am I the one who created the victor?

The imagination extends beyond the scale of a song since it's too creative to be bound by seven simple notes including those sharps and flats. It seeks new sounds, places between the major and the minor, breaking the ABC's and the do-re-mis and longing for the X's and the Y's and especially those breaking Z's.

This heart, uncorked and allowed to breathe, has perhaps drifted somewhere too high into the clouds. Perhaps its sight and its taste and its touch have all somehow been lost, all succumbing to the glory of the fantasy, to the tapestry of the creation.

Perhaps, after all is said and done and written and pontificated with as much poetic zest as I have, the truth is *not* a beautiful thing. Perhaps the truth is there is no beauty except in the creation of my broken heart, soul, and mind.

There is no truth in these hollow halls full of shiny, empty armor.

Memories

Etched in stone, love's letters can crack and crumble. Memory isn't cement, so rather than repairing, it can carve out something else entirely.

Sometimes you touch those hollow spaces, trying to remind yourself what filled them, trying to make out the words.

Big Picture

Do I remember you talking to me or do I hear a line from a movie?

Does my mind wander and will myself into some cinematic story?

Do I imagine my frail friendship bolstering to become one of your leading men?

Do I dare to believe those pretty words you shared . . . ?

Those colored birds flying away . . . ?

The imagination loves to create memories that never happened.

Maybe I shouldn't expect anything but I do.

Maybe I shouldn't wonder anything but I still do.

The world is bigger and brighter and bolder than it was when we were just kids. Yet it seems to smother and cover and cloak everything about you.

What happened?

Seriously, what happened?

Did I just not realize that you didn't have it in you?

I'm trying to find my way. Trying to figure it out. Wrestling with the things that every person—most every person—should do. This world and this place and this faith and this everything

So what about you?

What about you?

Why so still?

Tell me why so still? Why so stifled?

I want to shake you and show you and tell you how every single silent stifled little bit of your life has broken me and wrecked me and made me into somebody I didn't ever want to be.

I just wanted some damn connection.

I wanted somebody to simply make me feel alive.

Alive. To breathe the air and to hear the sounds and to smell the roses and to see the pretty pictures passing us by.

But all I get is choked up, unable to smell or breathe or see.

Every passing mile.

Every passing moment.

Every passing miracle.

I cannot bear any more stagnant standing by.

426

I cannot do this thing.

And so somehow the seeping inside suddenly found its way out.

And the thing that could never happen did. And I found myself gone.

The Wrong Clothes

Muffled and muted. The world, so already absent, suddenly turns a murky quiet. Leaving me to wonder. Leaving me to wander.

I go to the same places but she's not there. I arrive earlier, wait longer, change my times, make it later. But nothing works.

No connection I try connects. No attempt I make arrives. I'm suddenly feeling very much like the ghost that I am. I simply no longer see my shadow anymore, this beautiful alluring figure that always showed up nearby with a smile.

I still remember the winter when I was found. Those hours and those moments and the passage of time connecting. I lost myself but I was already a bit lost. I found myself when someone else decided to find me.

But now she was gone.

I go over the things I said, the things I didn't say. The things done and left undone. But nothing stands out. There's no bobbing black hat wading down the water, waiting for something to jump out of it. I'm left standing on the bridge, literally and figuratively. Standing and staring. Searching. Stranded.

Day after day I think that things might change, but they don't.

Night after night I think that words might be spoken, but they aren't.

The season rolls over into another and I'm left wearing the wrong clothes. Cold and chilled and confused about the temperature.

I wonder if she's going to show back up. Or if I maybe need to just go.

Smothering

I long for conversations but realize we never did talk. I would grab her hand and rush out with her and find some place to hold her and kiss her and love her. I'd listen by letting her wrap herself around me. We listened to words from strangers flowing through the speakers while we would take off our clothes and fit into each other.

I always thought we fit together so well. We did. For a while, at least.

My confidence. This hot molten core ready to explode and turn to ash. To blow and scatter over the ocean.

But so strong, this belief that we'd make it, that we'd last, that the longing would always be there like our tongues and our hands and our limbs. Always ready, always waiting.

But life pauses. And life occupies. And life lessens. And life smothers.

Foreplay

—Talk to me, I ask.

   —What do you want me to say? Tamara says.

   —Tell me something you've never said.

   —I don't know what to say . . . but I want to keep talking with you.

   —You've never said that before, I say.

   —We've never been here before.

   —Yeah.

So we start and we try. The trying starts over and over again. But the only way to start loving again is to simply try.

   —I used to dream about us being together, I tell her.

   —I always wanted to hear you tell me that, she tells me.

It's like playing tennis again after ten years. Grasping the racket feels the same but each stroke feels different. Running feels more vibrant and alive, yet we can barely try to keep our breath. But we keep serving and volleying and never really trying to score. We've already tallied the score. This is about simply practicing.

   Practicing to be civil.

   —Are you going to leave? she asks.

   —Do you want me to stay? I ask.

It's been so long since we were on the same page, since we knew we could even stay.

   A relationship begins to die when assumptions take the place of courtesy. When arrogance takes the place of curiosity.

   So we talk. Awkward at times. Trying too hard at others. But there's no television on. Nobody's on their iPhone. No child is screaming or tugging or running by. There's a look and a stare and a waiting and a wanting.

   Foreplay isn't necessarily about touching the skin. It's about touching the spirit. About finding something deep inside and grasping hold of it and simply saying you understand it. You know it. And you're *okay* with it.

   Intimacy is about someone believing in this and giving themselves up because of it.

RIVER DEEP (Trailer #13)

The pounding of the drums and the bass line follow the footsteps always moving and the hands always holding each other as an instrumental version of Coldplay's "Clocks" shares a meeting and a romance and a wedding and the happily ever after of a couple.

The colors and the patterns and the laughter and the brilliance all suddenly

STOP

Black silence on the screen. Then a shocked breath turns to a shaking sigh.

Light merges into ripples.

Cue "Washing of the Water" by Peter Gabriel.

The same young man is not so young and not so happy.

Something has happened. But what?

"Where did it go wrong?" his voice asks.

The young woman shows up looking not so young and not so happy.

The bliss has turned to bitterness.

"What could I have done differently?" her voice asks.

A love story turned into a tale of loss? So what's the selling point?

The fact that it's about everybody.

As Peter Gabriel sings, the couple looks distraught and at their end.

"Letting go, it's so hard. The way it's hurting now to get this love untied."

A couple hurting and alone.

"So tough to stay with this thing 'cause if I follow through, I face what I denied."

Soul-searching and angry arguments.

"I get those hooks out of me and I take out the hooks that I sunk deep in your side."

Children running in the mix. Decisions made. Choices. Pills. A knife.

"Kill that fear of emptiness, loneliness I hide."

Eyes open in the middle of the night.

"River, oh, river, river running deep. Bring me something that will let me get to sleep."

Blood dripping in the air and onto the surface of running water.

"In the washing of the water will you take it all away? Bring me something to take this pain away."

RIVER DEEP. IN THEATERS DECEMBER 25.

Embankment

I hear the hammer pounding my temples, the pressure from ten thousand hits. Still so solid, so wrecked, so going on.

The raging inside my skin.

I see her silk wrapped around hands, steady and secure and never torn. Always open, always waiting, always there.

God, I want you, I need you, Tamara.

A shore of regret. Soaking through and shoving back the sands. Seizing every bit of land it can with the last bit of hope before sunset.

This is all you have.

All you can try to hope for.

And there's a part that waits and watches for the moment when you can crash upon the shore like soldiers crossing Normandy through gun shells and hell and shock and awe.

You hope that somehow you can make it up the embankment in order to get to the foxhole she's hiding in.

Not to destroy but to save.

One Love

I suppose.

And yet I stumble.

I don't know much anymore.

I see you in passing. Through these doors and these walls and these moments.

I can't see you anymore.

I don't know who you are.

My heart breaks because we're supposed to be this one thing. This one love. This one unbreakable, bold thing.

I'm sure I disappointed you and left a bad taste in your mouth. And I'm going without every night, night after night. Longing. Feeling so alone. Feeling so very alone.

And we don't carry a thing.

We should carry each other but we don't. We're riding and flying solo. And the sleeping don't ever meet up with the awakened.

I try to wrap my mind around it all.

God knows I'm broken. God knows I'm so damn diminished. And I hurt you over and over and over again.

Bashing through your temple. Trying to wrestle my demons. Yet finding that you aren't some priest listening in the veil of some kind of confession.

So I try .

I keep trying.

The Clock Strikes Midnight

The biting cold chips cut against my face as I see this obscene weather amalgamation surrounding me. Mid-April hail is just not cool.

My feet make footprints in the icy pellets as I walk and try to find her.

Where is she?

Where's she been?

I've been on this trail of sadness, seeing familiar surroundings even as I stumble into something new and unknown.

Are you near, Lissie?

I enter that small restaurant where we first met but she's not there. Nor is she at the pub or the bar or the bookstore or the river's edge or the run-down apartment building.

Are you anywhere around here, Lissie?

Retracing yesterday wrecks with my memory. I wonder about the *really*s and the *maybe*s and the *never*s. I worry about the imagined versus the happened.

You told me you loved me, you told me you wanted me. I saw it inside your eyes and all over your skin.

Imagined, Spencer, imagined, imagined, all imagined.

I heard it through your words and inside your voice and you said I was important, I was something, I was needed, I was somebody.

The dank, dark underbelly of the buildings, the cold stone, the hard cement, the crumbling of the bridge and the faded lines of the street . . . I move past all and keep looking but I can't find her.

I can't find you. Did I imagine you? Did I create you?

The poster for the film playing at the old theater reminiscing in old relics such as matinees shows me (movie with a twist). I stare and think more about the trailer than the actual movie.

What have I become?

Where is my mind?

And where'd she go? Where?

Above the moving, haunting, dark waters of the Fox River, I think of the suddenly suffocating reality:

You were a two-minute trailer I concocted with the tools of my trade, with emotions supplied by music and true facts covered by melancholy.

The wind shoves me somewhere else, somewhere away from here. But I'm not budging. I have to find her. I have to see her one last time. Real or imagined. Sane or insanity. Meaningful or made up. Whatever.

I look at the time.

Once again.

The clock strikes midnight.

I wonder if it's me it's really, honestly striking down.

Yearning

I miss the country, the disconnect of it all, the turning off of everything during my teenage nights. That loneliness became a part of me. I could never shake it. Not even as an adult with my family in our suburban home and suburban life. I've come to learn that the parts of your childhood that are broken and messy are still pieces of the crossword you.

I'm reminded on a late-night drive with the sunroof open and the windows down. Do I need to describe? Even children know this sensation. Wind flowing and filling in those empty spaces. The parts of you that feel like a piece of paper half-shredded, now flapping in the breeze. It's glorious, the darkness, the alone of it all.

Maybe I still yearned as an adult because that's what I'd been trained to do as a child when the sun fell. Yearning for parents to sit beside me. Yearning for someone to laugh with me. Yearning not to yearn anymore.

Maybe all those faces on all the films I made trailers for were silent companions in the dark. Like the characters in the novels I read or the songs I listened to or the shows I watched.

Booze isn't the only way to numb your soul and life. You can do it in lots of other ways.

Forty-two years old, I realized I'd never *stopped* the numbing.

Like the sliding ceiling of the sunroof, the dark heavens above inspire memories. It's like opening a treasure chest full of pain. I wouldn't change it. These riches are my own and they've made me who I am. But maybe I can give a few of them away.

Lissie would take some.

I wonder where she is and whether it's night for her.

I wonder what it'd be like to just talk to her.

I'm yearning, of course. But I miss my friend. This is understandable. She understood about those teen years. She got the yearning. She knew what it was like.

So much points toward those difficult, deserted years. I still see that boy's shadow following his grown-up footsteps.

Have I really grown that much?

Have I really changed?

Sometimes I think youth is simply a fog surrounding us. The damage all around us is still there, we just don't see it. But the older we get, the more clear the picture becomes.

But maybe, maybe, we're surrounded by beauty. Stunning, epic beauty.

Maybe we just need to open our eyes to really look around and appreciate it.

It's late but I'm not done driving.

I think I'll drive by their place. Just to see. Just to watch.

Wild-Eyed

Echoes and echoes. Heartbeats beating, beating, beating. Nighttime quiet calm suffocating the breakage inside.

I wonder if they can see.

I wonder if anybody can ever know.

This torrential downpour inside my mind and my soul.

These torrents and turmoil deep, deep, so deep down inside.

Pouring out to simply get rid of the creative hurricane inside.

Dying to speak and say something to this silent, seeping world I'm living in.

Creating and carefully constructing and crafting and chiseling.

Sometimes I shiver suddenly, since nobody knows. Nobody can see. Nobody can know the raging and raging and rage against my own man-made machine.

Nobody except her.

Nobody except you.

And you were smart to have left.

Smart to have taken off before the damage could be done.

So now I sit here in the still. The shadows and the glow. The screens flickering and flicking more.

A story that could have been told in ten thousand words, yet so long and so troubled.

So much to say and so few to say it to.

And who were you, Lissie? Were you really there?

Sometimes the glorious crescendos come nearby to cushion the blows of life. Sometimes the volume can keep out the sinuous vanities.

So I turn it up and turn it up more.

Midnight knows these devices I work on and these vices that drive me to continue with each beat beat of the breaking heart inside.

I find more than I can handle, so I breathe.

Your breath, trembling beside me, long ago told a farewell, yet never forgotten.

It's time, Spencer.

I can't find the words.

I need to say it. Those two words or the one. Doesn't matter.

It's bad to say something good and it breaks to say some kind of bye. Yet you forge the words together and try.

Never knowing your wants and your needs and your desires and your dreams and your beliefs.

Breathless in this beyond. Breaking in every. Little. Step.

I can tell these tired treads are no longer leaving any prints in the mud. Maybe I'm stuck, at a standstill. Maybe I'm still trying to come up with the right name in my mind.

Hell to the Liars II

Only one of us believed in the better.

Only one held on to its hope.

Only one could stand and watch beyond the water.

Only one.

The other one.

I was the one who doubted and debated and drifted and dawdled. Stepping through the sand, hot and cold and hot again, sifting through my toes, standing in place, still, all while I'm staring out to the endless blue beyond, so full of f***ing doubt.

I'm not going.

So my doubt debated.

I couldn't see beyond the water spreading out on the horizon.

I could never see beyond my vision, beyond my breath, beyond my grip.

I could invent a soliloquy so effective, yet I couldn't imagine a single voice splitting through. Only one so singular could break through and break me.

Once upon a time, I thought I knew the meaning of brokenness. But its very essence is about breaking every possible meaning you think you know. Shaving and carving and cutting and scarring and finally tossing you aside to get busy pruning and shaping and slicing someone else.

There is little taste for this world. It's only an aftertaste, the hangover after the party never attended. It's a dizzy feeling without ever popping open the cork on the champagne. It's the effects of every loss and empty feeling ever felt.

This world, so broken and lost and empty.

And now in this moment of drifting, swallowing reverie, I stare over those waters and realize I need to get on the other side.

I need to see and believe hope that awaits.

It's not idle and not false and it's not imagined. It waits across the waters, pulling me toward it, a tide of hope unimaginable.

Is there time?

Is there *still* time?

Has too much time caused those tides to become still?

All I can do is venture out. To venture forth. To venture forward and forge on like some brave pioneer trekking into an unknown world.

Asleep

It's not the water splitting or the wake forming or the waves stretching out, but it's the still on the surface that hurts. The rush of the thrill gone in search of new waters.

It's a strange thing to silence the playlists of yesterday. I hear certain songs and they scrape my skin, clawing and letting bleed and never letting go. I'm angry for ever hearing them in the first place.

I go back to the songs of my youth, the tunes of yesteryear. Those passages try to protect me. They cover and then they start to lash out at any who seem to try to attack at my core.

The things we couldn't change then are the things we desperately try to change now. Yet they aren't the same.

"Deep in the cell of my heart I really want to go."

The cell of my heart. Everybody has one, don't they? Some have figured out how to unlock the door. Others have escaped.

Some are still there. Always there. Some want to but never are able to go.

Father's Day

She dances, and it feels like she's dancing with you.

When she moves, it feels like she's following your lead.

When she smiles, you can swear she's smiling at you.

Five years before meeting, and it still feels like the words were written solely for you.

She runs and maybe she's running toward you.

She laughs and maybe she's laughing at something you said.

And maybe you're there and she's seeing and she knows something you don't.

It's strange how the years can turn into seconds in the sanctuary of a song. How melodies and lyrics can burn my heart.

So light and bright and somehow it seems you've got the spotlight in your hand and she's grinning and making sure you've got it focused solely on her.

But she doesn't see you and can't run to you and won't be dancing with you.

The pain on her face doesn't have anything to do with you.

The struggle and the strain and the thrill and the beauty.

She looks so free.

If only she could look free because of you.

So beautiful, so buoyant. With this feeling and this breath that you so long for.

One thing at a time.

One step, she said.

Don't try to swallow the ocean, keep doing one day 'till one day you're free.

You remember.

I see you laughing on the other side.

You remember.

Where the walls have tumbled and the flowers grow wide.

You remember.

I see you laughing on the other side.

You remember.

With your broken heart.

444

And all these things and all these memories and all these hopes and all these dreams and suddenly all of these things make you feel this one thing.

—One day you'll be free, Lissie once told me.

She had a box of darkness given to her by someone she loved.

I want to be the light. I want to be the sparks that light the fire that will find you.

I've learned and I'm living and I'm longing.

But maybe.

Maybe there's more and maybe I can be someone you will be there for.

Maybe you could act out stories and scenarios for me.

Maybe. Somehow in my memories.

Yes. I'm here.

I am wild-eyed.

And yes, I'm waiting.

Mantra

Remembering Tamara and the girls.

Those memories move me. And they pinch and hurt and remind and remain.

I thought so much and didn't think at all.

The salt so free in the ocean tide of you. God, I let it simply rush and drown me. Yet I lived.

Or did I?

I still see you there. What happened. Where'd you go?

These snapshots I carry. Are they real? Will they remain? Can I take them back into real life?

I wonder.

I wait.

I'm wrong, thinking this way.

Midnight knows. Midnight remembers. Midnight maims.

The hurt of the night hurts.

The black of the ticking clock paints and conceals and suffocates.

Can you believe?

Can you breathe?

Can you and will you ever be?

It waits for you, ending today and beginning tomorrow.

The hover.

The balance of swept away and still a chance.

Midnight arrives to remind and to reset.

Noon is always in the middle of the action, the life of the party, the bright and sunny smile of chance. Midnight comes to pick him up and drive him home. To let him cry and let it out and let it go. To say there's always a tomorrow since, actually, it's today.

Noon is the choice and midnight is the chance.

Parachutes

It took too much time to figure things out and when I finally did, I'd already taken way too much. So much from others and from the world and from God. So much all for me.

I wonder how long and how far and how loud and how free I will really be.

Sometimes the melodies make me sit down and want to create something but sometimes I find there's just some random sadness I'm suddenly capturing on the screen. I could make an Adam Sandler movie melancholy without trying. It's my sensibilities. That outlook just makes sense.

If only.

Two words.

If. Only.

A parachute and a pull string.

Blinking

Time dances, skipping over creases in the book, dashing down the pages, refusing to stand still and be punctuated by any period

Hello

A candle waving in the wind, pulling me forward to its flicker in the darkness only to leave me stranded once it's blown out.

Stuck, seeing all sides and unable to find a road to steer out of.

—Are you there?

But of course there's no one to reply.

—Were you ever there to begin with?

But of course there's no one to give me answer.

Lost my mind in this place, this town. A heart can be full of helium, its surface so easily popped. I never sucked in enough to sound like a clown. My words were always funny enough.

I go to my place to find a note or a message or an autograph or anything. Nothing is there.

I retrace steps and find nothing.

I try to see if she was in my imagination, but I don't know. I'm left with the ghost on the screen.

The sidewalks don't see her. The streets can't call her name. The buildings haven't opened their doors and the restaurants haven't heard her order.

The red light turning green.

I see the stoplight and I'm half–color-blind, so I wonder if I meant to stay or if I should go.

I go to my home, my office, my little encampment and I close the door and I shut the blinds and I feel the night try to pound its way in. What's the month? Is it March or mid-September? Is that rain outside or flickers or hail or snow?

Where did you go, Lissie?

The tremor of the candlelight is the hope in my heart, flickering as I run to keep it lit, vanishing as I reach to grab it.

I go to see any sort of photos. But there are none. No videos. No selfies. No saving posts. Nothing.

—Are you gone?

Nobody can tell me yes or no.

—Do you hear me?

The you is nowhere to be found.

Rosebuds

Maybe every single thing is in my hand. Gripping on some kind of lesson learned.

Trending now. Sending it out now. The message and lesson of life. Winning. Learning. Loving. Letting go. Getting old.

I'm loving and learning and letting go. I'm also leaving soon.

I'm waiting for the car and it's waiting and the motor is running and all you need to do is follow your heart and soul.

Put the petal to the mettle.

Isn't that what they mean, not say?

Covering the clouds. Cover me. Cover it all with rosebuds.

True Love Waits

You can be alive but not living. Breathing without feeling breathless. Stuck in constant motion. Waiting and wanting and waiting and wanting for that mythical true love.

Does true love wait? Does it?

Are you the one to finally find that ghost in your attic, only discovering you've been tagged and now you're it? To hear the voices through the ceiling below, laughing and living and loving, all while you're longing simply to come out of hiding?

You once said, "Don't leave." Or did she? You once said this isn't a life worth living. Or were those her words?

A heart has to work despite the thumbtacks stuck inside it.

To bring home those lollipops with the dry cleaning. To hear the simultaneous interruptions and distractions and confusion. To see a trio waiting by the window, appearing by the door, rumbling with you in the hallway.

True love has always waited for you, Spencer. You've just bought the false lie saying it hasn't and never will.

It waits. There, just below, just through this drywall, just beyond this barrier.

Tiny hands and crazy kitten smiles.

Waiting for your love.

Waiting and wanting.

Dreamliner

The startling similarities. They strike down the passion and the humor. They make you surrender your spontaneity. They make you forget your punchline.

If.

This ball tossed up ready to serve. A potential ace. Struck with all your strength. But so often found stuck in life's thick net.

If only.

There they are again. The two words that ask over and over again a question that's unanswerable. Because the only can't be quantified. If only said. If only shown. If only seen. If only touched. If only listened to. If only a hundred times over.

If only we could begin again.

My mind wanders, wrapped up in the lines of the map. Yet I'm not searching out an address but rather a starting point for some kind of peace. Some kind of solution. Something I can believe in.

Begin again.

The two words over and over and over again. Spiral in a slide spotted in water park. Sliding down and down until crashing into the surface.

Mother's Day

This is what I want to tell Tamara. To text her or write a note on the fridge or carve it on the bathroom counter or simply whisper it into her ear.

Words I never said. Words I so want to say now.

You're not a good mother. You're a great mother.

You are consistent and kind. You awake and go to sleep with compassion. And you care. You always care, every second of every minute of every hour all day long.

You are steady. Steady and stable and secure in yourself. Unlike the unsteady, unstable, insecure parent you're secured to.

Your world is about structure and routine. This is the framework and this is how we fit inside it and this is what we do and this is what we continue to do.

Somehow, despite the stress and the chaos and the crazy moments, the girls understand and get it. They know this structure and they see this routine. It sinks in even when they seem to bounce around on the surface of insanity.

They can see the wisdom behind your ways.

You are patient. When they yell. When they whine. When they cry. When they fight.

And in the fog of parenting failure, and in the exasperation of everyday, you remain steady, even when your mate abandons ship.

You are a magnificent mother, one your girls will one day comprehend with age and then try to recreate when their time comes.

It might not seem like I notice, nor does it look like I appreciate it, but I do notice and appreciate all you do. I take it for granted, and I don't operate on that same level. I blow up while you dial back. I bark while you become still. No, you're not perfect, and neither am I, but you still have an idea of what you're doing and how you're doing it.

So many times, I have no clue whatsoever. But I do try in my own messy way.

Thank you for being a good mother.

The Same Sort of Melancholy

I'd figured out the puzzle but got all the pieces wrong. Color-blind and prying, I'd tried to devise some kind of image in my mind. So I tried and tried again and tried all those who couldn't put up with the intensity and the time and the pressures awaiting.

It was different but now it's like this.
It sounded a shade off but now the shadows cover me.
Melancholy riffs and minor chords that suffocate.
All with their time.
All with their haunted attics.
All with breathless abodes.
All true and all love and all lollipops and crisps.
It's a déjà vu to something ten years earlier.
To a decade snapshot backward.
To the same sort of melancholy except at the wrong damn thing.

Come On

Wake up, you sinner. The sights are blowing up in your face like grenades, and if you're lucky, you're holding the shards in disintegrating hands.

Blowback. This world. The news. The snapshots. The tweets and the posts and the pictures and the patriotic editorials.

Ruffles and blisters and blunders in the ocean of the noise.

Come on and come.

Come on, you f***ing chameleon.

What do you hear and what do you know and what are you trying to say?

Hear it? The symphony is beginning to play your song in some minor chord you've never heard. The kind you want to reject.

But it's you.

It's all you.

It paints its pictures with this melancholy sound.

You have it figured out until you hear these tunes and find yourself lost and wondering and wandering and bewildered.

Going Home

Weighed down and heavy. Limping along this long path.

I wonder if I was always this weak. Or had I never wandered this far from home before? Did this immaculate city rest right behind the hills beyond this safe shore I've stayed at my entire life? I can't say for sure but I can say I've rested inside the city limits.

Now the lights have been turned off. And I'm tired and simply wanting to drive back home.

Maybe I'll cross the ridge and start heading back down by the ocean and those glorious, amazing lights with flicker again. Maybe.

Maybe they'll reside in my mind.

This swinging bridge has too many broken maybes lining its steps.

I'm tired of maybes. I'm wanting to see something and feel something and touch something that's really there.

We can cut our lives with images and pictures that coax it to mean something but sometimes they're just assorted files for someone else to pick from.

Sometimes we need to take the story on a ride ourselves.

Sometimes we need to strap on the tale and take it out for a spin.

Sometimes we need to swim in the words for a while until they finally make sense.

I've spent so long in imagination that I seem to have lost my reality. I close my eyes and see more vibrant colors than when they're open. I want to edit others' lives. Want to mute and cut and copy and replace. But lives don't need a guy like me to come make a trailer for them. They need heroes and heroines to make a life that someone will desperately *try* to sum up with a two-minute collage.

The burden of broken pieces I'm always trying to make into some kind of story.

The burden.

My many broken pieces of burden.

They say a supermoon hangs outside in the sky. But I no longer need something super. I'm going to stop looking to the sky for inspiration.

Shells

I enter the family room of our house and feel the breeze of memory hit me. I see the shadows surrounding me in broad daylight. Shielding my eyes away from the bright glares locked on mine. Lost in a sea of me, in a storm of my own making, in defeating myself.

The place is empty.

The floors are all clean now, the carpet plush and white. There is no torn love seat with its blanket trying to cover it. The smell of dog and dried milk no longer lingers. I can't brush crumbs off the sofa since it's no longer there.

It's gone. The stains and the scents and the messes and the mayhem. The drowning noise and pulling hands.

It's hollow. Waiting. Waiting for joy and screams and cuddles.

All this time. Worried. Worried that it would be gone. That we'd lose it all. That I'd have to give it back. That we couldn't move ahead and that we would have to start over and that every single thing was my mistake.

This structure stayed in place. It's still here. But they're gone.

Something not there.

The something not there was me. Time and time again.

Lost in other worlds. Lost with clients and films and deadlines and art. This beautiful, exquisite, marvelous art.

I was gone. Gone in work and gone with worry. Gone with a weary mind and gone with a worried soul.

Gone Guy coming to a theater near you.

I was gone. And then, eventually, they were too.

My heart aches. Not in the metaphoric, romantic, brokenhearted way but in a very real way, the way it did before realizing I had to go into the hospital.

Why is my heart still hurting like that? I already died from a heart attack.

I hold it and can feel it pounding. Sweat dots my forehead. My breathing is strained.

This is what it felt like before.

Me.

Something not there is me.

I wasn't there then and then I decided to permanently not be there.

I kneel on the tile floor and clutch my chest not out of pain but out of knowing the truth. The inklings I've had and the denials that have been bubbling to the surface.

I'm still here. Very much here. Very much alive. Very much gone.

So where are they?

The excitement and the question and the anticipation. That's why my heart is beating.

I know now, I know it.

Yet I know I can't come sweeping in and riding a white horse. Only heroes do that.

I rush back out of the house. This structure. It's no longer my home or any kind of home. It's just a roof held up by walls. Rooms opened and closed by doors.

I thought the front door had been closed forever. I just never bothered to check and see if I could come back in.

Guess Again

So wait.

So this street is real and this turning left is right?

So wait.

Those waves are reality and this curb knocking my tire is doing some real damage?

Okay, so.

So this is it.

I'm not really Tyler Durden. No.

I'm not really dead and talking to the kid that sees dead people.

I'm Spencer Holloway. And I'm still alive.

The Thinner the Air

You.

Can't.

Breathe.

You can't think.

You can't do a fraction of all your fellow thousands of human beings can do. Love and live life and have sex and laugh and long for each other and go home and lie down and relax and let go and let go a little more.

The song sings.

Humming, stirring, pricking, praying.

Music was created by God. Why shouldn't it be sacred and holy?

The major and the minor notes were both created by Him.

Just like the light and the shadows.

Just like the morning and the night.

The moon hangs, hovering, shining its beam on you, chasing you down. Knowing far too much, overthinking when the rest of the world is clueless.

It was there at fifteen, you fool.

It was there at forty.

It was there when you weren't around and it'll be there when the few forget about you.

Shining and smiling and hovering and hanging on.

All while you've fallen on the wayside.

Unless.

Maybe.

Time won't fade.

The days won't splinter apart.

You won't fear a father down below.

You won't fear all those f***ed-up bedside manners.

I can create a whole world around you, you think.

But there's no reply.

I can tell you the reason why.

The End Is the Start

The only one in the train on the last trip back to my office. Shaking. Wet. Staring at my hands. Wiping my hair back. Shivering. Getting further away. Stop after stop. Closing my eyes and thinking back. Wondering when. Wondering how. Wondering what.

The night knows everything and stares at me through unmoving sunglasses. I see myself. Scared and cold.

For a second I try but nothing comes to mind. I tie my eyelids together into blackness and keep trying. But nothing. And nothing more.

It's no longer working.

Nothing is changing. Nothing is happening.

The vibration and the damp chill and the percussion of the tracks keeps coming.

I try to think of a song but none come. My phone is in the lake. My iPod destroyed. My computer—God knows where it can be.

I have cash and that's all.

No license. No credit cards. No little machine to thumb around with.

I try to imagine what words would go with this and what frame would be used but nothing.

I have nothing.

The night knows even if I don't. The night sees all and surely sees me.

I can't believe I got here so fast. A month has passed and now I'm here, alone and empty and riding toward a death. Without words to explain and without music to fill in the blanks.

The blank is sitting in this chair.

A blank slate. Ready to finally start talking and filling in the details to his tale.

Ready to start talking before I can't talk or breathe or blink anymore.

True Love Waits 2

You thought you could drown your beliefs to have your babies.

Yep, you thought you could.

You thought you could dress like your niece and wash your swollen feet.

But those thoughts somehow got caught in the back of your throat when you should have kept singing the song. When you should have called and pleaded and told her don't leave.

But leave she did.

Leave you did.

Leave is all that happened.

And just took off without you.

You thought it would wait, but true love wanted nothing to do with you.

True love grew impatient.

True love decided enough was enough.

True love wanted an attic to hide inside, but you had none.

So true love left.

Songs of Faith and Devotion

Hold on.

I'm alive.

I am alive.

I've become a living and breathing Pearl Jam lyric, the kind one of my best friends would mock. Eddie Vedder is swinging on a branch above me singing "I'm alive."

But all I can hear is a symphony of chaos and confusion and crazy thoughts streaming in my head like the loudest, lamest bunch of eighties lyrics torturing me.

What happened?

What did I do?

Where did I go?

How did I leave them?

What was I thinking?

When did it happen?

Where was my mind—?

My heart—?

My head—?

My soul?

I need to capture these thoughts and wrangle them in. It's morning time and not midnight. I can think straight again. I can see ahead.

I know something.

I know this echo of a song I once heard.

I know that deep down, in dark halls and dead ends, true love waits. It waits with laugher and light and songs of faith and devotion.

Where's My Mind?

Where is my mind . . . ?

    I'm trying to retrace my steps as the Pixies play in the background. *Where did I go and how long have I been gone?*

    My steps lead to Christmas Eve when I'm watching Clarence advising—in *It's a Wonderful Life.*

    My personal Clarence ends up showing up. Out of the blue, of course. I don't ask where he came from. I want to know where the hell I went.

    —I didn't die, did I? I say to him.

    —Do you feel dead?

    —I've felt dead for a long time. But I don't now. I feel alive.

    —Amazing to have some answers, isn't it?

    —I've been asking questions all my life. Never getting answers.

    —Have you found the answer now, Spencer?

    —I know the direction where it'll be found.

    —So then you probably know where you need to run to.

    —So the heart attack . . .

    —Wasn't a heart attack, was it?

    No.

    Of course not.

    —The doctor told me there was no way I was having a heart attack and then I told him . . .

    —You mentioned you had just gotten a bad case of strep, and he laughed and said it had nothing to do with it.

    —But it did . . .

    —It did, indeed.

    This is the part the trailer didn't show, the footage the movie begins to spill all over you. The rest of the story. The *real* story. And it's one not involving death but rather the fear of it.

    The trailer made me believe I was going to be watching a ghost story.

    —They said I had rheumatic fever, I say.

    "Where is my mind? Way out in the water, see it swimmin'."

    —Yes. And you thought that was some disease from the

seventeenth century.

—Of course. Nobody gets rheumatic fever.

—But you got quite the bad case of rheumatic fever, didn't you, Spencer?

Christmas Eve in ER and Christmas Day in a hospital room with my heart being coddled and monitored because of something called rheumatic fever.

I mean, seriously. What the—?

—Don't, the angel says.

—What?

—Don't finish that thought. Cursing your salvation isn't something a smart man does.

I laugh.

I would have thought this entire conversation with an angel was the imagination of an insane man, but then again, I just forgot about my freakin' rheumatic fever.

A sane man never forgets getting rheumatic fever. Perhaps the fever can undo the sanity.

—So all this time?

"With your feet on the air and your head on the ground, try this trick and spin it, yeah."

—Your mind is fine, the angel tells me.

—I haven't imagined all of this?

—You haven't imagined anything. Forgetting is the absence of imagining. You paint over the colors of yesterday and replace them with black.

"O"

Out of time but still here. Out of breath but still running. Out of luck but luck doesn't control a bit of this. Out of mind but didn't have much to begin with.

I still can't believe the truth, but then again how many hours have I lived in fiction? Working on others' stories, piecing together the best parts. Making up voices that don't belong there. Moving frames in place that don't belong together.

Maybe this was my destiny but I'm tired of designations. Tired of fate and fortune and following. I want to run ahead of the pack even if I'm only the one running.

I want to fly and soar straight to you.

I missed out on so much but I'm not missing out on this.

Four souls are better than one.

Four souls free the one that's mine.

Four souls wait, wondering where I've been.

Four souls need a little and that's okay 'cause I only have a little to give.

Your Stories

Remembering can be the hardest thing. Because you know now it's not something you lost but something you chose to leave behind. Something lost by the choices you chose to make.

There's still time, the wry grin of the moon says.

There's still time, the spectacle of stars state.

There's still time, the breeze dancing around you shares.

Moving on . . . It's so hard to do. But sometimes it's moving back that's the hardest.

Time plays tricks, hiding in the dark, then evaporating in the sun. Pounding its ticks in the afternoon, then fast-forwarding with a single blink.

The man you might have been and the husband you could have been and the father you should have been.

Time tries to taunt, spinning its dial, attempting to haunt. But you still have a voice reminding you now.

There's still time.

So Lissie said. So she urged and encouraged and warned.

Time.

Short days and long years and loud voices and shared laughter and wonder and hope and love.

In the still, with the surface calm and reflecting the moon, you can remember. You can know, too.

You can go back home. You can return. You can try again.

Your story isn't over. And until you do in fact take that last breath, it's not over.

Life doesn't always have to cover you with sky blue.

Life isn't over after forty.

Life is about taking every breath you take.

Life is about making sure you never let go.

Life can be summed up as marvelous and wonder and awe and glory.

Life keeps tellin' you don't stop believin'.

The Best Me

There's a manual for this madness but it's still stuck inside some kind of maze you never get out of.

Turn right and breathe in and fall down and follow your heart.

Yep.

Turn left and rush around and reach the near end only to see the roadblock.

Yes.

This is your life and this is your legacy. A maze moving around your brain and your smile and your throat and your waist and your heels. Piece by piece. Problem by problem.

We see them all worrying and waiting and weary-souled.

Trying to grip to control.

Trying to type out to share some soul.

Smiles and happiness galore. All while our life is torching apart.

Then you come like this breath and like this eagle of hope I can simply hop on the back of to ride far away coasting down the valley of my despair. Riding up to the clouds to rapture. To bliss. To better days. To the best me I could ever imagine.

I'll Keep Loving You

I want the ripples to stop. Seriously.

I've been seeing the swans swimming far too long. Call me merciless but I want to shoot them. White, sleek, sensational swans.

Yes, I have this whole thing deep inside and yes, it's like this giant ocean I find myself stepping into and then wading out into and then starting to struggle inside and then feeling the cramps and the waves and wondering if I'll suddenly sink.

I always land on dry ground. Wet, gasping, weary, dizzy.

Those ripples keep coming.

Yes, it'll always be there. Immense, deep, dark, silent. But there's nothing more I can do with it.

The surface of the water is a mirror for a reason. It poses the question before you dive into the deep. It allows you to see yourself for that brief, beautiful moment.

Yes, I swallowed the salty water and now I'm trying to simply dry out.

There's a part of me that feels . . . confused. Crazy. Concerned it'll never go away. The tide. The sound of the crashing waves. The soapy, bubbly aftertaste left behind in the corners of the beach.

Bare feet stamp prints into sand, then get wiped clean with salty words I cannot keep at bay. They sting as they soak into open wounds.

So yeah.

The sigh, the stare upward, the sound out here, the footsteps standing still. Lord knows I want to run.

To clutch and then carry and then climb and then crawl into some hole and then to collapse into you.

Yeah.

You want to know, really you do, don't you? These bubbles blown float around and I try to toddler them up with waving hands but I never even get close to a single pop.

Not even close.

I stop and stare and there you are waving in the distance. The smile, the serenity, the scene in the background. Seriously. I mean, *really*? It's not fair and it's not even right. It's not much of anything except this giant tsunami approaching and I'm just digging sandcastles out here on the beach.

Why the beach metaphor? Why not? I'm a little like the crusty sand and you're a lot like the endless ocean. I get stuck between toes and you wade out with hands and feet. Everything about me is directly related to you. Your waves and your tides and your surf and your rush. I'm solid when you're near and then I start to drift apart when you stay away.

Uh-huh.

Maybe I'm just a desert in search of an ocean. Dreaming of those swells, of the surf, somewhere in the middle of the Sahara.

It's a good thing to dream, to imagine, but it's no fun to be stuck, to be living in a fantasyland. It's no good to be the poor kid from North Dakota dreaming of the Disney World or Disneyland or any kind of Disney vacation.

These hands held up waving aren't inviting you in. Not anymore. They're signaling submission. They're saying I give up. They're telling you no more.

Oui.

Sí.

This is all I can absolutely say in my most honestly absolute way.

My wish watching the seven seas? To be free. To escape the beachfront. To head back to the hills. To see the city. The flatlands. The boring and the breathless place.

It's been a nice vacation but I'm ready to go back home.

The Raging Sunset

They say a hurricane is going to break Florida. They've given it a name but all I can see is Lissie.

I wonder. Captured and callous, these hands and this heart, I wonder. I wonder and wonder and wander around searching in vain for an answer to my wonder. This collection of pieces of parts circulating around. The parcels of my soul.

A brilliant and bright-blue ball floating down the stream in front of me. Landing by my feet and waiting, wading, wanting me to pick it up. My clasp is a terrifying thing. Because I know the ball doesn't belong to me. I was just fortunate to find it in the first place. Maybe I should toss it back out to the streams. Or maybe I should just set it on the side of the river.

Or maybe I should run toward the raging sunset with ball in hand.

I think I tried. And I think I failed. The sun forgot to fade away. And it forgot to rise the morning after.

I see lessons in drops of dew, these constant tears, these simple reminders. I can stand and feel the cool wet and know I'm alive. Know I'm real. Know I'm still standing. Know I'm somehow still on my own two feet.

Hypnotised

Maybe this has been some kind of story you were having while sleeping. A dream turned to nightmare turning a movie into a memoir.

Maybe you've been filling playlists to find meaning when God simply wants you to sing your own songs regardless of what you sound like.

Maybe the trailer you made oversold the story. Maybe you pitched another picture, only to be stuck and confused in the theater seat.

Maybe there's something waiting better than you could have imagined. Maybe the image and the vision and the picture and the sound and the fury all were built up inside of your own mind and passion and soul and imagination. Perhaps it's not that complicated but it's far more creative than you could have ever arrived at yourself.

Stability can still be complex. Sensibility can still be creative. A talent at art doesn't require losing one's self.

Open Your Eyes

It's not Christmas Eve 2013 but it's much later than that.

It's May 2018.

Five years.

Can it really be five years? Have I been gone all that time?

I try to look around at my surroundings but find myself in black. Nighttime? In a dream or nightmare? But no. I see a flickering light like the steady beat of a heart.

This is the computer screen before the trailer has been assembled.

This is the blank canvas I've always worked on.

This is where I've been lost for so long.

I see many pictures I can put up here on the monitor. Birthday parties and anniversaries and Christmas mornings and holidays.

I'm in those pictures, at least in most of them.

I'm trying to understand.

Then I have a sudden memory. A piece of the puzzle. One of a million.

Tomorrow

She cries saying she is going to miss her friends and I can't say how life is going to bring lots more of that her way. I divert and dispel and can't help but think of myself at her age when I was plucked and put somewhere else over and over and over and over and over and over and over again with all of these overs serving as a reality and not a simple redundancy.

Friends will leave you, sweetie.

So I want to say.

Things change and people move on.

So I want to explain.

Finding new friends is a good thing for you.

So I want her to believe. But she's six and she's stubborn and she has to figure it out herself.

Loss is a part of this life, little one. The tough part is leaning on the One who loves you the most, your Creator and Father and Redeemer.

That brittle, beautiful heart is something to behold at her age, when life hasn't left its tread marks over her impressionable soil.

Turn the sadness on its head and pour it out of you like salt.

Don't worry about tomorrow since today's certainly got enough problems of its own.

Things I wish I could say now. To her and to them and to myself.

K

Brief, so brief.

Like being jerked by the undertow until swimming back out of it.

Yet in that blink of an eyes-wide-open stare, I know.

The little isn't so little anymore.

The young girl will soon be moving into becoming a young woman.

But no, she can't and won't, not now, she's still so young and there's still time, just getting through one more day is exhausting enough.

The blustery, blistering days that cause your bones to ache are nothing compared to those blinks that suddenly find one or two or three years gone, leaving you to wonder where the days went to.

The fullness riding with you can feel so heavy at times. The weight can be hard to carry but it's also deep and keeps you planted and grounded and forces you to forge ahead. So you do.

So it's hard to sometimes step back like you used to. Stopping to survey the scene and to make sense of it all and to try to clutch it in appreciation.

This life feels like grasping at those massive floating bubbles that hover over you until popping. Your hands are empty and soaked and yet you're suddenly running after another.

Every day, a fresh batch of bricks are carefully set into place, positioned and patterned in her unique way. You try to help shape them, yet it seems you can barely keep up with this road she's on. You blink and you're a mile from where you were standing just one moment ago.

Held in your hands and held next to your heart. This sunrise of a smile. The greatest laugh you'll ever hear. She's a newborn and next thing you know, she's nine and she's so absolutely remarkable. Nothing you can ever do will make you that remarkable, yet every glance she ever gives you makes you feel exactly that way and more.

Growing but not grown-up. This tall, bighearted little baby girl. The firstborn and the first princess and the first father-daughter dance and the first of many firsts.

Tonight you hold your eyes open and keep them open and don't let them blink. For this brief little time, you want to stop everything else and just thank God for her. Once again. And to wonder where and how and when it all got from back then to suddenly now.

So tiny while wrapped inside your arm. Yet she's still not too big to be carried up the stairs though you know you need to work out more to keep doing that. She's not too cool to kiss your cheek before leaving for school or climbing out of your car. She's still madly in love with you and you're still shaking your head like a lottery winner holding the biggest payout ever given out and knowing you'll never be able to spend it all.

This dark world is a little brighter because of her. And the shadows that follow your footsteps suddenly fall away when she's by your side.

The sun and moon don't stand still and continue to go back and forth like volleys in a tennis match. Yet sometimes, it's important to stop both and look out at the stars. Just for a moment. Just to let their beauty sink in.

Time never stands still, even if you step back and realize your heart always will when it comes to this little universe.

Bloodstream

The weird thing is that Lissie's still there. I see her. See the lines on her face when she frames a smile. I hear her voice staring straight at me as she talks. And she speaks to my soul. Saying words I could only imagine someone with that smile saying. And all along each passing second I'm thinking, *I know her and she knows me and she somehow loves me.* But of course I'm wrong. Of course it's not real. Of course it's just a movie and of course I'm just doing my job. Yet I don't know.

Fast, steady, ceaseless, gone. Unless you're swimming with it.

The truth about the mirage of a motion picture is like that river. It's everything poured into this narrow bloodstream pumping through your heart. It's all you can see yet it's only a tiny fraction of the entire you. Yet your hands and your feet can't help but try to paddle their ways out of the desperate dark. Toward a light they're unsure will ever come.

If you reach the shore, you sit drenched and sucking air and realize that all you've ever been and all you ever knew is still heading downstream. Passing you by even though you desperately tried to stop it.

Some streams are unstoppable. Some storms, unthinkable.

Some shimmers unspeakable. At least in the fraction of the heart and soul you keep buried.

477

Rivers

Sunlight hovering above as I look down below.

You stood next to her and the river and watched, but which one did you look at? Which deep, flowing vessel did you stare at and try to comprehend? Which did you desire to jump in?

And so I wonder.

I wonder lots. But at the core it's about what Tamara wonders about. I wonder if she thinks of me and what she thinks if she does.

When I was a little kid, all I wanted was to be wanted. To be needed. To be thought about. I'd lived this kind of life passed over, pushed through, pulled back. I wanted to belong. If not to a place, then to someone's heart.

All this time, longing for some kind of anchor to catch me, to pull me to a standstill.

Then I died—or I thought I died—and then suddenly Lissie showed up.

But she died, right?

Lissie's gone and I know it and I'm not sure how or why but I know. The truth, yes. The reality, okay. I don't understand. Maybe you don't either and that's okay because maybe one day we can talk about the magic and the mystery. I don't get it. But I want to. I want to get it and explore it and move on.

What I really want is for Tamara to be there right next to me laughing and smiling and needing me.

Needing me.

Yeah.

I can't be haunted by imaginary ghosts. Like some kind of rare bird I spotted in the fog.

Somehow, someway, the bird flew on.

Somehow I was watching through binoculars while the bird didn't bother waving while it flew away.

I want to know the why. The lesson. The takeaway. The message.

Yet all I know is that I'm heading back to a place. Full and empty. Hot and cold. Safe and hollow.

I know better, now. But I also know more. I know better. I know that more is there, that the grass is not just greener but fuller and softer and thicker and deeper than ever. Thick and deep enough to make snow angels in. Even if only for a blink of a moment.

Yeah.

You wait your whole life and you spend your time in the story until the goal shakes you and tells you you're sharing a seat.

Yeah.

The story is done and I'm a bit broken but I know that I need to just go. Just head back to where the world makes a little more sense. Even if that sense isn't soft and pure and warm and wonderful.

It's logical and it's right and I'm okay with it. I have to be. I plan to be.

You Can Choose

Headspace chugging helium. I just don't sound so funny speaking like this.

But like my buddy told me, you have a choice you can make.

You can *choose* to be happy.

You can *choose* to let it go.

You get help, maybe, hopefully. But it's still a choice.

God or gin or going gonzo. A choice.

Right, Spencer?

A choice.

And I wade through the ugly weeds and pull out some golden vines of happiness.

I guess it's so easy to get stuck. It sneaks up and taps you on the shoulder and then runs into an empty garage to race the engine with the door closed. Intoxicating and dangerous.

Yeah. Stuck.

You can choose to get in the car and move on.

You can turn on the stereo and pick your song.

You can decide how loud to play it and how many windows you can roll down.

You can determine whether you have a sunroof or not and if you do, then you better damn well open that sucker.

And get going.

Rolling down the road.

Passing the scenery by.

Getting out of this town and the county and this state.

Getting far beyond this culture and this climate.

The flick of a switch cracking down the wall and shaking the surface.

That easy. Just crawl out of the swallow, then find some dry ground.

Stay in under the sun. Crack and brush off the chips. Then step up into the new.

The Swirling Storm

The technology connects. Your voice, your face, the melodies, the pictures in motion, the moving parts seen and unseen. I watch Tamara and want to ask and listen and wait and yes, wonder. Always full of so much wonder.

Are you really there?

I wondered that before and wonder it now, even though I know the truth.

I'm alive and so is Tamara. I know this because of the text messages I continue to receive from her. Seen there, I question the parts and the pieces of what I'm hearing and seeing, of what I'm feeling.

I question me as the familiar song plays in the background.

"In the swirling of this storm . . ."

Speak to me around this time.

"When I'm rolling with the thunder but bleed from thorns . . ."

The moment is near, is here, is ready, and is wondering.

So if I speak back, will she really hear me? When I type, can she see me? Am I simply a mirage, or am I an actual memory?

Talk to me, I want to say. But don't.

Tell me something, I want to write. But won't.

Soon the pictures pop off, leaving the desperate dark, the hovering stark empty black mirror. For now.

Sitting solitary, listening and remembering doing the same in some numbered seat, watching the clouds below while forgetting to breathe because of the ache of missing her.

Oceans 2

Fortuitous. Our meeting. Our falling. Our forever.

I find myself stuffed by shadows. All over my soul. All over my skin.

I don't like the feel and I don't like the fortune. I don't like anything.

I like the feel of falling. Free. Looking up. Forever flights. Free.

What does it mean, exactly?

Breathless, I surrender to a bit of loss. To a bit of failure. I grasp in the hole of your storm. Of your shallow soul. Of your thin eyes. Bitter, hell-bent.

I stand strong.

But I fall.

Strong but falling.

Strong but failing.

Strong but faltering.

And it all goes bad and wrong and oh so not right with a click of the night.

The girls gone and the adults staying put. Silenced, angry, so mature, so there.

So we forget to try. Forget how we got here. Forget the reason why.

We seize yesterday when all we want is tomorrow.

And every word and every action and every single desire. Shot to space.

Hidden and buried. I thought I belonged but now I know I'm stored away in some crawl space.

Longing for laughter but getting the linger. Looking for the light but getting flickers.

Stale showers, softly put, falling storms, stars off center, in your sight.

And we dream. To be better. To belong. To be free. To be singing songs. Our rights and our wrongs. In those lips that smile and scorn.

K-M-B

They've grown. More than I ever could have imagined. And I've spent the last decade imagining.

You blink and suddenly become someone else. Someone boring. Some kind of boorish adult.

But I look and suddenly see.

The amusement of those light eyebrows and eyelashes. The strawberry swirl inside the blonde. The height staring down at others her age. And a supernatural smile that could solve most of the problems in the world if only allowed to.

The contemplation of that far-off stare and wide eyes. The wavy, messy hair. The soft nudges and the hand always reaching for yours. The thoughtfulness amidst the noise, and the sensitive way of leaving the scene of turmoil.

And the thrill of the intensity from the fiery glance. Bright and white locks bouncing back and forth. The always-moving and always-acting fire shielding the fragile and delicate soul inside.

How did I miss all of this and why?

What if I could embrace it?

What if I could fully see them and then let them know just how truly awesomely authentic all of them happen to be?

I see the sort of grins that overshadow falling stars on a pitch-black night. The sorts that melt the early February morning windows of a Chicago car sitting outside all night. The kinds that stay with you on a trip to try to escape it all. A kind that will be tucked away even if the plane goes down and you parachute to some remote island in the Pacific.

And that's what I'm looking at right now and that's why I'm sort just crying all over the place.

I need to get back home to them.

In Your Eyes

Seen through those eyes, I'm bigger and bluer and such a beautiful creature. I don't want to believe it but it's like taking a bad movie and making it look amazing. With the right perspective and the right context and the right music, anything can look brilliant.

I make trailers for a living but she sees me in trailers. An endless set of two-minute story songs. The kind that makes me look compelling, mysterious, thoughtful, deep, profound.

Beautiful.

But it's smoke and mirrors, as they say. The songs fill the soul but I'm not the one singing them. The language is altered to say something magical, but I'm not the one saying them. I'm putting both pieces together.

Still, I'd love to believe. Sometimes I almost do.

I've always believed that we are accompanied by soundtracks all day long. Not just by our making but by others. A song playing at the gas pump. A melody in the medical office building. The outdoor mall with their selective speakers everywhere. The radio and the music in the background on ESPN and the opening alarm of another ordinary day.

The world creates a soundtrack for us, like it or not.

We are all characters in our own trailers. It's simply up to us to make the movie interesting.

Mine . . . well, I already know that film. It's not that exciting.

Maybe there's time.

Yes. Of course. 'Cause forty-two isn't sixty-two, right?

Maybe I can change.

Yes, of course. But I'm just trying to deal with the ramification of all the glory years I failed to truly pass with flying colors.

I'm cleaning up the debris day after day after day. Sweeping them up bit by bit.

And maybe I'm no longer forty-two. Or whatever forty I seem to be when I writing the number down.

I want my forties to feel a bit better than the first few years have.

God, please.

Twisted Logic 2

I have to say goodbye to Lissie before I can get back into the real world. But how?

Without words it feels raw and real and a reminder of the fuzzy noise. What was behind all those affirmations and affections and armed threats?

Could it be so long ago? Could I have been so blind, so belligerent? So stupid. Silly. A stool. So long ago.

I can't turn up the volume any louder. It won't let me. I want to feel the couch shake and feel my skin tremble and see the sun pause to rise for one more second before it catches its breath and lets me have this deep, dark reminder of that silly, stupid sot.

Words are there like shadows in the still. They wait. They watch. They grow weary because they want to be heard.

What have you done?

Where have you gone?

Have you gone that far?

Have you gone anywhere at all?

Who are you and what have you become?

You're remembering without all the details. Just the emotions, just the energy.

Youth is wasted on the young, but you went ahead and wasted it once again.

—Are you there?

Nothing answers.

—Were you a dream?

Nothing appears.

—Did I really die?

Nobody answers.

—Did we really meet?

Lissie doesn't say so.

I don't know the reality, whether it was a dream and whether I died and whether we really met. But in the end, I guess it doesn't really matter.

She was there. I found her, and I heard her words, and I

discovered her soul, and I felt like somehow, in some way she did the same for me.

Maybe I was simply on the other side of the rope, watching her perform, seeing her with the lights pointed her way, standing and watching in darkness.

That's okay.

It took a while before the birds finally all flew away. Before I realized they weren't going to be coming back around. Before I heard the silence and saw the still.

The shadows they left are gone. The sky is back again. And when I stare up, I don't do so with regret. I can only look and listen and remember Lissie.

The Hurt

Suddenly the dead come back to life. The ghost makes her appearance once again.

Before I'm gone, Lissie arrives back on the scene.

—I didn't realize . . . , I start to tell her about everything.

—You didn't know.

—You never told me . . .

—You never asked, she says.

I stand, watching the unseen wind circling her like an exclamation point.

—All this sadness . . .

—There are reasons, she says.

The melancholy no longer looks romantic. It's a splinter in the thumb, rubbing against raw skin and cutting it open over and over again.

—I'm sorry, I say.

—Me too.

—I wish I could . . .

—Don't, she says.

—Don't what?

—Don't do that.

—Do what?

She looks at me and I know she knows far more than I know. She sees deeper than I can see, and she can spell out those depths in a way I never could.

—I'm not trying to do anything, I say, already knowing neither of us believe those words.

—It's nothing you need to try to help me with, she says.

—What if I want to?

—I want a lot of things, and life has had its way with me. Humbling me time and time again. Showing me that want and need are two different solar systems.

—In one big universe, I say.

She doesn't answer me for a moment.

—It'll all work out, she finally says.

—Easy for you to say.

—I say it because I believe it.

—You believe in a lot.

—It's better than not believing in anything. Both are choices you know.

—I'm sorry, I say.

—Sorry for what?

—Sorry for . . . for what happened to you.

—Are you? Really?

I try to understand.

—Or are you just sorry to see me this way, no longer wondering and sparkling and pining and grinning? No longer helping you?

—Lissie, that's unfair.

—Is it? Is it? Are you sorry that things got messy and suddenly didn't seem so romantic? No longing with the background music pounding against us like ocean waves of love and lust.

—Stop.

—Why? You know I'm right.

—I'm sorry to see you hurt, I say.

—I'm only showing you the hurt I carry. I've tried to do what Pastor Rick Warren once wrote about. That my greatest life message and ministry could come out of my deepest hurts.

I don't say anything. I can't. I just think over the words she's spoken.

—I need to go now.

I nod.

—Of course you do.

She flickers, like some kind of frozen frame on a motion picture. *Flickers.*

—I will see you again.

I nod. Again.

—Of course you will.

She pauses, not pausing but seeming to suddenly be absolutely still. I stare and wait and try to figure out what I'm seeing.

—I recognize how much I've lost, she tells me.

This time I don't reply.

I'm just looking. She's larger than life. The smile and the glow and the grin and those curls and that healing, graceful, sympathetic, caring, sweet, soul-sister love.

—But I cannot face the cost, Lissie says.

And I stop, startled, silent. I can't breathe. The world seems to be suddenly sucking me in.

What'd she just say?

But of course I know it already before my rational mind can actually say it.

—'Cause I love to be loved, she says.

Yes.

Absolutely.

The shudder. Visibly shaking.

Lyrics to a song long ago, one meant for Tamara and I, one used in my art, one forgotten and tucked away like some farewell note from a distant love.

God, what is happening here?

I see Lissie saying these words on the screen. The big screen, the television screen, the tiny screen. Any screen. But it's a screen. A very definitive screen.

"I love to be loved."

Yeah. So do I, Lissie. So does Tamara. So does every single person in this world.

Suddenly I'm seeing my movie creations coming to life and crashing into mine.

—Can you hear me? I ask.

But I'm asking a movie, an actress, a persona, not an actual person.

No no no no.

But it's true.

"Only now do I see the big picture," says London Grammar.

"In this emptiness and fear, I want to be wanted," says Peter Gabriel.

Obviously all of us, every single soul, loves to be loved. But it's been a long time since I've felt like I've been loved.

Except this shiny, glistening rock skipping and jumping and tapping and bouncing over the water's surface.

And suddenly . . .

Yes.

I realize every conversation and every smile and every touch and every laugh and every single word ever spoken has been some spectacular imagined tomfoolery. It's been portions of the films I've done trailers for and even ones I haven't but only recently discovered.

I've made an entire movie out of emotional imagination, casting myself as the hero who knows he will never get the heroine. She will already be taken, time and time again.

Lissie is not my film and not my story.

The reality is really and truly painful. It rips against my skin, against my chest, against my beating heart and breakable bones.

The words, the facade of my sudden good fortune. This lovely love in front of me, but never, ever truly in front of me.

"I love to be loved."

That I do.

And love won't come anywhere close around here.

Secret World 1

We all build it and live inside it. This secret world of ours, beyond the public and even beyond the private. Our personal, single point of view.

Yet every movement and every action, every step and every snapshot, every scene and every sound, are trailers for one.

For the One.

Our lives are films God watches, and they are all sorts of genres. Comedies and love stories and coming-of-age tales and horror sagas. All known with all their minuscule intricacies.

We're making it up in our secret world.

The kind you never invited anyone else into. Including her.

And I hear and I realize and I know.

"Seeing things that were not there. On a wing on a prayer. In this state of disrepair."

The goose bumps get me as I stop working and I just look up to see the images on the screen. The music still plays.

I see me.

I see Tamara.

I see the girls.

I see it all.

I finally see.

Burn the Witch

The deep, endless dark of the ocean requiring that single, solitary thing. To walk on water buoyed by your belief.

Cracked rivers overflowing pavements. Lined up ready for you to sprint over.

The shore sees you. The sky watches on the surface just below. The waves shake you alive. All tell you the same thing. Faith is a life preserver.

Free

The strings sound the strain a decade in the making. Long live and long last and long love.

And we begin to believe again.

In death, we find life.

Unshackled and unashamed.

Victorious, our steps and our breath.

What will it be like to stare up at the sky's torn sacrament and lie down? The heavens pulled back allowing us to enter, free and fortunate and completely forgiven?

Leaving Appleton

Passing without a passion to be seen. So casual, so mundane. Just passing time. Just giving a simple nod to a simple soul.

I stand and reel and wonder.

That's it?

You carve your skin and cut out a piece and carry it over in your hand to give to her. And this—*this* is what you get in return?

Maybe she's simply holding back because of the reality. But there's this doubt—this little demon inside your mind that's been there your whole life.

You're not worthy.

You're not wonderful.

You're not something to wait for.

So very whatever. That's what I get? That's all it will be?

The real, painful goodbyes in life are never grand. They're simply moments you have to try to get through. They're not accompanied by rapturous music or memorable words. Usually they come with pauses and regret and open-ended sentences without punctuation.

I want the closing credits accompanied by the last meaningful song on the soundtrack. I want to leave this feeling like I got my money's worth. I want to stand in the dark and proceed down the aisle feeling this joyful rush of inspiration follow me out of the theater and into life.

But life is not a movie. It's not a song nor a poem. It's not a sweet, little love story.

Life doesn't have a two-hour limit that can be summed up by a two-minute trailer.

Life consists of inconsistencies, with broken character arcs and unresolved tension and plot points going nowhere.

Life is a messy structure that would be rejected in the first round of a Screenwriting for Dummies contest.

Life is that goodbye that's really never uttered. The awkward, stilted, circular sort of conversation that stays with you simply because it could have been so much more.

Life is seldom more than you want it to be. Yet you meet people

494

who can never be summed up by a simple story or a sappy song or a shiny painting. People—magnificent, imperfect, and complicated creations—are God's artwork running on its own. Faults and all. Precious and peculiar.

Fly on, ride through.

Yes.

Fly on, ride through.

Maybe. Of course. One day.

Fly on.

That's what people and life do. They fly on past you without giving you a chance to truly say goodbye.

My telltale heart trembles, scratching graffiti over the gray wall, waiting for the colors to bleed and perhaps free me.

Can it be that simple, that standard course for storytelling? That saw-it-coming? But there's no seeing the simple, standard, seen-it-before when it's in the shadows.

I'm deluded, delirious, and very, very far away from reality.

What am I doing here—right here and right now?

I realize I need to leave this town and go and get something.

I need to get my life back.

Imagined

So here's the truth.

There are plenty of ghosts in our life that haunt us. They might be flesh and bone but it doesn't matter 'cause they somehow see through us and manage to go bump in the middle of the night.

There are parts of ourselves—whole pieces—that we shove and bury away. That somehow get sidetracked and driven around.

There is pain that we part from in whatever way we can. To survive. To not succumb. To somehow keep breathing.

Maybe this is what I did.

Yet I know Lissie was not imagined.

I think God allowed her to be in my life for a reason.

The First Trailer

"You're there," I tell Tamara over the phone.

"What do you mean?"

"I mean you're really there."

"What are you talking about? Is something wrong?"

"Yes."

"What is it?"

"I'm not there. I'm not in this picture."

"That was your choice."

Of course it was.

"I'm sorry. It was the wrong choice."

"Spencer, please, I can't—"

"I want to bring you something. Something to watch."

"What is it?"

"It's a trailer."

"I can't do this now."

"No. It's a gift."

"For who?"

"For all of you."

"Spencer . . ."

"You'll see. This will be the first trailer of mine that you won't mind watching."

When

And when you know.

And when you see.

And when you look up and you can feel this sweeping sort of insensitivity.

And when you gasp just to get some fresh winter air.

And when you slow down when the garage door shuts.

And when the footsteps head up beyond your downstairs.

And when the love seat serves as an armchair for one.

And when the lights turn off with your fingers.

And when the breath of the day brushes your cheek good night.

And when you hear the quiet breathing next to you while you settle in.

And when you know that tomorrow will serve the same sort of helping.

Knowing and not doing anything.

Wondering but not figuring anything out.

And the morning comes.

And you're still there.

And you'll be there tomorrow.

Hard To Find

I'm standing in the empty house we lived in and built a home in and just sold. There's a light where the shadows used to be. The sound of footsteps in places I used to hear only the still. The wonder of knowing better when it used to simply be at the knowing. Sparks die. It takes more—a lot more—to keep a light aglow. But still, sometimes you have to keep that other light on.

I don't understand it all. I can't comprehend how every curve and corner permitted me to allow it all to fit into this beautiful and mosaic puzzle. The kind I want to frame and hang on the wall. The sort of picture that will remind me forever of this particular time when the lights were all turned off and the doors were shut and locked and when I decided to let nothing in.

There are nights of sliding open the glass doors to let our dog outside near midnight when I'll step onto the back porch with him. To feel the chill and hear the nearby buzz of the interstate or to see the stars that link us all together. A snapshot like this reminds me we're all connected. And it reminds me that I'm still alive and human and have a little more life left to live.

I'll pause, peering up above, wishing to connect those celestial dots. Yet the moment I'll find one to start with, it will fall and make me start over. So I will try and keep trying. I won't ever stop staring up since I know those starry-eyed reminders will still be up there, mapped out and watching, endless and still changing.

Great art doesn't start with a genius behind a piano or a keyboard or a camera. It begins with the breath of life and all the abilities we're given. Our world and life shapes us, but we're still all simply made in God's image. Even if we don't believe we are.

There are hiccups that arrive like songs from The National, the sort that dredge up a little bit of everything awful about yourself. The kind leaving you alone in a booth in some lonely bar with too much to say. You're so much better and brighter than this, but then someone comes along and reminds you that you're not a beautiful and unique snowflake. And when your subconscious says that's a pretty cool metaphor to be thinking, you then promptly remind it that you didn't come up with that but rather Chuck Palahniuk did. And frankly, you are not Palahniuk.

A long ways after it all, I still sit back wondering what I actually am. I don't know.

I do feel like a song by The National. But nine times out ten, people I would tell that to would simply give me a look as if I'm speaking Russian. And maybe I am. Maybe my whole life has been spent speaking in another language while understanding all the things others have been talking about. Life has been lost in translation.

On this concrete step overlooking the back canvas of suburbia, I glance up at my midnight summary. An evaluation set in the stars. I stare but never like seeing the score I receive. Yet I don't dare look down. I'll face every single falling star like the hero I've never been.

A Sky Full of Stars

Wash over me like some Amazonian waterfall. Gushing warm water that sends me deep holding my breath and closing my eyes. Waiting for the gasping open.

Let me knock and know.

Let me open and see.

You.

Let me know that you're there.

Let me know that the life follows you with tiny footsteps.

Let me somehow hold a little bit of this life in my hands again. Bigger, bolder, more absolutely wonderful.

Little laughter pounding away. Running feet. Giggling souls.

The broken parts that never worked are okay. For now. Because there are so many parts that fit into them. That shift and transform into the glue that bonds.

I want the embrace. The wraparound little figure against me. The tiny little voice against my ear. The smile. The rapture.

And yes.

I believe.

I believe that somehow and in some way God gave me this gift. He gave *us* this gift to remind us that there's more. Than us. Than two. Than those pieces. Than the major chords of life.

All these minor keys come alongside and fill in the major ones.

Wake Up 3

Resuscitated.

That's how I would have to summed it up. Breathing and breaking and finally trying to believe.

Breaths. Bit by bit.

Tangled and torn and thorny and intertwined.

I debated about what to call this summary. The best titles aren't the forced kind but rather are the ones that greet you with a smile at the doorway.

Once I thought it would be perfect to call this narration "Wake Up." Because that's what I've done. That's been the story.

But that's half the story, if I'm being honest.

I'm standing in the middle of a field in Grant Park in Chicago. Arcade Fire is capping off an amazing day and an amazing performance with one of their most amazing songs and I'm realizing it's the end of something. Not just an era but a whole state of being. The next time I come to an event like this—*if I come to an event like this*—I will have three children and will be middle-aged and should really and truly not be here.

But I'm going to fight.

I'm going to fight like I've fought my whole f***ing life. At the turbulent moves and the insane emotions and this innate sense of not-knowing-and-never-knowing.

I remember standing there and feeling like I was the only one being sung to.

I resonate with the words in "Wake Up."

"Our bodies get bigger but our hearts get torn up. We're just a million little gods causin' rainstorms, turnin' every good thing to rust."

I don't want to cause a rainstorm and don't want the good things to rust but God knows I'm afraid. I'm terrified, to be honest. Music reminds me and motivates me and tells me how equipped I might be (not so much).

Rapture comes in the melodies and the beats and the guitars and the harmonies.

Beautiful things, bringing some kind of peace amidst my fears.

The music is an exclamation point on a life already examined far too many times. But maybe there will be more. And more. And more.

And maybe I've finally woken up. Truly woken up. In a way they sing and shout about. The kind worthy of songs and memories.

A Beautiful Song

A great song is like a message in a bottle showing up on your doorstep and ringing the bell. It sounds off and gets you out of your chair and brings you to the doorway of surprise. It's written specifically and only to you, and somehow it's finally found you.

When particular tunes have come this way—unexpected, like a hitchhiker on a desolate road or echoes in a barren desert—they've prompted me to create. To figure out how to use them, even in temporary ways. I'm selfish that way, making it only and always about me. The spark is lit and all I want to do is find my latest batch of fireworks to show off to others.

When these songs come by my side, they're sympathizing with my plight and summing up the feelings I can't say. And God knows I can't sing them. But I dream I can, and I long to shout them out and hum along with the singer. Often I do, in the confines of my car with the windows mercifully shut.

A storyteller has a million ways to tell their tale, and a filmmaker has even more weapons at their disposal. But a musician is so limited, so suppressed in what they can create. So when the familiar becomes fresh and original, it seems like a treasure suddenly found, and you bury it deep inside your heart. A beautiful song tells its own tale because it's speaking about *you*.

A Sky Full of Stars 2

What do I say or do or aspire to say or do?

Angels dance in the dark.

Earthquakes swallow souls whole.

But the day and the dark meet in this strange twist and I find myself full of writer's block. Full of a soul's block. Yet every smile you give breaks away the stone.

Chipped fragments surround me as I feel . . .

Free.

As I feel whole.

As I feel me.

The mirror held up high is waved around like some colorful wand, like a glow stick in the crowd. And it pulses and prances and every bit I feel it.

You stare at me through the stars, little lady.

Wonderful and watching my weary little soul.

Held and holding and always hearing, always hearing.

Always hearing me.

God, I love you.

And the storms coming before and the circling clouds coming today can no longer compete with the coming joy clawing deep down into the everything that I know.

I want to sing and I want to soar.

New and no longer old I'm free.

Healed and no longer sick I can see.

Ten million. Bursting. Hovering. Breathing. Touchable and teachable and nameable.

Let me name them all.

Let them all be named you.

You mend them all and mind them all and somehow you remember. You remember and you know and you let go and you let it be.

Academic

Doubts still debate deep within me inside this empty house with the Sold sign on its front lawn.

The thing that sucks about the first eighteen years of your life being the cement blocks that define you is that they're completely out of your control. And when those years that are so out of your control end up being unstable and uncertain and utterly uprooted every chance it can get, it can make the rest of your life a bit unusual.

There have been far too many *un*'s in my lifetime.

Regret is a weed that can't easily be killed. Pay someone as much as you can but they can never kill those curling fingernails coming out of the soil.

Maybe I'll never be one. I'll never be that. I'll never be with. I'll never belong. Maybe I'll confiscate the nevers and lock them in a box and set them adrift down the Fox River to never see them again.

Possibility trumps never, but then again, I might choose to never use the word *trump* again in the same way. Everything has meaning until, of course, something renders it meaningless.

I want to destroy the meaning of *never*. To chip away at the cement and stone of the *n* and to allow *ever* to stay.

One Thing Left to Do Before I Leave

What if?

And what if now?

To step into your artistry and paint a pretty picture. All for her?

What if you take the very sore spot and build something bright around it, so bright it absorbs all the black, ugly pain?

To make this brief and beautiful trailer to us.

What if all that passion and pain and potential could have simply been put on her doorstep?

Maybe it would have made it better.

Maybe all the things I could have done but didn't can still arrive.

Maybe after all this . . . maybe after everything, we will survive.

Pieces

I still can't help but wonder.

Have you solved my case and have you closed the books?

Did the murderer ever get abducted?

Did the dead come to rise again?

Did they tell you secrets and stories and confessions?

I walk with hands clenched full of chunks of you. These broken pieces I will set adrift.

I will watch as they fly and flicker away, like the ashes of the deceased.

That's all we've been to each other anyway, right?

The smoke in the center of it all.

The broke coming around the bend in it all.

Every single piece, every one, picked up and collected and carefully dissected.

Who am I to you?

I'm not puppet master.

I'm no puzzle piece collector.

I simply stop and scan these broken bits. I've tried to put them back. All of them.

But they are so many. Just like mine.

Everyday Is Like Sunday

I thought so but I wasn't. Self-effacing to hide the selfish belief, I skimmed the surfaces because I still couldn't see what I now see.

Absorbing and sucking and draining isn't special. The special ones squeeze the pride out and let their soul be a sponge.

The spotlight, the kind I've steered away from, yet still steering the noise my way. Deceptive in my ways, even my misery.

Forced to give isn't giving, and buckled into submission isn't bowing. I've fought and fought and tried to forge on myself in my way in my own fashion.

Pride can be poison and petty and porous.

Now the work seems so lackluster.

Slight, all of it, focused downward without focus and without a center.

The downward melody and its minor declarations fit without me having to say why. Maybe God, not Morrissey, wants every day to be like Sunday, full of worship and rest.

Where We're Going

"Here's what I want you to do: Climb into the hills and cut some timber. Bring it down and rebuild the Temple. Do it just for me. Honor me. You've had great ambitions for yourselves, but nothing has come of it. The little you have brought to my Temple I've blown away—there was nothing to it."

There was nothing to it.

Nothing.

I see all the trailers and their accompanying awards and credits and industry kudos.

Nothing.

Like the Depeche Mode song goes. "Nothing."

I had great ambitions for myself and I tried and I scaled the heights but the Bible is right. Nothing's come from it.

Nothing.

So I try to do something honorable. To give back. To give to God as a sign.

I begin to tear apart the desk given to me by my parents as a wedding gift. A *wedding gift*. A desk for me. Not for us but for me.

That represents nothing. Nothing but the nothing quoted in this verse. Nothing but those great, vain ambitions.

Nothing.

So I take it apart piece by piece by piece.

A desk doesn't define me. Nor does a childhood desire.

God knows me by name and knows my heart and everything good I've ever seen or tried to be comes from His love.

DAD doesn't define me.

I'm more and I'm better and I deserve something other than this. I deserve nothing, but when it comes to God, He loves me enough to show I'm worth something.

I'm worthy of sitting down and working. I'm just not all that. I'm not magical or mysterious or enigmatic. I'm just Spencer, who's loved by God and who's still so full of himself.

But piece by piece by piece, I see that Spencer statue to himself going.

510

Watching HBO

Follow your dreams.

Forge your desires.

Foxes yield dogs.

But sometimes foxes can outrun them.

When the wind brings a scrap of memory, I can crumple it and toss it over the railing and watch it float down the river.

But I won't forget.

There's no way to unfortunately.

The complex, the deep, hidden in the dark, buried underneath the facade, unseen behind the mischief. They don't know. But you do.

And floating, the balloon on the blister of the sun behind it begins to wave away. My neck is sore from looking up, so I stare back down at the ground. Bidding Lissie bye.

The Truth

I lost my mind. And then I lost it again.

I remember the moments, the love, the urgency, the rush. So hard to find. So eager to get lost in the darkness.

Where did they go? Those moments. Figuring out how to hide, fitting together in the dark?

The beating, burning breath of the songs playing while we made love. Without many words. Just feeling. Just the breathless want.

I wonder how long ago and how recently it went away. How long the love lingered until it started to leave.

I don't know. But I know something.

I'm not done.

I'm not done with you.

We're not over.

We're not finished.

And all those foggy windows and all those crushing choruses and all those secret hours and all those little everythings are something that can happen again. They can come around again. We can begin again. The songs can start playing over.

They're not done and neither are we.

Supersymmetry

I watch the video again in all its splendor. Two minutes of glory and wonder. Then I make sure it's saved to the computer and then shut it off. Another productive day of work done. I feel joy. I feel full. And I feel like I can't wait to see what's next.

All these thoughts and feelings that used to follow me—they're gone. It's amazing in one sense to think how they can be. But then again, I walk outside the stone building and see the blue sky and realize all the love that is there. Waiting. Watching.

I find myself lucky to be free.

I set the computer in the back of my SUV and feel a sense of déjà vu. It still happens every now and then. It's a blessed reminder, as some have called it. Others call it a nice blast from the past.

I start to drive home, listening to music and humming to its melody.

This feeling—this freedom—I'd love to say it was earned. I'd love to say it's here because of something of my own making. But I can't. I'm here because of grace. Pure and simple. Every moment I breathe in air, I remember this. I feel it. I *know* it.

The sun hangs in the evening sky. The air blows through the open window as I drive down the street, seeing a few passing cars, waving to them as I move along slowly.

The song that starts to play makes me smile. It belongs to Lissie. I know the song well and start to sing the lyrics.

For a few moments, I look out at the sky and remember her. It doesn't make me sad, not anymore. But I do tear up because of the stirring inside.

All the things that used to matter so much. All the waves that never seemed to find their shore.

I drive for a few more minutes; then I start to slow down. Soon I find the nearest turn.

I turn right and start to drive. Clouds seem to watch me, following me.

I'm there in just a little while. It's funny—this notion of time. This beast that used to hover over my shoulder and soul. It's not there anymore. The ticks don't pester me like flies. The alarms don't jolt me like they used to.

I soon find a dirt road I turn off. It doesn't have a name but I know it. I've passed it by already and have thought about driving down it many times.

Today my car doesn't slow down.

The white house on the hill stands so beautiful in the midst of the trees and the rolling hills.

I slow down and then stop my car at the massive, multiarmed oak tree standing like a doorman alongside the road.

I get out and walk toward the tree.

The beautiful thing isn't what it used to be. The thrill of not knowing what's next used to be the driving force. Now it's the tranquility of not worrying about the outcome.

I feel a slight wind nudge my neck and my cheeks. I find myself under the tree and I wait.

For how long, I don't know. But it's not long. And I haven't worried for one moment.

Lissie walks toward me, knowing, seeing, smiling.

She is so marvelous, and my smile says exactly that.

The end of the day and here we are. Finding each other by the first tree in. Figuring out finally what to say.

—Pretty, isn't it? she asks.

—Always, I say.

She hugs me for a long moment, and I feel good.

I stare and look into those familiar eyes. Like the sky above me and the birds that sail through its currents, I love seeing them.

—How are you doing?

—A busy day, I tell her. And how about you?

—I performed in a play today.

—You need to surprise me a little. Tell me you got stage fright.

—Is that possible?

I laugh.

—For you? No, I don't think so.

It's so peaceful here, and I don't have the urge to go back home. To go anywhere. I don't need to be here or don't need to do this or don't need to do anything.

—This is the tree, Lissie says.

—I knew it had to be.

For a few minutes or hours, we talk. I can't tell. The sky turns colors and the wind blows from one direction to the next but I'm not worried about leaving. I'm not worried about what the outcome will be or what I'm supposed to do next. We talk about songs and movies and then we hear the silence.

—I probably should head on home, I tell her.

I remember maybe saying this at some point without ever believing it. But now I know it's time. It's not like I won't see her again.

I might see her tomorrow. And the next day. And the day after that.

—Spencer? she asks.

—Yeah.

—Did you think it'd be like this?

I look at her for a moment and think.

—Did you think heaven could ever really, truly be like this? she asks again.

I shake my head.

—I had no idea. None.

—I dreamt and hoped but I just never knew. But here I am. Here we are.

I smile.

—Every day, every moment, I thank God, I say. For this gift. For my little place. For my purpose.

—You've always known your purpose. It's just the world that hasn't known what to do with it.

I laugh. The constant encourager.

Lissie looks younger, but then again, so do I. But it doesn't matter. Those things aren't as important as they used to be. They don't elicit the same sort of things.

But those piercing eyes and glowing smile—now *those* are the same.

They make my soul shine.

—It's good to see you, I tell her.

—You too.

—Maybe I can come by tomorrow.

—Maybe, she says. Or the next day.

I look at her and smile, then hug her.

We look at each other and know. The way we used to know. The way we used to somehow dream. Late at night and in our imaginations.

Maybe there's a better place and maybe we'll find each other there.

I've found her. I'm here. She's there.

And time and the world and the rest of eternity won't bother us.

Then again, I'm okay with leaving and seeing her again on another day.

These words known as peace and love and joy—they used to be mocked, overused, diluted. But here they are real and they are powerful and they are now.

They are what we know.

—It's good to see you, Spencer, she says.

I hear a song playing and wonder if it's my imagination. The wind can sometimes do that here. Sometimes it can blow by a melody.

—I'll see you soon, I tell her.

—I will enjoy when you do.

The song continues to play, and the smile continues to pierce, and the sky continues to applaud. I belong here, and I don't have to worry or wonder why.

I'm fully awake and will continue to be. For the rest of it all.

Reality

But that's the dream. I'm back in the reality. A place I want to stay.

Life, so much longer than two minutes, is waiting to be filled. Waiting to be played at the beginning of the experience. Waiting to catch and claw your attention. Waiting to make you want more. Need more. Have to have *more*.

And I want and need and have to have more.

I'm not done.

There are sunrise shots that I can still create. There are still sunset moments I can still settle on. There are kisses and long looks at the sky and running down streets and holding hands on buses and trains and windswept wonderful moments that I can create.

We are not done.

The trailer of my life has yet to be finished.

The trailer of our love has yet to be fulfilled.

The trailer of our family can finally be returned.

The trailer of my faith can finally be restored.

It's not too late. If you're reading this, it's not too late.

You are not a ghost and you're not see-through. You have a shadow and it's called life and it follows you everywhere you go.

She might be a million miles away. Or she might be on the couch right across from you. Feeling the same. Being the same. Unreachable. Untouchable. Unknowable.

But that's a different movie now.

This one is different. Not necessarily better. Not necessarily with more explosions and more sex and more money on opening weekend. Yet this is going to be one that lasts.

The kind of film you find yourself watching when nothing else is on.

The kind of story you find yourself thinking about when the other tales wash away.

You like this one because it's not predictable. It makes you wonder what's going to happen. Because really and truly, anything can happen. Right?

You just can't wait to watch it yourself.

Secret World 2

I finally hear it. A chorus of angels finally getting my attention. The soul and the vibe and the familiar song from a favorite.

"I stood in this sun-sheltered place. Till I could see the face behind the face."

That expression. "Sun-sheltered." It gets my attention.

I feel goose bumps ripple and ride the waves of my skin and soul.

I keep listening. Mesmerized. Awakened. Realizing and terrified.

"What was it we were thinking of?"

Oh, dear Lord.

Really?

I've spent my life and my love under the shelter of the burning sun.

God knows I've hidden so many things.

I've spent my life swimming underwater. Time spent wading in the make-believe.

So many hours with my brain spinning round.

So many days spent running from sorrow.

And the something not there. The something the angel asked about.

It's me.

I wasn't there.

I was missing.

And the one and only thing we need now is prayer.

Lots and lots of prayer.

I've finally understood that good ole angel of mine.

"On a wing, on a prayer," Peter Gabriel sings.

A state of disrepair.

Can I fix something when I've never fixed a single thing in my whole freakin' life?

The drums say yes.

The guitars prod on with their movement and motion.

The bass hums a simple affirmation.

And the song begins to fade, urging me to not do the same, to keep the song going, to keep trying to go out and figure it out all again.

518

Driving

The signposts seem to say it. So I keep driving down I-65, straight and flat and stoic, trying to spot the exit.

Our imagination is stretched by everyday reality, so why should we believe in those simply beauties?

The whispers of wonder spill over. I question the currents and every single other thing. Maybe it's me, and maybe it's the simple memory.

Compass and Guns (AKA Death and All His Friends)

I'm driving east, then north, toward the edge of a time zone, toward another chance, toward tomorrow. And I can barely manage to not drive thirty miles over the speed limit.

This is the epilogue, the final scene in the story, the one where the character pushes the boat into the sea and then jumps off the sand.

Wind behind my back blows me forward.

With the whispers of so many films behind me:

"There's no place like home."

"My mama always said life was like a box of chocolates. You never know what you're gonna get."

"Of all the gin joints in all the towns in all the world, she walks into mine."

"May the Force be with you."

"You had me at 'hello.'"

"Ask 'em to go in there with all they've got, win just one for the Gipper."

"E.T. phone home."

But there's only one, really. The one I've always had following me, the one line I've lived (and died) by:

"Get busy living or get busy dying."

I used to think the hardest lines to write in a screenplay were the ones that became catchphrases in pop culture. I know now they're easier to imagine than sharing simple, basic truths every day. To stop and share a fear or to stop and give a compliment or to stop and just be silent. To allow the other to speak truth.

The most powerful sentiments we can imagine with typing fingers will never compare to the vulnerable thoughts we share with others.

There's the last song on a favorite album of mine that comes on, so I turn it up in my SUV.

"All winter we got carried away over on the rooftops, let's get married."

So Chris says.

"All summer we just hurried. So come over, just be patient, and don't worry."

520

So Chris suggests.

Don't worry. Yeah, right, Chris Martin. Easy for you to say.

"*And don't worry,*" he repeats.

Chords of yesterday begin to play. Reminding and refusing to part ways. I no longer hear it as part of a video, however. I'm no longer in a two-minute-trailer.

I'm steering this vehicle down the road in a very visible life.

"*I don't want to follow Death and all of his friends,*" Chris sings.

Coldplay is right. I don't want to follow Death and all his friends. Not now. Not yet.

Brooks was here. So was Red. And so was Spencer.

Rushing

So there's this thing and it's called life.

It's a bumpy dirt road that sometimes seem to go to nowhere.

It's a helium balloon that a toddler lets go of and starts to slowly drift away.

It's a series of smiles and tears and songs and fears.

It's the orchestra swell and the silent pause.

It's the grace in the flight of the birds, over and over and over again.

It's beautiful beauty sown with words and with music and with pictures.

But it's real, too. Fully all there. Worth recording but worth living, too.

Metaphors are great but so is breath filling lungs that make you walk faster. That's what's happening now.

Running, rushing, racing to get to her.

Racing to get to them.

Knowing their smiles will break the train.

Knowing they change so much.

Midnight 3

Silent but stirred. Shadowy whispers disturbed. You step, unsure, trying not to wake tomorrow.

These breaths that belong hover overhead, listening and longing. Wondering if you're willing. Wondering if you're worthy.

The still starts to break.

You feel the ground start to shake.

And in the midst of all this mind-numbing heartache.

You smile, knowing it's there.

This little light on.

Waiting for you.

Wanting you.

Watching you.

Bubbling and blistering and belittling, you find yourself at the doorstep once again waiting to knock.

So knock.

And wait.

And watch.

And hope Tamara left a light on.

Stars

Those stars they've watched you all this time growing and failing yet they've stayed strong. Winking. Knowing. Believing their shine can disperse the shadows.

Where We're Going 2

I want to tell them . . .

I don't know.

I'd like to picture the emotion and the quotations and the images together and simply let them press Play. But life isn't about pressing anything to play. Life plays.

I stand in front of the house, staring. I feel a blast of wind, urging me onward or backward but urging me to do something and anything.

I'm afraid of believing.

I'm afraid this won't be real.

I'm afraid I'll be standing on the edge of a monitor watching souls smile at me through some kind of flat screen.

I'm afraid of hearing their laughter and seeing their smiles and wanting to step inside a world that is no longer mine.

Go ahead, step forward. Give it a try.

The best things are the most terrifying. Love always comes with the potential for ache.

So I step forward. Just one step.

The wind still blows. I look back at the fading sun and I suddenly remember. I look at the grass on each side of the driveway and I remember. I stare at that dent that's still in the garage door and I remember.

I remember driving up this drive so carefully, so cautiously, with our new baby girl in the backseat.

I remember pulling into the garage with the twins swallowed in their car seats, sleeping so sound, so light and tiny.

I remember them walking and running over this drive.

Laughing and lunging. Attempting to ride a bike and screaming to stop.

The lemonade stands. The chalk scribbles on the sidewalk. The red wagon with the door that opens. The bicycles and the scooters.

I'm here. I'm back. I'm standing here wondering whether I should be back. Wondering whether I'll be welcomed. Wondering if I'm real at all.

All I want to do is see them again. All of them. Tamara's peace. K's joy. M's compassion. B's passion.

Am I allowed to simply knock? To ask for a door to simply open? To be invited to simply walk inside?

There is nothing simple about this. At least that's what I think. My heart and soul tell me something else.

It's easy. You have to believe and you have to know you're sorry and you have to realize you can be saved from being the ghost you happen to be.

Can a door open as simple as that? Can a miracle happen simply by believing? Can a life change simply by being sorry for the crap that's come in the past? For believing that there's more to life than this? That life can and should come from death itself?

So I walk.

I believe you are there.

So I keep walking.

I'm sorry for all the things I've done in my life. For my self-centered selfish actions and my anger and my confusion and my doubt and my despair and my lust and my longing and my self-destruction.

And I keep walking. Then I knock and the door in front of me opens.

I can't see who opened it, but I can tell someone is behind it.

I wonder if I can start over.

Yes, you can, Spencer.

I wonder what I have to do to be allowed to move on.

You've already done it.

I close the door behind me knowing they're inside. Knowing they're upstairs. Knowing they breathe breaths that I'll be able to hear. All of them.

I want to see them and stand by them and stare and thank God for them.

So I do.

I walk up the stairs, so quiet and so absent. Then I walk into the first room to the left, where our twins will be.

Their shadows and their forms on the beds without their blankets

526

covering them reminds me of the warm day. I see B curled up in an almost-angelic and comfortable pose. She looks so peaceful, so calm. Then I see M, sprawled out and mixed in with the covers like she's been digging for gold.

I seem to stand there and stare until the sun rises the next day. But I don't.

I want to see K.

I want to know for sure if this is real.

Sure enough, she's sleeping, looking so grown-up, yet also still so young. So peaceful. So beautiful.

I can't make this up. I can't imagine such beauty.

Only God can.

Somebody 2

And so there she is, and there I am.

The tears fall like familiar chords of a favorite song. I stand and see her, so tall, so alive, so beautiful, so real.

So much to take in.

I've been gone. But I'm back.

I wipe underneath my eyes.

Why you're mine, I'll never know but I know exactly why I'm yours.

You sleep and I stand and smile.

Thank you for this life beside me.

I want to believe in this breath next to me. To picture hope, like the sun coming up tomorrow, like the arrow pointing north, like the wind blowing you forward, like the sunset beginning to fade in the distance. I want to believe there's more and I'm meant for more and we're all in this together. Together for something much greater.

I stand and wait.

Tamara

Your heart beats. But only I can hear it.

I wait here for you.

Every breath, every second, every single thing.

We stare and we see the storm. I watch and I wait for you.

Standing here.

With or without you.

Wondering and waiting and wishing I could live with or without you.

Do you hear me here?

Do the echoes shake?

Can I ever cross the waters and enter into your world?

Can I take these ashes from this home and build them into something more?

Can you hear the heartbeat from the West Coast?

The song can sum it up in a single chord. My little lover. My love unknown. She's got soul, sweet soul, and she teaches me to sing and I can't sing since I'm a comedian.

But sunrise comes and for the first time I feel love.

And all the haters and the debaters can't tell me anything I don't know.

For the first time, I feel it. I feel love.

Running far away, I see streets paved with gold. The lovers and the takers all can't see this atomic sky, but I feel the rain that burns. I wipe the tears away.

Telling you and telling me.

I'm wandering.

Away from the Zen mountain and the peaceful isle.

Can you say you want the Kingdom but don't want God in it?

Can you hear a voice sounding like Cash?

See the signs and hear the voice and know you will return to me.

So now I'm a showman and I can show you anything you want. I'm a broken man with a broken back but that doesn't matter because this whole scene is reminiscent of a heart attack.

The heart is bigger than that and you should always know that.

Stay or Go

Rain reminds us just outside, steady and consoling and sounding the same as it did in our youth. We could be stranded but we have each other. We could be the last two souls on earth but we're still both here. Safe, secluded, somehow in this sanctuary.

"Am I dreaming?"

I can't help sounding like a love story cliché.

"You've been dreaming from the moment I met you."

My wife always had a way with words . . . and she still does.

"Where are we?"

She smiles and takes my hands and presses them against her.

"We're home."

I kiss her and hold her and find that everything fits once again. So wrong for each other in so many different ways yet finding her again to be the only other piece in my crossword puzzled life.

The need and the want and the love and the desire clasp hands amidst flickers of the storm outside and the glow inside.

Hemingway knew words were overrated and Depeche Mode said they were violent and broke the silence. They might be right or they might be fools but it didn't really matter to Tamara and me. Words were spoken—yes, quite a few—but they weren't covering the past or addressing the present or figuring out the future.

These were timeless and belonged to the two of us. Only the two of us as they rightfully should.

I knew the wrongs of being so many miles away and the rights I was still so far from but I felt full again. Emptying myself out and immersed completely with her.

Breathing in and out, I have to ask her. And she tells me.

"Yes."

I can stay.

Lucky

Breathe.

Then let it all out. Every single bit.

Nobody's asking you for anything but assume you're having to shut out the beggars and the offers.

Stand still and watch the sun begin to rise and think of how utterly lucky you are.

Each day you're given an opportunity to take the very thing you love and do it in ways only you can. So do it with joy.

A SKY FULL OF STARS (Trailer #14)

For a brief second on the black screen, a soft giggle, the kind of intimate thing only shared between two. Then the song and the trailer begin.

"Bluebeard" by Cocteau Twins starts and then we see the evolution of a relationship. The shy girl and the mischievous guy. Walking by one another and having various moments until the big one.

"Will you be my partner?"

She's asking him.

"I already agreed to be Dee's dance partner," he says.

But of course, they become partners.

Then in a blink, we shift to various scenes set to Enya's "Caribbean Blue." A proposal, a wedding, a honeymoon, matching gold chains around his and her wrists. A couple who can't stand to be apart at any time. Two souls clutching to be one. The passion and the joy. Different, yes, but excited by the different worlds they bring to each other.

The trailer doesn't suddenly come to a halt with a scratching record and a black screen. It trails off as if this is the happily ever after. Then we see our lead played by someone resembling Edward Norton shutting off his laptop like this is the video he was watching. And maybe it is.

Then he begins to narrate what seems to be a letter as we see the half-lit, half-awake face in a half-full bedroom. Thomas Newman's delicate and heartbreaking "There Was Snow" from The Horse Whisperer plays.

"I want to know if I've been the one to create this stranger or if I've become one myself," he says.

"I miss those days when I didn't walk around missing. Missing parts of myself. Missing parts of us. Missing the old you who used to care."

Images flood the scene. Good. Bad. Angry. Silent. Hurt. Tears. All while the music builds. Coldplay soon begins to play, of course. And Chris Martin begins to sing amidst the piano chords, of course. A montage of snapshots play against "The Scientist," of course.

"I don't bother to even try anymore because I know it won't work. There's nothing that matters to you, not about me. I don't bother to tell since you don't bother to ask. I don't wait and wonder because I know you're not about to act."

We see this letter being typed on a computer while a hand types another message. Both saying goodbyes in different ways.

"I want to know how we went so long without going far at all. But then I hear my words and know that I focus on the 'I' in my life way too much. And all I want to get back is us instead of me.

A continued montage of love and loss and growing up and being a family all while Nancy Wilson strums her guitar on "We Meet Again" from Jerry Maguire.

Then it stops and we see the newborn baby. The theme to Finding Nemo is there. It shows a baby becoming a girl, then two more babies, then crawling and walking and talking toddlers. The melancholy Thomas Newman turns into Coldplay again, that back-and-forth volley known so well. "Adventure of a Lifetime" shows just that as three girls grow up and get older and older.

The great thing about this trailer is there are no licensing issues. I can make whatever trailer I want with whatever music I desire. All I want to do is move the heart and soul of one.

And the last batch of pictures and videos, I show the joy and the love and the hope that's easily been forgotten on a screen and inside an exhausted soul. I put "A Sky Full of Stars" on again to show the lift and the rise and the rocket soaring.

And the feeling of those wonderfully warm goose bumps come at the 3:20 mark of the song, when the key changes and goes up. And there's the picture of the two of them, the two of us, then all of us, this group of five.

From Spencer Holloway, the creator of dozens of your favorite trailers, comes the movie event of a lifetime. A SKY FULL OF STARS. Playing now and in theaters for the rest of our lives.

Yeah, it's corny and over-the-top, but it brings the good sort of tears you love to see.

Mantra 2

I attempt to capture life, creating little moments, puzzle pieces put together with sight and sound, a summary of a story to come.

For so long, I've been editing others' creations, weaving work out of their content, crafting my own tales out of their talking pictures. Somewhere along the way I forgot to figure out my own life and forge my own path.

The footprints in the sand and snow stopped showing up behind my steps.

There's no retracing them, discovering them again. They've been swept out to sea and have melted into streams.

I need to make new ones. This time sealed in cement.

They don't have to have the grooves and impressions of my unique boot prints. My tracks can belong to anybody. It's not about what they look like but where they point to.

It's not about what you leave behind. It's about where you're headed.

Don't show others those prints, because they'll blow and wash away. The destination won't, however. Not when others are noticing and paying attention.

Walk. Or better yet, run. With the passion you put into those moving parts from those motion pictures.

You carry the brush, but the paint was made by your Maker. So capture the colors He made. You'll only get a fraction of them, but they'll still be beautiful in every single way.

12:01 a.m.

They sleep above me just like they used to. And here I am, one more time, staring at the screen, at one point white and then black.

Comfortably settled in. Perhaps I've taken that for granted, how easy it's been.

It used to always be so easy. Everything. I sometimes wonder if God decided to heap all sorts of blessings over me at the start of my twenties since He knew how miserable my turbulent and always-changing childhood happened to be.

Yeah, things came too easy. Even Tamara. Our love was sudden and satisfying and I believed it would always be that way.

Love and life aren't easy. They grow hard when you start to think they are.

"Good night," Tamara told me earlier.

"Good night," I said like so many times before.

We're taking baby steps, beginning again and believing. But we're not going to be naive. We're not going to get stuck back in the past.

I see a commercial on television for Sandals vacations. Gorgeous people in gorgeous locales. We went on a Sandals vacation for our honeymoon. Perhaps we were one of those on the screen. But we're no longer living in that sort of fantasy. Or I should say, *I'm* not living in it.

They're already dreaming right now. I'm still awake. In the distance, I can hear the midnight trains that have followed me from Illinois to Michigan. I think they'd follow me anywhere.

I'm not worried. Or at least I'm trying my best not to worry. Worry is a crowded red-eye flight nobody wants to take, where all they serve are shots you pay for but never get. But we board anyway, thinking we have to take this trip. Thinking we'll safely set down somewhere. But we stay airborne in those stormy clouds and believe that relief resides only with those standing on solid ground.

I'm open for anything. I know the joy I've held often burns quickly like gasoline, while the hurt has remained stored and locked away like cement, only to be chipped away at during midnight hours.

I'm always going to be a night owl. But I'm no longer going to fly on and ride through, hoping to find that next high to fly next to.

All I have to do is walk up the stairs and hear their quiet breaths in the dark to know they're there. And then fall asleep with the belief they'll still be there when the morning comes.

Cul-de-sac

That puddle looks deep enough to dance in.

Those seeds you planted are starting to sprout before the snow will cover them over.

The colors draping over the trees stand out better under the colorless clouds.

This countryside sort of scenery you used to never see breathes just outside, but it's not beyond your reach.

One step and you're there.

And all these parts paint this odd sort of picture. The stranger things in life that are simply standing there, right there in front of you, beautiful and often taken for granted.

Like the grace of ghosts that love you and leave you and linger like the glow of Christmas lights and campfire embers.

Peace isn't a parcel you can express overnight. Hope isn't a hurry-up antidote to a gushing wound inside your soul.

It's gonna take some time, Spencer.

Don't consider it some sort of season. Don't contemplate over missed opportunities that never came to fruition. That never even existed in the first place.

The places you can go are the places right in front of you. Ground you can plant a foot on and then see the print later in the evening glow.

The morning wakes and the wonder continues and the window remains clear until the daylight disappears. But it's okay to keep the blinds open.

You never know what sort of fireflies might float by. Or what the stars look like out here in the corner of this cul-de-sac on the crossroads between yesterday and tomorrow.

You thought you might be a ghost
You didn't get to Heaven but you made it close
--Coldplay

Made in the USA
Monee, IL
20 September 2022

14305834R10295